DAYS OF
DESTINY

Best Wishes

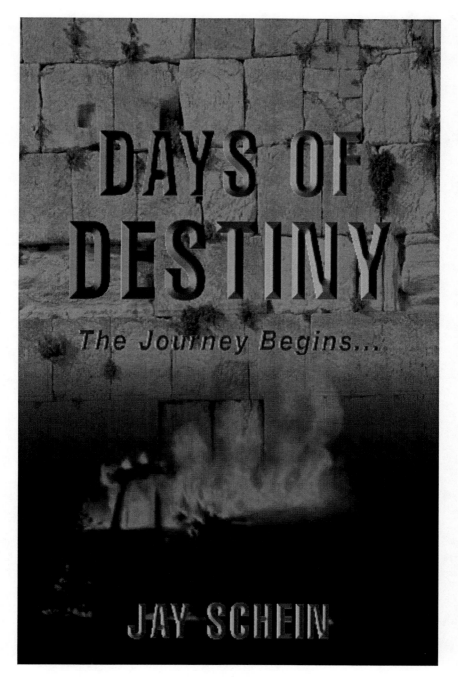

DAYS OF DESTINY

The Journey Begins....

JAY SCHEIN

TATE PUBLISHING & Enterprises

TATE PUBLISHING
& Enterprises

This novel is a work of fiction. Names, descriptions, entities and incidents included in the story are products of the author's imagination. Any resemblance to actual persons, events and entities is entirely coincidental.

Published in the United States of America

ISBN: 1-5988666-4-8
07.02.15

Tate Publishing
(888) 361-9473
www.tatepublishing.com

Acknowledgements

To Diane, Natalie, Brandon, Brittany and Jennifer
My Family—who has loved, supported, encouraged and believed . . .

For my precious mom, Trudy

Special Thanks To

Wendy Pieseski
For initial editing support
Bill Pieseski
For military information guidance

To Israel
May there be peace . . .

Any resemblances to the lives or circumstances of any person or persons living or deceased that are found within this book are coincidental and as stated previously, are a product of the authors imagination. Actual events, names of places and governmental agencies have, however, been used throughout this book but have been expounded upon and treated fictionally. All actual places are public knowledge and available as public information. However, the story and names of persons surrounding each circumstance that is portrayed is purely fiction. Specific details including descriptions and locations about universities, governmental agencies, hotels, apartment complexes, and the like, have been taken from public record. Jewish (Yiddish) words when occasionally used have been spelled phonetically for reading ease, with their English translation provided in parenthesis following each of the words.

Yiddish is a social language among the Jewish people and Hebrew is the official language.

"Destiny"—"Something that is to happen, or has happened to a particular person. The predetermined, the inevitable or irresistible course of events."

Synonym—FATE

Days of Destiny

Contents

Chapter One

Destined for Ministry

Nathan was totally confused. He suddenly found himself in surreal-type surroundings, and he had no idea how he got there. He felt an oppressive heat and was sweating profusely. Beads of perspiration were running down his forehead and his face, forming tiny droplets on his chin. Every few seconds, several would drip to the ground and make tiny wet impressions on the parched pavement. He focused momentarily on the teardrop-sized spots, as though evaporating moisture was the only thing that seemed real in his situation. ***Where am I? How did I get here?***

What was at first confusion quickly turned to fear. There was nothing but empty space surrounding him—no physical objects and nothing he could touch or feel. He looked around again and was shocked to see a huge wall of stone that had not been there just a moment ago. It was as though it appeared out of nowhere.

Panic emerged in the rapidly mounting shortness of his breaths and the unsettling sensations that were beginning to grip him within his chest. He tried to calm himself by focusing on the wall, as it was the only tangible object he saw. It stretched endlessly on either side of him and seemed to disappear at some point outside of his line of vision. It was as though everything in the world was swallowed up except for him and the wall. He was desperate to make some sense of this, for he was feeling as though he was losing his mind. He was far too much of a practical and methodical thinker to allow himself to panic.

As his eyes scanned the wall, he noticed that the larger stones formed the foundation; while higher above him the stones became progressively smaller. He noticed hundreds, if not thousands, of cracks and crevices between the stones, every one of them stuffed with tiny pieces of paper.

He had an impulse to run—*but which way, and to where?* He had no idea of where he was. *The wall must be the key,* he thought. Perhaps it was an illsion, or there was an opening he could not see—a secret door within the wall through which he could walk and be freed from this madness.

Nathan slowly reached out and extended his hands to touch the rough-hewn stones. He ran his fingers down the wall and realized he had no sensation or feeling. Perhaps the wall was an illusion all along? As he tried to focus, he sensed that someone was watching him. He even thought he saw a man and a woman walking toward him. It happened so quickly that it seemed like the flash of a camera—that sudden brilliant light that blinds you for the moment and then it's gone—leaving nothing but spots before your eyes.

Just then, he heard sounds like firecrackers. They were short, rapid bursts, similar to an automatic weapon—the sound of a machine gun he had once heard in an old-time gangster movie. His heartbeat increased by the second. The pounding within his chest seemed to be the only reality that he was still alive. Those rapid-fire sounds began again, only this time they seemed louder, as though they were right behind him.

Instinctively, Nathan fell to the ground. His body slammed hard against the coarse pavement. He held his arms over his head in an attempt to protect himself from whatever threat there was. The bursts continued, and now there was a second sound, the *clinging* of hundreds of small metal objects bouncing on the cement.

Bullet casings, he thought, but there were none that he could see. The same sounds continued for another minute or so, and then suddenly, they stopped. An eerie silence quickly enveloped all his senses, as he thought, *am I injured?* He knew *something* was wrong, but there was no pain or evidence of physical injury.

His attention quickly turned to a wet, sticky liquid that had not been there when he first fell to the ground. It was forming all around him in a puddle and growing larger as he watched. Slowly, Nathan reached out his hand to see what it was. He placed his index finger into the puddle, raised his hand, and saw that it was blood.

But whose blood is it? Where did it come from? I have no pain anywhere in my body, so it can't be mine, was all that he could reason for the moment. He abruptly sat up and examined his chest, his legs, and his arms. Then he heard tiny splatters on the cement behind him, resembling the sound that his drops of perspiration made a while ago. Nathan stretched his arms behind him as far as he could reach, attempting to feel his lower and upper back. His fingertips brushed against small holes in his skin, oozing his life-blood from each of them.

But how can that be? he thought. *I don't feel any pain!* There was nothing else to reason except that he had been shot multiple times by someone or something he could not see. He had only heard the sounds of the gunfire.

The entire event was so surreal that he felt there was no choice but to simply give up his will and accept his circumstances. His conscious life was seeping from his body so quickly that he began to feel a sense of weightlessness. His eyes drifted over toward the wall, and he sensed an overall peace within him as though everything would be okay. *Do I get to meet God now?* he thought.

A feeling of disorientation was taking hold of his conscious mind when the silence of the moment was suddenly broken by screams. They were deafening, high-pitched shrills that echoed all around him. As quickly as the fear had left him, it erupted from within as he was filled with an overwhelming panic. Nathan struggled to his feet. The intensity of the screams increased, and he also tried to scream, but no sound came from his mouth. He attempted to run, but his legs wouldn't move. He looked down at his feet and realized that he was standing in a puddle of his own blood. He tried to scream again for someone to help him, but no help came.

Suddenly the light around him began to dim, growing darker and darker, until finally it was pitch black. Sweat and blood were literally pouring from his body, and he was sure that he was dead because of the blackness. *This can't be, I'm thinking and reasoning. People who are dead don't think and reason—they are dead!*

It was a moment suspended in time; a moment of the known being unknown and the real becoming surreal. Nathan began to weep, and he fell back to his knees. He lifted his arms and cried out for God. He inhaled all the air he could draw into his lungs and exhaled a scream that magnified itself tenfold as it pierced the night.

The scream was so loud that it was heard by just about everyone in the college dorm. They all came running to his room to see what had happened. Several commented that it sounded as though someone were being murdered. When he realized that his sweatshirt and his sheets were soaked with his own perspiration, all he could do was to sit up and weep, his shoulders shaking from the sobs.

His roommate, Josh, and some fellow classmates attempted to console and calm him. In the twenty-one years of his young life, it was the most realistic and frightening nightmare that Nathan had ever experienced. It was too realistic, and he could not shake that sinking feeling in the pit of his stomach. It was so real that every now and then, without the slightest provocation, the memory of that nightmare would come back and touch his conscious mind. He was always left with the same sinking feeling, and regardless of his efforts to change his thoughts, he had a foreboding sense that the nightmare was some sort of a supernatural warning.

It was a proud day for Nathan's parents, as he was the third generation of rabbis about to graduate and be ordained. He was quite tall—a striking young man that stood out on the stage of the now-gathered graduating class of The Rabbi Isaac Eichanan Theological Seminary of Yeshiva University. Yeshiva is a private university, however not limited to just a seminary-type education for those pursuing Jewish ministry. The university has a broad educational base that provides extensive choices in curriculum. Located in New York, the university has an enrollment of about 5,600 students. Albert Einstein College of Medicine is affiliated, The Benjamin N. Cardozo School of Law, as well as many programs in medical and scientific research.

Nathan's father, Harry Blumberg, who was also an alumnus of Yeshiva, could distinctly see his son's face among the other graduates, even from the balcony of the auditorium. With all of Harry's acquaintances at Yeshiva, he was a humble man and refused any favors such as lower level seats. It was Harry's humility and wisdom that drew people to him.

Nathan, possessed a uniquely similar, warm personality that endeared him to everyone he met. His dark brown eyes would hold an intense, serious gaze, and just as it seemed he was about to challenge you, he would display the warmest smile that would capture the heart of the people he encountered. His 6'4" frame was lean but muscular, and he stood straight and proud as the commencement ceremonies began. His tailored pinstriped suit and burgundy silk tie had hung in his closet for months and had been freshly pressed for this proud occasion. Harry had presented the suit, shirt, and tie to him as a token graduation gift. He had planned a much larger gift after graduation, but Nathan never suspected it was a trip to Israel.

Harry had long dreamt of his son presiding over Temple Beth Orr—the synagogue he founded nearly thirty years ago. Now he was getting old, and a heart attack just a year ago had begun to slow him down. This once energetic and beloved rabbi knew it was time to retire. There was no mistake that Nathan was the apple of his eye, and Harry let everyone in his small congregation know that he would one day inherit his pulpit. Most of the congregation, having been there for many years, had watched Nathan grow up. They loved him and respected his devotion to Judaism, just as they loved and respected Harry. They had all encouraged Harry to retire and allow his son to carry on the family tradition of devoted rabbis.

She was sitting in the third row, staring intently at the stage. When Nathan saw her, he was instantly mesmerized. At first glance it seemed as though she was looking directly at him. She was lovely—no, she was exquisite—and a picture of natural beauty. She took Nathan's breath away the moment he saw her. She looked as though God had taken special time to chisel every feature and set her apart as an example of His handy work! This was not the best time to be gawking at a girl in the audience, Nathan realized, but he simply could not help himself.

The graduates were all lined up and began walking up the steps to the main stage. Nathan nearly fell over the man in front of him as he missed a step while focusing his attention on that amazing girl in the third row.

He had never seen a young woman so beautiful, and he was instantly attracted to her. Her skin was radiant, and he saw tiny shimmers of the bright lights dancing on her long dark hair. *I have got to stop this!* He thought. *I have never reacted this way over a woman before. Who is this angel?*

"Josh," Nathan whispered to his roommate who was standing to his right. "Look at the third row in the center and tell me who that girl is."

Josh Greenberg had been Nathan's roommate and his closest friend for the past four years. Josh searched the audience, straining his eyes and even squinting under the glare of the stage lights until he spotted her.

"Wow!" he exclaimed out loud. "She is incredibly beautiful—who is she?"

"If I knew who she was I would not have asked you!" Nathan replied and let go with a tiny chuckle. "After this is over, though, I intend to find out."

Josh smiled a knowing smile. He was pleased that Nathan finally set his eyes on a girl who he felt was attractive—and he didn't even know who she was! Nathan was quite the charmer, and yet Josh could not remember him being seriously interested in any girl during the past four years. Nathan was looking for a future wife and was not interested in passing relationships.

Josh's father was a prominent cantor in a reformed synagogue in Connecticut. Josh wasn't sure if he really wanted to start living the suburban life right away, or if he wanted to take some time off after graduation. Like Josh, Nathan did not want to immediately step into his father's shoes at their synagogue. They had both discussed the possibility of not working for at least a month so that they had time to think through their ministerial paths and perhaps even take a trip to Israel. Josh had relatives in Tel Aviv, so it would be an inexpensive trip if they could come up with discounted airline tickets. Nathan knew that his father also had a friend in Tel Aviv, and perhaps he might be welcomed to stay with him. At this moment however, both their thoughts were abruptly halted as the ceremonies began.

The sun rose with brilliant hues of orange and red over the plains of Moab, but no one was walking through the desert dust at sunrise to witness its beauty. This same sun brought rays of warmth and a sense of tranquility to many tourists who rose before dawn to capture this timely photograph, immortalizing their trip to the Holy Land. This morning's sunrise, however, was far from tranquil as it touched the rooftops of the Sajaieh neighborhood in the West Bank of Israel. The orange and red rays eerily bathed the fatigue-green uniform colors of the hundred or more Israeli soldiers who were quickly yet quietly approaching this small West Bank neighborhood. Only the occasional sounds of a dog's bark or a child's cry could be heard breaking the silence.

The past week had been one of the bloodiest since Israeli-Palestinian fighting had begun. About seventeen Israelis and nearly fifty-five Palestinians had been killed in fighting that appeared to be escalating rather than calming. Just two days ago, Israeli troops fired missiles, tank shells, and machine guns at Palestinian Authority positions in reprisals for a Palestinian ambush that took the lives of seven Israeli soldiers—one of whom was a top-ranking colonel. It was announced the very next day that Israel would begin focusing on small-scale counter-guerilla, counter-terrorist operations. It was obvious that the PLO terrorists were also focusing on a new strategy. They were attacking military checkpoints within the West Bank and Gaza, rather than infiltrating the borders of Israeli territory where the army outposts were heavily manned and protected. Their cry of "Get out of Gaza!" was now being announced in the smoke of surprise attacks that would soon bring the United Nations Security Counsel to an emergency session.

This morning's raid was an answer to the previous night's attack by the PLO on the Israeli checkpoint near the village of Ein Arik, west of Ram Allah. Every soldier was killed or critically wounded. Perhaps that was why only the top snipers and counter-terrorist teams from various operational groups were hand-selected for this particular raid—or Israeli reprisals, depending upon which side you were on. There was a house that Intel had scoped for the past week and was convinced it was a PLO storehouse for guns and munitions. Quick investigation had it that there was one family living there, but there were several suspicious visitors at all hours of the day and night.

They chose the timing of the raid to avoid there being a child inside the house who they knew was the subject's daughter. She had spent the prior day at a friend's home and was given permission to stay overnight since her friend lived less than a block from the schoolhouse they attended. The girls were just five years old.

At the appropriate light after sunrise, a warning was given over a bullhorn for the occupants to come out of the house and surrender to authorities. Within minutes, the Israeli officer received his answer as a rocket was fired at the lead tank in the line of armored vehicles. It exploded like a tinderbox, spewing shrapnel in every direction. It was a fraction of a second, a blink of an eye, catching everyone off guard. An immediate command to "commence fire" resulted in thousands of bullets penetrating the paper-thin, clay walls of the small house. A second explosion resulted after the bullets penetrated a munitions storeroom within the house, and a torrent of debris fell everywhere out of the raging flames that shot into the air. There must have been incendiary devices within the storeroom, as it resembled a scene from the fires of hell.

Three adult bodies were recovered from the rubble. Two of the bodies were the mother and father of Elanie, who was now sitting at a breakfast table with her friend and her parents. It was irony that Elanie and her friend were drawing with crayons as they waited for breakfast. She was drawing a picture of the very house that was now a heap of ashes.

The third body was later identified as a PLO assassin. A quick, secretive meeting took place at Intel headquarters later that morning, and a female officer and a government worker from the local orphanage were sent to pick-up this beautiful little girl just after she was dropped off at her school. Their assignment was to try and relate to Elanie that her parents were no longer alive and she would not be going home at the end of the school day.

~

"Ladies and gentleman and distinguished guests," the speaker began. "Welcome to the graduation and ordination ceremonies of Yeshiva University, The Rabbi Isaac Eichanan Theological Seminary. It is a time of rejoicing as we confirm the title of "rabbi" on each of these young men who stand before you this afternoon. Within this auditorium and the hallowed halls of this institution, many a famed rabbi has gone before these young men, serving God, and ministering to God's chosen people. Each and every man standing before you has good reason to rejoice in his individual accomplishments."

Several guest speakers followed the introduction and opening prayer, and finally the degrees and ordination certificates were awarded to each of the graduates. As Nathan's name was called and he walked forward to accept his diploma, he glanced up at the balcony and saw the proud smiles on the faces of both his mother and father.

The speaker congratulated the new rabbis, and the audience responded with a standing ovation. It was truly a joyous occasion for the graduates, their relatives, and friends. At the very moment the graduation caps were tossed into the air, Nathan bolted for the steps. Once on the auditorium floor, he headed directly toward the third row where he had seen the girl of his dreams. He did not really know why he was doing this; it was like an inner motivation that was now in control of his entire being!

During the past four years, Josh had watched his roommate and friend quite closely whenever there were women involved. Nathan would study them and have brief conversations, but he never followed through by asking any particular girl on a date.

"What *are* you looking for in a woman, Nathan—do you even know?" Josh would ask him from time to time. Nathan simply smiled and within a few moments would calmly respond with the very same answer he had given to Josh each time. It was no secret that Nathan was not seeking a casual relationship, but rather a wife. He purposed his heart to save his affections for the girl that would stand beside him through all the days of his life.

"When I see her, I'll know. I won't have to think about it."

Nathan approached the third row of the auditorium and saw the girl talking to another young man in the graduating class. *Oh no,* he thought to himself. *Not a boyfriend . . . and from my own class!*

He was contemplating backing off and simply walking toward the steps of the balcony to be with his parents when she turned and their eyes met. As she smiled at him, Nathan's mouth became as dry as cotton, his knees felt weak, and his breathing became somewhat labored. His heart began to pound, and he could feel perspiration breaking out in tiny beads on his forehead. *I can't believe I am feeling so out of control,* he thought as he managed to return her smile. Just one row away from her—so close—and it was as though the world stood still. Nathan could hardly speak. Everything around him seemed frozen in suspended animation! The woman standing beside the girl (Nathan correctly thought that she was her mother) sensed his instant adoration toward her daughter. She smiled, extended her hand and introduced herself.

"Hello, I am Ruth Wasserman, and this is my husband, Jeffery, my daughter, Rachel and my son, Allen. And who might you be, distinguished new rabbi?"

Nathan burst into his brightest smile. The young man who was from his own graduating class was her brother!

"My name is Nathan Blumberg, and it is so nice to meet you."

At that moment, Nathan heard his father's voice directly behind him.

He turned in time to receive an enormous hug from his father, while his mother waited patiently for her turn. They had observed Nathan starting toward the steps to meet them and then noticed his purposeful diversion. They saw him talking with this family and then saw this beautiful girl. Judging from the expression on their son's face, they decided to come downstairs because it was obvious he was not coming up!

"Hello," Harry said. "I am Rabbi Harry Blumberg, and this is my wife, Ruth."

"What a coincidence," replied Mrs. Wasserman. "We have the same first name!"

The two women embraced for a moment and congratulated each other on their sons' ordinations. Harry was already in conversation with Rachel's father, and Nathan simply stood there motionless, his gaze transfixed on Rachael. They were both obviously and instantly attracted to one another. Her smile was like a brilliant light, and at that moment, it seemed even brighter than the lights of the auditorium.

Rachel's mother broke the awkwardness of the moment by asking Nathan's mother if they would like to join them for brunch. Nathan glanced over at his father, and Harry instantly knew that look in his son's eyes.

"Of course," he replied, "we would love to."

It took nearly twenty minutes for Elanie to calm down from her convulsive sobbing. Her perfect olive-tanned face was being washed with the non-ceasing tears of a child who had begun to understand that her parents were dead. Aida, the social worker, had to hold back her own tears as she hugged and attempted to comfort this beautiful little girl. As they drove to the orphanage, a cell phone call came in for the officer.

"I do not want this to go through regular channels. Check any recent applications from Israeli citizens seeking a daughter and call them. Bring her directly to their home and process the paperwork there—short forms, no red tape, just an official adoption."

"I understand, sir," she answered.

At the very moment the jeep pulled into a parking space at the orphanage, the Feldmans were signing the final application papers to adopt a little girl.

"About five years old or so would be wonderful, since we both work," was their last comment as they handed the secretary the completed package of papers.

The Feldmans had one son, an older boy, Reuben. He had almost died at birth, and so did Mrs. Feldman after a complicated pregnancy that had demanded total bed rest for nearly five months if she had wanted to keep her child. The ordeal negated any future chance of becoming pregnant, and the Feldmans had discussed adoption for several months. They were in agreement, except for Reuben, who seemed to enjoy being spoiled as an only child—until he saw Elanie walk through the front door of the adoption center.

They were just getting ready to leave when the social worker and officer came into the lobby with Elanie. She was a captivating child with over-the-shoulder-length dark hair that was splashed with golden highlights from the desert sun. She had a captivating stare through huge, dark eyes that were now reddened from crying. She was absolutely beautiful, and the army officer saw the look on the faces of the Feldmans and the return stare from Elanie.

The social worker immediately touched Aida's arm and motioned for her to leave Elanie there and go into her office.

"I will be right back, Elanie. Why don't you wait here for just a moment and then we'll have some milk and cookies?"

The two walked into a nearby office, and Elanie simply stood there, returning that same look to the eyes of the Feldmans. Reuben was instantly mesmerized by this beautiful child, and had a sense that she was very special. If his parents wanted to adopt a sister for him, there she was. He had no doubt that this girl simply had to be the one.

The conversation and the call to headquarters took about ten minutes. When they left Aida's office, they stopped short of falling over one another as they returned to the outer reception area. There they found Elanie in the arms of Mrs. Feldman, who was crying right along with her as she kept telling them that Allah sent them because her "daddy and mommy were not coming home any more." The adoption was pushed through channels within twenty-four hours, and Elanie became Elanie Feldman, the newly adopted sister of Reuben Feldman.

~

Harry accepted the invitation to join the Wasserman family for brunch, and as they all walked together towards the exit, Rachel hesitated just long enough to be at Nathan's side. Rachael was silent for a few moments and then turned her head toward him with her warmest smile. Nathan saw the tiny dimples on her cheeks and the glow in her eyes that left him almost breathless. This was no simple attraction. This was the "Fourth of July," exploding like fireworks within every chamber of his heart. *Whoever said there's no such thing as love at first sight?* Nathan thought to himself.

Rachael congratulated him on his ordination, and Nathan thanked her, instantly attracted to her gentle voice. Little did he realize that in less than a year, Rachel would become his wife. Nathan saw beyond her natural outer beauty and knew there was something very special about her—almost spiritual in some way. He sensed that this must be what true love was all about. Rachael also was aware of something deeper than just a physical attraction to this tall, handsome rabbi walking beside her. Something within her very spirit told her that this was no chance meeting.

~

In less than a week's time, Reuben and Elanie were inseparable. It was an unexplained relationship of a new "big brother" who would watch her on her way to school and always be there when the school day was over. He would carry heavy objects for her, refill her water glass at dinner, and never neglect to say good night or read her a story. The Feldmans were delighted, since Reuben had been their biggest obstacle during their initial discussions about adoption. To anyone who was unaware that Elanie was adopted, they would appear to be a loving brother and sister who had been friends from birth! It was this very afternoon, after school, that Reuben and their father agreed to take Elanie to see the graves of her biological parents. There was some confusion as to where they were buried, and after an hour or so of searching two cemeteries and a hundred small markers, they finally gave up. On the way back to their house, Elanie told Reuben that she didn't want to look for them anymore.

"They are with Allah," she stated emphatically. "They are not here anymore." It was difficult for the Feldman's to hear Elanie refer to God as "Allah" but they knew they had adopted a Palestinian and in time, she would learn their ways.

Chapter Two

Israel

Accepting an all-expense paid trip to Israel was not a difficult decision for Nathan to make. Harry reasoned that this trip was for filling his son's soul with the historical beauty of their heritage. He insisted on paying for all the expenses so that Nathan could fully enjoy the experience of Israel. He would have plenty of time after the trip to begin the process of taking over the pulpit of their synagogue.

Nearly two months had passed since Nathan's ordination, and he and Rachael had dated every weekend. Nathan knew she was going to be his wife and made up his mind to propose to her after his trip. This gave him some time to think and pray about it while also planning the words of his proposal. Waiting to propose had nothing to do with his feelings for Rachael, for he absolutely adored her. It was simply his practical way of implementing important decisions.

Throughout college, Nathan would usually say, "All serious decisions need time and prayer." Josh and several of his other friends would often chide him about his serious ways, but Nathan simply refused to be emotional about any important issue, and marriage was surely something of importance.

Nathan packed for the trip on a Tuesday night, as Harry had obtained the tickets for a Wednesday mid-week departure. Now on his way to Israel, less than twenty-four hours had passed, and he had already worn out Rachael's photograph by handling it every moment since he kissed her goodbye at the airport. He could not stop thinking about her—during the flight to London, the layover, the connecting flight, and even now as he showed his passport to the officials at Israeli security after landing.

Tel Aviv seemed warmer than Nathan thought it would be for the month of June. The average temperatures at this time of year ranged between sixty-seven and eighty-three degrees. Today, it must have been near eighty-five. It was much too warm for the long sleeved shirt and vest his mother had insisted he wear in case the weather changed. Nathan walked beyond the customs gate and followed the signs to "Transportation."

Once outside, he hailed a taxi and asked the driver to take him to Jerusalem, the Old City. Placing his one suitcase in the trunk of the old Mercedes, he slid into the back seat and stretched his long legs across to the opposite side. It had been a long flight, and the seats on the plane were so narrow and close that he had felt as though his knees were the snack tray!

Turning his thoughts to his present surroundings, Nathan could not help but notice the difference in the interior of the Mercedes in which he was riding from those in America. He had only seen one Mercedes on campus—one that had belonged to a visiting parent. He was able to look inside but had never actually ridden in one. This car had cloth seats instead of posh, genuine leather. There was no air conditioning, no fancy dashboard trim, and it had a stick shift—a far cry from luxury. The car was identified only by the Mercedes symbol on the hood of the car and on the center of the steering wheel.

Nathan had purchased a "Guide to Israel" at Barnes and Noble before he left on this trip. He began to flip through the pages until he came to "Jerusalem" and read some of the highlighted historical facts. *No city has been as coveted and fought over as often as Jerusalem, City of Peace. From the Babylonians to the British and the Jordanians, fifteen conquerors crossed the paths of its bloody and anguished past.* As he thought about the incredible history of the Holy City, he felt his heartbeat increase. Among other things, he pictured the Wailing Wall, and he relished the opportunity of praying there. He wanted to place his written prayer for Rachael and his family on a tiny slip of paper and place it within a crack in the wall, just as thousands had done before him.

Harry had planned his son's trip well, rejecting any notion of him staying at a costly and impersonal hotel. Harry had arranged for him to stay with his old friend, Victor and his wife, at their apartment in Jerusalem. Victor and Harry had met many years ago while Harry was in Israel. They were praying beside one another at the Wailing Wall, and just when they were both leaving, a conversation ensued. Their like-mindedness had blossomed into a long-term friendship.

Victor's background had always been a bit confusing, so Harry reminded Nathan not to press Victor for any information about his work or his life. It didn't really matter what Victor did for a living—he had never discussed it, and Harry had never asked. In all the years since he had known him, Harry always felt as though Victor's occupation was very secretive. Harry identified those unspoken words as a possibility that Victor held a position in one of Israel's many branches of government service.

Nathan's tour guide, Ronie, was born and raised in Israel. He was educated at The University of Tel Aviv, and after graduation served his required time in the Israeli Army. He was promoted twice during the time of his service and had become a decorated officer. After his honorable discharge, he attended Israel's School of Historic Education and chose to become a tour guide. He formed his own tour company and guided both Jewish and Christian groups. His love for Israel was evident in every descriptive word he spoke during his meticulous coverage of the many historical sites on his tours. Nathan listened carefully as he taught.

"Today as we visit the Kidron Valley, I would like you to consider both the geographical and the historic information—especially referencing those who passed through this valley in ancient times. The valley begins north of Jerusalem in the Valley of the Walnuts and is situated about 2,600 feet above sea level. The Kidron Valley reaches to the Valley of Jehoshaphat, and, of course, we know that the prophet Joel prophesied The Day of the Lord, declaring this site to be the valley where God will judge."

Nathan could not write fast enough in his notebook, much less even *begin* to absorb the incredible knowledge his guide possessed. He was glad he took the tour. He was not one for letting someone else shuffle him around, but this was a tour steeped in historic value, and his tour guide knew it well. He recalled these facts from his own study of scriptures; however, seeing it in person brought it all to life in both his mind and within his heart.

The tour continued throughout the day at a grueling pace, with an unscheduled but voted upon stop at Absalom's Pillar and the Tomb of Zacharias. Ronie began pointing out the significance of where they had stopped.

"Here you will find controversy," Ronie explained. "We have two religious groups, Jews and Christians, each claiming to be correct regarding who is actually buried here. The Jews proclaim that this is the Zacharias portrayed in 2 Chronicles 24:20, while the Christians believe that this is the Zacharias portrayed in the New Testament's Matthew 23:35. Perhaps some day we will know the answers to these controversies." With that said, the group wandered about for a few minutes, taking pictures and discussing the dispute. Ronie then announced it was time to go, and they headed back to the city.

Returning to Victor's apartment by early evening, Nathan was so exhausted from the tour that he had no appetite for dinner. He requested only to take a hot shower and get some sleep. Victor and his wife fully understood, as they could hear the weariness in his voice. They also knew that he had trekked all over Israel in a pair of dress shoes! Nathan knew he should have brought another pair of shoes but wanted to only pack what he could carry on the plane. Sometimes practicality had its downside!

The next day, as Nathan approached the Wailing Wall, the excitement of the history of the stones began to move him. This was the site of the temple that was destroyed in 70 a.d. and was never rebuilt. It was just a wall of stone, but it represented the history of ancient times and the struggles of the Jewish people. Those who were now standing before that wall were praying with reverence and a sense of their oneness with God. He looked out over the area and he saw the Dome of the Rock and the guards with their machine guns strapped loosely around their shoulders. They were carefully observing every person that passed before them. In the area where he was, the Israeli Army was patrolling, heavily armed and visually searching the crowds for any would-be dissidents. It was far from ancient times, though, and Nathan wondered if they would ever rebuild the temple.

Nathan put on his hat to cover his head. Coming face to face with the wall, he could not explain the surge in his emotions as he began to pray. He realized, however, that these emotions were familiar. There was uneasiness within him, and he began to perspire. As he prayed, drops of perspiration were seeping down the bridge of his nose and beginning to drop on the pavement below him. His hands began to shake, and he ceased his prayer. *What is going on here? Am I that emotionally carried away by the Wailing Wall? I sense this is somehow familiar to me—yet I don't know why?*

It took him a few moments, but he managed to contain his emotions and reason them away to the experience of being there. After a while he reached into his jacket pocket and took out the small piece of parchment paper he had prepared. The tiny scroll held the brief prayer he was able to fit on it. His eyes searched for an appropriate place to insert it within the wall, and finally he saw an opening a bit higher than he was tall. He was able to stretch upward and insert the scroll into the crevice. Nathan was sure that particular crevice contained many pieces of paper filled with hopes, dreams, and prayers, including peace for Israel. He smiled from ear to ear, knowing that his own prayer was now a part of the temple wall. He also knew that the future would bring thousands of rabbis to the wall, and they all would be praying just as he did. He made a slight *bowing* gesture out of reverence, and he stepped away from the wall and headed back to Old Jerusalem.

He walked through the winding streets and stopped at several shops where hand-made souvenirs were being sold. As long as he was there, he decided to purchase gifts for his parents and for Rachael and her family—so many to choose from, so many to bring home. He would need a much larger suitcase than the one he brought, or he would have to carry several shopping bags aboard the plane.

The trip home was slightly less exhausting than it had been getting there, and Nathan slept most of the way. Now that many of his questions and curiosities about Israel had been satisfied, he was anxious to get home to Rachael.

Israel was everything he had anticipated it to be, and Nathan knew he would return someday. Upon landing in Florida, he felt rested and very much ready for the tasks before him as the newest Blumberg at the pulpit. Harry met him at the airport, and once Nathan went through customs, they embraced as though he had been gone a year.

"So, how was your trip home?" Harry asked as Nathan searched for the baggage carousel that indicated his flight number. It was all very confusing to a non-seasoned traveler.

"The trip was incredible! I will remember it always, and I can't thank you enough for sending me. I love you very much, Dad." The two embraced again.

"Touring Israel instilled a great deal of love in me for the Holy Land and our people. Academics alone could not provide that spiritual connection. Being there is like history coming alive and capturing the essence of our faith."

Harry smiled, knowing exactly how his son felt. He had experienced the identical feelings when he first visited Israel many years ago.

Finally there was a buzzer, a flashing red light, and the baggage carousel began revolving. A moment later, the luggage came flying down the chute. *The whole process,* Nathan thought to himself, *resembles a huge mouth spitting out bag after bag.* Nathan chuckled as he watched it for the first time.

"Why did you check your bag?" Harry queried, knowing Nathan had taken only one carry on suitcase to Israel.

"I purchased several things in Jerusalem and had to actually buy a new suitcase while I was there. It was a used suitcase I found in a flea market, and it was quite reasonable. Besides, I needed a new one, anyway."

"And what happened to the old suitcase?" Harry asked, his voice reflecting the usual frugality that made Nathan laugh.

"I gave it to Victor in appreciation for allowing me to spend nearly ten days as his guest."

"I see!" Harry laughed as he stroked his beard.

Nathan finally saw his suitcase and retrieved it from the carousel. They left the baggage claim level and after exiting the terminal, took an elevator to the street level parking lot for short-term parking. In less than twenty minutes they were in his father's driveway.

When they walked to the front door, Harry insisted that Nathan go ahead of him. Nathan gave his father a curious look, shrugged his shoulders, and walked into the house ahead of Harry. He looked ahead and dropped his bag where he stood in total surprise. Nathan could not believe his eyes as he looked into the face of his beloved Rachael! His parents had invited her to come over earlier in the day, knowing that Nathan would likely come home, drop off his bag, give them each a hug and a kiss, and head out the door to Rachael's house. This way they were sure to get more time with their son! Harry might have been getting old, but he hadn't lost one bit of his shrewdness.

Rachael lived nearly an hour away in Martin County and that, too, was a sign from God as far as Nathan was concerned. How else would the girl of his dreams appear at a Yeshiva graduation up north and yet also live in Florida—within driving distance!

"Rachael!" Nathan exclaimed with excitement. The two embraced, never wanting to let go.

"I hope you don't mind, but your parents . . ."

"Don't say another word!" Nathan commanded in a loving way. He kissed her on the lips and on both cheeks until Ruth, standing beside

Rachael, made a remark about becoming "second fiddle" now that her son was in love.

Nathan let go of Rachael and hugged and kissed his mother as she laughed and pushed him back toward Rachael.

"Go ahead, she's younger!" And that was when Harry finally asked about dinner.

"The boy is starving after all that flying. Less kissing and more eating!"

Nathan went into the bedroom to wash up before joining them at the table. As he wiped the cool water from his face, he heard a light knock at the bedroom door. It was his mother, who entered the room and quietly closed the door behind her.

"Thanks so much for bringing Rachel down here." Nathan's gratitude was evident in his voice.

"Don't be silly. We had selfish but loving reasons. We wanted to spend some time with Rachael before you landed, and then keep you at home for a while as well. Nathan, I have something that I want you to have. I believe in my heart that this is the appropriate time to give it to you."

Nathan appeared surprised and wrinkled his brow with a curious sort of look. "What do you mean, Mom?" Nathan asked.

"Come, sit with me here on the bed." Ruth sat on the edge of his bed and patted the bedspread next to her signaling Nathan to sit down. He sat beside her and looked into her eyes with curiosity, waiting to see why his mother was being so secretive. Ruth reached into her apron pocket and brought out a white handkerchief. The four ends of the handkerchief were tied, and when she untied them, Nathan saw a small black velvet box. Ruth picked it up from her lap and handed it to Nathan.

"Mom, what is this?" he inquired.

"Open it," his mother insisted.

Nathan opened the box. When he saw the beautiful diamond ring, he took a deep breath. Tears began to fill his eyes. As he looked up at his mother, he saw that she too was tearful, and they simply embraced.

"Mom, I love you and Dad so much! You have been such wonderful parents that I will never be able to repay that much love in my lifetime," Nathan expressed with the utmost of sincerity. Ruth smiled and glanced at the nearly one-carat diamond engagement ring that had belonged to

Nathan's grandmother. In her usual soft voice and with the tone of a proph-etess, his mother said,

"I believe that tonight is the right time to give this ring to you. I see a girl at the kitchen table who loves you very much. Your father and I love her as if she were our own daughter." She leaned forward and placed her hands on his cheeks. She then looked into his eyes with wisdom and a mother's love.

"God has sent you the wife you have waited for."

She smiled, stood up, and left the room. Nathan watched her quietly open and close the bedroom door, and then he stared at the ring. Beaming a bright smile of joy, he lifted his eyes and thanked God for this blessing. Surely this was the night to ask Rachael to be his wife.

As soon as Nathan came into the room, Ruth excused herself, making a remark about "getting dinner on the table." Rachael looked at Nathan with a puzzled look. He watched as her right eyebrow rose just a bit. She would do this whenever she was questioning something. He smiled at the thought of his already being aware of her eccentricities.

"Why did Ruth leave?" Rachael asked.

Nathan maintained his boyish smile for a moment and came around the table to Rachael's side. He took her left hand in his and nervously stated,

"Calling her Mom instead of Ruth would be more appropriate."

He knelt down on one knee in front of her. He cleared his throat in a nervous sort of way and looked directly into Rachael's eyes, which were beginning to glisten with tears of joyful expectation. She tilted her head ever so slightly, gazing down into his eyes, and smiled in a way that Nathan had not seen before. It was as though she was looking right into his very soul.

"Rachael, until I met you at my graduation, life for me was about ful-filling the desires of my parent's hearts, especially my father's wishes. It was about serving God and taking over the pulpit from my father. I prayed for God to send me a partner in all of this: a wife who would share my values, my commitment to the synagogue, and who would share my dreams. The moment my eyes met yours that day, I knew you were the one. Only God Himself could have sent me His most beautiful creation. Would you do me the honor of becoming my wife?" Rachael knelt down beside him and melted into his arms.

She embraced him and whispered,

"Yes, Nathan, with all my heart and my life."

He took the black velvet box from his pocket and opened it, holding it out for Rachael to see. Nathan removed the ring and placed the empty box in his pocket.

"This ring belonged to my grandmother, and her mother before her. My mother handed it down to me, as is the family tradition. My father gave it to her when he proposed, and now, with my commitment of eternal love, I give you this ring and ask you to be my partner in life for all time."

Nathan slipped the ring on the fourth finger of Rachael's left hand, and the two embraced so tightly it appeared as though they would never separate! As if they were right on cue, Harry and Ruth came into the dining room and took turns embracing and congratulating the newly engaged couple.

During the meal that evening, conversations ranged from wedding plans to the honeymoon. *Rachael will make the perfect rabbi's wife,* Harry thought to himself as he watched her pass every question back to Nathan for his opinion or approval, depending of course on the question at hand. Harry now had his own confirmation that God had just arranged his retirement.

Chapter Three

Perfect Unions

The Board of Directors of the synagogue had established a custom that when a rabbi was named to join the staff, he would sit with the board and receive what they called "the charge." It was a time of acquainting the incoming rabbi with the policies and decisions the board had voted on in the past. Nathan knew what this traditional interview was about. He thought that the procedure was especially amusing when one considered that his father was the founder and only rabbi since the synagogue's inception. He prayed that they wouldn't explain *all* the decisions they had made for the past thirty years!

"Gentleman," Harry began, "this is a very proud day for me, an occasion filled with joy. On this day, the old generation retires and the new generation receives his charge. It is the day we charge him with his duties, his continued faithfulness to God and the synagogue, his family, and the community."

Harry turned and looked directly at his son.

"Nathan, as the new rabbi of this synagogue, God willing, you must not only teach the Torah, but you must also live it. You should be an example for the community, one who is above reproach. You not only represent the synagogue, but more importantly, the laws of God. You must reflect the values and the rules of our faith so that they may be instilled in others. You must be involved with all aspects of running the synagogue from administration to finances. However, no institutional leadership shall come above spiritual leadership and your responsibility to teach Torah and lead our people to a higher understanding of the Jewish faith. As far as religious questions within the synagogue, we know that Torah confers authority on the rabbi as spiritual leader of the congregation so that he may discern and answer any religious questions brought before him. In doing so, you must possess a complete knowledge of the law so that you may uphold the law in the execution of your duties. You must be faithful to the law, to its principles, and its axioms of faith."

Nathan stood and pledged his acknowledgement and acceptance of these things. Harry prayed a short prayer and all said "amen" as they stood and congratulated him. Nathan thanked them and then practically ran from the small room to drive to Rachel's, where she was anxiously waiting for him. They were to meet with her parents and begin making plans for their life together—the wedding, their honeymoon, and where they were going to live.

~

Americans have no idea how young terrorists are recruited. One would think that the terrorist organizations waited for them to turn a certain age, such as seventeen years old, when an Israeli enters the army for his or her expected tour of duty. But a boy named Reuben Feldman? An Israeli? From the very moment Reuben learned that the Israeli soldiers had killed Elanie's parents, something snapped in his young mind. He had never been religious and did not really follow any of the traditional practices of Jewish boys. Now, nearly twelve, he wanted no part of a Bar Mitzvah and was beginning to actually believe the many brainwashing conversations he had overheard at school.

A boy in his class who had secretly converted and became a Muslim, influenced his rapidly developing disdain for the Israeli way of life. No one in the school knew about it or the boy would have been expelled from the predominantly Jewish school. The distorted and misguided conversations about the killing of innocent Palestinians in the West Bank had finally touched Reuben's sympathetic side for his sister's tragic past. He became angry, and several conversations later, he turned against all he was raised to believe in.

He would study about the Quran and would never let his parents know. *I can now worship with Elanie,* he reasoned. Their parents had attempted to teach Elanie their Jewish customs, but she was as stubborn as she was brilliant. She refused, but did so in a way that was never disrespectful to the parents who gave her a new life. The Feldmans quickly discontinued their efforts so as not to force Elanie into any situation that would compromise her adjustment and the love they felt for her.

There was, however, no doubt about her intelligence. At five years old she could solve math problems that were usually taught in the fourth or fifth grade. She loved to talk about nature and the flowers, the bees, and how they go from flower to flower. A five-year-old girl was actually becoming aware of the process of pollination! She didn't even know how close she was to becoming the brightest student in the school. Her teacher recognized how smart she was and began allowing her to slowly delve into more difficult projects each week—beginner's science and biology being her favorite. She was also very popular, and her classmates were drawn to her captivating beauty and precious smile.

"I can only imagine great things for your sister," her teacher remarked to Reuben one afternoon when he came to walk her home. Reuben simply smiled, took Elanie's hand, and walked away.

Nathan and Rachael's wedding rekindled wonderful memories for Ruth, as not many customs had changed from when she and Harry were married. They even had white starched tablecloths and napkins, now supplied by Harry's friend who attended the synagogue. Brandon Nussbaum had a commercial laundry operation, and whenever there was a function at the synagogue, he declared, "It is an honor to dress up God's house."

All the details of the wedding were perfect. The *huppah* (a trellis-like covering over the bride and groom) was simple but beautiful, adorned with an array of flowers that Rachael had handpicked from her parent's back yard. She had wanted everything to be from their families and not purchased. Her mother's wedding dress, handed down from her grandmother, and her engagement ring, handed down from Nathan's grandmother, were the most significant ties to that tradition.

The small vases of pink and white carnations on each table were modest, but they added just the right touch of color. The room comfortably seated a hundred people and was used for every social function.

Ruth's thoughts were quickly turned back to the moment as Eli, their resident pianist, began playing select background music, a signal that the wedding was about to begin. Ruth took her place with Rachael's mother. Ruth Wasserman leaned close to Ruth Blumberg and whispered, "Did you ever think that from a brunch at graduation we would see such a joyous day?"

They both smiled as two mothers who could not have asked for a more blessed occasion—not counting their expectations of a first grandson, of course!

Allen, Rachael's brother, and Josh, Nathan's best friend, were both serving as best men. Allen held the gold wedding band intended for his sister, and Josh held the ring for his best friend and fellow Yeshiva classmate.

After all participants in the ceremony were in their proper places, the music went from background music to processional, and the wedding party started down the aisle. When everyone reached his or her designated and well-rehearsed places, there was a brief pause in the music. Then, "Here Comes the Bride" echoed throughout the synagogue, and everyone turned and watched the back of the sanctuary. Rachael's precious blond-haired niece, who was five years old, walked just ahead of Rachael, sprinkling flower petals on the white cloth runner.

Rachel gracefully walked down the aisle while her father held her arm. There was a radiance emanating from her that seemed as though God had sent several angels to be at her side. The brightest and purest of lights seemed to shine from her smile. She wore her mother's wedding dress with only a few added modern touches. It was as lovely as the day her mother had worn it to her own wedding.

As soon as Rachael was standing beside Nathan, Harry asked everyone to be seated. The cantor chanted the blessings bestowed on every new couple, and there was hardly a dry eye in the entire synagogue. Just witnessing the way Nathan and Rachael looked at one another was enough to set the tears flowing. It was nearly impossible for Harry to get through the ceremony without pausing every so often to keep himself from being overcome with emotion. Nathan then turned to Rachael, beholding her in the fullness of their mutual love. Josh handed him the ring and he placed it on her finger.

He then declared in Hebrew, *"Harai at mekudeshet lee, b'ta-ba-at zu, k'dat Mosheh v'Yisrael"* (Be sanctified to me with this ring in accordance with the Law of Moses and Israel).

Rachael then placed Nathan's ring on his fourth finger and also vowed her love and devotion. Traditionally, as in all Jewish weddings, Harry took a glass wrapped in a small towel and placed it at Nathan's right foot. Nathan raised his leg, and his foot came down on the glass with such force that even the guests in the back seats of the synagogue heard the sound of the glass being shattered.

Everyone shouted, "Mozeltov!" (The glass is broken as a tradition in commemorating the destruction of the temple in Jerusalem in 70 a.d. by the Romans.) Harry's emotions were about to spill over as he pronounced them man and wife. Nathan kissed Rachel with a kiss that was sweeter than anything that had ever touched his lips. Her smile spoke a million words to his heart, saying, *"I am yours forever and will stand by your side through all this life and beyond."* This was part of their personal vows they had made to each other. They spiritually sensed the depth of their love, something they could not explain in their finite wisdom. They simply knew that God had brought them together.

As they walked back up the aisle, Nathan experienced such overwhelming feelings of love that all he wanted was to share their souls, intimately and tenderly. Nathan sensed that tonight the stars would fall from the heavens and light up their honeymoon suite. He imagined an array of brilliant fireworks over Biscayne Bay that was being set off just for them. Nathan had always expressed a vivid imagination but on this night, his imagination would turn into a blessed reality.

They were to stay at the Sonesta Beach Hotel in Key Biscayne. It was a beautifully appointed hotel with a reputation for service and attention to every detail in satisfying their guests. Harry had held several functions at the hotel over the past several years, and George, the banquet manager, complimented them with the bridal suite for two days.

Nathan saw Rachael glance at her wedding band as they neared the end of the aisle. Nathan thought, *we are really one now—we are married! I have a wife who is as beautiful within as she is in her appearance.* They headed for the stairs toward the back exit of the synagogue. Before the ceremony, Harry had requested that they wait at the bottom of the back staircase to allow the guests to exit the synagogue through the front doors and walk around to the back. This way, they could line up along the single pathway to the street and see them off where their limousine was waiting for them. The limousine ride was a wedding gift from one of the congregants.

Harry had suggested that just before Rachael got into the limousine, she should announce, "The next girl to be married shall be . . ." and throw her wedding bouquet over her shoulder—a traditional gesture, predicting that the girl who caught the bride's bouquet would be the next to marry.

As they waited for Harry, they leaned against the wall at the foot of the staircase, and Rachael practically melted into Nathan's arms. "Oh, Nathan, I am so happy! This is so right—I feel you within my very soul and cannot wait to be with you tonight. I have kept myself for my husband."

Nathan felt a hot flush pass through his body and he nearly lost his balance. He promised himself that he would make these moments last forever, inscribing them with indelible ink on the pages of his most beloved memories. He bent forward and kissed her tenderly, whispering words of love that came pouring out of his heart.

She tightened her arms around him just as the exit door swung open and a voice exclaimed, "Okay, okay, there will be a whole lifetime for that, but now you have about eighty people lined up in the afternoon sun, and they are all waiting for you, so let's go!" It was Harry, and they saw the tears of happiness in his eyes.

Harry opened the door and the newlyweds, Rabbi and Mrs. Nathan Blumberg, walked along the line of guests as shouts of blessings were heard over and over.

When the driver opened the door for Rachael to get into the limousine, she followed Harry's earlier request. After she shouted, "The next girl to be married," she tossed the wedding bouquet over her shoulder and high into the air. Rachael's cousin, Melinda, who was just sixteen, caught the bouquet, and everyone laughed and joked about her future wedding. Nathan and Rachael slid into the plush, black leather seats of the stretch Lincoln limousine. When the doors closed, the sounds of the world disappeared, and the driver sped away toward Biscayne Bay.

~

It had been nearly three months since the wedding and Harry wanted to give Nathan and Rachael ample time to set up their modest home. It was two bedrooms, and two baths, just east of Federal Highway in Pompano Beach. One of Harry's old-time friends had inherited the house from his aunt when she passed away. It needed a great deal of interior work as well as a new roof. However, with the prices of homes in Pompano Beach at that time, a modest investment would bring the house back into its original cottage-type décor—restoring both the house and its market value.

The house was only minutes from the ocean, and they both loved to spend their Sunday mornings at the beach. They would walk together, hand in hand, holding their shoes and allowing the surf to gently roll across their bare feet. They would stop occasionally for a look at a curious shell in the sand or a jellyfish that was beached by a wave, but mostly they would just walk and talk. You didn't have to look twice at this couple to see how much in love they were.

The younger Blumbergs would attend the synagogue faithfully every Friday night and Saturday, and Rachel always made a traditional Shabbat dinner before services. Harry and Ruth were there every week by Rachael's invitation. They loved her excellent cooking. *Oh what a blessing she is,* Ruth would think to herself with the first sip of her homemade chicken soup. Rachael seemed to simply beam as she faithfully attended to God's business. It was her gentleness; her poise, her soft voice and her love for God and for Nathan that had made Ruth fall in love with her from the moment they met.

This Friday night, Harry had some serious business to discuss with the family. Just as they finished their first cup of coffee, he asked for their undivided attention—as though Nathan could stop staring at Rachael long enough to be undivided! Harry cleared his throat slightly as he usually did before he was about to give his message at the synagogue. They could see that he was most serious about whatever it was he had to tell them.

"Children, your mother knows this already because we have discussed it, and we have decided that tonight would be the best time to tell you of our plans before we leave for services."

Harry glanced at his watch and realized they had only twenty minutes, so he pressed on.

"I am going to retire as of this weekend and turn the pulpit over to my son."

Harry now had the full attention of both Nathan and Rachael. Nathan was quite surprised by this sudden announcement. There had been no prior warning or even a discussion before tonight. He had received his indoctrination, but no date had been set as to when he would take over. He was very content being the assistant rabbi to his father and having fewer responsibilities so he could spend more time with his new bride. Nathan stared directly into his father's eyes as many thoughts began to fill his mind. *I can't say no to him,* he thought with a sense of urgency. He could see that his father was waiting for some kind of response from him. *My father has sacrificed his whole life to educate me and send me to the university to study our traditions and our laws and to be ordained. I cannot let him down. I pray that Rachael feels as I do.*

Nathan slowly broke into one of his famous, warm-their-hearts smiles. Harry beamed with obvious relief, for he knew the answer was a positive one. There wasn't an expression on Nathan's face that Harry didn't know.

"Dad, Mom, it will be an honor to take the pulpit in our family tradition. And as this is news to me, I have some news for you."

Harry was a wise man and instantly glanced at Ruth. The two of them looked right at Rachael, for it was the tone of his son's voice that gave it away.

"Do I have to guess," Harry began, "or do I simply embrace the mother of my first grandchild?"

Rachael and Nathan laughed, and Rachael stood up as Harry and Ruth jumped up and practically ran around the dining room table to embrace her.

"Mozeltov!" Ruth declared, obviously elated at the news. Harry wept for joy as he hugged Rachael. Nathan embraced both his parents and was simply reveling in this joyful moment.

"This is how we should do this," he said as he attempted to calm his emotions.

"Tonight at the closing of the services, I will make the announcement that the Blumberg family is blessed once again to have the next generation of rabbis stepping up to the pulpit because I am retiring. I will pause, and as most of our congregation will know exactly what I mean because they know me, I will then talk about my son, whom everyone also knows. Then I will ask them to pray for yet another generation that is now on the way! I don't suppose God has told you yet if it's a boy or a girl?"

They all laughed.

"That announcement should encourage some reactions from the congregation, and they will be prepared for the change of leadership."

Despite his age and failing health, Harry knew how to handle his congregation. After thirty years, Harry had not lost his eloquence at the pulpit. With that, he suggested they leave for the Synagogue.

Rachael and Ruth finished removing the dishes from the table. They wrapped some of the leftover chicken and side dishes and put them away. It took but ten minutes with the four of them helping, and they were walking toward the synagogue with just enough time for Harry to enter through the back door. It would take only two minutes to change into his black robe, his tallis, his head covering, and walk to the front of the stage to begin the services.

What a blessed day, Harry thought to himself, and his heart welled up with thankfulness and spiritual strength.

After Ruth and Rachael were inside, Nathan approached the door of the synagogue and motioned for Harry to go ahead of him. Harry smiled at Nathan and exclaimed,

"No, my son, you are the new rabbi of this synagogue, and I will hold the door open for you! And by the way, did I mention that you would be sitting next to me on the stage tonight and tomorrow? Pull your chair from the assistant side to the rabbi's side."

Nathan hugged Harry. As he walked ahead of his loving father, he glanced back and watched Harry pull the door closed, lock the top and bottom locks, and kiss the Mezuzah that was proudly mounted on the doorpost. (This is a custom and obedience to God's instructions declared by Moses to "bind a sign upon the doorposts of your house." The Ten Commandments are inscribed on a rolled parchment located within.)

Nathan imagined him having done the same routine for the past thirty years. He smiled to himself as he pictured himself doing the very same thing for the *next* thirty years.

When Harry made the announcement, it was as though the congregation already knew what was going to happen that night. Everyone who attended the synagogue was there—which was unusual. Perhaps Harry had let the word out in a brief mention to another member, or perhaps it was after Nathan received his indoctrination. On this night, however, Harry wanted the entire world to know that his son, Nathan Blumberg, would be the next rabbi at the pulpit of the synagogue.

Chapter Four

God's in Charge

Nathan was the only man sitting in the waiting room of Dr. Strauss's office, flanked on both sides by several pregnant women. Noticing their huge bellies, he could sense how uncomfortable these mommies to-be must feel! He tried to picture Rachael with such a large belly and almost began to laugh at the thought.

Sid was one of the most sought-after OB/GYN physicians in Broward County. He lived in Boca Raton and maintained this office on Oakland Park Boulevard so he could see his Ft. Lauderdale patients two days a week. Nathan was beginning to feel somewhat nervous, although he purposed his heart that morning to remain calm and strong for Rachael, who was in the process of receiving an ultrasound. She had been with the nurse technician for over an hour. ***What could be taking so long?*** he wondered, and he began wringing his hands together.

One of the women sitting across from him (the one who appeared ready to give birth at any moment) asked in a kind voice if this was his first child.

"Yes, it is. Can you tell?" She smiled at him with a knowing kind of look.

"Yes, since this is our third! After a while you can spot the first-time fathers."

Nathan was amazed—she didn't appear to be a day over twenty-five years old.

"When I was pregnant with my first child," she continued, "my husband paced these floors until the nurse finally came out to get him. The nurse calls all the husbands in so they can be with their wives when the doctor gives us his findings. His hands were as red as yours are right now!"

Nathan laughed and thanked her.

"May I also respectfully suggest that it is all in God's hands anyway, so why worry?"

Nathan looked at her and in that instant felt somewhat faithless, as he of all people should be telling her that and not the other way around.

"Thank you for those important and powerful words. You are absolutely right—it *is* in God's hands. Does that mean I can stop wringing my hands now?" Nathan chided himself, and they both began to laugh.

The woman introduced herself. "My name is Suzanne Stoltz." Nathan returned the introduction but left out the title of "rabbi."

"It's nice to meet you, Mr. Blumberg."

"Please," he insisted, "call me Nathan."

"I should really call you Rabbi Nathan, should I not?" she replied, catching him totally off guard.

"How did you know I was a rabbi? Are you Jewish?" Nathan asked.

"No, I am not. However, my best friend whom I went to college with is Jewish. We have been friends all these years. I am definitely not a psychic!" she joked. "However, you were quietly praying when they first took your wife into the examining room, and a few words of Hebrew rose above your silent prayers. You are also carrying a Jewish prayer book that my friend's rabbi also carries."

"You noticed all of that? Am I that much of a giveaway?" Nathan asked with a warm but somewhat embarrassed smile.

"Actually, while you were praying you were moving your head up and down ever so slightly, which is what the religious Jewish men do when they pray."

"Well!" Nathan exclaimed as he regained his composure from the surprise. Here was a total stranger who had pegged him for a rabbi, just from her slight familiarity with Jewish customs! She had obviously learned all these things from her Jewish friend.

"Tell me," Nathan went on, "where does your friend go to synagogue?"

"Oh, she attends a Messianic synagogue in Tamarac."

"Messianic?" Nathan questioned.

"Yes," Suzanne replied, that's correct."

There was a moment of silence as Nathan thought about this. He had heard of that synagogue, as well as another in Boca Raton.

"What is your friend's name?" Nathan asked.

"Esther Rabinowitz—do you know her?"

"Is that the same Rabinowitz family who own the Ramada Inn?"

"Yes," she replied, "it is. Do you know the family?"

Nathan hesitated again, for the story was rather complicated.

"Yes," he finally responded, "I believe my father knows them. You are speaking of his daughter who would be around your age now, aren't you?"

"Yes, I am," Suzanne answered, but this time her voice took on a more cautious tone.

Nathan discerned that he needed a quick way out of this conversation and took it. He was not about to relate how Esther broke her religious father's heart when she turned away from Judaism.

"I really only know *of* Esther. I do not know her personally since we've never met. The relationship was actually between my father and her father."

"I see," Suzanne replied, but she sensed there was more to this and the rabbi was simply avoiding controversy.

It was the perfect timing for an interruption in the conversation as the nurse walked over to Nathan and asked him to follow her to the doctor's office. Rachael's ultrasound and exam were completed. He smiled and thanked Suzanne for her kindness and her support and wished her well. She smiled and wished him luck. He caught up with the nurse, who had already opened the door to the doctor's office.

"Thank you" he said as he went past her and shook Doctor Strauss' hand.

He was standing behind his desk, waiting for Nathan to come in. Sid wore a white jacket over a starched white shirt and colorful tie. His slacks were khaki, and his shoes were Docksiders. He had a stethoscope tucked into the right, outside jacket pocket and a penlight and tongue depressor clipped within the breast pocket of his jacket.

Sid was about medium height and build with silver hair and blue eyes. He always boasted a deep tan, which usually kept its bronze color from his time on the golf course or boating and fishing on Wednesdays. Friday afternoon and Sunday were both golf days. Sid adored Harry and Ruth and had attended their synagogue until he moved to Boca Raton. Every once in a while he would drive down on a Saturday morning with his wife and attend a service.

"Dr. Sid," Nathan greeted him, "I haven't seen you in what seems like years!"

"Yes, I know. I have been busy with the practice and trying to balance Boca and Ft. Lauderdale with three to four deliveries a week. I haven't seen you for a while, since you went off to Yeshiva—and by the way, congratulations. I hear you took over the pulpit from your father. How is he?"

"Harry is fine, and thanks for asking. Where is Rachael?"

"She is getting cleaned up and dressed. We use a lot of "belly jelly" during the ultrasound, and it takes a while to remove it all. She will join us here in a moment." As Sid looked deeply into Nathan's eyes, it was that very moment that Nathan suspected something was wrong.

"What is it, Sid?" Nathan asked in a direct tone of voice.

Sid looked down for a moment and then asked Nathan to wait until Rachael came in so he could talk to them as a couple. Rachael was now fifteen weeks and had been suffering with morning sickness, but she never really complained about any other symptoms. The larger of their concerns was her spotting. There were small spots of blood that she found on her panties and on the sheets in the past few days. She had tried to hide her concern from Nathan, but he knew she was quite upset.

Just then Rachael came in. Nathan stood and kissed her on the cheek, taking her hand as though to lead her to sit down next to him.

"Is something wrong," Rachael asked, "or are you two simply talking about golf?" Nathan and Sid laughed and they sat down. Sid began in a quiet tone, his hands folded on the desk in front of him. He appeared very professional instead of relaxed, as a long-time family friend would be.

"Rachael, Nathan," Sid began, his voice now becoming quite serious. "I do not want to alarm you, and I surely do not want you to misconstrue what we are going to talk about, but I have some concerns with this pregnancy."

"What's wrong?" Rachel alarmingly responded. Her right hand went up to cover her mouth as she did when she was emotionally excited—good or bad news alike. Nathan took her hand and held it tight, giving her a reassuring look.

"Rachael, the key word here is caution. There are several complications that will need to be closely monitored."

Sid stood up and walked around his desk as Nathan and Rachel turned their chairs to face the opposite wall in his office. Hanging on the wall were several charts and pictures of the various stages of pregnancy. Sid pointed to one of the pictures and began to explain. It was as though the doctor's words were inaudible, for all she could hear were the words "lose the baby, stay off her feet for most of the pregnancy" and something about her uterine wall.

Rachael did not have to hear all the medical or technical details to feel the sudden, crushing sensation that seemed to envelop her chest. It was like a wall of sand slowly sifting down on her, burying her in slow motion. There were tears and medical terms exchanged, and thirty minutes later, they left Sid's office. As they entered the elevator, she took Nathan's hand and held it so tightly that he began to lose all feeling in his fingers. She was visibly trembling, although she was trying to hide the emotional pain sweeping her away in a tide of disappointment and denial.

When they reached their car, Nathan opened the door, and Rachael got into the front seat without so much as single word or glance. Nathan walked around the car and got in. From the time he started the engine until the moment they were almost home, Rachael remained silent. Suddenly, she began to sob and kept murmuring, "I am so sorry, Nathan," over and over again. He heard the heartbreaking pain in her voice, and he had to bite his lower lip to keep his emotions under control. He saw a gas station a half block ahead on Federal Highway and pulled in, parking the car in the farthest space from the front door of the convenience store. He turned toward her and held her face in his hands in an act of comfort and understanding.

"Rachael, after God, *you* are my life. If this child was not meant to be, then it's God's will. He is in charge, and if He wants us to have a child, then we will have a child. Sid said you should be careful, plan a strict diet of high protein, and stay off your feet as much as you can. You must take medication and pray—that is all you can do. These things happen, and it's not your fault or some quirk in your genetic makeup! Sid will monitor you once a week. If he thinks there is the slightest chance that the situation is worsening, he will do what is morally, ethically, and medically correct. I trust Sid, and I will not jeopardize the life of my wife. We know that the chance of going full term has many risks. We will wait, we will pray, and we will trust God. Okay?"

Through her tears, Rachael stared into his eyes and saw the undeniable love he had for her. She threw her arms around his neck and whispered how much she loved him, over and over again—but it did not ease the gnawing pain of fear and disappointment within her. Breaking the news to his parents was not going to be easy. There was a fifty-percent chance they could lose the baby. Worst of all, there was the stark medical reality that Rachael would never be able to have another child. This was their only chance. Whatever happened, they would trust God's will. Nathan knew that if all turned out well, it would surely be a miracle, and that's what he was praying for.

~

Nathan and Rachael readied themselves to join Harry and Ruth for their weekly Shabbat dinner. Rachael had not slept well Thursday night, and Nathan decided to stay with her and not go to the synagogue on Friday morning. They talked some, prayed for a while, and spent a quiet day together, supporting one another simply by each other's company and an occasional hug or prayer. Until today, Rachael had usually prepared the meal each Friday, but Ruth insisted she was going to cook this week. She had not received a call from Nathan or Rachael after their visit with Sid on Thursday, and she instinctively knew something was wrong. She also stopped Harry from calling Sid or Nathan and Rachael after their appointment. She reasoned with him that "If I cook dinner and the kids come over, they will be here, and they will tell us."

It was time to drive over to his parents, and Nathan locked the front door while holding on to Rachael's arm with his other hand. They walked to their car in the driveway, and he opened the front passenger door for Rachael. Waiting until she was comfortably seated, he shut the door and walked around the front of the car and got into the driver's side. After starting the car and before backing up, he turned to Rachael with a reassuring look and told her he loved her very much. Rachael smiled and responded with her radiant look of love.

"I know how much you love me, Nathan, and together we will get through this. I simply needed a day to adjust, to pray, to regain my composure, and to allow my faith in God to replace the panic. I also thought about the fact that if we are all praying for our child to fight for his life, we need to have a name for this child in our prayers. Even if God's will is that he does not survive, a name will be required to bury him."

Nathan admitted his surprise at the calmness and correctness of Rachael's statement. "Wouldn't you rather wait a few weeks when you might be feeling stronger to do this?"

"No," Rachel replied with a firmness that told Nathan she was quite serious. "We will ask your parents to help select a name, and we'll pray that God will instill that name in all of our hearts. We'll choose a boy's name since the ultrasound and blood tests that Dr. Sid conducted indicated that it's likely a boy."

Nathan nodded, acknowledging her wishes, and started the car. The drive to his parents' house took only a few minutes. When they arrived, Ruth was waiting outside the front door as if she had timed their arrival. Ruth gave Rachael a warm smile and threw her arms around her as she came to the front door. Both he and Rachael surmised that his parents would know there was a problem when they didn't call them after the doctor's appointment.

Harry came to the door and saw the scene on the front porch. He lowered his head for a moment, and then embraced Rachael before motioning for them to come inside. Nathan followed, and they all went into the dining room and sat down at the dinner table. Nathan explained the details of the problem while Rachael could hardly speak. She simply sat there and shook her head in disbelief. When Nathan finished explaining the risks as well as the hardship that Rachael would have to endure in order to have this baby, he paused and asked his parents if they had any questions.

"No," said Ruth, "not right now. It is more than obvious that Rachael is the one who has to make certain decisions. If Doctor Sid is sure about this, Rachael will have to practically spend the next five months in bed. What did Sid say about another pregnancy or future children?" Nathan looked over at Rachael. Her eyes were lowered, and she was silent.

"This is our only chance for a child. We cannot take the risk of a future pregnancy. It could be too harmful to Rachael," Nathan answered.

Ruth did not react but rather rose from the chair and walked around the table to Rachael and gently stroked her hair. "We will face this together, as a family. I would like you to both think about Rachael moving in here with us. Since I am home most of the day, I could care for her. Have you shared this news with Rachael's parents?"

"No, we have not," Nathan replied.

"May I ask why you haven't?" Harry queried. He had remained silent until that point but chose to express the inappropriateness of their not sharing this with Rachael's parents. Nathan addressed his question by apprising him that Rachael's father was recently diagnosed with a heart condition. They felt the news would be too much for him to handle at the moment.

"I see," Harry commented. "Rachael," Harry began after a minute or so of silence. "Would you like Ruth to call your mother, invite her to lunch, and break the news to her—mother to mother?"

"Yes, please," Rachael answered gratefully.

Harry abruptly stood up as though he had just received a revelation.

"We will take this challenge on together, and we will win. God will deliver a son to you, a grandson to us, and although it will be tough on Rachael, just think about all the movies and books she can catch up on!"

For the first time, Rachael looked up at Harry and smiled as though new hope had been pumped into her veins.

"Yes, I *will* catch up on reading and some good movies. Ruth, will you teach me how to knit?" Ruth was still standing behind Rachael, and a tear gently rolled down her cheek.

"I will be happy to teach you knitting, and we'll spend some wonderful time together—and I want to see some movies with you also. If you are going to knit, we can begin the baby's wardrobe right away!"

Ruth glanced over toward Harry and looked into his eyes with so much love and respect for her husband's wisdom and giving heart. Harry was a fighter and never gave up on any challenge that life threw his way. Once he made up his mind to meet an obstacle head-on, he would not give up until he either won or was convinced that God had another plan. At the very least, he would put up a good fight. He may be growing old, but Ruth could see that he still had plenty of spunk. This was the man she fell deeply in love with; the man she had always respected and stood beside, supporting all he believed was right and just. Now they were faced with a challenge they never expected. Somehow, Ruth believed deep within her that this would turn out okay. One healthy grandson to carry on the family tradition would be wonderful. *So who needs a whole house full of kids in this day and age anyway?* she thought to herself.

"I am going to prepare the guest bedroom for tonight. It is only a double bed, but you two are newlyweds, so you will be able to snuggle."

For the first time since they arrived, they all laughed together. It was a cautious sort of laugh, but nevertheless an expression of relief, and perhaps an exclamation of family unity and hope. Dinner was delicious as usual, and Harry left for the synagogue after he finished eating. He asked Nathan to stay with Rachael.

"I'll take the services tonight. You stay with your bride and the mother of my grandson!"

Ruth would not let Rachael lift a finger to help her with the dishes and insisted she relax on the couch in the living room. When the last dish was dried and put away, she took fresh sheets and pillowcases from the hallway linen closet and changed the linens in the guest bedroom to cheerful floral patterns and colors. They decided they should indeed pick a name for the baby, but it was getting late, and waiting until breakfast was a much better idea than rushing through it when they were tired. Rachael was in agreement and expressed that Harry and Ruth should be a part of that process.

Harry and Nathan awoke very early the next morning and prayed together as the sun came up. Ruth found them in the living room, sitting on the floor and talking about Biblical names. They were both led to select a name from one of the kings of ancient Israel. Nathan extended a hand to help his father stand up, but Harry waved him away.

"What do you think, I can't stand up on my own two feet?"

"No, Dad, just being polite."

"Sure, sure, and I suppose you think that my heart has weakened my legs as well."

"Okay, you two," Ruth interjected, "this is not a contest, and we need to move a little faster or you will be late for services. It *is* Saturday, remember?"

"Yes, my loving wife, I know what day it is." Harry smiled and winked at her.

"So . . . with all your prayer, did God give you a name?"

Nathan looked at his father, but Harry was silent. He simply went into the dining room and sat down. Nathan and Ruth followed. Harry took his pen from his shirt pocket and reached for the paper napkins that were tucked into a butcher-block holder at the center of the table. He lifted several of them and handed one to Nathan and one to Ruth.

"This is what I suggest we do," Harry began. "Let's each take a napkin and open it from right to left, with the solid fold facing left so there are two sides. We will each write the name we have on the right side and fold the napkin back over again. When Rachael wakes up, we'll explain to her what we're doing."

Nathan smiled warmly at his father's detailed instructions to what was actually a good use of handy resources! Nathan also commented he was sure Rachael had been up for a while and had been praying during the time they were talking. Ruth stood up and said she would check on her and left the room.

The moment she left, tears began to flow as Nathan cupped his head in his hands.

"Why, why did this happen to someone whom God blessed with every beautiful attribute? She is a gift, a good person who has never had a bad thing to say about anyone. Why would God allow this to happen?"

"No, Nathan, don't blame God," Harry quietly interjected. "God does not cause sickness, suffering, or human misfortune, and you of all people should know that—you are a man of God! You're a rabbi whom people look up to for their strength and their support in times of their own suffering and human frailties."

Harry was attempting to calm his son's emotions as he watched him becoming more and more frustrated.

"Man, in his frustration and humanity, questions God about things he cannot understand. Then he attempts to reason through those frustrations with finite wisdom."

"To me, Dad, nothing about this makes sense, and there *are* no answers." Nathan wiped the tears from his eyes with one of the paper napkins. As he did so, Nathan looked away from his father. He then heard his wife's voice as she was coming down the hallway with his mother.

"Let's not talk anymore. Rachael is coming."

Harry leaned closer to his son and in a whisper replied, "Then look *up* instead of clouding your faith with frustration, and allow God to be God!"

Their eyes met, and Nathan saw his father's wisdom and his love for him. He managed a smile as Ruth and Rachael came into the dining room. Rachael walked around the table to Nathan and kissed him gently on the lips and then on the top of his head. She was very affectionate, and Nathan enjoyed the benefits of being the sole outlet for those affections.

Ruth told Rachael about the method for selecting a name that they had agreed upon. Rachael agreed and took a napkin, unfolding it to the inner fold. She then looked up at Harry with a slight smile.

"Dad, did you want the fold left to right or right to left?" she chided.

"Okay, okay, so it doesn't matter which way you fold or unfold it."

Ruth leaned over and kissed him on the cheek. "You are still adorable, and still my charming Harry."

As Rachael unfolded the napkin, Nathan could not help but notice her small feminine hands and delicate fingers. There was not a single thing about Rachael that was not beautiful. Her hair was pulled back in a ponytail, and she was wearing a white lace robe that Ruth had given her as an engagement gift a few days after Nathan proposed.

"I have also been praying this morning, and I believe that God has given me a name for our son." Rachael looked right at Nathan and continued.

"I also have faith that He will allow us to have this child. I believe it's going to be a boy, and he will be a very special child. I sense there is a reason God wants us to go through this, and He will bless this pregnancy."

"Amen, from your mouth to God's ears!" Harry exclaimed.

Rachael took the napkin, reached across the table, and took Harry's pen. She cupped her hand in front of the napkin to cover the name she was writing. She placed the pen back in front of Harry and folded the napkin.

"You shouldn't have bothered hiding the name or folding the napkin," Ruth quipped. "You should go first!"

"No," Rachael replied. "I would prefer to hear *your* choice of names, and then I will let my choice be known. I told you, God gave me this name, and my husband should also have chosen the same name—perhaps all of us will."

Harry looked over at Ruth and opened his napkin. Harry had written the name David. Ruth became teary eyed, for she, too, had chosen that name. She looked at Nathan and motioned for him to open his napkin He tucked his lower lip inward with a slight smile. It was something he would always do when he tried to hide his emotions. Rachael and Ruth knew that look.

"You chose the name David also, didn't you?" Rachel asked Nathan with a smile, who was now beaming from ear to ear.

"Yes, I did."

They all took each other's hands and began to pray for the unborn David. He was no longer a fetus or an unborn child. He now had an identity, a link to historic greatness, as well as a link to their hearts. They all sensed that David would indeed be born and would also be a healthy baby. They were unified in their belief that God would use David for great things. Perhaps he would become the most renowned rabbi in the Blumberg family.

Rachael silently daydreamed, while Harry prayed for his coming grandson and for God's mercy in allowing this child to be blessed with life. The next few months would be a tough road, a journey of trials and complications, but they would deal with each challenge as it presented itself. More importantly, they would be bound together in hope and trusting God's perfect will. Rachael was willing to make *any* sacrifice necessary to give Nathan a son and a possible heir to the Blumberg pulpit. It was a commitment that went beyond most people's understanding.

The guest room was located just a short distance from the kitchen and was ideal for delivering three meal trays every day. Being next to the kitchen gave Rachael the freedom to get something to eat or drink without feeling helpless or totally dependant. Though she did not want to intrude on Rachael's privacy, Ruth had made up her mind that she was there for one reason and one reason only—to make Rachael as comfortable as possible and simply be there for her. It was not an easy task to stay off your feet for nearly five months.

Dr. Strauss was monitoring Rachael closely, intending to conduct any and all necessary tests. Sid was simply an old-fashioned doctor, and his close association with Harry made this a personal challenge for him. He took his patient's illnesses and individual needs very personally. He was unable to agree with his colleagues on not getting emotionally involved with one's patients; therefore, this pregnancy in particular was very important to him.

The weeks passed quickly, and Rachael commented that it wasn't as bad as she thought it would be. She openly thanked and praised her loving mother-in-law every day, who in return would tell her it was more of a blessing for her than being alone all day. Rachael's days were basic and routine, which presented an ongoing challenge of not becoming bored over the next four or five months. She would read for a while, chat with Ruth, learn a new knitting technique, and even watch a few T.V. programs. Rachael commented that she never realized there were so many soap operas on television. She decided to rent some videos and spent several afternoons quizzing Ruth about some of the older movies.

One morning Ruth paused at Rachael's door and lightly tapped on the center panel. It was a bit later than usual, and she had waited to see if Rachael would call her. It was nearly 8:30, and there had not been a sound from her room. Ruth knew she was still sleeping and did not want to intrude. She was also a little concerned since Rachael was usually an early riser.

Ruth knocked again. Not getting a reply, she opened the door quietly and saw that Rachael had actually been sleeping. However, Rachael heard the door open and was awakened when Ruth entered the room. She stretched her arms and legs to work out the stiffness in her joints from so much bed rest.

"Good morning," Ruth greeted her. Rachael looked up and squinted as Ruth opened the curtains. The morning light beamed across the room and onto her bed.

"Good morning, Mom," Rachael replied in a sleepy voice. Ruth placed the bed tray on the dresser and turned to help Rachael out of bed.

"How do you feel?" Ruth inquired as Rachael slowly slipped her legs over the side of the bed and adjusted her nightgown.

"I feel good, I really do." She managed a smile and placed her hands on her belly, which was growing larger by the day!

"Good morning, David," Rachael quietly said as she looked down at her stomach.

Ruth smiled and then remembered, "Before I forget—you *do* remember your appointment with Dr. Sid this morning? You are scheduled for an ultrasound—at least that's what I *think* they said. Sid asked me to remind you to drink a pint of water before you arrive at his office. I left a bottle of water in the refrigerator earlier this morning."

"Yes, thank you, Mom," Rachael gratefully replied. Ruth kept track of every test and logged them along with the results when they came back from the labs or the hospital.

Rachael slowly got up from the bed and hugged Ruth, holding her tightly and whispering, "Thank you, thank you."

"I love you, Rachael. You are like my very own daughter," Ruth whispered.

She then grasped Rachael's shoulders and took a step backward. "Look at you, the daughter I've always wanted, ever since Nathan was destined to be an only child. Now, you, too, have a son growing within you that could possibly be your only child."

Rachael lowered her head and stared at the floor but did not reply.

"I know," Ruth continued, "it's not easy to face truths such as these, but you must be strong. Take one day at a time, and trust in God to do His will. Who knows, maybe David will one day find another Rachael in this world to give you a daughter as well."

Rachael smiled as she walked past her and out into the hallway toward the bathroom. Ruth looked back at the food tray she left on the dresser and knew that the toast and the tea would be cold before Rachael would get to them. She picked up the tray and walked back into the kitchen to reheat the tea and warm the toast. The appointment was at 10:30 a.m., and Ruth knew that Nathan would be there to drive her. Sid had prescribed several medications that she was to take immediately upon rising each morning before she could get out of bed and walk around the house. Ruth kept track of them and readied them on the table with a glass of cold water.

Rachael came into the kitchen, laughing. "I feel like a pregnant turtle! If I move any slower, I won't walk a mile before it's time for the baby to be born!" She slowly and carefully eased herself into the kitchen chair. Ruth smiled and placed the reheated breakfast in front of her.

"What would I do without you?" Rachael asked as she slowly picked up a piece of toast and took a bite. Her words were said with a tone of sincere gratitude and love.

Ruth adored Rachael more and more with each passing day for her sweetness and genuine humility. *She is truly a prize,* she thought to herself as she placed a loving hand gently on her shoulder. Rachael looked up and could not hold back a few tears of thankfulness as she grabbed Ruth around the waist and hugged her.

"Shush now," Ruth said softly but firmly. "Don't you allow those beautiful eyes to become swollen before your husband arrives." Rachael smiled and told her how much she loved her.

At that moment the front door opened, and Nathan came into the kitchen with a big smile on his face.

He kissed his mother on the cheek and jokingly asked, "Who's the good looking pregnant woman at your table?" He bent down and kissed his wife on the forehead while stroking her hair.

"I would kiss you on the lips but you have raspberry jelly all over your chin!"

The humor was timely and appreciated. Rachael finished her tea and went to her room to dress while Nathan had breakfast with his mother.

The test results were the same as they had previously been, and the recommendations for Rachael's care were without change: She was to stay off her feet most of the time, get plenty of rest, not exert herself, and take her medications. There was to be no bending or lifting and very little walking. The baby was healthy, and as the weeks passed, their hopes were mounting.

Rachael mentally counted the weeks of her pregnancy on the way back home. *Let's see,* she thought, ***three months until we knew, a week of preparing to come here, seven weeks since I've been here—that would be about twenty weeks. Another eight weeks and the baby will be seven months! He will have a fighting chance—I have got to stay positive, I have got to trust God, I have got to . . .***"

~

The PLO leader watched as Reuben removed his shoes. He then motioned for him to enter the makeshift Mosque, located in the back of a house that was frequented by known terrorists. Reuben felt an overwhelming sense of pride, knowing that this was his time of indoctrination. He vividly recalled the scene of the Palestinian Fattah, wearing their black masks and holding their rifles in the air on the streets of the Gaza. They rallied together and cried out chilling chants of death to Israelis and Americans, and now he would be one of them.

"It is a time in history when the Israeli pigs will finally realize that we will no longer allow their oppression to smother our people and take from us what is rightfully ours. This is *our* land," Reuben's mentor declared, and Reuben had actually come to the point of believing him.

It was Reuben's day to receive his acceptance into the PLO. It was indeed rare for an Israeli born citizen to join their ranks, and it was a feather in the cap of the recruiter. There would have been only one witness on Reuben's side—one person to agree and to cheer him on—but girls were not allowed within. Elanie waited outside, under the care of a Palestinian woman who spoke with her about Muslim tradition and what was going on inside.

Reuben's convictions were put to the test the very next morning. Along with a group of young, would-be terrorists, he was taken to the Palestinian town of Beit Furik. It was a village located about six miles from Joseph's tomb. It had also been an Israeli Army outpost and a Jewish seminary in the Palestinian-controlled town of Nablus. It had been only one week since the Israeli troops had finally withdrawn from the area. The indoctrination that Reuben would face would be his witnessing the assassination of a Jewish Torah teacher who had immigrated to Israel and settled in the Jewish West Bank settlement of Elon Moreh, near Nablus. The teacher taught at the Joseph's Tomb School and was marked for death when he crossed paths with this group who had decided to ransack the Joseph's Tomb shrine. He was at the wrong place at the wrong time, caught up in the hatred and inner drive to expel the Israelis from the West Bank.

As the group raided and destroyed the shrine, the teacher drove up in his jeep and was fired upon by several of the terrorists who thought he was going to try to stop them. Wounded at first, they dragged him from the jeep and carried him off into a nearby cave. Reuben stood next to his terrorist mentor and stared down upon the bleeding Israeli teacher, who begged for his life. He had six children. The terrorist looked at Reuben and touched him on the shoulder. As Reuben turned his attention to his mentor, he handed him his revolver.

"Shoot him Reuben, and you will be glorified."

The teacher was discovered several days later with a single bullet in his left shoulder and a fatal bullet in his heart.

Chapter Five

The Miraculous Will of God

It was almost 3:00 a.m. when Ruth heard Rachael's scream. Nathan was not there. He had slept at their house that night to get some work done and prepare for the coming Shabbat message. Ruth ran into Rachael's room to find her lying in her bed, crying hysterically and sobbing,

"No, dear God, no! Please, this can't be happening. Not my David!"

Blood covered her pink nightgown and her legs. Ruth handed her a towel and ran to the phone to call Nathan. She only had to say, "Come quickly!" and then called Sid. She glanced at the kitchen clock and realized that it was the middle of the night. She was thankful he had given Harry his private home number. After many rings, Sid finally answered. He was drowsy but quickly responded to Ruth's urgent tone as she described Rachael's condition.

"Keep her in bed. Tell her to press her legs together and lay back. Do not allow her to get out of bed. I am sending an ambulance, and I will meet you there as soon as I call the hospital E.R. and have the surgical team prep what I need."

Ruth hung up the phone just as Nathan came bursting through the front door. When he got to Rachael's room, Harry was already kneeling and praying. Nathan took the chair from the corner of the room and sat beside her.

"Don't let her get up!" Ruth shouted, repeating Sid's orders. "He is sending an ambulance and does not want her to move."

The shrillness of a siren could be heard a few moments later. It sounded far off, but every second it was getting louder. Ruth wondered if she should call Rachael's parents.

"Rachael, do you want me to call your parents?" Ruth asked, and

Rachael shook her head to indicate no. She was still crying, but she was calmer than she had been before. Ruth noticed that there was no indication of any further bleeding and took that as a positive sign.

Nathan was attempting to comfort her while holding back his own tears. For the first time in his life, he actually felt helpless. He had always known what to do in an emergency situation. He was usually the calm one, but not this time. The blood on the silken gown of his precious wife could be that of his own son. Nathan wept within his heart, while the fear of what was to become of both his son and his wife swept over him. Outwardly, however, he remained steadfast for the sake of his wife and his parents.

The siren of the ambulance was now almost deafening, and then suddenly it stopped, indicating they had arrived. Ruth started for the hallway just as the EMT's knocked on the door. Moments later, two paramedics with a gurney entered Rachael's bedroom, began an I.V., and had Rachael on her way to Coral Springs Medical Center.

The hospital was located just off University Drive in Coral Springs, a town that had grown into a city over the past thirty or so years. The hospital had a highly advanced maternity unit, and Sid had wanted Rachael to have the best prenatal care when he made arrangements for her to be seen there for testing. Since she was in the throes of this unexpected crisis, it was the logical hospital for her to go to.

Both Harry and Ruth went with her in the ambulance, and Nathan followed in his car. Nathan could not keep up with the ambulance as it sped along route 95 with its lights flashing and siren wailing. At this time of night there was very little traffic. Had it been during the day, getting from Ft. Lauderdale to Coral Springs would have taken far too long in an emergency situation.

After what seemed like an endless drive, Nathan pulled into the emergency room entrance of the hospital parking lot and parked his car, nearly slamming his hand in the door as he closed it. He ran toward the emergency entrance, and the automatic doors swung open. The ambulance that had carried Rachael was just outside the main entrance with its doors wide open and no one inside. Nathan ran through the entrance and saw his parents, who motioned for him to follow them. They practically ran toward the trauma-room door when a nurse approached them. Her badge identified her as Natalie.

"I am so sorry, but you will have to wait here for the time being," Natalie stated with an authoritative but soft voice.

"Where is my wife?" Nathan asked.

"She is with Dr. Strauss and Dr. Brandon Halpner, our surgical resident. They are prepping her and will likely take her to surgery within a short while."

"How is she, and do they know about my son yet?" Nathan blurted out, allowing the tears to flow freely.

"Your wife appears to be stable, and they are hooking up the equipment to monitor the baby's heartbeat. I will be staying close to this situation."

Just then, a woman touched Nathan on the shoulder from behind.

"Are you the husband?"

"Yes, I am," he replied.

"My name is Trudy Stein with administration. I am so sorry to have to bother you in the middle of this emergency, but I will need you to fill out the appropriate medical and surgical consent forms. Your wife will likely be in surgery within the next thirty minutes." She handed Nathan an official looking form.

"This is the emergency surgical release, and I'll need your insurance card so that I may begin processing the hospital admission paperwork. I assure you that it won't take five minutes."

"Go ahead, Nathan," Ruth urged. "I'll stay here, and if I hear anything, I will come and get you. There is nothing we can do right now except pray."

Nathan nodded in recognition and proceeded to follow the admissions clerk.

Just then he heard a loud bell going off and saw several nurses running toward the set of doors that guarded the trauma rooms. Suddenly a voice coming from loudspeakers in the hallway of the trauma rooms blurted out, "Code one, E.D. three, stat. Repeat, code one E.D. three, stat."

Nathan panicked. He ran in the direction of the doors that stood between him and his wife and unborn son. Several nurses and two men pushing a cart with some type of a machine on it were rushing through the doors, and Nathan followed behind them. He watched as they all crowded into trauma room #3. It was the room Rachael was being treated in, and Nathan stopped just short of the door, nearly slipping on the polished linoleum floor. He took several steps backward and leaned against the wall opposite the room. His hands hung helplessly at his side, and he felt as though his entire life was being drained from him. Right there in that room, the person whom he loved more than his own life was lying there helpless, while a man placed two metal paddles on her bared chest.

The sound of the man's voice yelling, "Clear!" echoed through the hallway. Nathan felt as though he was in the middle of a nightmare from which he could not awaken. He gasped, holding back the sobs that were trying to erupt in his chest and throat. His eyes were transfixed on that room, but the figures moving about became blurred objects. Just then, the sounds from the room began to fade—the voices diminishing as though they were becoming farther and farther away. The lights in the hallway seemed to dim, and he suddenly felt cold, despite the perspiration dripping from his forehead.

Then, as the lights appeared to be fading to near blackness, he suddenly heard screams echoing within his head. From out of nowhere, a huge stone wall rose up and blocked his view of the room where Rachael and his son were fighting for their lives. He tried to jump up to see over it, but it was growing higher and higher. Then there was nothing but darkness.

~

Reuben was in the process of undergoing a psychological metamorphosis. His loving ways began changing to impatience and intolerance for any sign of human weakness. It was a matter of a hardened heart—especially after his indoctrination by the PLO. All he could think about was the injustice of Israeli dominance over the Palestinians. He would sit with Elanie for several hours on the weekends and talk about the poverty and oppression of those on the West Bank when compared to the living conditions and freedoms of the Israelis. Slowly, one convincing argument at a time, Reuben was penetrating the innocence and naivety that was once the shining, angelic smile of a girl who found a loving family. She was inching towards the thinking and the heart of a budding dissident. The sweetness of a pure soul was beginning to turn into doubts and tainted opinions as the shadows of the "dark side" began to creep into her thinking. Reuben was bringing her to a point of turning away from all she knew and had once believed in—slowly and methodically through his own disappointment and souring regard for Israeli justice.

~

Nathan heard a voice, faint but recognizable. It was the E.R. physician, and he was calling Nathan's name.

"Nathan, do you hear me?"

Nathan heard the voice and began to open his eyes. He tried to focus on his surroundings.

"Nathan, don't try to open your eyes too quickly. Take your time. I also don't want you to sit up yet. You should not have been outside that room where we were attending to your wife. You fainted from severe stress and have been unconscious for about ten minutes."

"Rachael . . . my wife, my son; what's going on?" Nathan managed to blurt out as he slowly tried to lift himself on to his elbows.

"Mr. Blumberg, your wife is in surgery right now with Dr. Strauss and our obstetrics specialist, Dr. Brandon Morgan."

Nathan sat up and rubbed his eyes, trying once again to focus.

"Doctor, what is the status of my wife and baby? When did she go into surgery?" Nathan was obviously scared now that he was lucid. He could feel the gut-wrenching pain of fear beginning to gnarl up in his stomach. He took a deep breath in an attempt to fight it off.

"Your wife went into surgery about five minutes after you passed out in the hallway. Your wife's heart stopped. The time clock that was started the very moment the incident occurred read out at precisely one minute and six seconds. That means there was no serious deprivation of oxygen to her brain or to the baby. Your wife began hemorrhaging, and Dr. Strauss made the decision to perform an emergency C-section."

Nathan shook his head as though acknowledging what the doctor was saying, but not wanting to believe all of this was actually happening. His thoughts were running out of control, and he mentally caught himself, managing to clear his throat and ask for a drink of water. He swung his legs over the side of the table that left him facing Jennifer, a nurse with large brown, sympathetic eyes and a pleasant smile. She handed Nathan a plastic cup with water from the stainless steel sink in the room, apologizing for it not being very cold. He sipped it slowly, draining the small cup.

"Doctor, are you saying that her heart began beating normally and that she is in surgery now?"

"Yes, that is correct."

"On what floor is surgery located?"

"O.R. is on the second floor. There is a surgical waiting room where you will be a lot more comfortable. Let's try to get you up, but slowly, please."

Nathan managed to thank the doctor for his help before he slowly got to his feet. *Oh God,* he thought. ***Where are my mother and father?***

"Excuse me, Doctor?" Nathan called, as the physician was about to leave the room. Nathan asked about his parents.

"They are both in the waiting room upstairs. Come, I will ride up with you and show you the way."

Nathan followed the doctor to an elevator that had stenciling indicating, "Medical Staff Only." He watched as the doctor placed a card in a slot that electronically signaled the elevator and the well-polished stainless steel doors opened. They rode up to the second floor in silence. When they exited the elevator, Nathan followed the doctor down a sterile-smelling hallway to the surgical recovery area and through another set of automatic doors.

When Nathan entered the waiting room, his mother and father literally jumped from their seats to greet him.

"My son!" Ruth exclaimed as both she and Harry hugged him so hard he could hardly breathe. ***God, they must be scared right now,*** Nathan thought to himself. Neither of them knew about what had happened in the trauma room, and Nathan was not about to tell them. He had to fight back the tears from his tired, reddened eyes. When they finally sat down again, Nathan sat next to his mother and simply stared into her eyes.

"Has there been any news yet?"

"No," his mother replied in a disappointed tone. It was as though she wished she could comfort her son with something positive, but they had not heard from anyone since they were ushered up to the second floor about a half hour before.

Nathan got up and began to pace the floor. After a few minutes, he told his parents he would be right outside and left the room. He began walking back and forth in the hallway, silently praying and realizing how helpless one was in these situations.

Just then, the twin set of electric doors from the surgery area swung wide open. A man in surgical clothing walked towards Nathan, removing his mask and cap. It was Sid. He was sweating profusely, and when he saw Nathan, a faint smile appeared on his face. Nathan turned to call his parents to come out, but Sid motioned to let them stay inside. He approached Nathan and placed his arm around his shoulder, ushering him back into the room.

Sid embraced Nathan, and with tears streaming down his cheeks, announced, "Congratulations, Rabbi, you have a beautiful son. Rachael is resting and doing well. The baby is in an incubator in the Neonatal Intensive Care Nursery and you may see him in a half hour or so—after he is cleaned and the nurses have completed what they need to do. However, you will not be able to see Rachael for about an hour or more until they bring her up from the surgical recovery room. They will bring her to a private room in maternity when she is fully awake and her vital signs are stable."

Nathan released a sob and wept tears of both thankfulness and guilt, as he knew in his heart that he had doubted God's sovereignty. Throughout this trial, he had not been as strong in his faith as he should have been; however, Nathan was totally convinced that God had a mighty plan for their son. Harry and Ruth gleefully hugged Sid and Nathan. Sid reminded them that David would have to stay in an incubator until he was strong enough to come home. He was premature and had been through a great deal of trauma already in his young life.

Although tradition called for the circumcision of their son on the eighth day, it could not take place until David was strong enough to go home. To comply with Jewish law, Nathan held a small ceremonial service in Rachael's room exactly eight days later, but David would remain in the nursery for at least another couple of weeks. He was physically strong, his reflexes were normal, and he was generally doing well. His lungs were functioning perfectly, and the nursery staff said he was absolutely beautiful for a premature infant. Sid called Nathan's son his miracle baby of the decade.

Nathan blessed the wine and the bread as the small but grateful party of immediate family and close friends looked on. They drank the wine and then prayed for baby David. Rachael was still officially in the hospital, but Sid said he would release her in another day or so. He wanted to make sure she was well on her way to healing from the ordeal before allowing her to go home. Rachael, however, was adamant about staying at the hospital until she could leave with her son in her arms. Since the hospital could not allow her to stay that long under insurance regulations, Sid intervened and spoke to the administration staff. Rachael would be officially discharged but could board in the room rather than be registered as an inpatient.

She appeared more radiant than before, possessing the vibrant glow of a new mother. Nathan hardly left her side, and Harry covered for him at the synagogue. The board insisted that he take the time off and care for the "next Blumberg rabbi."

It was several days later that he was sipping a cup of tea with his father in the hospital cafeteria when Nathan asked,

"Dad, with all this talk about David being the third generation of rabbis, how would you feel if David didn't want to become a rabbi?"

"Ridiculous," Harry retorted, seeming annoyed at Nathan's question.

"Do you really believe that God would give us such a miracle child if He did not have something worthy and wonderful planned for David?"

"I suppose not," Nathan replied.

He consciously chose not to challenge his father's wisdom. After all these years, he knew he would lose. Somewhere in his heart, however, Nathan wanted no part of any discussion pertaining to the future. For now, it was living each day with gratitude. God had given them a son, and they were bringing him home to the Blumberg house, and in perfect health.

Chapter Six

Life Continues

At Nathan and Ruth's urging, Rachael finally agreed to come home just two days before David was to be released from the hospital. There was a great deal of preparation to be done around the house, including the plans for the actual circumcision, or Briss, as it is ceremonially called.

"Are you certain you invited all the people from your side of the family that you want to attend?" Nathan asked.

"I've invited everyone who needs to be there," Rachael replied. "Do you want me to begin calling them?"

"Yes, please," Nathan answered as he adjusted his tie. He appeared to be looking for his briefcase. "There is no time to mail invitations if we want this to take place next week. David is coming home tomorrow, and that will give us some quiet time together before we snip him."

"*Ugh!*" Rachael exclaimed, and made a grimacing face at the thought. "I went through enough just getting him into this world, and I am not happy about some rabbi taking a piece of him." Nathan saw the awful look on her face and laughed.

"I'm only kidding," she said, and she laughed along with Nathan. Then she pointed to the den.

"What?" Nathan asked, and she chided him about his never being able to find his briefcase.

"It's on the coffee table. You were putting some notes in it last night before you went to bed." Nathan smiled and kissed her on the forehead. He walked into the den and picked up his briefcase. On the way out, he repeated the same kiss, but this time saying, "I love you" before he left for the synagogue.

Today would be rather trying for him after having been away from his duties for several weeks. There were many appointments scheduled, and his secretary, Karen Levine, had given him advance warning that he would need a good night's rest. Most of his appointments were repeat counseling sessions, comprised of those who did not take his counsel the first time.

When will people learn to follow God's advice and not the world's advice? he thought to himself as he pulled out of his driveway. In less than ten minutes, he pulled into his space at the rear parking lot of the synagogue and entered through the back door. As he closed the door, he paused just before his right foot was about to take the first step to go upstairs.

He thought about that very same spot he and Rachael stood when they passionately kissed as man and wife. He thought it was curious that it should come to mind today. He remembered they were waiting for his father to come and get them as the guests lined up in the back driveway. He relished the memory and the sweet joy of that kiss. He recalled (almost laughing aloud) when Harry told them that everyone was waiting "out front." His father was so used to coming in the back door that the back became the front to him whenever he made reference to an entrance in the building. Slowly, he lifted his right hand and gently pressed his palm against the painted concrete as though he could touch that very moment, reliving the sweetness and the passion. He could almost see Rachael standing there in her mother's wedding gown. His lips curled into a smile as several tears of joy found their way from the corners of his eyes.

Ruth and Harry were waiting for them the next day as they pulled into the driveway. There was an intense smile of sheer joy on Harry's face. Nathan walked around to the back door of the car and took David from Rachael. He was all wrapped up papoose-style in a powder blue and white blanket and wore a tiny knitted blue cap on his head.

Rachael stood up, and the two of them walked toward Harry and Ruth. Harry opened the front door and stepped aside as Nathan carefully stepped up and through the doorway. He walked straight to the nursery and placed David in the crib. Rachael came up beside him and carefully removed his tiny hat. It was truly a touching sight to behold, the four of them standing

The Journey Begins...

there and staring at their tiny miracle child. His hair was silken, and his red cheeks stood out as if to encourage someone to pinch them! He was so tiny, but at nearly eight months, the doctors said he was strong enough to come home, although he cautioned them to be watchful for the next few weeks.

Ruth motioned for them to come out and have lunch. The ordeal of the pregnancy and birth were over, and Nathan looked forward to raising his son. They had accepted the reality that David would be an only child. *For sure,* Nathan thought to himself, *this will be one spoiled little boy!*

~

It had been nearly a year since Reuben had been secretly indoctrinated into the PLO, and his parents still had no idea of his activities. Prominent in his mind was the incident at the Joseph's Tomb, for there was a great deal of publicity about the death of the teacher. An uprising of Jewish settlers on the West Bank, clashing with Palestinians, flashed across the screens of the world's television sets for months. The initial headlines read, "Teacher Attempts to Save Torah Scrolls at Tomb."

The Feldmans sat in front of their TV with Reuben and Elanie and shook their heads in disbelief.

"How could anyone murder a man for wanting to save what was precious to him?" Mrs. Feldman asked.

"He shouldn't have interfered," was Reuben's immediate response. His father shot a glance at him that was an expression of shock and disbelief that those words came from his son.

"What did you say?" his father asked.

"He should not have gotten out of his car when he saw all the Palestinians there, that's all."

"Do you feel anything for that man, Reuben?" his father asked. He was deeply concerned that there was something within his son he hadn't noticed before now.

Elanie excused herself and went into the kitchen. She did not want to actively participate in a family squabble. She already knew Reuben's commitment to the Palestinian cause and that he had become a Muslim. She knew because he prayed several times a day on a mat when their parents weren't home. The prayer mat was hidden in his closet. He would unroll it and pray and had even begun to teach Elanie the words. Reuben had also been successful at planting the seeds of sympathy for the Palestinians. She would respond positively to the conversations he had with her when he sounded anti-Israel, mostly because she loved him.

The conversation between Reuben and his father lasted only a few minutes. The final remark by Mr. Feldman alluded to the fact that Reuben was a Jewish boy who certainly has not shown one iota of faith during his entire religious upbringing. It was at that moment that Reuben admitted to his father that he had no faith in his *assigned* religion and was pursuing other beliefs. That was the day that Mr. Feldman suffered from what they thought was a heart attack.

~

No one would suspect that the parents of the new baby who were greeting family, friends, and members of the congregation at their front door had just come through trials that would challenge the most vivid imagination. In fact, one would never suspect that anything had ever happened out of the norm if one did not know the circumstances of the pregnancy and birth of this beautiful baby boy. Rachael was her vibrant self, and Nathan stood at her side, greeting everyone and welcoming them to this wonderful, traditional occasion.

Rabbi Tannenbaum had performed hundreds of circumcisions and had assured Rachael before everyone arrived that it would be forgotten by David's next bottle.

"I promise you, Mrs. Blumberg, it will be fast—over in an instant."

Even with all the words of comfort from the rabbi, Rachael still felt queasy each time she thought about it.

David was on a table in the middle of the room, covered by a single folded white sheet. Rabbi Tannenbaum stood on the opposite side of the table. His sterilized instrument kit was laid out before him, and he donned a pair of latex rubber gloves. Nathan raised his hand, and a respectful silence came over the room as the rabbi opened his prayer book and began to recite the traditional prayers. When he had completed praying and blessing

David, he picked up his surgical instrument and the eyes of the guests that had just been wide open, were now tightly closed.

He recited the law given to Abraham; there was a moment of silence and then a moment of David's cry.

"Okay, you can open your eyes now and take your son—it's over."

Rachael quickly wrapped David in a blanket and took him into her arms. Drawing his tiny form close to her and lowering her cheek to touch David's face, she whispered soft, comforting words to her infant son. Rachael turned to Ruth, who immediately picked up on her look to rescue her from the crowd.

"Everyone, may I have your attention, please?" Several of the women began peeling the layers of saran wrap from the platters and bowls on the buffet table along the far wall of the living room. "Lunch is now being served."

Chapter Seven

Blessings and Tragedies

The clock of time waits for no man, and thirteen years can pass by very quickly. From kindergarten and a Hebrew school class to the most important event in the life of a young Jewish boy, the Bar Mitzvah is conferred on his thirteenth birthday. It is the Jewish tradition of a ceremonial "passage" from boyhood to manhood. After his Bar Mitzvah, the young man is allowed to worship among the men and no longer has to sit with the children.

For Rachael, this was a day to be proud and to rejoice, but there was also an unexpressed sadness within her heart. Rachael could not come to terms with the fact that thirteen years had passed since she was nursing David in the small bedroom next to theirs. He was now the image of his father, tall and handsome, with big brown eyes that held an expression of confidence and intelligence. But most of all, David possessed a true love in his heart for everyone.

Nathan would conduct the services, and sadly, Harry would not be called to the pulpit because of his health. The years of his heart condition and arthritis had not been kind to him, and his medical issues were taking their toll. Nathan knew that his father would not be with them much longer. He was grateful, however, that he was there for the Bar Mitzvah of his only grandson.

Rachael looked at David sitting in the chair on the stage next to the president of the synagogue and the senior board member. Nathan sat opposite the arc that housed the sacred Torah.

Rachael found herself staring at David. She would sometimes wonder, just before she fell asleep at night, what David would be when he grew to be a man. *What is his mission, Lord?* she would think to herself, and she would dream about the things God might have in store for her son. Her thoughts were suddenly interrupted as Nathan stepped to the pulpit.

"Shabbat Shalom," Nathan began. The congregation responded with the same greeting aloud. "This morning, as you all may be aware, we have the Bar Mitzvah of my son, David, so let us begin," Nathan announced. The entire congregation became silent and bowed their heads.

Nathan finished the prayers and turned toward David. He introduced him, and David stood and walked about ten feet to join his father and stand at his side. Several tears rolled downward from Nathan's eyes, as he could no longer control the emotions of gratefulness for his wife, his son, and their entire life.

"Today," Nathan proudly announced, "three generations of the Blumberg family are before this congregation." He then walked from the pulpit to the Torah reading table.

Just as Nathan was about to recite the prayer before the reading of the Torah, there was a loud scream that broke the sacred silence of the moment. Every eye turned to the front row where the Blumberg family was seated, and people were getting up and running toward the front seats. By the time Nathan was able to make sense of the confusion, a crowd of people had gathered and completely blocked his vision. He ran from the stage, down the steps, and cleared his way toward the front seats. It was then he saw the reason for the scream. That shrill sound had come from the lips of his mother, who was now sobbing uncontrollably. Nathan saw Dr. Sid kneeling over his father and applying CPR.

"My God, this can't be!" Nathan exclaimed in a choked whisper. He looked to Rachael, who got up and grabbed hold of him. She, too, was sobbing and silently praying, her lips forming silent words to God. She was trembling and continued to hold Nathan tightly. Rachael's parents were standing to the side of Sid, their faces ashen white with utter shock. The sound of a siren could be heard as several people had called 911 on their cell phones when they realized what had happened. Nathan gently moved Rachael's arms from around him and knelt down beside Sid. He stared at the frail, lifeless figure of his father.

Harry had fallen forward and simply collapsed onto the floor in front of the seats. It had happened so quickly that at first, the people behind the family had not even realized what occurred. Ruth had screamed, and Sid ran to the front row and began CPR—although he instinctively knew that his efforts were in vain.

Harry had suffered a massive coronary—his third and final one.

The paramedics arrived and worked their way to the front row. Sid stopped applying CPR and looked up at one of the paramedics. He shook his head to indicate Harry was gone. The young man looked down at Harry and knelt next to Sid. He placed several fingers against his neck to feel for any sign of a pulse and to confirm Harry's death for the records. His partner had a stethoscope placed on Harry's heart, and he, too, acknowledged the painful but obvious truth. Harry was dead. Sid was physically and emotionally drained as he gazed at the dead body of an old, dear friend.

As this was all taking place, it occurred to Rachael that she had not seen David since this had happened. She literally pushed her way past a few onlookers and saw David sitting on the steps to the stage. His expression was totally blank, and his color was ashen. He sat there as though he were frozen. His arms were motionless and hanging at his sides. His knuckles were white from his grip on the steps.

"David, David!" Rachel cried out, but her son did not respond. He simply continued staring straight ahead while gripping the steps.

"David, please speak to me!" Rachael quickly sat beside her son and tried to hold him, taking him into her arms. As many times as she repeated his name, David did not respond. He appeared as though he had turned into stone. Rachael jumped to her feet and looked around for Sid, calling to him in almost the tone of a scream to be heard above the commotion in the sanctuary.

Sid turned and saw her, and then saw David on the steps. He quickly made his way to their side.

"Sid, what is wrong with him? Look at him. What is it?"

Sid took one look at David, looked into his eyes, and opened his eyelids wider with his thumb and second finger. He removed a penlight from his jacket pocket with his other hand and clicked the tiny button to produce a single beam of bright light. He passed the light in front of David's eyes, left to right and back again, watching David's pupils.

"He's in shock, Rachael—I need to get him to the hospital."

Sid ran back to where the paramedics were now placing Harry on a stretcher and covering him completely with a plastic sheet. Sid said something to them, and one of the paramedics picked up his radio and called for a second ambulance. He received an acknowledgement that one was dispatched. As he did, Sid asked him for a blanket and then walked back to the stage where David was sitting and wrapped him in it.

It was also at that very moment that the Paramedics were wheeling the gurney with Harry's body, out of the Synagogue. The beloved founder of the synagogue had died in the very house that he built to worship God, before his only grandson and a synagogue of over four hundred people. It was only after they placed Harry's body in the ambulance that the people began to leave, their heads bowed and hearts filled with grief.

David was later taken to Holy Cross Hospital in Ft. Lauderdale. He was kept under observation for twenty-four hours, given medication, and released the next day. Once he was home, David slept most of the time—or so it seemed.

David's mind actually continued to replay the tragedy of his grandfather's death each time he awoke. He would ask God for answers, but none came to ease his deep, emotional pain. Several times during the night, David began questioning life itself.

Harry's death had a traumatic effect on David. He was now subject to the greatest of inner enemies—failing faith. He had entered a battle with depression, evidenced by a fading of his outer glow that was obvious to those who knew him. What was once a passion for life was now a look of lifelessness. He was a young man whose questions about life could not be satisfactorily answered by any mortal. Sid told Nathan and Rachael that it was his system's way of dealing with the trauma. He would continue to fall in and out of sleep and question God until he was ready to deal with the realities of what had occurred. Each time that Rachael looked in on him, he was curled up in a fetal position, clutching the edge of the comforter that was pulled over his face.

She knelt down and kissed him gently on the top of his forehead.

"I love you, my son. Please, rest and come back to me."

Rachael quietly left and closed the door to the bedroom. She walked toward the kitchen to see how Ruth was feeling. Ruth had been sitting at the kitchen table the entire morning, quiet and very still. When she passed Nathan's office, he was on the phone with the cemetery, making the necessary arrangements. Rachael stopped at the door and stood there for a moment. She whispered, "I love you."

He looked up at her from behind his desk with reddened, tired eyes, acknowledging her expression of love. She then went into the kitchen and sat down next to Ruth, taking her hand and caressing her cheek. Ruth looked at her and smiled a warm but briefly held smile.

"Thank you, Rachael. I love you, and my Harry loved you very much, too—you know that."

"Yes, Mom, I do know that, and I loved him very much, also."

~

There was a not a seat to be found in the sanctuary of the Star of David Cemetery. Harry was truly a beloved man, especially among his peers. Rabbi Lefkowitz from Miami had agreed to perform the memorial service. He was hesitant at first when Nathan called him, but after recovering from the news of the passing of a dear colleague and friend, he consented. Nathan knew that he was one of the few who would be emotionally strong enough to carry out the appropriate prayers and properly memorialize his father.

Rabbi Lefkowitz walked up to the pulpit, and a hush came over the crowd. The services began, and the rabbi asked all who mourned to recite the prayer for the dead.

When it came time to call people to the pulpit who were to deliver their eulogies, a man came walking down the aisle. He was standing beside the rabbi before anyone realized what was going on. Nathan looked up and thought that his face looked familiar, and then he recognized him. The man leaned over and whispered something to the rabbi, just as Nathan told Rachael's who he was. Rabbi Lefkowitz looked at the man for a moment, nodded his head as though approving of whatever it was the man said to him, and stepped aside.

The man was Victor, Harry's dearest friend and closest tie to Israel and Harry's favorite place, the Wailing Wall of prayer. After learning of his friend's sudden passing, Victor flew from Tel Aviv and came directly to the funeral from the airport. His eulogy was short, and it cut to the heart of the true character and unyielding faith of Harry Blumberg. He explained how they had met at the wall when Harry began taking his annual pilgrimage to Jerusalem. He related how the two befriended each other and how all the Orthodox rabbis at the wall's hidden office loved Harry. His brief statement was nothing short of eloquent, and when he stepped down, the only sound in the sanctuary that could be heard were people weeping.

Later that day, Victor met Rachael. He told her about Nathan's first trip to Israel and how he had taken a tour and walked the plains of Moab in leather walking shoes! Then Victor met David and stared at him, realizing how much David's eyes resembled Harry's. He looked like Nathan, but he was so much of Harry that Victor had to turn away and walk into another room to gain control of his emotions. He had lost a very special friend. Victor left for the airport that evening and flew back to Israel.

~

Five years had passed, and the changes that took place in David were apparent to all who knew him. Nathan and Rachael attributed this to the tragedy, yet they discounted any thoughts of permanency. David slowly but methodically began questioning God's will, His timing in the lives of His earthly children, and all the things one can never understand about God. It was as though he was attempting to exhaust all intellectual knowledge so that his doubts could be replaced by natural faith.

Nathan tried to answer David's growing list of questions with a father's love and a rabbi's mind. He did, however, try to avoid any deep, theological issues or conversations that he discerned were negative toward their beliefs. Rachael instinctively sensed that David's inquiries were becoming more intense. It seemed that the more he learned about life, the more David questioned man's conclusions about the wisdom of life.

Something was drawing him away from traditional Jewish religious precepts and he was searching for something he claimed was "missing."

His own destiny was his deepest concern. Before the tragedy in the synagogue, David had been totally open to God's will. He believed he was meant to become the third generation rabbi in their family. Now he sensed that every human being had an individual calling on his life, and he was determined to find his own.

David was graduating from high school, and unbeknownst to him, Nathan had longed for this graduation so *his* son could attend Yeshiva University. It seemed as though there was never a doubt in Nathan's mind that David would one day become a rabbi, so securing a place for him would naturally be kept a surprise. He never bothered to consider that he had never discussed this with David. Since Nathan was an alumnus, he was able to take David's records to the dean of admissions, Josh Greenberg, who was Nathan's former roommate from his graduating class.

A letter of acceptance was sent to Nathan within a few weeks of his submitting David's transcripts. His acceptance was based solely on David's incredible record of outstanding grades and not Nathan's contacts. David had maintained an "A" average in all his subjects, was elected president of the senior class, and was slated to be the class valedictorian. Graduation was seven weeks away, the senior prom was coming up, and there was an elaborate dinner being planned at the Blumberg household—a family celebration before the school's festivities began.

~

Elanie could not possibly have known that her participation in the research of a deadly gas known secretly as Bio47, would one day lead to the largest coup in Reuben's career as a terrorist. No one at PLO headquarters believed that he had any chance of getting into the Biotech center. If he did, they never thought he would be able to get out with canisters of a newly developed biological gas—the results of a special biomedical research program at the lab. The gas was determined to be so deadly, that they placed a hold on any more testing until further studies could be completed.

However, getting to the gas and getting it out of the country was not a concern to Reuben. He knew that even if and when the Israelis discovered the duplicate empty canisters and realized that the filled ones were missing, the government would never admit they were gone. It would start a panic throughout Israel—especially in Tel Aviv, where the lab was located.

There were two critical factors in his plan. First, he had to obtain the key card to get into the lab and second, he had to get the canisters out of Israel. Reuben had obtained access to the key card for a period of up to ten hours. The five canisters containing the gas would be replaced with empty canisters that Reuben had obtained with Elanie's help. The real ones would be taken to a ship at the docks in Tel Aviv and be out to sea before dawn.

This way, should the theft be discovered before their plan for usage was ready, they would never find the canisters in Israel. They would be across the sea; ready to be brought back when the overall mission was planned and ready to be carried out.

It was 3:00 in the morning when Reuben was being lowered down the ventilation shaft within the Biotech building. It would take three persons to successfully carry out the theft. Elanie would serve as the lookout, and Yael, their best friend, would assist Reuben. A nylon climbers line was attached to a harness that held him suspended within the shaft. It was several hundred feet straight down from the roof of the building to the lab level. For safety purposes, Yael looped the line around an exhaust stack next to the opening of the shaft. One slip of that rope would send Reuben to his death. The emergency ventilation shaft that they had obtained access through was used for venting the outside air into the building in the event of an accidental, biohazard leak. If that were to occur, safe-zones would be sealed off from the contaminated areas of the building and the outside air would be used to supply oxygen to the sealed safe-zones.

There was one obstacle that he knew would be difficult. That was the ventilation intake fan that was approximately sixty feet down within the shaft. The fan had six huge blades, and one of them had to be dismantled in order for Reuben to continue down the shaft. It was decided that Reuben would wrap the second line around the blade he unbolted and Yael would lower the blade just enough for him to get by it.

They had planned to use a small, mechanical wench, but Reuben was not taking any chances on the sound of the gas-powered wench being heard by the guards. It was also too heavy to get up to the roof. During the planning, Yael said he would tie-off the lines one at a time in sequential order.

"The first line will lower you. Then I'll send down the second line for the fan blade. Once you tie it onto the disconnected blade and I have lowered it enough for you to get by, I'll tie the blade off, lower you and send down the third for the canisters when you have them. You'll have to send the canisters up, one or maybe two at a time to get them through the fan blade opening."

Elanie advised him on what she had seen on the mechanical plans of the fan. She had snuck into the engineering office during her lunch hour and found the blueprints.

"The fan blades are connected by giant bolts, larger than your hand. I know they can be loosened because I have seen them service the system. If you drop one of them, or the blade itself gets away from you and it falls, the sound sensors within the second shaft passage leading into the other research labs will set off the alarm. Once the alarm sounds, the Special Forces team who protect the facility will be all over the building in less than seven minutes. You would never be able to get out alive. If Yael is helping you and he's on the roof when the alarm sounds, their helicopter would be on top of him before they came after you. That is their method of deployment in the event of any intrusion."

Elanie knew the drill. She also knew that once Reuben made his way into the lab and got away with the canisters, she would not have to disappear—even if they somehow discovered the entry. She suspected that entries and exits were recorded electronically. However, Elanie was not the sole person to hold the only key card to the lab and gas storage vault. There were seven members on the research team, and for security reasons, each person wore the key card on a chain around his or her neck one day each week. The day it was in any team member's possession was never constant. Possession of the card was alternated between the seven members of the team. If the substitute canisters were found, they would never be able to tell which of the seven held the key card at the time they were stolen.

The team would assemble each morning, go through metal detectors, and their purses or bags would be x-rayed. They would then meet a security guard in a holding area. They would all walk down a video monitored corridor, into a decontamination room. Each team member would put on specially designed safety suits and masks. When they had all finished, the security guard would accompany them to the main door of the lab. None of the team members knew the person who had the key card that morning. Once that person opened the door, security would retrieve the key card. At the end of the day, the security person would close the inner door to the vault containing the canisters, and all members of the research team would leave the lab together. The outer door was then secured. All personnel would go back through the decontamination process, be searched, and then leave the building together.

Each night, a member of the security team would come to one of the team member's residences and have them sign for the card. In this simple, yet carefully executed security operation, no one knew who had the key that night.

There was no activity in the lab from Friday afternoon until early Monday morning. It was rare that out of forty-plus canisters, someone would decide to test them *all* for content, especially if there were no alarms set off or the key card and the person having the card were not missing on a Monday. What was ironic was the physical location of the building's outermost point of the rooftop. It was near the outer perimeter and hidden from the heavily guarded front gate. Reuben had long determined that coming in from a dirt road on the other side of the property line would provide hidden access and egress. Scaling the outside wall to the roof could be done with a rope ladder and scaling hook, totally out of the front gate guard's line of vision. They had less than fifty minutes to carry out the operation, as security patrols passed that location every hour on the hour.

They had to wait for Elanie to be given the card on a Friday night so that Reuben would have two days for the canisters to be taken out of the country. A Lebanese-registered freighter that was secretly funded by the PLO and sailed from the port of Tel Aviv would be waiting for the canisters. Their destination was unknown to anyone, even Reuben, who was only to deliver them and walk away. No questions, no discussion, and no one else to know about the canisters or what they contained.

Chapter Eight

The Turning Point

The table in the dining room was adorned with a hand-embroidered, Damask linen tablecloth. Matching starched napkins stood at a perfect point on each of the English bone china settings. The sterling silver flatware glistened in the light of the twin tiered, brass chandelier that was polished to perfection. The dinnerware and silver were service for twelve, handed down for three generations. They were mainly used for special occasions such as the Jewish holidays, Thanksgiving, and occasions such as this.

Tonight Rachael insisted on taking out the family's best, as Ruth had given her the china and sterling silver flatware after Harry died. The tragedy was now long behind them, but the pain of loss was still there. In celebrating David's graduation from high school, Nathan planned to raise a glass of wine, toast his son, and present him with the letter announcing his acceptance to Yeshiva University. It was a surprise he had not even shared with Rachael as of yet. He had received the letter just the day before and decided to surprise both she and David on the same night.

The aroma of cooking flowed through the house from the large roast and potatoes in the oven. She heard Nathan come in and listened to the familiar sound of him dropping his briefcase on the living room coffee table. *Some things never change,* she mused to herself. *By tomorrow he'll forget where he left it!*

Nathan headed for the kitchen and stopped short when he reached the dining room. He was genuinely impressed and paused to admire his wife's talents.

Rachael watched his expression and laughed aloud. "If you could only see the surprise on your face!"

She practically knocked him over, lunging at him and throwing her arms around his neck. She clung to him with all her weight as he exclaimed, "Hey, I'm not a kid anymore!" He laughed aloud but also let out a wheeze. Rachael also laughed and kissed him on the lips.

"You're home early. Did an appointment not show up?" Rachael asked.

"Yes, actually, the very last one, and I didn't bother calling them. I wanted to come home early because I have a surprise. Is David home?"

"No, he went over to Jacob's house. Several of the boys from David's class are there. It seems their graduation gowns didn't fit very well, and it's a bit late to send them back. Jacob's mother has a talent for sewing. She offered to fix the hems and sleeves for all the boys in her son's class. He should be home shortly.

"What's the surprise?" Rachael asked. Nathan reached into his pocket and took out the envelope from Yeshiva. Rachael took the envelope, and when she saw the return address, her right hand went up to her mouth. She inhaled with surprise and made a funny "oh" sound, as she did when she was caught off guard.

"He was accepted!"

"Of course," Nathan answered with a look of surprise as though she should have never doubted he would be.

"Oh, Nathan, I am so blessed, and I know David will be thrilled." Just then they heard the front door open and close. Nathan quickly took back the envelope from her and placed it in his jacket pocket, just before David walked into the kitchen.

"Wow," he exclaimed. "Who's coming to dinner? The dining room looks like we're expecting someone really important!" Rachael smiled and kissed David on the cheek.

"There *is* someone very important coming to dinner, and he's standing right here," she said, pointing to David. Rachael threw her arms around her son and smiled.

"It's a pre-graduation celebration for our valedictorian."

"Oh, Mom, you didn't have to go through all of this trouble."

"Nonsense," Rachel retorted. "This is a blessed and joyous time, and we *should* celebrate." Nathan smiled and placed his hand on David's shoulder.

"Hi, son." David gave him a hug.

"I have the greatest parents in the world!" David exclaimed. He kissed both Nathan and Rachael on the cheek, one after the other, with the brightest smile of love.

"Go wash up for dinner and call your grandmother, but please do it gently—she's been napping."

Nathan kissed Rachael once again and went to wash and change his clothes before dinner.

Rachael took several potholders from a drawer, opened the oven, and the aroma of the pot roast filled the kitchen. Just then, Ruth came in, sleepily rubbing her eyes. She asked Rachael if she needed help.

"No, thanks, Mom, I'm all prepared. Why don't you sit down at the table and talk to Nathan? He will be back from changing in a minute." Ruth had become frail over the past five years since Harry died. She had also become quite withdrawn, perhaps even depressed, and chose not to engage in conversations when she was not asked a direct question.

The doorbell rang, and it was Ruth and Jeffery. Nathan answered the door, and Rachael's mother gave him a big hug. Jeffery shook hands and they exchanged greetings. They walked into the dining room and greeted everyone, saying hi to David and Ruth, who were already seated at the table. Jeffery sat down, and Ruth Wasserman went into the kitchen to see her daughter.

"How are you, sweetheart? How do you feel?"

"I am really fine, Mom. I feel wonderful. Why don't you go and sit with everyone? I want you to enjoy home cooking for a change!"

"You look lovely, even in an apron."

"Thanks. With the exception of Nathan, you're my biggest encourager, and I love you." Ruth kissed her on the cheek and then went into the dining room to join Jeffery. Everyone took his or her seats. Nathan offered up the pre-meal blessings, and they began eating.

Usually, Rachael's parents ate at 5:45 at a restaurant just a few blocks from their home. They liked to arrive before 6:00 p.m. for the early bird special offered at many of the local restaurants in South Florida.

Ruth Wasserman disliked cooking. She maintained that a chicken dinner at one of the restaurants was less expensive on the early bird menu than cooking at home. She reasoned this out by considering the preparation time of a three-course meal; the cost of the food; waste, clean up, and hot water for the dishes; and the cost of electricity. By the time she finished this reasoning process, she actually thought they were saving money by closing the kitchen!

David had been silent for much of the evening. Finally, Jeffery asked him about his plans after graduation. It was a simple and normal question to be asked of a young man who was graduating high school. David, however, looked sheepishly at his mother and then glanced briefly at his father before clearing his throat. At that very moment, Rachael sensed that something was about to happen—something unexpected. She could always tell when David was nervous. He had a certain look in his eyes, and there was a change in his posture. He would slightly drop his shoulders and appear slumped over.

"I applied to a school in Pennsylvania and was accepted—with a full scholarship. I was going to announce it tonight and surprise everyone."

David lowered his eyes and Nathan nearly choked on a piece of potato pancake he was eating.

"You're going where?" Nathan blurted out in a tone of utter shock. He dropped his fork and wiped his mouth with his napkin. Rachael remained silent but looked sternly at David with total disappointment in what she just heard her son tell them. *How he could do such a thing is inconceivable,* she thought, watching her son struggle to face his father. Nathan's forehead was beginning to turn beet red as it usually did when he was very upset, and that wasn't often. He balled up his napkin and practically threw it down on the table.

"Answer me, David. Please, share with me what was going through your mind when you did this."

Rachael knew that Nathan was devastated by David's announcement, so she got up and walked around the table to be near him. She also saw that Jeffery was somewhat shaken. He obviously regretted having asked that question in the first place.

David noticed his grandmother staring at him with a look of shock.

"David, I never dreamed that you would not want to go to Yeshiva like Harry and your father. You would be another generation of rabbis in the Blumberg family, a tradition—a solemn responsibility to your family, your synagogue, and God!"

David looked at Ruth lovingly—even after that guilt trip statement. Regardless, he would never show the slightest sign of disrespect to his grandmother.

"Grandma, the college I am going to was at one time a very Jewish school. It is now mixed, but there are many Jewish kids attending. Michael Feldman, the pharmacist's son, is also going to Pitt. I have a full scholarship to a great school, and Pittsburgh is not that far from Florida, so I will be able to come home often. It's not as though it's at the other end of the world."

Nathan looked at Rachael and then returned his attention to David. He reached into his pocket and removed the letter from Yeshiva. He placed the letter in front of David, who did not take his eyes off Nathan's face the entire time. David had sensed some time ago that his father would obtain acceptance to Yeshiva for him. That's why he had applied to Pitt as soon as he was able to obtain a transcript of his final grades. David had his acceptance letter before Nathan even applied to Yeshiva on his behalf.

"I know what that is, Dad. It's from Yeshiva, isn't it?" Rachael saw a painful look in David's eyes. It was as though Nathan had actually betrayed him instead of him obtaining the letter of acceptance, only out of love for his son.

"I did it for you, David. I—"

"No, Dad," David interrupted, "you did it for *you*."

"David!" Rachael called out in sheer disbelief at what she heard her son say.

"How could you even think that there was a selfish motive in what your father did?"

"Because he didn't ask *me!* He *assumed* I wanted to go to Yeshiva without ever once thinking about what his son wanted to do with his life. It's *my* life, and in all due respect, Mom, I have to begin making my own decisions. I am also prepared to live with the consequences of my decisions, as long as they are my *own* decisions."

Rachael's parents got up from the table. Ruth Wasserman turned to her daughter and thanked her for a wonderful meal; however, it was late, and they had to go. They practically ran out the front door.

Rachael looked over at Ruth, and asked if she would help with the dishes.

"Of course I will." She started to clear some of the dishes on either side of her, and then she and Rachael went into the kitchen.

Nathan and David were now alone in the room, sitting next to one another. For the first time in his entire adult life, Nathan felt totally inadequate. He was groping within himself for the appropriate words.

"David, tell me, when did you make this decision to go to a secular university?"

"I have been thinking about it and praying about it for nearly the entire year. I faxed in my application as soon as I was able to get a copy of my grades and the letter for valedictorian."

"I see," Nathan answered. "What made you reject the idea of going to Yeshiva—besides the point that I never asked you?"

"Dad, I have far too many questions that remain unanswered, and I would be nothing short of a hypocrite if I went to Yeshiva next year. There is an unfulfilled emptiness in me from too many unanswered questions. I believe only God can answer those questions—in time. I do not know what God wants for my life. I don't know what I'm supposed to do as a useful human being. I seek some type of sign every day, something that would confirm where I should go and what I should do. Because of these things, I know Yeshiva is not in my best interest—at this time in my life."

Nathan was at a loss for words. He felt as though he was losing his son—the son that he had almost lost eighteen years ago.

In the kitchen, Rachael had said goodnight to Ruth who went off to bed. She was fighting back tears as she scrubbed the roasting pan. The exchange of words that was going on in the dining room was between the two men who comprised her entire life—her husband and her son; one who completed her life, and one to whom she gave life. She silently began to pray for both of them to come to a place of peace with all their differences.

Please God; don't allow this to tear our family apart. Bring them together in thought and in Your Spirit, Lord. I know that You have your hand upon him, and I know that one day You will show him the way to his destiny. Whatever it may be, I pray that Nathan and I do not stand in the way of it because of our selfishness in never wanting anything bad to happen to our son. I give him up to You and ask You to forgive me for being so protective. Amen.

As Nathan and David continued talking, Nathan slowly but surely regained his composure. He realized that he could not personalize the events of the evening. He had to address it as though he were counseling the son of a member of the synagogue.

"Do you think that this will be for a time—like a year or so, until you face these issues and prayerfully resolve them?"

"I'm not sure, Dad. I have never lied to you before, and I'm not going to now. I need some time to figure out the plan. I sense that there is something deeper, some sort of mission perhaps that has not been revealed to me. Dad, you know I have a profound love for Israel. Even *you* wanted to go there before you started your career. I still very much want to visit Israel, to stand in Jerusalem, and . . ."

"And what? Be blown to pieces by terrorists?" Nathan interjected. "Now is not the time to be in Israel, David! Even the State Department has issued warnings. They have not restricted travel to Israel but they are warning travelers of terrorist attacks on Americans."

"I don't live in fear, Dad, just in frustration. If that happened when I finally got there, then that would have been my destiny. I trust in God, and He did not intend for me to go to Yeshiva this year. That's all I know."

Nathan sensed his sincerity and his convictions. This was a huge blow to Nathan and Rachael, and he was upset with himself for not seeing it coming. The problem was he could not deny the integrity of David's argument. Nathan reached over and picked up the letter from Yeshiva.

"I will call my friend at Yeshiva tomorrow and inform him that you are going to put off a decision for at least a year. Perhaps God will lead you back to where you need to be—rather, where He *wants* you to be."

David rose from his chair and went around to his father. Nathan also stood. They hugged, and David began to weep.

"I did not mean to hurt you, Dad. I love you."

"I know you do, David"

Rachael walked in and saw her husband and son embracing. She became instantly joyful, setting aside the pain of the change in David's plans. In the depths of her heart, she had never doubted that God would eventually lead her son to the place He intended. God gave him to her, and God had the right to deal with him as He chose.

~

Graduation was only a week away, and Rachael thought it was strange that David hadn't mentioned the senior prom. He didn't have a steady girlfriend that Rachael was aware of, and like his father, he also wanted to wait for the one God would send to be his wife. Perhaps that's why he had not dated very much during the past four years. He had also wanted to maintain his focus on his grades, and dating always distracted him from that focus. After the Yeshiva disappointment, both she and Nathan were hesitant to engage David in any personal conversations. They were hoping that things would first quiet down and then they would eventually find an appropriate way to reason with their son.

Tonight, however, while Rachael was preparing dinner, she mentally toyed with a way around any direct questions regarding the prom, as she was not about to have another episode as the last tragic dinner fiasco. She did want to know about the prom, as she actually had a pleasant surprise for David if he was planning on going.

Ruth was feeling a little queasy and wanted to skip dinner, choosing to just have a bowl of soup in the kitchen while Rachael was cooking. She had hardly finished half of it when she said goodnight and went off to bed. Rachael was very concerned and thought about calling her doctor and taking her in for a check up. She was, however, quite relieved that Ruth would not be at the dinner table in the event the conversation did not go smoothly.

Rachael called out to Nathan and David that dinner was ready. She brought the food to the table and sat down. Nathan recited the usual blessings and they began to eat.

"Is everything okay, Nathan? You seem preoccupied tonight." David looked over at his father and actually joined in.

"Yeah, Dad, you are kind of quiet. Is there anything wrong?"

"It's nothing," Nathan answered. "I just have a lot of things going on at the synagogue, and I'm trying to sort them all out."

"And how is dinner?" Rachael asked.

"Delicious, thank you, and I'm sorry, but what were we talking about? I need to get my mind off of synagogue business for a while."

"We were really not talking about anything in particular, but I do have a surprise for David."

"A surprise?" David remarked.

"Yes, David. How would you like a tuxedo for the prom that was worn just once?"

"That would be wonderful! How did you get one?"

"I was talking to one of the women today whose son graduated last year. They bought a new tuxedo, and he wore it that one night, dry cleaned it, and hung it in his closet. It's just your size!

"That would be great, Mom. Is it black?"

"Yes. All you would need would be a tuxedo shirt."

"Thanks. I don't know what to say!"

"Well," as Rachael saw her opening, "you could tell us if you are even going . . ."

David laughed, but it was an uneasy laugh.

Rachael felt that same nervous sensation, and for a moment she wished she had waited until after dinner for this conversation.

"Of course I am going, Mom. It's the senior prom! I wouldn't miss the last function of our entire senior class. Everyone will be attending and we may not see one another again until our first reunion. The tuxedo would be a blessing, and I'm grateful. I was going to wear a dark suit. I didn't want to rent a tuxedo for just a one time use—especially when they doubled the rental prices because it was prom night."

"Well, now you have one. I'll pick it up tomorrow. By the way, whom are you going with? It would be nice for us to know, wouldn't it?"

David threw a quick glance at Nathan to see if he was listening. He was not only listening, however the question Rachael just asked gained his undivided attention.

"I am going with a girl in my class. I don't think you know her. She's a very nice girl, and we've been in the same class for two years."

"What is her name?" Rachael asked.

"Diane." David stopped short of giving her last name.

"Diane? I don't think I know a Diane. Does she go to our synagogue?" Rachael asked, as though ever considering that this girl may *not* be Jewish.

David remained quiet and again dropped his eyes and sat very still. His shoulders rounded, and Rachael knew right then that the girl must *not* be Jewish.

"David, what is her last name?" Nathan questioned. "Your mother asked and you seem to be avoiding the answer. Is she a terrorist or something—on the FBI's most-wanted list?" Nathan mused, attempting to ease any further tension. However, the tension would shortly turn into another bout with parental dismay.

"Her last name is Kelly. Diane Kelly," David finally disclosed.

Rachael looked over at Nathan. He gave her a look that indicated he was going to deal with this, so Rachael kept silent.

"I see," Nathan said calmly. "She must be a lovely girl who is very proper, very nice, and very intelligent. You two are simply getting together to go to your senior prom—a one night date, so to speak. Is that it?"

"Yes, Dad, that's *all* of it."

"Well, then, that's perfectly fine."

Nathan's expressions and tone of voice were not divulging his disappointment. He purposed his heart not to lose his regained line of communication with his son.

Rachael understood her Nathan's approach and remained just as calm. She smiled and commented, "Well, then we certainly would love to meet Diane. Perhaps you could invite her over to dinner before the prom."

"I don't know about that, Mom. There are so many things to do before the prom that she may be occupied all week—you know, the things that girls do!"

"Oh, I am sure you can talk her into a short dinner, and it can be on whatever day and time is convenient for her."

David now looked annoyed. He stared into his mother's eyes for a long moment before his tone of voice changed from delighted to "you're pushing it."

"Mom, why is it so important for you to meet a girl I am going to take to a dance just so I don't have to go alone?"

Rachael hesitated, trying to curb the disappointment in her son's recent attitude. She never dreamed she would see this in David.

"Because I do not believe you, David, that's why." Rachael jumped up from her chair and threw down her napkin.

Nathan was in shock, never seeing her so visibly angry before.

"I won't have my son deceiving me or his father. If you can't trust us with the truth *every* time, then we have failed you as parents."

David was in a momentary state of disbelief. His mother had *never* spoken to him like that, and he knew she was deeply hurt. After the dinner last week and finding out he was not going to Yeshiva, he instinctively knew they both must have felt deceived. This was the only other "skeleton in the closet," and now he did not know quite how to handle it.

Rachael was standing at the end of the table, her hands placed firmly on her hips. She stared at him, waiting for a moment of truth, and then it hit her.

"David, answer this question for me. What college is Diane going to next year? *Perhaps she is the reason that David chose Pitt instead of Yeshiva,* Rachael thought.

"She's going to CMU, Carnegie Mellon University," David finally answered.

Oh, thought Rachael, *she's not going to Pitt!*

"I see," Rachael replied, nodding her head ever so slightly as though she approved. She was very much relieved, but she did not have a clue where CMU was. It sounded familiar, and she thought that Sid had once mentioned something about his daughter going to a CMU, or was it . . . she could not recall and dismissed it altogether from her mind.

"May I please be excused now?"

"Of course, David. And if you can invite Diane over for that dinner, I would love to meet her. If she is going to the prom with my son, she must be lovely."

At the very least, the edge was off the conversation. Nathan sat there and simply appeared to be assessing the whole dialogue. Carnegie Mellon sounded very familiar to him, and he thought for the moment that the school was *also* in Pittsburgh. He would call Phil Weiss after dinner. His older boy had graduated from Pitt, and Phil had been up there several times over the years.

"Is there anything else before I clear my dishes and see if Mom needs some help in the kitchen?" David asked his father.

"No, that's fine, son. And if Diane can come for dinner one night, that would be nice, but if not, that's okay, too." Nathan smiled, got up, and kissed his son on the head before walking away.

David was relieved because he knew in his heart that Diane would *not* be coming to dinner anytime soon. David was also aware that his father knew that, also.

Nathan never made the call to his friend about CMU. He had barely finished eating when the phone rang. Rachael answered it and motioned to Nathan that it was for him. A member of the synagogue was in the hospital and in critical condition. His wife called and asked if Nathan could come right away. He excused himself, kissed Rachael, and told her not to wait up for him.

She asserted her usual "drive safely and be careful" and went about cleaning up the kitchen. She told David to go and visit with his friends.

"It's graduation week. Go out, enjoy yourself, and don't be concerned with washing dishes."

David left the house soon after his father did. While it was still quiet, Rachael decided to finish in the kitchen, but the question of the mysterious Diane was nagging her. Was David being truthful with them? Was this *just* a girl from his class to go to the prom with, or was there something more, perhaps a relationship David didn't want them to know about?

~

With the prom matter behind them, Nathan chose not to have any further discussion regarding Diane. Rachael also dismissed the whole matter as a passing event with no serious threats. If her son was going to Pitt, then she must show her support in his first year. She heard of far too many parents breaking the lines of communication with their kids because of an argument or an unresolved issue.

Deeply within her spiritual discernment, Rachael believed that David would find his way, perhaps enrolling in Yeshiva after a year at Pitt. She maintained that it was something David had to get out of his system. All she could do now was to purpose herself to get involved in whatever he did. She wanted David to always know that she was there for him. She had called the administrative office at Pitt and had all pertinent school information mailed to her. Perhaps this *was* best, she reasoned. At least he can never say that his parents forced him to pursue a career he did not choose for himself. Besides, a year goes by rather quickly, she reasoned, and Pitt seemed like an excellent university. She would visit him on every occasion, even if Nathan could not get away.

~

Rachael sat in the auditorium, waiting for Nathan to get there from an emergency that he had insisted on attending to. Constant exposure to death and sickness was a way of life in their family. When they needed the rabbi, Nathan never hesitated, regardless of the time of day or night.

Just then, the attending crowd became silent as the speaker walked on stage from behind the tall, black curtains. Everyone applauded, and still, Nathan was nowhere in sight. He had assured Rachael that he would swing by the house and pick up Ruth when he finished attending to the emergency. He felt there was no sense in having her sit in the auditorium, waiting for the program to begin.

It was then that Rachael realized it was their son who walked onto the stage! Then she heard Nathan's voice. She was so focused on her son that she didn't even see Nathan and Ruth walk up the aisle to the empty seats.

"Excuse me, are these seats taken, Miss?" Rachael smiled and kissed Nathan on the cheek as he sat down beside her. Ruth sat to the left of Nathan and reached over to touch Rachael's hand for a moment.

"Look, its David," Rachael excitedly exclaimed.

A moment later, the voice of their David boomed through the immense auditorium speakers.

"Good morning, honored faculty, parents, guests, and fellow students of Nova High School of Ft. Lauderdale." The faculty was seated in a long row of armchairs across the front section of the stage. They, too, were wearing caps and gowns, but theirs were purple instead of the black gowns worn by the students. David wore a gold sash around his gown as the valedictorian.

David continued his address.

"My name is David Blumberg, and I am humbled to be standing here today as the graduating class president. This is a wonderful day for every student who is seated before you. By our donning these caps and gowns, we have made an all-important and profound statement. We have risen above the perceived mediocrity of our times and have set our sights on higher education and the pursuit of excellence."

The crowd began applauding loudly as David signaled the entire graduating class with a sweep of his hand and they all stood to face the audience. The applause was deafening and lasted for what seemed to be about five minutes.

They had arranged to meet David in the student parking area after the ceremonies. The school had hired several photographers to take outdoor pictures near a setting that was roped off for that purpose. After the ceremonies, they would drive to the beach and choose a restaurant for a celebration lunch. Rachael insisted that perhaps she should cook, but Nathan would not hear of it. "The chef is off today," he joked. "The Blumbergs are dining out."

Chapter Nine

Welcome to Pitt

The trip to Pittsburgh was without incident. Nathan did most of the driving, and Rachael was elated to have all that time together as a family. They talked about the city of Pittsburgh, school academics, and David's courses for the semester. David talked about anything and everything *except* religion.

Rachael had received the information she requested from Pitt, including brochures on the local attractions near the university. She was beginning to become a Pitt enthusiast as she came to realize the rich history of this famed school. Pitt was founded in 1787 and at that time was named The Pittsburgh Academy. It was originally located in a log cabin near Pittsburgh's three rivers. The student attendance was currently about 32,300 with approximately 9,600 faculty members.

"Nathan, I'll bet you never knew that Gene Kelly graduated from Pitt, did you?" Nathan was jarred out of his private thoughts as he kept his eyes on the road.

"No, dear, I didn't. That's really something. He was quite a movie star," Nathan replied with a look on his face that he was genuinely impressed.

"Nathan, I am so glad that we decided not to stay in one of the modern hotels in Pittsburgh. I wanted to sense the history and culture of the city that our son will be a part of for the next year."

Rachael began reading from a brochure on the hotel they had booked.

"The Club Hotel is in the Oakland district. It was founded in 1890 and was hailed as the most reminiscent of a European bed and breakfast in all of Pittsburgh."

The hotel had only four rooms, and Rachael had called at the right time to obtain one of them for this trip. She was surprised she was even able to get through to the hotel, this being just before the opening of the fall term.

The residence hall would open the next day, August 25th, and David's freshman orientation would take place over a four-day period. It was almost unbelievable to Rachael that here she was, taking her only son to college. It seemed like a lifetime away from the night he was born.

The brochure she had read in the car that described the hotel did not even begin to do justice to its charm and touches of elegance. In the center of the ceiling hung a five- arm, brass chandelier that somewhat resembled the one they had at home, but this one was much bigger and looked very expensive. The tall, paned glass windows were covered in old world draperies and sheers. The lamps on either side of the cherry wood end tables were old-fashioned stick lamps with white pleated shades, and the bedspread was embroidered with tiny flowers that were the same colors as the draperies. Rachael was very pleased with herself for having found this darling hotel. She vowed to remember it for the next time she and Nathan visited.

The hotel was conveniently located adjacent to the school campus, and many of the attractions that Rachael wanted to visit were within a couple of miles.

The Byham Theater, Point State Park entrance, the Andy Warhol Museum (which Nathan insisted they skip), and, of course, Heinz Field, home of the Pittsburgh Steelers, all seemed to be interesting. Nathan also noticed that the Pittsburgh Zoo was only four miles away.

Rachael opened her small suitcase and removed her toiletry bag. She noticed a hairdryer in the bathroom attached to the wall and thought that she should have asked about the amenities *before* she packed her own.

Nathan called out to her, "I'm going to go out and get us lunch to go."

"I just want to take a hot shower and change my clothes," Rachael replied from the bathroom.

"Okay, but dress very casually. I'll be back in about twenty minutes or so."

Rachael turned the huge white porcelain handle to hot and felt the needle setting from the showerhead hit her hand with a slight sting. *Why couldn't we install a showerhead like this at home?* Rachael thought. She got into the shower and thought how wonderful it felt to simply stand under the hot water and not be concerned that it would run out!

After Nathan returned, they decided to briefly tour the main building and then find a place for their picnic lunch that Nathan had purchased. Rachael was quite surprised to see the list of famous graduates from Pitt as they walked along the hallway of the reception center. There were pictures on the wall of Gene Kelly whom she mentioned to Nathan earlier, and Jonas Salk (the Salk vaccine for polio was researched and discovered at Pitt). The history of his research and findings were printed on a card that also stated there had been over 57,900 cases of polio, and that the number had dropped to a handful after distribution of the vaccine. There was Mike Ditka, who won NFL's Rookie of the Year, and Tony Dorsett, winner of the Heisman Trophy in 1976, having completed the season with 1,948 yards and twenty-three touchdowns.

Rachael was thoroughly impressed as she continued reading the cards that were posted along the hallway. Each one represented a well-known person who had graduated from Pitt. Rachael also heard that their School of Medicine was internationally renowned. The first human transplant was accomplished at Pitt, and she thought, *Perhaps David might choose medicine if he decides not to become a rabbi.*

They left the building, got into their car, and drove down a road leading to a nearby park less than three miles away. Nathan simply wanted to find a park location, spread out a blanket, and eat a quiet lunch with Rachael. As they approached the park, Rachael saw a sign and another college campus.

"Nathan, stop the car!" she suddenly called out in a tone of surprise.

"What is it?" Nathan asked as he pulled the car over to the side of the road near a bike path.

"Look at that sign and tell me why we stopped."

Nathan bent his head and leaned toward Rachael to peer out of her window.

"Carnegie Mellon University."

"So?" Nathan asked, feeling as though he was missing something.

"What was the name of the school that David told us Diane Kelly was attending?" Nathan suddenly realized what she meant.

"You're right. This *is* the school. Perhaps it's just a coincidence that the university she is attending is right next door to Pitt . . ."

"I don't think so," Rachael replied. "I've had this feeling ever since David mentioned her name and the name of the school. It sounded familiar to me, but I quickly dismissed it along with all the other details. I didn't want to become jaded. I purposed my heart to wait, to get involved and to support David—no matter what."

Nathan nodded his head in understanding.

"Is this considered no matter what?" Nathan asked in a facetious tone.

"Yes," Rachael answered but with a slight hesitation.

"Okay, so she goes to this school. There was no mention of her and certainly no dates with her *after* the prom that I'm aware of," Nathan reasoned. Rachael continued to ponder the issue with deep discernment over this new finding.

"Perhaps you're right," she finally declared after a few more minutes. "This could all be a coincidence and we're making too much of it. Come, let's go find a tree and spread a blanket. I'm hungry."

~

The August sun was surprisingly kind to the first year students at CMU as they adjusted their chairs and awaited the opening address of the orientation. Temperatures were climbing, but there was a cool breeze. It seemed more like spring weather rather than a hot summer.

Diane sat in the second row just a few seats to the left of the podium. She adjusted her skirt to allow for the stack of papers that were about to fall off her lap. There were class registration papers, drop-add papers, rooming information, location of buildings, and classes and programs for just about all of the scheduled events of the coming week. Sunday-to-Sunday was very much a full agenda.

"Good morning," was the greeting of the middle-aged woman standing at the podium, and every conversation ceased among the students.

"Allow me to introduce myself to our first year students. My name is Anne Mishner, and I am the director of admissions. It is my pleasure to present all the activities that our staff has lined up for you over the coming week. We have chosen to do this outdoors today since we are having a BBQ lunch this afternoon. I felt it would be more of a relaxed atmosphere for everyone."

Mrs. Mishner was around forty-something and had been on staff at CMU for nearly twenty years. As she continued to announce the week's coming events, Diane allowed her thoughts to wander and turned her gaze toward Pitt. David was there, probably in a class by now, as they started earlier than CMU. With such a short distance separating the two huge schools, perhaps they had to have orientation several weeks apart or the traffic would be out of control.

Diane's thoughts turned back the clock to the prom and how handsome David had looked in his tuxedo. They both had agreed that it would be better to meet at the school and avoid any questions from their parents. It was supposed to be a casual date, but for the past seven months they increasingly found that they were attracted to one another in a way that they could not explain. It had simply happened, and they both committed to take one day at a time. There were to be no promises, nothing serious, everything virtuous, and they would see where the future led.

She was beyond her years in maturity. At eighteen, she was more sensible than most adults David knew. Her mother was an ICU nurse at Holy Cross Hospital in Ft. Lauderdale. Diane's father had died from a massive heart attack when she was quite young, and her mother had never remarried.

David and Diane's biggest problem was that David was Jewish and she was a Christian. There was also the reality of David's father being a rabbi and expecting his son to become one also. The acknowledgement of those facts weighed heavily on their relationship. David had been taught early on that there was to be no dating or attractions to a *shiksa* (a non-Jewish girl).

"It will only lead to heartache," Nathan had reminded him in one of their father-and-son talks.

"Can a non-Jewish girl who had no Jewish upbringing, relate to the members of the Synagogue?" he had once asked David.

Diane had been in one of David's classes. Although he glanced her way several times, the real attraction began that day in the school hallway. She was speaking with several of her friends on the girls' soccer team and had just come out of the locker room and was readying herself for practice. She was wearing shorts and a t-shirt, soccer socks, and her sneakers. The moment David seriously stared at her, his heart began to race as never before. She had an attractive, turned-up nose, high cheekbones that accentuated her sculptured face, several small freckles on both cheeks, and dimples that made her face light up when she smiled. Her hair was long—well past her shoulders—dark brown, and appeared to glimmer in the hallway lights. But there was something else, something he had not been quite able to comprehend at the time. Her expressive, huge green eyes turned their gaze directly toward David when she realized he was staring at her. Their eyes locked for that moment, and she returned his captivating look with a smile of sweetness—a smile that simply said, "Hello."

She was talking with her friends and then saw David. She cocked her head to one side ever so slightly, squinting her eyes in a questioning stare, as if to say, "Who *are* you?" David smiled back and then turned and walked off toward the front hallway. The fact was that her demeanor—cocking her head and the faint smile—was what his mother did when she was interpreting a look from his father. It wasn't until several minutes later that he realized that in his moment of being mesmerized by her, he hadn't locked his locker. He turned and walked back to where he had just come from, and there was Diane as he turned the corner of the hallway. He abruptly stopped, nearly running into her. Her friends kept walking, but Diane lingered to talk to David.

"Hi again," she greeted him with a smile. David, instantly captivated, introduced himself with a quasi-nervous handshake.

"David, oh yes," Diane reflected. "You are in my social studies class, aren't you?"

"Yes, I sit on the other side of the room, and honestly, I hadn't noticed how lovely you were until today." Realizing what his heart had said instead of his brain, he turned three shades of red. His reaction was a nervous chuckle.

"Did I just say that? I didn't mean to be forward."

"No, that is a charming and honest thought, and I assure you that I accept it as such. Thank you—it's very sweet. However, I am not sure if I am smitten by what you said or upset that you've never noticed me!"

Her face appeared serious at that moment, and David almost lost it!

"I'm only teasing," she said, and she gave him her warmest smile.

"My name is Diane. Diane Kelly." David's reaction to her last name almost gave his disappointment away. *She's Irish,* he thought, *surely not Jewish. What am I doing? No, better yet, what am I starting?*

Despite her not being Jewish, David and Diane began an innocent friendship. David walked her to the soccer field that afternoon and watched the practice. Afterwards they sat in the bleachers and talked for about an hour until they both had to go home. In the time they spent together that afternoon, they both realized that they shared many similar thoughts. They were literally drawn to one another but remained cautious in their relationship. They agreed that there would be no amorous involvement. They would strictly approach this beginning relationship as friends until they saw where it was all going. Although neither of them wanted David's parents to even think there was a romantic "thing" going on between them, after David described his mother, Diane desperately wanted to meet her.

"Your mother sounds like an incredible person," she commented the second time they got together after classes.

"She is," David agreed. "She is an extraordinary woman and very much adored by anyone who gets to know her."

Suddenly, Diane gave up her daydream and returned to the reality of CMU as the announcement was given for all to stand for the singing of the Star Spangled Banner. The senior choral group was now assembled, and the school band came marching onto the field. There was something very patriotic about the singing, the band, and the fields around them. When the band concluded, the students were all seated and Mrs. Mishner returned to the microphone.

"We know that going away to college is a major transition in your life, which is why this orientation program is held. We want to help make that transition easier. Be assured that all work and no play can be very dull, so be ready for lots of activities. There are over one hundred students from the upper grades that are participating this week to make your orientation a smooth one. Events such as our giant icebreaker will surely provide a great start, as well as our 'Kick-off to College Life,' which provides information on all of your first year's involvement here at CMU. That would include classes, academic meetings, theme dinners, and the cultural events that take place on campus."

Diane began to feel the heat of the sun, and reached down beside her chair and retrieved her bottled water. She took a long sip, and realized that the water had grown warm.

~

David could already tell that Pitt was going to be a challenging school. He was sitting in the very last row of the lecture hall in his first class. The removable "Session" sign at the door read "Geology I." As impressive as the professor tried to make his introduction to the class, David could not bring himself to get excited about rocks. He had questioned his decision to take the class from the very moment he registered. It was simply not of interest to him. Perhaps that's why Roger called it the "Rocks for Jocks" class, an easy "A" for first semester students. Listening to the first lecture, David was sure Roger was being sarcastic. David's roommate was a simple but brilliant young man who hailed from Philadelphia.

Their room was in Tower B, and they had arrived at the dorm within moments of each other. When the two surveyed their living space, there was an immediate joke made about who would take which bed—it was an easy choice. One was on the left wall and the other on the right wall. At the head of each bed was a small desk that was the same width as the bed itself. There was a small closet for hanging clothes just at the walk-in area, and a single window overlooking the campus. They had lockers under their beds that Roger couldn't even close from all the food his parents had stuffed in it. They had taken about five seconds to throw their bags on their chosen beds. David had simply taken the right side, as he was closest to that bed.

"Nice view," Roger had commented. He had opened the window a crack to let in some fresh air. David walked over and looked out of the window. They were just about in the middle of the campus. The building at the forefront of their view was The Cathedral of Learning. Within this huge edifice were classrooms located on the lower floors and offices located on the upper floors.

After classes, David stood at the window in his dorm room and stared out over the campus grounds. He appeared deep in thought when Roger entered the room and threw his books on his desk. The thud startled David, and he gave a "thanks a lot" with one of his expressive looks.

"Roger, do you have some time to talk, or are you on your way somewhere?"

"I am a little pushed, but what's up?"

"I'm just having a tough time with . . . kind of a situation." David paused and looking a bit pensive. He stared down at the floor. "I need to air it out and perhaps get a sense of direction."

"Is it about Diane?" Roger knew about Diane and approached everything one way—black and white, right and wrong, and true and false. His transparency and forthright ways were almost identical to Diane's. It was one of the characteristics Diane possessed that drew David to her, not withstanding the fact she was utterly beautiful!

Roger turned his desk chair toward David. "Talk to me. What's going on?"

David glanced out the window as though he was laboring to gather his innermost thoughts.

"I am starting to get overly stressed out, and I think I'm also getting depressed, or having bouts with depression, whichever it is. Issues are getting all jumbled up when I try to sort them out."

Roger leaned forward, giving David his undivided and caring attention.

"It's my father, the synagogue, Yeshiva, my beliefs, Diane—and I guess they are all connected and not easy to unravel. The problem is I keep trying to separate them, and I can't. I figured if I could solve one problem the rest would fall into place; however, it doesn't seem to be working out that way. My father is the synagogue. My father is the one who dreamed of me going to Yeshiva, and he is the one who wants me to take over when he retires—just like he did from my grandfather before he died. He is also the one that gave me a hard time about Diane."

"I still don't understand something," Roger interjected, seriously in deep thought. "You are making one problem into many problems—don't you see it?"

"No, I don't," David, responded, staring intently at Roger.

"David, the whole thing is about your father. You're trying to unravel something that is very much inseparable. You followed a strict Jewish path because your father *placed* your feet on that path instead of *leading* you to it. Your Grandfather Harry encouraged you, but he also placed your father's feet on *his* path. There were no choices, no personal commitment except to please your parents. When you finally found out that your mother almost lost her life bringing you into the world, you felt you had no choice but to accept your father's choices. You have been trying to please the rabbi and forgot about David. That is the root of the problem."

David hardly blinked, instead maintaining that intense stare into Roger's eyes. His roommate was a psych-major and wanted to counsel children. He was becoming a family therapist, he recalled Roger mentioning.

"This all came to the surface since you developed a relationship with Diane, didn't it?"

David thought for a moment. He realized that his roommate was possibly striking at the very truths that were buried in the recesses of his heart that he could not honestly face—a growing relationship with a non-Jew. But was that all of it? Was it *just* Diane, or was there more? David held up his hand as if to say, "Stop talking, I am getting some insights, give me a minute."

"It's my faith, Roger. I don't feel what my father feels or what my grandfather felt. There is something missing, something I can't explain. It's an emptiness that never gets filled. I could pray all day and all night, and in my *mind,* I know that I am praying to God and God is listening. Then, somewhere within me, I sense that I am alone and my words of prayer are bouncing off the ceiling and not going into the ears of God. I can't really explain it.

Roger looked very serious.

"David, you just haven't found your own personal destiny."

Chapter Ten

The Visit

The warming rays of the sun over Pittsburgh were beginning to set earlier as the fall season turned the leaves to the colors of gold and red. Many piles of leaves stood waiting to be burned, bagged, or simply become diving targets for young active spirits. Oktoberfest tipped many a glass of lager as the chill of the early winter months caused most of the students to close their dorm windows for the coming winter.

The family weekend was not without consequence. Nathan and Rachael flew in for the weekend and had to stay at a motel some fifteen miles away. They arrived on Friday afternoon, and within a few hours, Nathan was searching for an appropriate synagogue for the Sabbath. David was visibly annoyed, as he wanted their time together to be meaningful and private—just the three of them. He didn't want to sit in synagogue. He even suggested they pray together and said that surely God would understand that he had not seen his parents since orientation. Upon hearing this, Nathan became annoyed and challenged David as to where *he* spent his Sabbaths. David would not answer, not wanting any unpleasantness. Nathan was led to divulge the one untruth between them that he did not intend to reveal.

"I'll bet you've spent your Sabbaths at CMU, didn't you, David?"

David realized that they knew, and he became instantly defensive.

"Are you talking about Diane Kelly, Dad?"

"Yes," Nathan replied. "I am certainly talking about Miss *Kelly.*"

Rachael became very upset and begged Nathan not to pursue this. She insisted that they had just arrived, and this dialogue could be pursued at some other time. David, however, was now in a totally defensive mood, but he tried to remain calm and not reply disrespectfully.

"No, Dad, I did not spend Saturdays at CMU. I actually spent the few

Saturdays since August right here, studying for exams and hardly sharing *any* social life. If I am going to live up to your expectations and be at the top of my class, I do not have time for a social life. I see Diane on Sunday afternoons for a few hours. We usually go out and grab a burger and talk or go for a long bike ride. We are friends, Dad—just good friends."

"Can I meet her?" Nathan challenged.

"You mean right now?" David replied. His voice was beginning to sound a bit annoyed at the rhetoric over Diane and his not attending Shabbat services.

"No, I'm more reasonable than that. I'd like to meet her anytime, is what I meant."

Rachael broke in, and Nathan was taken by surprise. Rachael never interrupted him in the middle of a sentence.

"I apologize for interrupting you, but I, too, would like to meet Diane. How about Sunday afternoon, and let's *all* go for burgers?"

David looked into Rachael's eyes and immediately realized what she was doing. Aside from intervening and putting a halt to this fencing dialogue between them, she was giving David an out. Their plane left at 3:40 p.m. On Sunday, Nathan would realize there was little time for going out for burgers when he finally calculated the time to get to the airport, turn in the rental car, and catch their plane. If there were *any* time to meet Diane, it would be brief. David smiled and agreed, and Nathan finally gave in. They would wait until Sunday, and David would call Diane when he got back to the dorm and make the arrangements as to where and what time. *Late,* David thought to himself, very late.

"Hi . . . were you studying?" he asked, excited to hear her voice.

"No," Diane answered, "I was actually thinking about you."

The remark brought a smile to his face but also made him a bit nervous. He pulled back on the phone but forgot he had the phone cord wrapped around his wrist. The phone fell from the bed but stopped short of hitting the floor.

"What were you thinking about?" David asked, purposely seeking her verbal affections.

"I was thinking that our friendship after a year is really more than friends."

"I know," David replied. He sensed that warming feeling throughout his body. It was a sensation that he had whenever he was with Diane or when they talked on the phone.

"Are your parents having a good time?"

"I'm not sure," he replied. His smile diminished to a concerned sort of frown as he pictured his father's disappointment during their conversation. His biggest concern was that the entire evening and all the next day were yet ahead of him.

"I'm meeting them for dinner at 7:30 to give them time to rest. How would you like to go out to dinner with us? It would blow them away if I showed up with you on my arm."

"Are you serious?" Diane asked.

"Yes, I am serious. I don't want them to meet you over some burgers on the way to the airport, but rather spend an entire evening with you. Then they'll get to know you."

"That's very sweet, David, but I don't think your parents are ready to meet me just yet. They will totally blame me for you going to Pitt instead of Yeshiva."

"I don't think so. Not if we simply portray our relationship for what it is."

"And what is that?" Diane asked with a note of challenge.

"Friends. We are *good* friends, and that can be stated with truth. We have never been intimate, and heck, I've only kissed you goodnight once, maybe twice, and it was certainly not a lover's kiss. It was a loving kiss that close friends exchange—well, maybe very close friends."

"David?"

"Yes?"

"We both know that our relationship is becoming more obvious to both of us. Your parents will see right through the *friendship.*"

"And just what will they see?" David questioned, yearning for her to be the first to say it.

"That I love you, David, that's what." Tears began to brim, and her voice became somewhat choked. Diane had never spoken those words at any time, and neither had he spoken of love.

"I have an idea," David blurted out, breaking the moment of intense emotions.

"Why don't we avoid your meeting them until we go home for Thanksgiving?"

"I think that's a good idea," Diane agreed.

Now David would not have to endure a weekend full of scrutiny and questions.

Thanksgiving was traditionally a family meal, and the questions would not be as personal or as serious. Even though David had prayed about this relationship many times, there were no answers to his prayers because he *knew t*he answer that had come from Rachael's talk with him several weeks ago.

"You stay with your own people and please, I beg you, don't break your father's heart." In spite of her spoken words, he was confident that his mother would love Diane once she got to know her. There were so many identical traits between them, but he was unsure of what her response would be if Diane were to be more than a friend.

The weekend went by quickly, and there was no further conversation regarding Diane or his not going to synagogue regularly. He and his parents dined together, went sightseeing, and on Sunday morning, Nathan decided (as anticipated) that there was little time remaining before the flight to go out for burgers. Instead, he opted to have a late breakfast and bid his son goodbye until Thanksgiving.

In the year since David and Diane began developing their relationship, they did not discuss the subject of religion. The differences in their beliefs went unstated because they were unmistakable and very real to both of them. David had said early on that as long as Diane didn't mention anything about her faith, he would not try to make her Jewish! They both knew they were in love but were too scared to admit it openly. Diane was the first to verbalize her love, but David chose to withhold further discussion on the subject. He was better at hiding his feelings and would change the conversation instantly if he felt it was becoming overly intimate.

Thanksgiving was a few weeks away, and David was looking forward to going home. Ruth was still struggling with health issues, and David prayed daily for the Lord to keep her around just a little longer. At last he felt he was ready for his parents to meet Diane.

"After all, Mom, we are still good friends, and you've wanted to meet her." Rachael knew differently about the "good friends" statement, but she was not about to discuss, divulge, or dissuade David from the relationship. She was not going to lose her son over religion. She had nearly lost him during childbirth, and nothing was going to stand in the way of her relationship with him. She told David that it would be a pleasure to meet Diane, and Thanksgiving dinner would be a perfect time. Now, if he could only get his father to think like his mother, all would be fine.

~

Professor Erick Todd not only had tenure, but he also had earned the highest respect from all his colleagues at Pitt. He had taught Comparative Religion for over twenty years, and everyone thought he would not retire until he was unable to stand at the front of the lecture hall. His reputation was firmly established over the years by consistently leading his students to seek truth and spiritual awareness rather than what man professed was absolute.

"Nothing is absolute to you," he would say, "unless it is believed from within—a belief you are willing to die for—then it becomes absolute." His students quickly learned to trust his openness, as well as his non-judgmental nature in his religious discussions.

That day's lecture was based on the lack of understanding in American history of how Jews helped make America a great nation. The professor's lecture on Jewish history was delivered with a passion. His knowledge of how Jews withstood the persecution during Hitler's reign in Europe was fascinating to his class. It was not that a third of them were Jewish, but rather knowing that this was the first monotheistic religion that withstood insurmountable trials and still survived.

The lecture hall was now quiet, and the professor looked up from the podium, walked to the center of the room, and began. "The Diaspora—the disbursement of the Jewish people to the four corners of the world. We covered this in a previous lecture as to how, when, and why. Today we look at five empires that were hosts to the disbursed chosen people. These were individual empires that did not persecute the Jews. Instead, they actually offered a safe heaven for them. Did you know that Babylon was actually the place where the main version of the Talmud was created? It was this setting, this community that led the Jewish world for nearly a thousand years. Then other teaching centers developed, namely Rashi's Torah academy in Troyes, the Kabala school in Gerona, Moses Maimonides' oracle teaching from Cairo, and of course, the debates over his teachings that took place in Provence and Ashkenazi.

"Then there was Muslim Spain, where the Jewish people escalated their learned reputations in science, poetry, statesmanship, and military genius. This was halted, of course, with the Christian return to power around 1492. Here we have persecution and a great expulsion with mass conversions— although those conversations were questionable and mostly temporary. It was then that we saw the third age of the rise of the Jew, with Constantinople at the heart of it. Hence, four centuries of prosperity that ended in a strange shift from Islam to Christian Europe. Am I getting ahead of anyone yet?" Not a hand was raised, for most hands in the hall were furiously taking notes.

David allowed himself to mentally drift from the professor's words. He knew the history of his people well and could afford a moment of thought. Thanksgiving was almost upon him, and he had not slept well during the past week. He was thinking about Diane actually joining his family for the holiday. Now that it was truly a reality, he was becoming quite nervous. She had told him about her conversation with her mother after David confirmed her coming to dinner. Her mother decided to visit her sister, for a few days since Diane would be visiting David's family.

"It will be a good experience for you to spend a couple of days with a Jewish family, especially someone as respected as Rabbi Blumberg," her mother concluded in their telephone discussion. Diane also told him that her mother asked if she was seriously dating him. Diane spoke of her feelings for David, and her mother responded, "It's between you and the Lord."

The night she told him all of this, she had jogged over to David's dorm. She was dressed in sweats, a wool cap, and a pair of gloves. After stretching for about five minutes, she ran the three miles along the bike path until she came to his dorm. She was actually sweating in the frigid November night air, which chills right to the bone in Pittsburgh. Winters could be extremely brutal there, and that was the one thing that she found difficult becoming accustomed to.

It was dark and a little after 7:00 when she called David from her cell phone. David met her downstairs, and they walked to the study hall, where there were several overstuffed chairs in which to relax. David recalled that as they were walking, he had actually placed his arm around her shoulders and did not even realize it. They were talking about Thanksgiving, and he had sensed her nervousness about meeting his parents. David's response was automatic—a way of reassuring her and offering his support. Diane was surprised for a moment, but she realized that it was simply David being strong. She moved closer to him and commented that the air was not so cold anymore. David had a strong impression of the look in her eyes from that moment, and he held it mentally—even in the middle of a lecture.

Chapter Eleven

Thanksgiving

David had been home for less than twenty-four hours and felt as though he had been gone for years! Rachael fussed over him, and Ruth not only cried when she saw him, but she became teary-eyed every time he hugged her. Nathan was also genuinely happy to see his son. It was as though their conflicts during the October weekend had never occurred. Because his room had become Ruth's room the day he went off to Pittsburgh, he was the one who would be sleeping in his father's study on the new futon. His mother insisted that it was much more comfortable then the pull out couch that had been there before. David walked into the dining room and watched as his mother laid out the silver, the napkins, the water and wine glasses, and it appeared she was somewhat nervous.

"Would you like some help, Mom?"

"No, thank you, David. Were you watching me all this time?"

"Yes, I was standing in the hallway and never remember seeing you so meticulous about a dinner table before—except when you made my graduation dinner. Is there anything different about this night?"

"You are very precious to me, David, and I want this night to be more than a Thanksgiving dinner. I want it to be a memorable holiday. When you return to school in a few days, I would like you to take this memory with you. This way I know that when you are away from us, the warmth of our home and the love of your family are always with you. You have never been away from us like this, so I guess . . ." Rachael lowered her eyes and several tears rolled down her cheek. She missed David terribly and wanted to keep that loneliness from him but could no longer do so. David smiled a loving, caring smile at his mother and gave her an extra tight hug.

"I love you, Mom. Thanks for everything you do."

Perhaps she was nervous because Diane was coming to dinner and was scheduled to arrive in less than an hour. He did not want anything to hinder the joy of having Diane at his family dinner table for the very first time.

The doorbell rang, and it was the Wassermans. Rachael's parents were looking quite healthy and vital for their age, and while David was greeting them, he outwardly acknowledged that he should only look that good when he gets to be "fifty."

Ruth Wasserman laughed and remarked,

"You should really become a rabbi. You've got that natural charm to hold a congregation together. Fifty indeed!"

As Rachael was hugging her mother, the doorbell rang again. This time, David knew it was Diane.

"I'll get it," David stated. Thoughts of how he was going to introduce her ran through his mind. He opened the front door, and her face was like a beacon of light. She looked radiant. David expressed those feelings, and she smiled and hugged him. Rachael watched as they embraced. She stood directly behind them, waiting to be introduced.

"Hi, Diane. I'm Rachael, David's mother. It is so nice to finally meet you." She gave Diane a genuine hug.

"Thank you, Mrs. Blumberg. I have been looking forward to sharing this evening with your family."

"Please, call me Rachael," David's mother replied.

At that moment, Nathan came over to them with a charming smile on his face. David nearly broke out laughing but managed to control himself. *This must be so difficult for him,* David thought as his father introduced himself to Diane and shook her hand. David also noticed that his father did not seem the least bit uneasy and was actually very pleasant in a warm and natural sense. This put David more at ease, and they all walked into the dining room together. Rachael proceeded to introduce Diane to the Wassermans and to Ruth, who must have come to the table while they were at the front door. His grandmother managed a softly spoken hello, and Diane went around the table and gave her a hug. Ruth acknowledged her expressed affection with a warm smile, staring at Diane for a few moments as she went back to take her seat. David caught his grandmother's look. He knew Ruth was an extremely good judge of character and saw immediate approval in her eyes.

Rachael had prepared a feast, as she always did for the holidays. The food was placed on the table, and everyone became busy passing the various dishes to one another. Rachael served everything on platters or in large bowls, family style

He was also thinking that his mother had introduced Diane as a friend of David's who lived in Ft. Lauderdale and was also home from school for the Thanksgiving break. Diane did not change her expressive smile, nor did she blink through the introduction. She simply chose to accept it as she went right on shaking everyone's hand, saying how nice it was to meet them and how thankful she was to share this holiday with David and his family.

Diane wore an attractive dress that came to about two inches above her knees. It was cotton with a simple floral design, puffed-up sleeves with elastic around the arms, and a fitted waist that accentuated her athletically lean figure. Her hair was almost identical to Rachael's in color and was cut in almost the same style. David took notice of his mother's glances when she arrived and saw her smile of approval. She observed Diane's lack of any visible makeup and also noted that Diane appeared to be the epitome of the "girl next door." She was naturally beautiful, inside and out—as Rachael had appeared to Nathan when he first set eyes on her at his graduation. Nathan saw this as well. David caught his father studying Diane from time to time in a series of glances. The conversation was flowing very smoothly, and everyone appeared to be very much at ease.

There was absolutely no hint of religious conversation at the dinner table that night. Rachael had obviously schooled both her parents and Ruth that Diane was not Jewish and that out of respect for Diane and David, anything *except* religion could be talked about over the course of the evening.

Ruth excused herself from the table. She picked up her soup dish and salad plate and slowly walked into the kitchen. David watched his grandmother, thinking how frail she looked as she left the table. It was not a moment later that a loud noise broke his silent thoughts. He looked up to see his mother and father run toward the kitchen, followed by Rachael's parents. Diane looked at David with concern and asked what he thought had happened.

"I don't know," David answered, immediately getting up and quickly following everyone into the kitchen. Diane was close behind him.

As he looked past the door, he saw the broken dish fragments scattered over the kitchen floor. His parents and the Wassermans were on their knees, circled around Ruth. She was face up on the floor, her arms at her side, and simply lying there very still. Her eyes were open, and she seemed to be breathing without any difficulty, but she was not moving at all. She simply stared straight up at the ceiling and had the strangest expression on her face—as though she saw someone or something and was transfixed on an invisible sight. Then David saw her hands begin to shake, and her right leg twitched as though it was in a spasm. Ruth, they would later learn, had suffered a major stroke. Not the type of stroke that immediately threatened her life, but one that would have irreversible physical and mental consequences and would, in God's time, surely take her life.

~

It had been several hours in the E.R. waiting room, and Nathan was trying very hard not to reflect on the night that Rachael was rushed to the hospital—but that was a very long time ago. Now, instead of being a patient whose very life was hanging on a string, Rachael sat next to him and was attempting to comfort him by stroking his hand. She looked into his eyes, squeezed his hand, and they reassured each other in those unspoken words of love that they would endure this tragedy together.

Just then a man with curly gray hair partially covered by a green surgeon's cap came walking toward them. Diane and David were sitting on the opposite side of the waiting room when they saw Nathan and Rachael stand up and talk to the doctor. They immediately rushed over and stood beside them.

"This is our son, David, and his friend, Diane," Rachael introduced them. The doctor acknowledged them and went on talking about Ruth.

"As I was just telling your parents, David, your grandmother suffered a major stroke. I cannot assess all the physical or mental damage at this time. She is unconscious and we are going to need to conduct a CAT scan. The chief neurologist will likely order several tests. For now, she is not in any further danger; however, in situations like this, we never know."

Nathan began to softly cry. Rachael placed her arm around his

The Journey Begins...

waist, drawing herself closer to him. Nathan placed his right hand over his eyes and wiped away the tears, regaining control quickly. It was what he had to do so often from the pulpit when something touched him spiritually.

"Rachael, why don't you take my car and drive Diane home since it is already after 11:00? It could take hours before they get Mom into a room in ICU. David, you should also go home and get some sleep."

Diane then suggested that Rachael drive *her* back to their house, as her mother's car was parked there.

"I will have to go back to your house anyway to get my car, so I could drive back here and stay with David and Rabbi Blumberg."

"Diane, that's a very kind suggestion. Rachael, go home and get some rest. These two are young and can stay up half the night and it won't affect them."

After nodding in approval, Rachael hugged and kissed Nathan on the cheek. Diane turned to David and told him how sorry she was.

"David, why don't you go with them since Diane is coming right back?" Nathan suggested. "I don't want them to be alone this late at night."

"Okay, Dad, good thought. I'll be back soon."

The three left, and Nathan walked over to a chair in the corner of the waiting room. He picked up a magazine, sat down, and stretched out his legs. He rubbed his eyes and scanned the counters and furnishings for a coffee machine. He saw one and brewed himself a cup of coffee just as the doctor walked up behind him.

"Rabbi Blumberg, I have some preliminary results back. Why don't you take your coffee and we'll go to the consulting room so we can have some privacy and talk." Nathan picked up the hot coffee and followed him to a room with a punch-button lock. They stopped momentarily as the doctor punched in some numbers, and they went inside. The doctor motioned for Nathan to sit on the couch as he pulled up a chair in front of him so he could face him.

"Rabbi, your mother suffered a severe stroke. I do not have all the details yet; however, the area of the brain that was affected involves her speech and the coordination of her movements. There is a strong possibility that your mother may be bed ridden for some time, perhaps the rest of her natural life. I am truly sorry to tell you this, but I believe that will likely be the case, though one never knows. I am going to keep her in ICU tonight, and tomorrow morning I'll have our neurologist examine her. She is sleeping now, as I have given her a strong sedative as well as anti-seizure medication. If you would like to see her, she will be assigned a room in ICU in just a short while. I will have the duty nurse come out and bring you back when your mother is settled and we have the necessary procedures accomplished."

Nathan did not even answer the doctor. He simply nodded his head. The doctor told him that he could stay in this room until the nurse came for him.

"No, that's okay. My son and his friend are coming right back here, and they won't know where I am."

"Okay then. I am so sorry, but there is always hope."

"Thank you so much for your concern and professional help."

The two men left the room. The doctor headed toward the E.R., and Nathan went back to the waiting room. He decided not to relay this news to David or Rachael. He would simply go back to ICU to see his mother when he was permitted. He would then go home, get some sleep, and come back in the morning to get the appropriate diagnosis from the neurologist. He would inform the rest of the family when he had more concrete information.

Rachael used the driving time back to the house to get to know Diane a bit more and engaged her in several areas of conversation. She thought that it was actually uncanny how much Diane was like her—sensitive, caring, and mature in areas of thinking that were uncommon for a younger person. Rachael actually found herself growing quite fond of Diane by the time they pulled up in their driveway. Diane's car was parked in front of their house.

"Thank you, Mrs. Blumberg, for everything you have done tonight. The dinner was so much like my own mother makes. Your family's devotion toward one another has truly made me feel as though I were home."

"Thank you, Diane, that's so sweet" She gave Diane a hug. David then embraced his mother and waited until she was inside the house before they left. While driving back to the hospital, there was hardly a word spoken between them. It was after midnight, and they were both feeling the effects of the long evening.

"I am so sorry, David. I know you are very close to your grandmother."

"Yes, but I am more concerned about my father. First Harry, and now Ruth. It seems like just yesterday that Harry died. The scary part is that both events occurred at a family occasion. I told you my grandfather died at my Bar Mitzvah, didn't I?"

"Yes, you did, and I know how terrible that was for you," Diane replied comfortingly.

"Now my grandmother has a stroke on Thanksgiving, the one Thanksgiving that you are here with me."

When they arrived at the emergency entrance once again, they went inside but did not see Nathan in the waiting room. They determined that Ruth had been placed in ICU. When they found the room, the duty nurse saw them and announced,

"I can't let you stay very long. It's almost 1:30 in the morning. We still need to do some blood work and several other procedures."

"Thank you," David replied. He assured her that they had returned to the hospital to drive his father home. "We'll likely be leaving shortly after my father knows we are back."

They entered the room and saw Nathan. He was quietly sitting there with tearful eyes, staring at Ruth. She was lying there so very still, her situation accentuated by the numerous tubes and wires connected to her. She appeared very pale, the pallor accentuated by her silver hair on the white pillow. He glanced toward Diane, who had sat down at the foot of the bed and closed her eyes to silently pray. His father was also praying, and he stood gazing between Nathan and Diane. His father finished praying, rose from the chair, and turned to him.

"Let's go, David. Diane, thank you for coming back. There is nothing we can do here, and we should all go home and get some rest. I sense that tomorrow will be a very long day."

"Has she regained consciousness at all, Dad?"

"No," Nathan replied with sadness in his voice, "she hasn't. I have just been praying that God will not let her suffer. Come, let's go."

Nathan placed his left arm around David's shoulder and placed his right hand on Diane's shoulder as she stood to leave with them. They walked silently toward the door to the emergency room exit and then out to the parking lot. She unlocked her mother's car, and Nathan reached for the back door as David entered the front passenger side. Diane got in, and the sound of their seat belts clicking was the only sound that broke the silence at that time of night. Diane drove Nathan and David home, expressed how sorry she was, and then hugged David goodnight and left.

When they entered the house, Rachael was asleep, exhausted by the day's events. David said goodnight to his father. As he headed for his father's office and the futon, he instinctively stopped, turned toward Ruth's room, and chose to sleep there tonight.

Chapter Twelve

A Life-Changing Event

David tapped his finger on the edge of his desk as he mentally struggled with an assignment for Comparative Religion. He was about to close his books when he made a conscious decision to complete it. He had been back at Pitt for several days and was already feeling the strain over his grandmother's stroke. She was in a coma, and there was no telling how long she would be that way. Both Nathan and Rachael had insisted he return to school. He was already several days late; however, the extra time was granted when Nathan called the school and explained the circumstances. Nathan promised that they would call him if there were the slightest change in her condition.

Diane had returned to CMU the day she was supposed to be back from the regularly scheduled vacation, but David had not seen her since his return. Just then the door opened and Roger came in, throwing several shopping bags on his bed.

"Hi, working hard?"

"No," David replied, "I am past the assignment and was just thinking about some things."

"Do you want to talk about it?"

"No, thanks, that's kind, but I think I'm going to take a run and then shower and get something to eat."

David picked up his jacket from the back of his chair, slipped it on, and saying goodbye to Roger, left the room. He headed down the steps to the main lobby area and out the front door. Once outside, he began a jogging pace and turned toward CMU. The early December air was very cold, and he pulled his jacket hood over his head and slipped on his wool gloves. It took no more than a few minutes to realize the futility of running the three miles. It was not so much the run going there as it was coming back that made him rethink his decision to run in the extreme cold. He headed back to the dorm storeroom and got his racing bike, a Motobecane twenty-four speed-racing bike. He slipped his sneaker into the pedal strap and began to pump all of his inner frustration into attaining a racing speed. He considered surprising Diane and perhaps spending a little time with her, feeling somewhat guilty for not calling her for the past few days.

When he had reached a suitable pace after a few minutes, huge snowflakes began pouring down from the sky. It was beautiful as the sun began to set. The hues of light across the campus were filled with piercing colors of red and orange against the backdrop of raining snowflakes. Snow had come late for Pittsburgh that year, and David was grateful. He was not used to having his life hampered by several feet of snow.

The snow began coming down heavier, and as he passed the huge oak trees that lined the biking path along the park, he began to regret that he started out in the first place. The snow was sticking to the leaves and the grass, and he knew that he would not be able to ride his bike back if the accumulation continued at this rate. David had no way of knowing that a major blizzard had begun in the Pittsburgh area. The rate of snowfall was heavier than the weather forecasters had seen in many years. As David pushed down on the pedals to propel himself even faster, a knife-like pain shot through his left hip. He stopped peddling, realizing that he had not stretched sufficiently and his left thigh muscle had seized up on him. He got off his bike and attempted to walk out the cramp. The pain was significant, however, and he knew from experience that he was finished for the night. He was also painfully aware that he still had at least a mile before he would reach CMU. The snow was piling up fast, and he knew he had to decide whether he should walk his bike back to Pitt or continue on to CMU. The pain was getting worse, not better, so he grasped the handlebars of the bike and hobbled painfully on.

A moment later, he saw the lights of a car coming up the road behind him at a slow pace. Immediately David was relieved and thankful. He was alone, and the snow was making it impossible to go on with his bike. It was already dark, and he knew he was in a bad situation and needed help. He limped toward the roadway and waved at the oncoming car as it came closer. The car slowed and pulled off the road just past him before stopping. *Thank God!* David thought as he tried walking toward the car. All at once, a sinking feeling grabbed him in the pit of his stomach. All four of the car's doors opened, and four young men with black ski caps got out. David stopped dead in his tracks at this menacing sight. **What's going on here?** he thought to himself, a knifelike fear now shooting through his gut.

"Hey man, what's wrong—you in trouble?" came the heavily accented words from the driver of the car. The other three stood by their doors, not saying a word and glancing back and forth between the driver and David. Maybe they really were college kids and they wanted to help him, but something instinctively told him that this was trouble.

"Yes, I got a cramp in my leg, and with the snow and the cold—well, I was trying to make it up the road to CMU. Can you give me lift?"

"And what about the fancy bike, bro? You gonna leave it here?"

"Well, I could chain it to a tree and come back for it tomorrow."

"No, that's a bad idea, man. We'll put it in the trunk for you."

The two who were in the back seat were walking toward David. He tried squeezing his leg to see if he might be able to run, but the pain was so severe that at best he might be able to hobble off into the park. It was the first immediate instinct—drop the bike and leave. His instinct was correct, as the man to his right let go with a punch that caught David in the stomach. He doubled over from the wind being knocked out of him.

"Nice bike, *hos. It* must be worth big bucks. We'll make sure that it finds a nice home. Got any cash on ya, bro?"

David kicked forward with his right leg and caught the man in his groin. It was his biggest mistake. He heard a clicking sound and then felt a sharp sting in his chest. Then he heard another sound, which was the heel of a boot connecting with his forehead. It was the sound of leather on flesh and bone, with a crunching impact that closed the doors to the world around him.

The sounds of a hospital are distinct, especially if you've just spent a great deal of time waiting for your grandmother to come out of a coma. David blinked a few times from the glare of the light as he tried to focus his eyes. There were two men talking to one another at his bedside—one a policeman, and the other who appeared to be a security guard. The policeman noticed that David was awake and walked over to the side of his bed.

"Hello, I am Officer Monahan from the Pittsburgh Police Department. This is Bill Sardis from the campus security at Pitt. Your roommate," he read from a small notepad, "Roger, notified campus security when you didn't return from your run. Mr. Sardis found you on the road less than a mile from CMU on the park side of the street. You are a very lucky young man. It appears that you were stabbed, but the blade missed your heart by a fraction of an inch. You lost quite a bit of blood, but according to the doctors you will be okay. Do you feel up to telling us what happened?"

Stabbed—at school? How could this be possible? David thought.

"You also have a very nasty bruise and some swelling on your forehead—possibly a mild concussion. From the looks of the mark, it appears that someone used the heel of his boot on your head."

"Yes," David answered. "One of them kicked me in the head after I was stabbed. I was riding my bike toward CMU when my left leg suddenly cramped up. I couldn't peddle any longer and could barely even walk. I got off the bike and saw a car coming up the road so I hailed it down, hoping for a ride. The snow was getting thick, and I was freezing cold."

"Did you happen to notice what kind of car it was?" asked the police officer as he scribbled some notes on his pad.

"Yes, it was a four door, blue or black car. The snow was beginning to cover it but not the back. They stopped past me, so I was able to get a good look at it."

"Did you happen to notice the license plate?" the officer asked.

"Yes, it was something-8114. I can't seem to remember the first numbers or letter."

"That's great, especially after what you have been through. That will give us enough information to trace the plate. You said the other one kicked you. How many were there?"

"There were four of them."

As David answered the police officer, sharp pains began to shoot through his head. His expression of pain was obvious to the police officer, but every detail that David could provide was needed. The police officer pressed on in the event he passed out or could not go on talking.

"Son, take your time. I know you are in pain, but I am sure you would like to see these guys get caught."

"It's okay," David answered. "Please, go ahead."

"You did not have a wallet in your pocket or any identification. Did you have one when the attacked you?"

"Yes, I did. They must have taken it from my pocket after I blacked out."

"Please give me your full name and home address." David provided his home address and telephone number.

"Is there anyone you would like us to notify?"

"Yes, would you please call Diane Kelly at CMU?"

"Sure, I would be glad to do that." He wrote down Diane's name on his pad. "Just a few questions more. I know you have been through a traumatic experience, but we need to find out as much as we are able to—I'm sure you understand."

"Yes, sir, I do," David replied in a tone that related his physical pain.

"Okay, can you describe any or all of them for me?"

"Yes, I think I can. There were four of them. The man who stabbed me was about six foot and medium build. He wore a leather jacket, blue jeans, and had boots on like bikers wear. The other guy was shorter—less than six feet tall. Now that I think about it, they were all wearing blue jeans and leather jackets with huge silver snap buttons on the front. The guy who kicked me had a tattoo on the back of his hands."

"Can you recall anything about that tattoo; what it looked like; any words or colors?" the police officer asked.

"Yes," David replied, "they were huge diamonds, like the ones on playing cards."

The police officer and the security guard thanked David and assured him they would call Diane as soon as they left his room. They also asked if he would be willing to pick these men out of a lineup should they be apprehended. He decided not to inform his parents since he was in no apparent medical danger. That's all they needed, he thought, another family member in the hospital. What concerned David were the contents of his wallet. He had some cash, but his Florida driver's license and credit card were also taken. He would ask Diane to call and cancel the card and report it stolen, as well as his license.

Life was beginning to appear as a complexity of nightmares instead of the joy David had known earlier in his youth. It seemed as though his life had turned sour beginning with the day of his Bar Mitzvah. He felt the gut-wrenching pain of disappointment and loss as he closed his eyes. Several tears of heartfelt pain flooded his eyelids and rolled down his cheek, dropping to the pillow and leaving tiny spots.

He fell asleep quickly but was soon awakened by a nurse who wanted to take his vital signs again. Another woman he did not know was also in the room and was waiting for the nurse to finish. She explained that she was with the hospital administration department and needed to get some information from him. That would include his medical coverage, and of course, the card was in his wallet. When David informed her of what had happened, she said it would be okay and asked him for his name, date of birth, social security number and the name of his medical insurance. She said that would be enough information to establish his coverage. She appeared to be in her twenties and was staring at David quite intently while she was getting the information from him.

"I will process your information, Mr. Blumberg, and if there is anything you need, please do not hesitate to call me. My phone number is listed on the back of my card."

David took the card from her, and her hand lingered for a fraction of a second. It was as though she was touching him with a sympathetic and caring hand. She was quite lovely and young looking. She had long, almost chestnut brown hair with blondish streaks and large, dark eyes. Her skin tone was olive; she was on the thin side, but judging from her muscle tone, appeared to be quite athletic. They finished up quickly and she smiled at David. She told him that she hoped he felt better soon and left the room. The nurse who was taking his vital signs was surely the opposite of this charming young lady. When she left the room, David looked at the card the woman had handed him.

Her name was Elanie Feldman, which seemed to David like an Israeli name. David noticed that the phone number she had written on the back of the card was not her office number, but rather her home number. He knew that because she had written beneath the number, "call me if you need anything." He was about to close his eyes again when he heard Diane's voice. David saw her through the glass window, talking to the nurse that had just left. She looked toward the room, nodded her head in affirmation, and then entered the room.

"David, oh David, I am so sorry. Roger drove me down here and is in the waiting room. They will only allow one visitor at a time in ICU."

"ICU?" David questioned. "Is that where I am?"

"Yes," Diane answered. She reached for his hand and touched him gently and lovingly; being careful not to touch the I.V. needle and tube that was taped to his skin.

"I thought that there was something familiar about this type of room."

He attempted a smile, but his head bore too much pain. There was a sticking sensation in his chest from the stitches that closed the knife wound.

"How do you feel?" she asked with deep concern in her voice.

"I feel like someone who just got stabbed and kicked in the head—terrible!"

"May I stay with you, David?" she asked.

"Of course. I would be grateful."

He began to feel a bit lightheaded and deducted that the nurse must have injected something into his I.V., but also felt the warmth of her hand on his. A soothing effect came over him, and he closed his eyes. It only took a few minutes for David to fall asleep. Diane took off her ski jacket and sat down on the chair at the foot of his bed. She had an instant flashback of sitting like this and praying when she was in Ruth's room in Florida. She prayed silently for David and became teary-eyed, sensing his pain physically and emotionally with all he had been through. Diane simply stared at him, very much aware of her deep feelings for David. At the very least, the wonderful friendship they shared was better than no relationship at all. She believed that real love had many phases, and perhaps this was simply a preliminary phase for better things to come.

It was nearly 2:00 a.m. when David opened his eyes again. He rubbed them, feeling the edge of the gauze bandage wrapped around his head. Then he saw Diane, sound asleep in the chair at the foot of his bed. He stared at her and felt the comfort of her presence. Just then, she awoke and stretched, covering her mouth as she yawned.

"You're awake!" she happily said as she saw David smiling at her.

"Yes, I woke up about five minutes ago. Your back must be sore from sleeping in that chair."

"No, I'm okay. How do you feel—any better?"

"Yes, a bit, but my head is throbbing."

David stretched his legs under the sheets just as Diane put her hand to her mouth and exclaimed,

"Oh no—Roger! I left him in the waiting room when we first arrived. I'll be right back. I have to go out and see if he's still there."

"If he is," David called to her as she was going out the door, "tell him to come in for a few minutes. Then he can drive you back to campus and drop you off at your dorm. It's already after 2:00 in the morning, and I don't want you staying here all night—you have classes in the morning."

Diane nodded in approval of his wishes and continued walking toward the ICU waiting room. Roger had indeed fallen asleep on one of the couches, claiming it was more comfortable than the beds in their dorm room. He walked back to see David after Diane woke him up.

"Will you drive Diane home and make sure that she is safely inside her dorm before you leave her?"

"No, I can't," Roger emphatically stated.

David looked at his roommate with a puzzled look.

"What do you mean?"

"David, there's almost five feet of snow on the ground, and it's still snowing. There is a major winter storm out there. I'm not going anywhere in this weather. Besides, the couch is soft, there are vending machines if I get hungry, and I have minor classes tomorrow. It *is* Friday, you know."

"Wow, I knew it was snowing when I was heading for Diane's, but I had no idea it was this bad. I wouldn't have continued, but I missed Diane and wanted to see her."

"I understand," Roger smiled, "so let me go back and get her so that . . . " Just then Diane came through the door.

"How did you get past the nurse at the desk?" David asked.

"I don't really think she cares about one more visitor at this hour."

David looked into Diane's eyes with love—the love that emanates from a mature relationship developed over time.

It was nearly daylight when Diane and Roger left. The roadways were being plowed, and Roger felt it was okay to venture back to the campus. He promised David that he would drop Diane at the front door of her dorm and wait until she was safely inside.

After they left, David was once again alone with his thoughts. He was still feeling the pain in his chest and the throbbing in his head. He was fortunate—there would be no permanent damage, and he was young and would heal quickly. Perhaps he needed to call his father and let him know about the situation and that he was not badly injured. He did not like the idea of keeping something from him—aside from his true feelings for Diane, although somewhat suppressed.

Nathan reacted calmly to David's call, just so long as David assured him that he was all right. He jokingly promised that he would not panic and take the next plane to Pittsburgh. He did, however, insist that he speak with someone from the hospital and with the police officer that took the report. Nathan wanted a copy of the report faxed or e-mailed to him so that he had the official status of the incident on file. Diane called him at about 10:30 a.m. and Roger also called to see if he needed anything. He was due to be discharged in a few days and said he was fine until then. The bandage around his head was to be taken off the next day, and just to be sure there were no other complications, a CAT scan was ordered for that afternoon. He was also being moved out of ICU to a regular room.

Once David was settled into his new room, he turned on the television and clicked the remote control until he found the news channels. Fox News had just begun airing a breaking news story about a terrorist bombing in Israel. It was a live broadcast from the scene, and there was no way to hide the graphic bloodshed. All the news people could do was to not show any extreme close-ups at the heart of the devastation. There were bodies without extremities among the dead, and several victims holding on to life by a thread from their injuries. The bomb was powerful and had killed numerous Israeli adults as well as several children. Fortunately, the cameraman on the scene was sensitive and did not show the dismembered children lying in the street. The death count had not yet been established, and David watched tearfully. It was a street in Tel Aviv, and he sensed a surge of anger at the thought of such senseless killing. The small television screen became a living portrayal of the ageless conflict between Palestinian and Jew.

"A horrible sight, isn't it?"

David looked into the eyes of the beautiful administrative person from last night. She had entered the room while David was engrossed in the news story.

"Yes," David replied, wiping tears from his eyes.

"You look much better today. You have some color returning to your face, and the swelling seems to have gone down considerably. Are they removing your gauze head bandage today?"

"Yes," David replied, "probably this afternoon." She had come back to see him. He wondered if this was an official visit or perhaps just a random stop to say hello.

"It's nice to see you—thanks for stopping in to check on me."

"Oh," Elanie smiled, "you are a charmer as well as being handsome!"

With that she moved closer to the bed. Her body pressed up against the bed rail on the left side of David.

"Your insurance came through, and you are totally covered, less a deductible of two hundred dollars, which is the maximum toward any hospital stay. I also spoke with your father this morning—Nathan, isn't it?"

"Yes, he called you?"

"Well, not specifically, but he was connected to my extension when he asked to speak to someone in administration. We had quite a chat."

"You did?" David exclaimed with much surprise in his voice.

"Yes, he is a nice man, and it seems we have something very much in common."

"What would that be?" David curiously asked.

"Our love for Israel—our homeland. We *all* hate terrorism and have only disdain for this senseless violence taking place day after day."

"Well, you and my father obviously had more than a short conversation!"

"Your father was just upset about what happened to you, and in the process of assuring him you would be perfectly fine, one thing led to another, and the topic of Israel came up. He also provided his credit card number for your two hundred dollar deductible."

"I see," David commented as he took a closer look at this beautiful woman. His eyes explored her face and her slim, well-endowed figure. She was absolutely lovely, with highly pronounced foreign features. Elanie knew he was studying her. She smiled as she reached her hand across the bed railing and rested it on David's hand, which was holding onto the left bed-rail.

"Seriously, I simply wanted to comfort your father, and I am here now as a friend. I am not a nosy person who is trying to measure your feelings for Israel."

"How do you know so much about Israel?" David curiously asked.

"I was born in Israel and left for the United States after graduation. I was about fourteen when my mother and father visited a friend on the

West Bank. My brother—his name is Yael—was not with them that day. I was in school, and he was in college. He was a freshman at the time, and I was a freshman in high school. One afternoon, terrorists planted a bomb where there were several shops. My parents had stopped to buy their friends some figs and fresh fruit. They walked into the shop just moments before it went off. They were killed instantly, along with several others in the shop and some passers-by on the street. After I buried them, I lived with an uncle until I entered college and worked my way through."

David was shocked by this tragic story and considered that perhaps his own situation was not that bad in comparison. "I am very sorry about your parents. It must have been both tragic and very painful for both you and your brother." David looked at her face and could see the wondering look in her eyes as though she just relived the entire incident. She was truly beautiful, but he had already noticed all that when she came to the room to inquire about his insurance. Why was he now so intent on studying her face, her features and her mannerisms? It was a thought that crossed his mind because it *was* his mind. It was how his thinking process actually functioned—striving for collective awareness, searching for truths, and trying to unpeel all the surface layers from people to see who and what they were really like on the inside, where it mattered the most.

Elanie was doing the very same thing to David—probing, watching his emotional reactions, and studying his eyes—and David knew it.

"So how do you feel about these bombings in Israel, David?" she asked. She pulled the single chair in the room close to where she had been standing and sat down.

"I am tired of seeing our people being killed for no other reason than hatred. I am sick and tired of seeing innocent people, who only want to live in peace, being blown to bits or being disfigured for life."

"I know exactly what you are saying," she assured him. She moved her chair a bit closer to the bed. "I came here for the work, but I miss Israel and have considered returning. I have a small apartment in Tel Aviv that I bought several years before I came to the United States, so I do not have to worry about a place to live. I could easily get a job teaching or even working in a hospital. The trouble is," she sighed, pausing and looking down at the floor, "I can't bear to see any more of our people suffer. The terrorists are taught to hate us from the time they can understand their first words."

"Yes," David replied, "I know exactly what you are saying, but I can't feel what you feel. It is *your* country, and they are your people. I view *all* murders and bombings as senseless and evil."

Elanie tightened her jaw and stared at David for a long moment. It was as though she was studying his face and evaluating what he had just said.

"You are an honest man, David. You are obviously transparent with people whom you trust. I do sense a guarded tongue, which is a good thing."

David smiled, almost in a shy way. She had read him in so short a time that he was at a loss for words. Elanie got up from the chair and pushed it back to the head of the bed. She hesitated for a moment and then turned toward him, but only halfway, as though one were glancing back to convey a forgotten thought.

"I will see you later, David Blumberg. I have to get back to work. My lunch break is over."

With that she left the room, but as she approached the glass window on the outside wall, she stopped, turned halfway toward him and smiled warmly. Then she walked away. David held that image in his mind as a young girl came into the room with his lunch tray.

Chapter Thirteen

The Betrayal

Three weeks had passed since the incident, and David was back in school. He was still healing, taking it easy and missing his racing bike. He and Diane spent some time studying together, but with limited conversation. His professors had heard what happened to him and allowed a great deal of leeway with his homework assignment and the exams he missed.

David had managed to convince Nathan and Rachael that he was recovering wonderfully and there was no sense in their coming up there while Ruth was still in a coma. Ruth had been moved to a nursing home from the hospital since she did not meet the criteria for hospice. She also required far too much medical attention for them to keep her at their home. She remained in a coma and no one, including the medical specialists, knew when or if she would recover. She was breathing on her own and being fed intravenously. Nathan and Rachael spent numerous hours praying and discussing the matter, finally deciding that they could not give her the daily medical attention she required. Perhaps she would simply wake up one day, and although weak or perhaps even bed ridden, God would grant them His infinite mercy and keep her around a few more years. Without Harry, however, Ruth was lost. She missed him so much that her heart had been broken with his passing. Nathan knew his mother wanted to leave this life, and to be one in spirit with Harry again. He was beginning to believe that it was probably the best thing that could happen, but he did not allow himself to even mentally meddle in God's affairs.

David stared at the snow-laden trees on the campus from his window and continued reading and studying. It was nearly 10:30 p.m., and his eyes were growing heavy. He noticed that Roger was not back yet. He had said something about getting some good food for a change and was driving into the city.

The swelling on David's forehead had subsided, and the wound in his chest was healed–except for the scar that would be his reminder of the incident for the rest of his life. David felt fortunate that he was alive and simply wanted to put all this behind him.

On one corner of his desk was a business card. He had placed it there the first day he came back from the hospital. The card had the hospital logo, name and telephone numbers. On the bottom right side was the name "Elanie Feldman, Administrative Assistant." It was a business card, but David held back from turning it over. That was the personal side of the card—the "call me" that was written directly above what he assumed was her home telephone number. He had not called because he felt it was almost like cheating on Diane, and that was not within David's character. He had thought of Elanie on several occasions, perhaps more than he ought to. Her image kept popping into his mind, provoking sensual thoughts rather than the loving, friendship thoughts he shared with Diane. He quickly dismissed these feelings as being inappropriate. Just then the telephone rang. He put down his textbook and reached for the receiver. It was Roger, a thoughtful call to see if he wanted some Italian food.

"So that's where you went. Thank you, and sure, I would love a portion of good-old lasagna. I haven't had that in years."

"You got it," Roger replied. David was about to thank him for thinking of him when he thought he heard Diane's voice in the background, asking Roger whom he was calling. *No, it couldn't be. He had to be mistaken.* He thanked Roger and hung up the phone. David replayed the voice and the noise from the restaurant over and over in his mind, convincing himself that he was mistaken. He picked up his textbook, but something started gnawing away at him. He just couldn't be absolutely sure that he heard what he thought he had heard.

Feeling guilty that he would even *think* that Diane would go out with Roger, he ignored the matter until several hours later. Roger had not returned, and David finally reached for the phone and dialed Diane's dorm room.

"Hello," was the greeting from her roommate.

"Hi, this is David. I'm sorry for calling so late, but is Diane there?"

"Oh, I'm sorry, David, you just missed her. She was having a hard time sleeping—she said something about an assignment and went over to the library with Charlene to study." David thanked her and asked that she tell Diane that he had called and would speak with her tomorrow. He sensed some guilt over his suspicions, and within a few minutes of reading one of his textbooks, he fell asleep.

He did not hear Roger come in, nor did he hear him leave again. It was dawn before David awoke and saw that Roger had not been there all night. *"I'll bet he met a girl and spent the night with her! So much for his self-professed chastity, if that's what really happened,* David thought. He quickly dismissed that thought and even felt bad that he was conjuring up all these negative thoughts about his best friends. *"What is happening to me lately? One minute I am who I have always been, and the next minute I feel like a cynic."*

David saw a sticky note on his desk that read, "Lasagna is in the fridge in the closet." They had each chipped in and bought a tiny dorm refrigerator that held a few cans of soda and perhaps two portions of leftovers from a restaurant. David was pleased and smiled that his roommate had actually thought of him. But it also occurred to him that Roger had returned and had left again, and that thought was confusing!

Roger walked into the room at about 6:00 a.m., looking as though he had very little sleep. He stripped off his jeans and shirt, wrapped himself with a towel, and was heading back out the door to the shower when David awoke.

"Hey, where have you been all night? If you were not back when I woke up, I was seriously going to call campus security." David was a bit drowsy as he sat up in bed and reached for a bottle of water that was on his desk. He took a long gulp and then looked at Roger, awaiting some kind of answer. Roger looked a bit guilty of something, and David began to laugh.

"Don't tell me, I already know the answer. You met a girl and were at her place all night. Now you are going to call me a virgin for the rest of the semester, aren't you?" Roger smiled a guilty sort of smile but remained silent.

"I knew it, I really did," David declared. He began to laugh aloud.

"Okay, I'm going to take a shower. I have a class in an hour, and I need to prepare a few things."

Roger opened the door to leave when David exclaimed, "What, no details, not even a name?"

"Listen to you," Roger retorted as he let go of the doorknob to turn and answer David. "Aren't you the Jewish Mr. Rogers who will not have an intimate relationship until he is married?"

"Well, yeah, that's what I've always believed."

"And you're questioning me as though you don't believe that anymore?"

"No," David snapped back. "I still believe in chastity until marriage, and I don't mean to sound judgmental over what is between you and God. If you want to have a one-night stand, it's your business and your own beliefs."

"Oh, I see, not judging but. . . . never mind. I've got to get a shower." Roger opened and closed the door behind him.

The moment Roger left, the phone rang. It was his father.

"Hi, son. How are you feeling?"

"I'm fine, Dad, really. Except for a small scar on my chest and a bruise on my forehead, I really am okay. Even the headaches have stopped, and I don't take the medication any longer. I don't need pain pills if there is no pain."

"I am so glad to hear that. Hold on a moment, your mother wants to say hello."

Rachael's voice on the other end of the phone gave him immediate peace within. His mother had that effect on him.

"How is my handsome son?"

"I am almost recovered. I am fine, but more importantly, has there been any change in grandma?"

There was a silence on the phone, just a slight hesitation that told him the answer. Something had turned in Ruth's condition, and that was what this call was all about. Somehow he had suspected it when his father got on the phone. His calls in the daytime were mostly from his mother, and his father would call him in the evening, but never this early in the morning.

It was with a heavy heart that Nathan told him the truth. "David, Grandma had to be put on a respirator last night. She could no longer breathe on her own. The doctors told us that her heart is giving out, and there is little hope she will make it beyond the next few days. They have moved her back to an ICU unit at the hospital."

After a short conversation with his parents, David said his goodbyes, hung up the phone, and then suddenly jumped from his bed. With a single sweep of his arm, he shoved every textbook from his desk to the floor. Anger was pulsating through his body, and the anger was turning to rage for the first time in David's life. It was an incredible change in David's way of handling tragedy—rage instead of prayer—but he found that he couldn't control himself.

In that rage, David flipped his bed over on its side. The phone line had been wrapped around the bedpost and the telephone receiver was flung across the room. At that very moment, Roger opened the door, returning from his shower.

"David, David, what's the matter with you? Sit down. Let me get you something." He was shocked to have witnessed such a violent act from his roommate. David's eyes were glaring, and he was breathing rapidly. Roger quickly grabbed a pair of sweatpants and a polo shirt from the closet and got dressed. "David, I am sorry, more than you will ever believe. It wasn't supposed to have happened. It was an innocent thing, dinner. That's all but..."

What did he say? David thought. He suddenly realized what Roger was saying and he turned towards him, his brow wrinkled in disbelief but his eyes quickly displaying anger. Roger was talking about Diane. He must have thought the call was about Diane and not his parents. Roger had no way of knowing, and guilt forced him to tell the truth. David slowly stood with a menacing air about him, his fists clenched. Roger stepped back and reached for the doorknob to quickly leave the room if he needed to.

"David, please hear me out. If you have never judged anyone in your whole life, don't judge this until you listen to what I have to say. It was not my fault entirely. David, it was partially *your* fault, and mostly the wine. "

David cocked his head just a bit and frowned. There was a questioning look in his eyes instead of anger. He relaxed his clenched fists and did not speak. For the moment, Roger remained silent, not knowing what to say except to tell David the truth.

"What are you trying to tell me—that it was *my* fault you had sex with my best friend, a girl with whom I had a deep and serious affection for and—"

"Stop," Roger broke in. "That's the point. A deep affection that has never been physically expressed, and she was confused by the fact that you never even kissed her like a girlfriend, much less expressed a desire for her as a woman! She would have never allowed you to have intimacy with her, even if you wanted to because she is a believing Christian. She just needed to know you *wanted* to—that you were physically, spiritually and emotionally attracted to her. We went to dinner because she wanted to talk about *you*, David! After it was all over, she sobbed like a child—we both did. She and I are so sorry that it happened that we are both broken people right now. It was a couple of inebriated moments and nothing more. I don't even remember how it started because I was half drunk, and so was she. We had a few glasses of wine with dinner, that's all. I didn't know she never drank before. We were almost wiped when we got back here."

Roger was crying by that point, almost sobbing. It was obvious that he deeply regretted having gone to dinner with Diane. David sat back down on the bed and Roger sat on the floor, tears streaming from his eyes like a little boy who had just disappointed his one true friend in the world. It was a heartbreaking sight; and the words coming from Roger were choked with such emotion that David knew they were not false.

"Tell me then why you stayed with her all night if it was a drunken mistake?" he demanded.

"I didn't!" Roger sobbed. "I was walking around all night, trying to figure out how to tell my best friend what happened. Diane is also devastated. It took only minutes for both of us to realize the sobering truth of what we had done in our stupor. I should have known that Diane never drank, but I didn't think about it and simply ordered a bottle of wine. I should have realized that she never drank when she stared at the glass in front of her for a long while—before she finally picked it up and took a sip."

"Where was she if you were not with her all night? I called her roommate and she said that she was out—at the library or something with a friend, studying."

"She was with a friend," Roger confirmed, "but she was being consoled, not studying. The girl she was with, Charlene . . . her father is a Chaplain in Colorado. They called him and Diane was on the phone with him for over an hour. David, you've got to believe me."

Roger was now staring at David with pleading eyes, and David knew that it was all truth. But the reality was that it had actually happened and nothing could reverse it.

"I believe you, Roger."

David then got up and grabbed a shirt from the closet and a pair of jeans. He dressed quickly and warmly, putting on a sweatshirt and then a bulky sweater. David put on a pair of heavy wool socks and his leather boots that were waterproof. He then took his wallet and some loose change from the top of the dresser and tucked them into his pockets. Roger just watched him without saying a word. He picked himself up off the floor and sat down on his bed.

After a slight hesitation, David remarked in a calm tone of voice, "You cried a lot, Roger, but you never asked for my forgiveness."

He opened the door and slammed it forcefully behind him.

He practically ran out into the early morning daylight and down the path towards the Cathedral of Learning. He felt as though he couldn't get away fast enough. He had a 7:30 a.m. meeting with Professor Todd in his office on the tenth floor of the building. David was to select the subject matter for his first semester paper, but as he approached the building, he began to cry. Instead of continuing, he turned away towards the park. The tears on his cheek were turning to ice almost as fast as they fell, but he didn't care.

He didn't take his gloves, so he dug his hands deep into his pockets to protect them from the bitter cold. It was then that he felt something like a card and pulled out the hospital business card that he must have grabbed when he took his wallet and loose change. It was only 7:00 in the morning, and he knew that Elanie would not be at the hospital for another two hours. He changed direction and headed for a payphone near the campus entrance. He pulled out the change in his pocket, inserted a quarter, and dialed the number on the back of the card.

The phone rang several times, and Elanie answered in a sleepy voice, almost a whisper.

"Hello, who is this?"

David realized that he must have woken her. He was going to hang up, but something made him stay on the phone.

"Hi, I am sorry to call you so early in the morning, but this is David— you know, from . . ." His voice faltered a bit.

"I know who it is. I know your voice. Are you all right? You sound very stressed. What's wrong? Where are you calling from?" Elanie sounded immediately more awake than when she had answered the phone.

"I'm okay but desperately need someone to talk to, and you are the only other person I know in this city—outside of the campus."

"Where are you? I'll pick you up unless you have a car?"

"No, I don't own a car. I am at the main entrance by the tallest building on the front campus. I'll walk down to the main road and wait there. Are you very far away, and are you sure you want to drive out here?"

"I am not that far from you, and yes, I will pick you up. Are you sure you're okay?"

"Physically, yes, but emotionally, no. I'm really not in good shape right now. I need a friend." David was struggling to hold back his tears.

"I understand," she replied in a soothing and sympathetic voice. "I'll be right there."

Less than twenty minutes later, David was glancing at the sign near the entrance to Elanie's apartment complex. It was a "Welcome" sign to the Chateau Perry Apartments. There were lots of huge oak trees all around, but at this time of year they were barren. A few inches of un-melted snow covered the spacious grounds. The building was four stories, all brick, and was at the north end of town. When they got upstairs, she told David to make himself comfortable and went straight to the kitchen and began making a pot of coffee—also putting some raisin-cinnamon bread in the toaster.

"Do you want some eggs, David?" Elanie called out.

"No, thank you. Just coffee and a slice of toast would be wonderful," he answered. He looked around at every detail, smelling the toast and the aroma of cinnamon that had begun to fill the air. *Elanie must be in her late twenties,* he reasoned.

"David, would you like to sit in the living room and have your coffee, or would you prefer the dining room?"

She was really pretty, David thought as he asked to have his coffee at the table. He did not want to get too close to this beautiful woman. Elanie poured the hot coffee into mugs and set one in front of David as he sat down.

David sipped the strong brew as Elanie gently prodded him to find out what had happened. David opened up like a gushing fountain. He left no detail out of the story and then, as he just about finished, began to cry. Elanie got up and came around the table, placing a hand on his shoulder. She tried to comfort him, but David's heart was broken. The only thing he wanted was to get as far away from all of this as he possibly could. He controlled his emotions and there was silence for a minute or two. Then David declared, in fact, that he was going to leave school.

"How can you do that in the first semester? You could ask for a transfer to another dorm or get another roommate if you want to. I truly understand your pain, David." Elanie continued speaking in that same soothing and understanding voice.

"Why did you leave Israel and come to the United States?" David asked.

"I can not tell you *why* I left, but I will ask you to trust the fact that I never wanted to leave my country. I left for good reason, and I am returning shortly."

"What sort of time frame is 'shortly'?" David was curious now.

"Within the next thirty days."

David was somewhat surprised. He had finally met someone he could talk to—not only intelligent, but she was beautiful as well—and now she was leaving the country and going back to Israel.

"Would you like company?" he asked.

"What are you saying, David—that you want to go to Israel?"

"The thought has occurred to me on several occasions. There is nothing here for me outside of my mother and father. I have no real friends—Diane was my only real friend. I do not know what I want to do with my life. Besides, I don't like Pittsburgh, and I know how my father loved Israel when he took his first trip there after college. He came back a renewed and dedicated man. Maybe it's what I need for a time."

Elanie looked at him as though she were seriously studying him.

"I have to go to work. I am already late. You can stay here and rest. There are many books and brochures on Israel in the bookcase in the second bedroom."

"I'm going to dress and go to work. Stretch out on the couch and rest yourself. The television controls are on the coffee table."

David heard her door close.

David drifted off to sleep as he lay on the couch. He slept for about an hour. He awoke about 11:00 a.m. and decided to look at some of the books and brochures on Israel. He went to the second bedroom and was quite surprised at what he saw. The room was an office, but there was also communications equipment. One piece looked like a short-wave radio, and there were several other machines that resembled recording equipment. Her desk occupied most of the right wall of the room, while the opposite wall with the only window had a single-sized bookcase. An oversized chair was up against the center wall, and across from the chair was a small table, stacked with books and brochures on Israel. David thought that Elanie was simply full of surprises. An administrator at the hospital who was a short-wave enthusiast and apparently enjoyed studying the Middle East, as all the travel and history books in the room indicated. David took several books on Israel and some of the travel brochures that were piled-up on the lower shelf of the bookcase. He returned to the living room and spread the stack of brochures on the coffee table. He began reading a tour book about Israel until he fell asleep again. He must have been very tired because the next thing he knew, Elanie was rubbing his arm and calling his name. It was already 5:30 in the evening.

"David," Elanie called. Out and he slowly sat up, trying to focus his eyes.

"Hi, I guess I fell asleep. What time is it?"

"It's about 5:30. Would you like to go get some dinner? I didn't take anything out this morning with all that was going on."

"Sure," David answered. "That would be great."

"There is a small Israeli restaurant not far from here. It is off the main road, and unless you know about it, you would never know it exists."

"How did you find it?" David asked inquisitively.

"It is owned by an Israeli man who came here a year ago from Tel Aviv. I knew him from the university. Why don't you use the guest bathroom and freshen-up while I change. Are you hungry?"

"I'm starving."

"Good, they have great food—you're Jewish, you'll love it!"

David smiled and got up, following Elanie up the four steps from the sunken living room and down the hall. She stopped outside the hallway bathroom, opened the door, and switched on the light.

"There are clean towels on the rack."

She smiled at David and gestured towards the bathroom. She then went into her own room and closed the door. David took off his sweatshirt and undershirt. He washed up, dried off and re-folded the towel, and placed it on the sink instead of back on the towel rack. He dressed and returned to the living room. Fifteen minutes later, they were on their way to the restaurant.

David could not remember the last time he had enjoyed someone's company so much, and the small restaurant was exactly as Elanie had described. The dining room had only eight tables, and the kitchen was behind a counter with a glass divider so that you could see the food being prepared. David thought it odd that there was not another person in the tiny restaurant, and no one came in after they were seated. Reuben, the owner and chef, came over to the table where Elanie and David had just finished a cup of Turkish coffee.

"So, how was the meal?" he inquired. He then asked if he might join them.

"Of course, Reuben, you're a friend," Elanie replied, and he sat down.

"So, David, tell me, how is it that you wound up in Pittsburgh from sunny Florida?" Reuben asked.

What does your name mean in Hebrew?" David asked, without answering his question.

"Reuben means 'A Son.' I am an only child. My mother almost died during my delivery, and the doctor told her that she should not attempt another pregnancy—it would kill her." David's face must have turned ashen in color.

"I don't believe this! My mother, Rachael, almost died having *me,* and I am an only child!"

Reuben opened his arms, got up from the table, and came around to give David a hug. Elanie smiled and mentioned something about them being "brothers in circumstance and fate." Reuben walked back behind the counter and brought out some desert, insisting that Elanie and David try his homemade pastries. David picked up the pastry and took a bite, declaring how delicious it was and that it tasted totally homemade.

"I taste cinnamon, raisins, walnuts, and something else I can't figure out." Elanie laughed. "It's his love for authentic food that he puts in it—that's what you taste!"

They all laughed together. Reuben sat back and folded his arms, almost studying David.

"So David, tell me, how do you like school here at Pitt?"

"I don't. I would rather be in Israel."

Reuben did not so much as acknowledge his remark but rather became more serious in his demeanor. He leaned forward and placed his hands on the table, folding them slowly. His thumbs arched upwards, pressing against one another. He glanced at Elanie and then turned his attention completely to David.

"What makes you think you would rather be in Israel—if you are serious, I mean."

"I am very serious. I have had my fill of tragedy, this cold weather, and the crummy circumstances in my life. I am tired of our people being blown up on the streets of Israel every day. These are senseless killings in the name of 'Allah'—it's in the name of 'hatred and madness.' That's what it's all about, and I am sick of it." David's voice quivered a bit with emotion.

"What is it to you, David? You were not born in Israel. Why should you care?"

David was taken aback, not only by the question but also by the tone in which it was asked. It was as though he was being challenged to explain himself.

"Look, we are here to eat, and I am glad to have met you. However, that does not give you the right to question my motives for loving my *own* people." David immediately took offense to this man's questions. Reuben's expression never changed.

"I was not questioning that aspect of your remark, David, just what you thought you could do about it."

Reuben had a very noticeable accent. David could tell that he had not been in the United States very long. He remembered Elanie mentioning something about him being there about a year.

"Reuben, I wish to God that there *was* something I could do about it. Don't you understand what I am trying to say to you without telling you my entire life of tragedy? I have nothing here anymore except my mother and father. My father is heartbroken because I won't become a rabbi. The only one who would truly miss me would be my mother, and I am sure she would get over it if she knew I went to Israel to do something worthwhile with my life. And now, I've lost my best friend in a stupid act of intoxicated behavior, along with my roommate, whom I don't even want to see again." Reuben was silent. He looked over at Elanie and then back to David.

"How serious are you about 'doing something,' David?"

"I don't know what you're getting at."

"I asked you how much you really wanted to be a part of defending our homeland," Reuben replied.

"If I had the opportunity, I would leave tomorrow."

Reuben looked at him with a long, curious look as though he was searching his face for absolute truth. He then excused himself, got up from the table, and went to the phone behind the counter. Elanie was simply sitting there and staring at him, as well. Suddenly, David sensed that there was something much more to this conversation and this particular restaurant than simply its authentic food. Reuben was speaking in Hebrew, and his conversation lasted only a couple of minutes. As Reuben pulled his chair back towards the table, David heard footsteps from a room that he thought was a storeroom behind the counter at the end of the dining room.

The footsteps were just that—someone coming down the steps from upstairs. *Of course,* he thought. ***There must be an apartment or a place to live above the restaurant.*** Just then, a man came out of the doorway and walked around the counter, intently looking at David. This was becoming a bit unnerving, and David looked to Elanie for an answer. She sensed his nervousness and took his left hand in hers. Elanie gave him a warm smile of comfort, as if to say, "It's okay, relax." The man was perhaps around Elanie's age and seemed incredibly fit. He wore a sport shirt, denim jeans and a leather jacket, which did not do very much to hide his muscular frame. His shoes looked like army boots. He came over to the table and smiled at David. Then he looked over at Elanie.

"Hello, my sister." He leaned over and kissed Elanie on the forehead.

"This is your brother?" David blurted out in surprise.

"Yes, this is my brother, Yael. In Hebrew it means 'God's Strength,' and he has certainly been all of that to me." David began to get up, but Yael motioned to him that he should remain seated.

"I am not very formal, David. In fact, I am quite the opposite."

Elanie laughed aloud, and David smiled at the way she threw her head back when she laughed.

"He is trying to tell you in a nice way that he's just plain rude!" said Reuben, and he laughed, as well.

"David, Reuben tells me that you would like to go to Israel and do something for the cause of our people. Is that right?" David did not answer immediately. David sensed that he was in over his head. He cast his eyes downward as though to ignore the fact that he was just asked a serious question. He quickly considered that the only way to find out what was really going on was to say,

"Yes, that is what I said."

Yael studied him for another moment and sat down, pulling his chair close to the table. Now three sets of eyes were on David.

"David," Yael began, "I am able to make that desire come to fruition—that is, of course, if you are truly serious. It would be nothing less than a complete and total commitment. Serving Israel as an able-bodied young man is not about volunteering to do bake sales and raise money for a cause on the weekends. It's knowing God has called you to defend 'His beloved,' 'The apple of His eye,' the land that He promised would be ours forever. That's what it's about. Is that something you are really prepared to do?"

"I don't know what you are saying. You ask if I am prepared to make a commitment, and I don't even know what you are referring to." Yael looked surprised and glanced over at Elanie who looked somewhat upset.

"You did not talk to David before bringing him here?"

"No, I did not," Elanie answered, appearing somewhat embarrassed.

"David has been through a great deal. He was beaten and stabbed, his girlfriend and his roommate. . . . well, it's been a lot for him. The opportunity did not present itself to go into any discussion. David made a serious statement that he wanted to go to Israel. I believe he is serious and sincere."

"I see," Yael acknowledged. "Well then, I have a lot of explaining to do. I apologize for my rudeness, but you were forewarned." Elanie and Reuben laughed. Reuben slapped the table and then placed his hand on David's shoulder as a friendly gesture. Reuben got up and said he was going to get something to "warm the sting of the winter wind!"

"I am going to use the restroom," Elanie said as she pushed out her chair and left the table. Yael and David were now alone.

"Why did they both leave?" David asked curiously. He appeared a bit nervous.

"Because there can be no second party around to hear our conversations. This way, if I divulge secretive information, there are no witnesses to our conversation. It's your word against mine," Yael explained. David nodded in acknowledgement. At the same time he folded his arms across his chest and leaned back in his chair—like a man who was waiting for a long story.

"David, I can offer you airline passage to Tel Aviv, as well as the completion of your education at the Tel Aviv University, all tuition paid. You will also have free room and board. Upon graduation, you will be required to do what every young man does who is a citizen of Israel. You will serve a tour of duty in the Israeli Army." David looked at Yael with surprise written all over his face.

"You're serious? You or whomever you represent is willing to fly me to Tel Aviv, put me through four years at the university, give me lodging, all expenses paid, and all I have to do is a tour in the army?"

"In a way, that's the short side of the details."

"Is there a lot more to it?" David asked.

"Yes, there is but it involves very sensitive information and I can not talk here."

"Where then *can* we talk?" David insisted.

"We will go back to the apartment. I can talk to you there."

"But there's no one here except us," David persisted.

"You will learn a lot in four years, my brother." Yael abruptly got up and extended his hand. David stood and shook hands.

As if on cue, Elanie came out of the restroom and warmly smiled as David looked over at her.

"Ready to go back?" she asked.

"Yes," David answered, and they left as Reuben said goodbye. He insisted that the meal was his gift of celebrating a brother coming to their side. They no sooner got into her car than David asked her to explain what was really going on. Her hand poised on the ignition key, she hesitated for a moment, looked over at David, and sat back in her seat, omitting a deep sigh.

"David, do you know how much I have to trust you to have even brought you here tonight?"

"Trust me? You don't really even know me!"

"Yes we do, David, better than you think."

"We? Who are we? What do *you* have to do with all of this, besides the fact that Yael is your brother? And what is your brother doing here in Pittsburgh? I thought your brother and sister were in Israel?"

"My family was my mother, my father, my sister, and Yael. I was a student at the University of Tel Aviv. I went to the University for my first semester and then was accepted into another program, a division of the university. Elanie stopped talking. She was shivering and started the car.

"Let's go back to the apartment. I can't turn on the heater until we warm up the car, and Yael will be waiting for us since he doesn't have a key."

She backed the car out of the street and did a three-point turn to get back on the main road.

"We were working on a program for the Israeli Defense Forces."

"What does that all mean?" David asked. He was beginning to sound interested and curious.

"We were working on understanding biological and non-biological entities."

Snow began falling, and Elanie turned on the windshield wipers. She saw that the engine had sufficiently warmed, and she turned on the heater. David was beginning to shiver a bit himself. The temperature obviously had dropped since they were in the restaurant. David was beginning to recall some of the Tom Clancy novels he read and wondered if he was smack in the middle of some kind of secret organization. He would have never taken Elanie for a spy!

"That's funny," he said aloud.

"What's funny?" Elanie asked as she changed the heat to defrost as the windows began to fog- up.

"I was thinking that you were a spy—too many conspiracy books in my brain. Tell me, what were you developing in terms of a product?"

"There were possibilities in the areas of pharmaceutical, environmental and advanced bio-inspired materials—the one most desired by the Israeli military. These were also very plausible possibilities in the field of security. Are you sure you want to hear all of this?"

"Yes, really," David replied. "It's fascinating to me."

"There was a study that was commissioned by the Ministry of Science in specific areas that I can't talk about. My mathematical and pharmacology abilities got me recruited by the staff to work on the project. I had to get military clearance first, and that brought my name and personal informa-tion into a database of project workers. Within six months we were close to a technological breakthrough in the area of a newly designed, biological gas. There was a girl in our lab with whom I became quite friendly. We were working on this project when we received threatening letters to quit the project or we would be killed. We each thought that someone was playing a cruel joke on us. Two days later, Daphne—that was her name, stopped on her way home to get some groceries for her mother that took her about fif-teen minutes. The shopping saved her life, but both her parents were killed. Terrorists bombed her building and it collapsed, killing everyone inside."

"My God," David exclaimed, shocked that these incidents really existed.

"What about you?"

"Thirty minutes later, the building where my family once lived was also bombed. Not only was our sister killed, but also our next-door neighbors and their newborn son. She brought him home from the hospital only two days before the bombing. My brother was not at home, and I was living on campus."

"You told me back in the hospital that your parents were killed in the bombing of a shop. Why did they bomb your building? They *must* have known they had killed your parents in a random act of terrorism previously."

"They wanted our sister dead—to make it known that they could get to us anywhere, any time."

"I see," David murmured, and he simply thought about the tragedy. At the very least, he thought, she still had her brother. They were only a few minutes from her apartment, and this time David recognized the sign as they turned into the complex. When she parked the car, David saw Yael waiting for them at the front entrance. He walked to the car and opened the door for his sister, and David got out on the other side. The snowfall was increasing in intensity, and the flakes were the size of quarters. *Very beautiful to watch,* he thought, *but I just want to get warm.* David pushed his hands deep into his pants pockets as the three walked to the front door of the building and went upstairs. As they entered, David kicked off his slush-soaked boots and left them on the doormat. Elanie went into the kitchen and asked if they would like some hot chocolate. David and Yael both said yes and went into the living room. Yael sat on the couch, and David sat in one of the chairs facing him. David began talking first, telling Yael how sorry he was to hear all the tragedy they suffered in their family.

"It must have been very hard for you. I don't really know what it is to lose your parents at such a young age, but I did lose my grandfather just before the reciting of my Haftorah at my Bar Mitzvah."

"You mean he died in the sanctuary?" Yael asked.

"Yes, in the first row," David answered.

"I am so sorry."

"Thank you. And now they are about to pull the plug on my grandmother. She had a massive stroke and has been in a coma since Thanksgiving."

"I am sorry again," Yael expressed.

"David, are these all of the reasons you want to go to Israel, or is there something else?" Yael asked him, searching his face and wanting only forthright answers.

"I suppose there is more than one reason for my wanting to go to Israel, but I really can't say there is something specific—just many reasons that add up to my conclusion. It's almost as though God is nudging me through all these events to do something with my life that goes beyond the norm—if you know what I mean."

"That's fair enough," Yael reasoned. He looked over at Elanie, who met his gaze. She nodded her head slightly as if to give him a "go ahead."

"David, what I am about to tell you is to be considered as secret information. You may not reveal any part of our conversation from this point going forward. Do you agree to that?" Yael looked quite serious, and David acknowledged his wishes by shaking his head.

"David, if you do speak to anyone, the deal is off. We will deny ever having talked to you, my sister being my collaboration. Have you ever heard of an organization called Mossad?" David had, as any Jewish person would. Whoever knew anything about Israel had heard of Mossad.

"Yes," David answered, "I have, but I don't know anything about their actual involvement in things."

Yael nodded his head in affirmation of David's directness.

"Do you know very much about the entire workings of your own CIA?" he asked.

"No, I don't. There are many divisions and departments, and sometimes I think that our own government doesn't know half of what's going on around the globe with the CIA."

"Good, that is an excellent analogy, and the Mossad is no different. They are our intelligence in defense of our country and are involved in top-secret missions and projects. David, if we send you to the University in Tel Aviv, you would be required to train on weekends with the Mossad. Initially, you will have some free time since this training will not begin right away. We would first like you to see Israel, learn our customs, and take some classes on Israeli citizenship. Elanie will introduce you to the local people and the local activities. I will be there to guide you for a short time, and then I will turn your training over to someone who will be your training coordinator. He will be the one who will pick you up and accompany you to the various sites where you will be trained in every aspect of Mossad. If you recall our earlier conversation, when you graduate from the University, you would be required to serve a term in our army. You do recall that, correct?"

"Yes, I do" David answered. Yael continued.

"You are committing to serve in the Mossad and not in the regular army for a term of seven years.

David never expected something like this, especially a term of seven years. He quickly calculated that he would be about thirty or so by the time he completed college and his commitment. Many thoughts went through his mind—his mother and father, his life here, the synagogue—and he instinctively knew that this could be the turning point in his life. Within his deepest thoughts, his self-esteem was in question, and this caused continuous emotional stress. *Was this of God or of man?* David reasoned and knew he had to give his answer, or at the very least, ask for time to think it over.

"Can I have until the morning to give you my answer?" David asked, and Elanie nodded affirmatively to Yael.

"Yes," Yael answered, "until morning. You can sleep in the office, and I will sleep out here on the couch. Good night, David."

It sounded as though he was being dismissed. He then remembered that the office had a desk and bookcases, but he did not remember seeing a bed. Just then, Elanie got up and told David that she would make-up the convertible chair. The large chair in her office turned into a single bed. That answered his question, and he remained silent—except to say "thank you" to Elanie. It was a difficult night for David, as he had a life-changing decision to make.

David did not sleep very well, as evidenced by the puffiness under his eyes the next morning. He slowly sipped a cup of hot coffee, trying to awake his tired mind. Elanie had said very little since he awoke.

Yael then came to the table, saying good morning to both of them. Elanie poured some coffee and passed it to Yael. After taking several sips, he looked at David and remarked that he too looked tired and did not have enough sleep.

"No, I didn't, but mostly because I was praying through the night."

"And did you receive your answer?"

"Yes, as a matter of fact I did. I have decided to go to Israel, and I am committing myself to the program you outlined last night."

Yael abruptly stood up and opened his arms wide. David also stood, and the two men embraced. Then Elanie came around the table and hugged him.

"Come," Elanie said, "let's sit in the living room and talk about a schedule for you so you have time to talk with your parents and—"

"No, I don't need any time. I will call my parents soon, and I would like to be on a plane out of here as quickly as possible." Elanie looked at Yael. He was staring straight into David's eyes and nodding his head in acknowledgement of David's wishes.

"Let me make a few calls," Yael said. "Do you mind if I use your office, Elanie?"

"No, of course not, Yael. Go ahead."

Chapter Fourteen

Open Doors

Nathan was sitting on the chair that was next to Ruth's bed when he felt his cell phone vibrate in his pocket. He tried to answer the call, but it stopped abruptly. With all of the medical instruments and the steel structure of the building, there was little if any signal strength in the hospital's interior rooms and corridors. He left the room and walked toward the waiting area that had a window where he might be able to obtain a cell signal. He opened his phone, saw that it was from home, and pressed the redial button. Rachael answered right away and sounded very upset.

"What's wrong?" Nathan asked, immediately concerned over the tone of her voice.

"It's David. He is leaving school and is going to Israel!"

"What?" Nathan practically yelled. "Where did you hear this—from David directly?"

"Yes, he just called! He is booked on a flight out of Pittsburgh for New York, changing for a flight to London, and then a final flight to Israel. He is flying into Tel Aviv!"

"Rachael, calm down and let me call him—" Rachael broke into his sentence to let Nathan know that he was not at the dorm.

"David said that he could not explain everything to us in one phone call—there are too many circumstances and many paths influencing this decision. He said he prayed about it all last night and had a perfect peace about the decision. He feels it was what he was meant to do. He did tell me something that almost sounds bizarre. I don't know how he did this, but he said he had been accepted into the university at Tel Aviv and has a complete scholarship for four years!"

"He told you that?" Nathan asked in surprise.

"Yes, and he told me that as soon as he arrived in Tel Aviv and was settled in, he would call us with all the contact information—his dorm, telephone number and the address to write to him."

"I am coming home. I need some sleep, anyway, and perhaps we can make some sense of this together. But the university at Tel Aviv is not such a bad thing—if all that he told you is true."

Nathan said goodbye to Rachael and closed the small cell phone. He struggled for the moment with the entire situation, both Ruth and now David's startling news. He had to go home. He needed rest and time to think all of this through. Nathan walked back to ICU and told the duty nurse that he was leaving. As he left the hospital and got into his car, he rolled down his window and allowed the breeze and coolness of the Florida winter to circulate through the car. He looked forward to this time of year, when the humidity was lower and one could breathe deeply without sweating.

Nathan was no more than a mile from the hospital when his cell phone rang. It was the charge nurse calling to tell him that Ruth had finally given up her silent battle. He thanked her for calling him right away and then pulled over to the side of the road. Nathan quietly sat there as the reality of losing his mother swept through him and he wept. That generation of the Blumberg family was now gone and he was afraid that he would be the last generation of rabbis in this family.

He sensed that David would never take his pulpit. Deep within his spirit he also prayed that David was perhaps destined for something far greater. He also hoped that David's decision to go to Israel was truly answered prayers and direction from God. The problem was, if God was talking to David, he surely was not sharing all of this with him. He decided not to inform David of Ruth's passing if he spoke with him. *Let him go to Israel with peace in his heart and not mourning,* he thought.

He pulled away from the curb and continued his drive home, considering how he would break the news to Rachael. *Faith is a tough road to maintain a steady journey on in this fallen and disappointing world,* he thought.

~

As David's plane touched down in London, he unlatched his safety belt and waited patiently for the more anxious passengers to deplane. He watched as several people nearly dropped their carry on bags on one another's head while removing them from the overhead compartments. He began inching his way from the window seat to the aisle. He opened the overhead compartment to retrieve his bag, and the compartment was empty. A rush of both fear and anger swept over him. Then he heard a voice from behind him from the opposite side of the plane.

"You may have patience, David, but you also need to keep your eyes on what is important to you." David turned around and saw a man sitting four rows back in the window seat.

"Who are you, and how do you know my name?"

The man did not answer but rather stood and picked up a leather jacket from the middle seat. He put it on over his sweater and inched his way out of the narrow space between the seats and he had David's carry-on bag in hand. David was surprised as well as confused. The man appeared middle-aged and had black hair and piercing dark eyes. David was at a loss for words, so he chose to remain silent and wait. The man came toward him and extended David's bag to him. David took it, but he never let his eyes break away from his gaze.

"My name is Isaac Selinsky. I work with Yael. I have been with you since we left Pittsburgh for New York.

David was too shocked to answer. His eyes searched the man's face, trying to understand how he knew so much about him. "You're from . . ."

The raising of the man's hand stopped David before he could say the word Mossad.

David nodded in recognition of his near-mistake and shook hands with him. He motioned toward the front of the plane to get off. The two walked off the plane and into the terminal building, following the signs for Customs. Once they were cleared, they left the terminal, and Isaac hailed a cab.

"The Abbey Court Hotel, please."

David looked at him curiously. "Why are we going to a hotel? I thought the layover here was only a few hours."

"It is," Isaac replied. "There is someone who wants to meet you. He's my boss, and Yael has told him a great deal about you and your family. He thinks you are very brave and have demonstrated your love for Israel just by getting on that plane in Pittsburgh."

"What is his name?" David inquired.

"I can't tell you that right now."

The Abbey Court Hotel is a four star hotel in the heart of London. It was originally built in 1830 and had been restored to its original, luxurious condition over the previous few years. The hotel had only three floors and twenty-two rooms, which were usually booked several months in advance. As the taxi pulled up to the front of the hotel, David studied the architecture while Isaac paid the taxi driver. He noticed that the entrance somewhat resembled the elegance of the United States White House. It boasted two massive pillars and was decorated with finely detailed etchings throughout the façade.

"This hotel is small, but classic," David remarked as he began walking toward the front steps.

"We're not going to the hotel." David turned to see Isaac walking away from the hotel toward the entrance of the adjacent building. He hurried to catch up and asked Isaac where he was going.

"This is a health club. There is an indoor pool and sauna room. We are going to visit the swimming pool area."

After they entered the building, Isaac opened a door within the inner lobby and walked down a flight of stairs. David followed close behind him. At the bottom of the landing, Isaac pushed open a steel door with a small glass pane covered with wire-meshed safety glass. As the door was opened, David felt a blast of humidity in his face along with the smell of chlorine. They entered the pool area and continued walking the length of the swimming pool until they came to the end. There was a steel door leading to a hallway. He held it open for David, and when it closed, the echo reverberated through the entire pool area. Isaac came to another door that appeared to be an office door. He opened it and then stepped aside, motioning David to go ahead of him. David slowed, and when he came to the doorway, he saw a man sitting at the end of a small, oblong table.

"Come in, David, please."

David walked through the doorway and into the small room that must have measured no more than twelve by twelve. The table was small, accommodating only four chairs. The man at the opposite side of the table stood and extended his hand, and David shook hands with him.

"David, my name is Agent Ross Schneider. Welcome to London."

David thanked him, and Ross motioned for him to take a seat to the right of him at the side of the table. Isaac put their bags under the table, reached for the pitcher of water, and poured three plastic cups to the middle level. He placed one in front of Ross and David.

"How was your trip, David? Restful, I hope?"

"Yes, thank you, but why am I here?"

"David, I simply wanted to meet you personally *before* you got to Israel later tonight. Thank you for coming here. It was the closest place to meet from where I need to be this morning for an important meeting. David, I sincerely hope you enjoy attending the University of Tel Aviv and that you quickly feel at home in Israel."

Ross hesitated for a moment, as though he were gathering some thoughts and then leaned forward in his chair again. His shoulders were slightly hunched and his head cocked to the side.

"Tell me, David, what made you trust Elanie and Yael? You did not know Elanie and Yael very long, but you trusted them enough to get on a plane for Israel."

David felt a slight twinge of panic run through his lower stomach. It was like the feeling you get when you realize that something was more than it seemed and you were on the receiving end of the bad news.

"I don't believe I told them very much except that I was sick of snow, cold weather, Pittsburgh, and people being slaughtered by terrorists in the streets of Israel. I called Elanie at the hospital, and I was put through to her office. My father had called the administrative office and was put through to her, as well. I saw her hospital identification and her story was sound. As far as Yael is concerned, I originally had some doubts about him, but the body language and eye contact between he and Elanie appeared to be normal for a brother and sister—or two people who knew each other for a very long time."

Ross continued to look into David's eyes. He then glanced over at Isaac and back to David.

"You have a keen sense of observation, and I believe you will do very well in the program that they set up for you."

Ross abruptly stood. He reached over and shook David's hand, picked up his briefcase, and walked out of the room.

Isaac stood, motioned toward the door, and simply said, "Let's go get some food and then head back to the airport."

David was relieved, thinking, *that's it? That's what we came here for? Were these men really Mossad?*

Ross appeared to be more American than Israeli. He did not have the slightest accent. At first, David thought that he sounded as though he were born and raised American. These and other thoughts raced through his head as Isaac led him toward the exit. He almost audibly sighed in relief as he began climbing the stairs to walk out of the building. However, David still did not know what that meeting was really about, but he was sure he would find out soon enough.

~

Ruth had died on Friday, and she could not be buried until Sunday according to Jewish law regarding the Sabbath. Many people attended the funeral for Ruth, and the chapel at the Star of David Cemetery in Tamarac, Florida, was full to capacity. Many had to stand at the rear of the sanctuary. Harry and Ruth had many friends, and those who were physically able to attend were there. Nathan, of course, had most of the synagogue membership attending the funeral, as well as other rabbis from all over South Florida. Nathan and Rachael sat in the front left row, facing the casket. The Wassermans sat beside them. The rabbi conducting the funeral was a long time friend of Nathan's.

The services took about twenty minutes, and the eulogies took another twenty. Upon completion, the pallbearers walked the casket up the aisle and out the front doors to the waiting hearse. Nathan and Rachael were motioned to follow and the Wassermans behind them. When they reached the hearse, the casket was slid inside, and the limousines pulled up to take them to the gravesite. It was only a few hundred yards away, next to where Harry was buried. Rachael had been emotionally overcome by the eulogies, and Nathan had his hands full just attempting to comfort her.

It is always the gravesite service that is so much more emotionally draining than the memorial service. It is here that the reality of our short time on this earth has its impact on one's reality about life and death. Eyes cannot help but wander from the rabbi conducting the graveside service to the pile of earth and the rectangular hole alongside of it. No matter how beautiful the casket or the eloquence in which Psalm 23 is spoken, our human frailty stands before the attendees in stark reality that life has but one conclusion about death. Tomorrow is guaranteed to no one.

~

Isaac had said goodbye to David at the gate of El Al Airways flight to Tel Aviv.

The flight was a time for him to rest, reflect, and not react to the confusion he felt.

Isaac was a mystery, and Ross was even more of a mystery. It was bizarre, considering that they had to go all the way into London and a health club to have a twenty-minute meeting. Perhaps he was simply being checked-out by the organization. After all, they *were* making a substantial investment in him. He slept most of the way as his young mind could not cope with any more input.

~

Diane looked at Roger in an intense, questioning way.

"I don't understand. Why didn't you tell me about this note when I spoke with you?"

"Because it states David's request on the front of the envelope; I simply respected his wishes."

Diane looked down at the unopened envelope on her lap. It was boldly and explicitly written, "Roger, please give this to Diane in person and not until tomorrow."

"Would it have made any sense to tell you about it yesterday and have you running over here to get it?"

"I suppose not, but I am still trying to make sense of all of this. David and I had a very special relationship." She lifted her gaze from the envelope to the roadway at the main entrance to CMU. They were seated on a bench outside her dorm and had been talking for only a short while. Diane stared off toward Pitt as if she expected to see David come bicycling up the road at any moment. Several tears rolled down her cheeks and Roger looked away. He sensed her pain but was unable to comfort her because of his guilt over their indiscretion. Diane looked back down at the envelope and slowly opened it. She read the brief note that was inside.

The message was that Diane would always occupy a very special place in David's heart. What was done was done. He forgave her and stated that he had no right to judge what happened. He would simply let the passing of time take care of the healing. He also said that he was sure they would see each other again. It was signed, "Love, your special friend forever, David."

Diane knew that David was right. She would see him again someday, and perhaps circumstances would be different. Perhaps somewhere down the road of life they would find a path to each other. For now, she had college to finish. She also didn't plan on seeing Roger again, but she also did not want to sever their friendship. She thanked him, got up from the bench, and went back to her dorm. Tears of heartbreak flowed freely as she climbed the stairs to the second floor.

Orientation was as exciting as David had anticipated. The initial welcome and introduction presentation was given by one of the professors. About an hour into the orientation, David saw a man standing along the aisle. He was leaning against the wall less than two rows up from him. He did not appear to faculty or staff by his mannerisms—and the way he was dressed. David kept his eyes on the stage and the speaker, but he quickly glanced over and saw that the man was watching him. It was unnerving, but perhaps he was growing slightly paranoid from all of this.

The speaker had been going on for about forty-five minutes and was covering the curriculum and some of the campus rules.

"You will receive a resource book that has been carefully chosen to provide you with a great deal of insight into understanding the complexity of Israel's society in this modern day and age. Study will focus on the 4,000 year-old relationships of the Jewish people to the land of Israel and their return to Israel during the last 150 years. This was as the Zionist movement implemented its national program and the final passing of Israel's statehood."

David understood why they were devoting this initial program to new students. How else could foreigners understand the challenges that face a small country made up of Jews, Christians and Muslims from extraordinary diverse social, cultural, linguistic and economic backgrounds?

"I thank you and look forward to seeing all of you in class. Shalom."

This was the closing portion. The students and the faculty adjourned to the cafeteria for lunch. They would be seated in the same section today so that any questions the new students had, could be addressed.

David bent down to pick up the papers and information packets he placed under his seat. As he sat up, the man who was standing against the wall was now standing at the end of his aisle. He glanced at David and made a motion with his head as though he wanted David to follow him. David had not seen this man before, and he appeared threatening. He stood and slowly walked toward the aisle, purposely allowing another female student to go in front of him. This placed another person between David and the stranger. He had no idea what he wanted, but he was feeling intimidated. David avoided eye contact with this man and walked to the main lobby, where he found himself among a sea of people. He instinctively maneuvered himself between a group of students and professors and managed to be hidden among them as they headed for the cafeteria. Just as they were all about to enter the other doors, David quickly moved aside and scanned the perimeter of the area. The man was waiting for him. His arms were folded, and he was leaning on a wall near the cafeteria. David walked toward him and stopped about a foot from where he was standing.

"Are you following me?" David asked, inching a bit closer with a stern look on his face.

"Yes, David, I am following you. I need to have a talk with you. Look over your shoulder to your right—that huge window. Do you see a line of trees along the entrance to the grounds?"

David turned, looked out the window, and saw the area he was referring to. "Yes, I see them."

"Do you see a van parked next to the fifth tree on that road?"

"The green one?"

"Yes, and in five minutes, I would appreciate you're meeting me at that van. We need to talk."

He abruptly walked out the door and toward the road. David stared after him, not having a clue as to who this man was. This was becoming more bizarre by the day, and David considered losing himself in the crowd. However, he reasoned, the man obviously knew him. He watched as the man got into the van, but not in the front. He slid the side door open, stepped up into the van, and closed the door. David hesitated for a moment and then slowly walked toward the double set of doors that led to that street. He began to walk down the path to the tree-lined road. *Perhaps I am overreacting*, David thought as he approached the van. Suddenly, the same side door slid open and there he was, motioning for David to get in.

What David saw as he stepped into the van was a miniature version of a mobile communications center. The man extended his hand and introduced himself as Col. Ya'akov Cohen of the Israeli Army. He reached into his jacket pocket and produced an identification card. The picture of him on the card was in uniform and appeared authentic. Behind David was another man who had his back to them. The man abruptly turned around, and David was in a state of shock. It was Ross, the man from London.

"I don't understand," David managed to blurt out in a tone of total confusion.

"I couldn't tell you very much when we met in London, David. I work *with* Mossad, but I am deep undercover and a foreign operative with the CIA. My office is located at the United States Embassy.

"Army Intelligence, Mossad, CIA—why are you so interested in me? I'm just a new recruit, and I do not even have to serve until I finish college—do I?"

"David, that's what *they* told you, isn't it?"

"Who are *they*? Aren't Elanie and her brother with you guys?" David looked to Ross for some type of confirmation that would calm the increasing beat of his heart. He knew something was not right.

Ross continued.

"David, Elanie and Yael are *not* members of Mossad. Yael is not even Jewish, although he bears a Hebrew name. Yael is a Palestinian, and his father is Lebanese. He is a terrorist who is working with an organization that used to operate out of Lebanon until a few years ago. They became a bit more sophisticated and infiltrated several universities and branches of those universities. They became recruiters on and off campus. They operate under the guise of being affiliated with Mossad. You were recruited under that plan because Elanie is one of their chief operatives. She is not in any way related to Yael except they went to the same elementary, middle school, and high school together. She was born a Palestinian, lived on the West Bank, and when her parents were killed, the Feldman's, an Israeli, Jewish family, adopted her. She works for the same organization that Yael works for. Reuben Feldman is her adopted brother."

David began to shake. He could not control himself. His left foot kept rapidly shaking up and down while his hands also began trembling. Ya'akov picked up a bottle of water and handed it to David.

"Here, take a drink. I know that this is a big shock to you, David, but you must be calm and understand that even we—Mossad and Army Intelligence—are taking a big chance by bringing you in and allowing you to know what is going on."

"Why are you telling me all of this?" David blurted out. His voice was trembling from the reality of the thoughts now racing through his mind.

"Because you are the first American they have recruited, David, that's why." Ross continued explaining. "You were to be trained over four years and would have become the first American mole they were able to plant in Israel. They knew we would find out, and Elanie would have later seduced you over to their cause. She's a beautiful woman and can be very convincing. They were grooming you to become a double agent. Do you remember the man on the plane who took you to meet me at the health club swimming pool in London?"

"Yes, of course I do."

"David, Isaac Selinsky is my boss. His office is in London, and he heads up the European Counter Terrorism Group. He is an assistant deputy director with the CIA. He is the one who contacted us to apprise us of what was going on. When he flew in from Pittsburgh to return to London, it was sheer luck that you wound up on the same plane. He was actually turning you over to me. I was in London to meet with him on other matters until this became a priority. The United States team, working with Isaac's men, has had Reuben's Israeli restaurant under surveillance for months. However, diplomatic diplomacy dictated that we turn the case over to the FBI in Pittsburgh.

"Let me explain. When you entered that restaurant with Elanie, it was the first time that the CIA had seen Elanie in a long while. Elanie, Reuben and Yael had dropped out of sight after they left Israel. They were recruiting international visitors to Israel—mostly Europeans and some Israeli kids who were out of work. They posed as Mossad operatives and even faked their identification."

"I don't understand," David interjected. "Elanie was at a Pittsburgh hospital. She held a responsible position. She had an office there. I know she did because my father called the hospital and he was transferred to her phone."

"Yes, I know, David, but she also had fake credentials when she applied for that job. She was hired out of the hospital's immediate need for an administrative assistant with strong computer knowledge. She had only been working at the hospital a short time, and the apartment in Pittsburgh was not hers. The couple that owns the apartment was in Europe for the winter. They were Jewish and found the Israeli restaurant two days before they left. Elanie was there, and for the rest of the story you can use your imagination."

"She seemed so comfortable in that apartment," David mumbled out of shock.

"They are very good at what they do. Did you find a lot of travel brochures in the apartment?"

"Yes," David recalled, "I did."

"The couple who own that apartment are travel agents."

David nodded his head, now understanding a bit more.

"Do you know why she took that job at the hospital? Don't answer or stretch your imagination—I'll tell you why. It was a college town. Any of the students who wound up in the hospital or received any kind of medical services from that hospital were processed through her. She had all their insurance information, including their date of birth and Social Security number. With that, she could find out everything she wanted to about that individual and decide if they were recruitment material."

David shook his head and rubbed his palms together.

"I don't get this. What would they want with me, a nineteen year-old American, well, almost nineteen who . . ."

Ross cut David off in mid-sentence.

"Who is at Pitt because his father is a rabbi and wanted his son to go to Yeshiva and hates his life?"

David was now shocked even beyond all that he had heard already.

"How did she—they know all of that?"

"Your father called Elanie, remember? That's when she led your father down a conversational path that revealed to her why you were in Pittsburgh. 'It would never have happened to my son had he gone to Yeshiva' is what I believe your father told her—unwittingly, of course."

"Okay, how do *you* know all of this?" David demanded.

"Simple—the FBI. They have a tap on her phone at the hospital and at the apartment she is occupying. Once she stepped foot into Pittsburgh, she was in America. That placed her under CIA jurisdiction because we were investigating her organization in Israel, Lebanon, Yemen and other countries—including a cell that was operating out of London.

"However, because it was on U.S. soil, we asked the FBI to intervene and takeover the entire surveillance operation there since we were working with the local officials in Israel and our jurisdiction is primarily international. The concern is that there is the possibility of a threat stemming from their mission to Americans as well as Israeli citizens."

"I don't understand—what mission are you talking about?"

Ross told David that he would find out everything—in time. For now he needed to calm himself and understand that he was an innocent recruit who fell for their sting operation. It got him to Israel and paid for his first semester's tuition at Tel Aviv University.

"My *first* semester ... that's it? That's all they paid for?" David felt even worse than he did before.

"Yes," Ya'akov answered. "Any schooling after that would require further commitment, and they would suck you in deeper and deeper until there was no way out for you."

Ross then mentioned that it was growing late and that they could not keep the van in this location much longer. They had several people around the campus, and they were professional terrorists who knew what strange, parked vans were all about. They could get suspicious.

"I want to see your offices or a military base or something that bears out who you are and what you have told me, or I am going right to the police."

Ya'akov looked at Ross and looked back at David.

"And tell them that you have been recruited by a terrorist organization that has been blowing up our people for several years and your tuition at school was paid with money that is symbolically soaked in Israeli blood? Tell them that you want to go back to the United States? You would be assassinated the minute you stepped foot in Pittsburgh or in Florida, and you would also expose your family to that danger. They love bombing synagogues."

David was now pensive and did not really want to talk anymore. He had barely registered all of the information he had already received. His brain was on overload.

"Look," David exclaimed in exasperation, "I came here to get an education and possibly give something of myself to a cause. I did not commit any crime; I did not do anything wrong. I simply believed some people who were not who they represented themselves to be. I want out, and I want out now. I am willing to pay for my own transportation home to the United States and forget all of this."

David now sounded like someone who was pleading rather than demanding. They knew he was scared. Ya'akov looked at Ross and nodded his head. Ross turned around and opened the edge of the curtain that separated the back of the van with the communications equipment and the front seats. David never realized there was another person in the van—the driver.

"Go," Ya'akov ordered, and the van pulled out. It turned around and sped away from campus.

"Where are we going—where are you taking me?" David demanded.

"Relax, David. We are taking you to the American Embassy," Ya'akov assured him.

"Look, I have no right to even be telling you what I've already told you. I did so because of what you have been through–the way you were duped into quitting school and coming to Israel. The people at the American Embassy will sort this all out—besides, you are an American, and that's how this should be handled."

The drive to the embassy did not take long, and the guard at the gate seemed to recognize the van. David assumed this because he did not bother to ask for any identification or hesitate in opening the gate to pass them through. David noticed a sign on the gate,

By International Law, the United States Embassy will be closed on all official U.S. and Israeli holidays. Please make your plans accordingly.

In the event of an emergency, please contact the American Citizen Services Unit through the Embassy switchboard at 03–519–7575.

The van pulled around the back of the embassy and stopped just short of a rear door to the farthest point of the building. The driver came around and opened the side door to the van. Ya'akov motioned for David to get out, which he did. Ya'akov and Ross stepped out after him, in that order, and a United States Marine, who resembled a commando in his fatigues, opened the door to the building and then stood at attention. As they entered the hallway, David saw a red runner carpet protecting highly polished wood floors. They were obviously in the back section of the building. There was a set of double doors just a few feet from where they were standing. Just as David noticed them and the huge, polished brass handles, the door opened. A man in a dark pinstriped suit, burgundy tie and a white shirt came walking toward them with a huge smile.

"Ya'akov, Ross, so glad you could make it. This must be David." The man with white hair and blue eyes that looked like Antarctic ice extended his hand, and David simply shook it.

"David, my name is Bill Shanks." He reached into his suit jacket pocket and extracted a wide billfold. He flipped it open and held it at the height of David's eyes so that he could see his identity card from the CIA.

"David, I am the senior representative of the Central Intelligence Agency here in Israel. I work with Ross, who is the senior man here at the embassy. I also work with the embassy in the area of international diplomacy. In a few seconds we are going to walk through the double doors that I just came out of. Although this is the United States Embassy, there is a single room used for secret meetings with the Israeli Government. That is the room we will be going into. Let me explain what and whom you will see in that room. There is a long table with chairs around it, and the United States flag and the Israeli flag are side by side on the far wall. The flags will be above two men who will be sitting in the end chairs at the very head of that table. David, one is the prime minister of Israel. Alongside of him will be the United States Ambassador. To his right will be the assistant director of Israeli Army Intelligence. After him and going down the left side of the table will be the director of a branch of Israeli intelligence, whose name I cannot share with you as of yet. Next will be a man whom I also cannot talk about, as he is a deep undercover operative in the Mossad—the real

Mossad—and his name will not be used. Are you beginning to see a picture here, David?"

David was feeling better than when he first came into the building. That sense of excitement replacing his initial fear was rapidly building inside of him. He actually began to feel somewhat important and was not curious beyond his years as to why he was being taken into a room with all of these important officials. What was it, and why was he involved?

"Allow me to continue. On the right side of the table, as you are facing the prime minister, from his right to your right—down that side of the table will be men who will not be introduced. One of them is a scientist who works within a research program in the Department of Biomedical Engineering of Technion.

"Yes, I remember. Elanie mentioned a program she was working in when her parents were blown up because of the project she was involved in."

"No, David. That is a lie. Her parents were never killed that way. An Israeli family adopted Elanie when she was five years old. Her parents were blown up, all right, but by their own doing. They housed arms and munitions for the terrorists. The house blew up because she fired on Israeli troops, who returned that fire and hit the munitions within the house. Elanie grew up with the Feldmans and after her education and completion of her post-graduate work, she was involved with the Interdisciplinary Center for Technology Analysis and Forecasting at Tel Aviv.

"There is a connection in all of this, but you will learn of these things as we go. There will be two more men who are both Israeli Intelligence. One is the director of Shin Bet, which is one of the three branches of Israeli Intelligence organizations—a group most Americans are not aware of. The other man is with Army Intelligence, a top-ranking officer who also will not be introduced by his name. He, too, is deep undercover within the framework of this situation. Are there any questions you have before we go inside?" Bill asked as he glanced quickly at his watch and realized they should be going in.

"Yes, sir, just one. May I leave now?" Bill smiled and placed his right hand on David's left shoulder. He guided him toward the two men, who took positions outside of these doors.

"David, relax. It will all turn out fine."

David heard a loud clicking sound from the other side of the doors, and the two doors were opened from inside. At first he thought that the wood must be very thick. He then realized as the doors opened a bit more that the wood was a façade on the outside and the doors were solid steel. They just kept opening until David estimated about six inches of steel by the time the opening appeared. That would mean that the walls themselves were about six inches or more in thickness. Bill motioned for David to step inside, and he did, immediately looking at a sea of important faces. As David approached the chair at the direct opposite end from the prime minister and the ambassador, Bill pulled the chair out and asked David to sit down. He did so quickly, as his knees were beginning to buckle! As he stared at the faces and uniforms before him, David suddenly felt weak, and a lump was in his throat.

"David Blumberg, welcome. I know that this must be somewhat overwhelming for you, to say the least, but I assure you that by the time you leave this meeting, it should all be clear to you. Please feel at ease."

The ambassador was speaking to David, and he could not even blink.

"You, David, for some reason that only God knows, have fallen into a situation that is a matter of national security for Israel. You have somehow managed to walk into a web of terrorist activity that we have been trying to unravel for a very long time. You have actually been instrumental in bringing us closer to finding out certain information that our own intelligence agencies have been unable to confirm. I know that may be hard to believe, so one of our Israeli Army Intelligence officers will explain this all to you and perhaps answer any questions that you may have."

The man that Bill had told him about was staring at a blank legal pad on the table positioned just to the right of him. David turned slightly in his chair to face him.

"David, I can not tell you my name, but I can tell you that your name has been praised in certain circles of the intelligence community." "*My name?*" David blurted out in a tone of complete and honest surprise. "Yes, the name of David Blumberg. Considering all you have been through, you persist in persisting—the endurance to move ahead and serve the State of Israel. Your involvement in all of this could have consequences of the highest proportions. If the terrorists carry out their plan, thousands of Israelis could die. It could change the tide of our struggle with the Palestinians, the terrorists, and the surrounding countries that would love nothing better than to see Israel annihilated. David, we have Hizbollah on our borders to

Lebanon, we have Palestinian dissidents in the Gaza, and terrorist funding, training, and munitions supplies through Syria and Iran. There is the Egyptian Islamic Jihad, Al Qaeda, the Taliban, Hamas . . . am I painting a picture for you as to what we are up against as a small nation?"

"Yes, of course," David nervously answered. He never realized all of this and wondered how many Americans truly realized what was truly going on in the Middle East.

The officer paused and reached for his glass of water. He took another slow, deliberate sip and then continued.

"Elanie and Yael are terrorists, devoted to the PLO. Their convictions are centered on bringing down Israel. They hate America equally, if not more."

He picked up a leather briefcase from beside his chair, unsnapped the lock, and removed a legal size folio. He placed it on the table and placed the briefcase back on the floor beside his chair. He opened the file and looked through several pages. The room was silent. There was not so much as a whisper or a comment from anyone in the room. "David, it seems that there were three people in Pittsburgh—two men and Elanie—weren't there?"

"Yes, Yael and another man, Reuben."

The man speaking to him turned another page and read some notes.

"Did he or Elanie tell you that Yael was her brother?"

"Yes, they did," David answered.

"David, Yael is her boyfriend, not her brother."

"Yes, so I have been told." David replied with a tone of disappointment.

He had never been lied to and manipulated so much in his young life.

"Reuben Feldman is her adoptive brother. He is also the organizer and leader of this terrorist cell within the PLO. One of our greatest concerns is that the organization they are running is nameless. We do not know how many people are involved; where they are located in the Middle East, Europe or the United States; or exactly what they are planning. What we do know is that they have been working on a project that was launched and funded legitimately in the name of Israel's security. It was, at first, a joint project among several research organizations. It was a division of Tel Aviv University in biomedical research. In the past several years, the group infiltrated nearly four major programs. They now have operatives at high levels of research and management."

"The programs you are speaking of, don't they involve biomedical research and technology and not weapons or bombs?" David asked.

"Yes, that is correct, except several of the projects are in the area of biochemical warfare."

David was beginning to see a picture, and Elanie was written all over it.

"Allow me to ask you a few questions and also explain some history to you before we take a brief recess and have some refreshments. It should also help you to understand why you are here. When you spoke with Yael, did he mention anything to you about his life or his past?"

"Yes, I told you, he claimed to be Elanie's brother, not her boyfriend."

"I see, but he never mentioned anything about his father's life?"

"No, he did not."

"David, Yael and Reuben are the masterminds that started this organization. Reuben turned Elanie at a very young age." He paused and took another sip of water.

"We believe that there are two distinct operations, and that you stumbled upon this at a time when they were ready to implement either one or both of them simultaneously."

David appeared thoroughly confused.

"You said there were two objectives but only one was being implemented?"

"Yes, that is correct. One involves a shipment from the United States, and the other involves this gas from the biochemical research days. We have not been able to put them together. We know about the ship, but we are not sure of her cargo. We also know they have access to this biological gas, but are not certain if they actually have any. If they do, we do not know where it is being stored. We do know, that the lab where Elanie worked has five empty canisters that were recently discovered. We are not sure if this particular group has the gas, how they got it out or where it is. Somehow there is a link, but we have not been able to pin it down."

"I see," was all David could say.

He looked toward the other side of the room and saw that the prime minister and the ambassador were no longer there.

David was quite nervous, but attempted to appear as calm as he was able to be. How did *he* fit into such complex operations? He was a kid from Florida and didn't even know there were such things going on in Israel until he met Elanie. He felt like a total fool who had been duped by a pretty face and a sympathetic speech.

~

Elanie shuffled some papers on her desk in an attempt to look busy. She was intensely preoccupied with her thoughts of David. She liked him and sensed that he would make a good operative, but she was concerned about his forthright nature. In a word, he was *too* honest. She had spoken to Reuben about her concerns, but he had assured her that after a few months of processing, David would be fine.

"David is Jewish," Reuben had assured her. "He loves Israel, his life is in disarray, and he is filled with disappointment. He will come around quickly."

Elanie glanced at her watch and saw that it was only ten more minutes until lunch. She had an hour but always took a little more time so she could drive to the restaurant and meet Yael and Reuben. They were to decide if perhaps she might be needed to keep an eye on David in Israel. She was entitled to a two-week vacation from the hospital, and she could take it with only one week's notice.

~

Ya'akov and Ross were still standing behind his chair in front of the double doors. They had not left those positions since David entered the room.

"David, when we have completed this meeting, everything that has been discussed in this room shall stay in this room. Do you understand?"

"Yes sir, I do," he answered.

"As I mentioned, Elanie is not Reuben's biological sister but rather an adopted sister. Reuben grew up with hatred for the Israeli Army because of what happened to Elanie's parents—an unavoidable tragedy, however their home was a munitions arsenal for the PLO. Reuben was also brainwashed into believing that the Israelis were suppressing and killing Palestinians. He was recruited into the PLO at an early age and was totally brainwashed against his own people. He conceived this terrorist plot based upon the biological research Elanie was working on. She is a full-blown terrorist and a very intelligent young woman. She knows a great deal about biomedical research and explosives. David, do you understand everything so far?"

"Yes sir, I do," David responded.

"Good, then let me pause here and ask you these questions. Are you in any fear for your well-being right now?"

David did not answer for a moment. He caught himself before he gave a response from his heart instead of his brain. He noticed that every eye around the table was on him.

"Sir, I am not fearful for my life but rather for my future. I was brought here to go to school, and now it appears that I will *not* get the education I had hoped for."

"That is not so, David. In fact, we want you to continue your education, the four years you were promised. There would be but one thing we would ask of you in return for our footing the bill for three of the four years."

Ah, here comes the catch, David thought.

"And what would that exception be?"

"Before I answer that, do you still have a profound love for Israel?"

"Yes, that hasn't changed."

"Would you like to serve the national security interests of Israel?"

"I don't understand. What would going to school have to do with serving security interests?"

"You are about to be sent to school by the PLO. They are going to train you to become a terrorist in a suit. That is to say, you will not be parachuting from airplanes, shooting guns or planting bombs. They will strive to groom you into becoming a double agent. They are not stupid, David, and must know that *we* know about your involvement with them. They have observed us meeting with you outside of the university—which is exactly what we want them to know. They will encourage you to cooperate, in fact, train you to even come to us and tell us everything that *they* want us to know. For simplicity, David, you will be working for both sides, but you will *only* be on Israel's side. David, you would become the youngest member of our counter-intelligence network."

"Has any other American ever done this before?"

"No, you would be the first."

"So you want me to become a double agent?"

"Something like that, David. We are asking you to do something that will have minimum risk. Mr. Shanks from the United States Embassy will have to approve the plan and sanction your involvement. We cannot simply recruit you because you are not an Israeli citizen. However, you are over the legal age, and we do not require parental consent. It's totally up to you."

David thought for a moment and looked up at Bill Shanks. David realized that he had some bargaining power.

"If I agree to do this, I would like something for taking all of these risks."

"Money?" the man asked in surprise.

"No, but I want to finish my education at Tel Aviv University, all four years, the last three being funded by the Israeli government—as you stated. I also want dual citizenship—American and Israeli. I will agree to serve a regular term in the Israeli Army after graduation."

The man studied him. A slight smile began to curl his lower lip.

"You learn fast, David. I don't believe there will be any problem in granting your request." He looked down the table to one man who had yet to say a word. He nodded in approval, and David watched as he did. *There are some powerful leaders at this table,* David thought.

"David, in a few days you will receive a receipt for your tuition, paid in full for your second through fourth year. I understand that they are also providing you with room and board. Is that correct?"

"Yes, sir, but as you said, for the first year only."

"We'll provide the other three, as well. If you drop out or flunk out, the deal is off. You must maintain a B average at minimum—especially if you want to become an officer when you graduate."

"An officer?" David repeated. He was quite surprised yet inwardly delighted at the thought.

"Yes. With the training you will receive over the next four years from the Palestinians and from us, you will have invaluable experience. We will want you in Army Intelligence."

He reached for his briefcase once again and removed a set of documents, which he thumbed through before handing them to David.

"I would like you to look at these papers as I explain them to you. I want you to thoroughly understand what they contain and all you are committing to."

David glanced down at the papers and asked when he was required to sign them.

"Today," was his answer.

David took the package of papers and began reading through them. As he did, several of the people at the table began leaving. Each one stopped and wished David good luck and God's protection. The man from Army Intelligence remarked that he would see David again very soon. David considered that he must be one of the officers who would be training him.

What they did not have was a mole—someone they could trust on the inside of the PLO. He did not have to do anything that was overtly dangerous or complex. He simply had to feed information on any new development and anything that he could provide in the way of names, descriptions, and those who were purportedly masquerading as Mossad operatives and were supposed to train him. The PLO trusted no one, but perhaps with Yael, Reuben and Elanie as David's comrades, they just might slip one time, and that would be the break they needed. David asked how he was to get this information to them.

Ya'akov was David's contact. He was to arrange for the exchange of information and provide David with some simple tools to get the information out to him. He would receive a miniaturized recorder; a cell phone that recorded conversations automatically, and other instruments that David was assured they would acquaint him with.

The United States Embassy would be his safe house if anything were to go wrong at any time. David was unsure of many things but assumed he would have all his questions answered in due time. What bothered him most was this *project* that was so dangerous to the national security of Israel. These details were still being withheld. He struggled somewhat in whether he should continue to inquire or just let it all become known when they were ready to share it with him. He decided to remain silent and knew that there was no turning back. He desperately wanted his dual citizenship and his four years at Tel Aviv University.

After David signed the documents, the man removed some additional papers from his briefcase. One of them was a declaration of citizenship signed by the prime minister. David only had to fill in one blank—his name. *They knew I would say yes,* he realized. The man who conducted the entire briefing stood. David gathered his copy of the papers, and after shaking hands and the usual wishes of good luck, he left with Ya'akov.

He was actually excited and asked when he was to start as he got into the passenger seat of the van. Ross was not inside, just a driver whom David did not recognize. Ya'akov did not get into the van.

"David, I will not be going with you. I will see you shortly."

The driver pulled away and headed toward the university. In the darkness of night, without anyone even near the vicinity of the tree-lined road, he was dropped off without a word spoken, and he returned to his room. The day's events were racing through his mind. He could only think of Elanie's deception and wondered how he could have been so easily fooled. He realized that they had known his emotional condition and took advantage of his need for friendship. Within moments of that thought, David was asleep, the events of the day, now filtered from his consciousness.

Chapter Fifteen

Nothing is what it Seems

The man who conducted David's briefings at the embassy sat at the kitchen table in his superior officer's Tel Aviv apartment. He was gathering background information on the Blumberg boy from Florida. Could David be trusted? What were his parents like, his background, childhood, school records and the tragedies that occurred in his young life?

If anyone could provide the inside information on David, surely this man could because he knew the family.

Army Intelligence had recruited Victor after his first year as a young officer. He had demonstrated a unique ability of fading into the shadows of any situation and was never under suspicion by the Palestinians.

Victor had met Harry at the Wailing Wall in Jerusalem when Harry was in Israel. The friendship grew, but Harry never knew of Victor's secret life. He was led to believe that Victor was a communications specialist with the IDF, the Israeli Defense Forces, and he never questioned Victor in all the years they remained friends. Harry would come to Israel at least once a year, and he and Victor always managed to spend time together during those trips.

Victor met David for the first time when he flew to the United States to attend Harry's funeral. Harry had tragically died during David's Bar Mitzvah. He had remarked that David had "a little Harry in his eyes, but mostly resembled Nathan." It was also the first time that Victor had met Rachael.

"Nathan had your picture plastered to his forehead," Victor had chided Rachael, but nothing eased the pain of their mourning for a man they all deeply loved. Victor returned to Israel and had not heard from Nathan since. At the time of the funeral, it had been nearly fourteen years since Nathan had stayed with him in Tel Aviv after graduating from Yeshiva. Victor had made a lasting impression on Nathan while he was there. Nathan had also marveled at the authority in which he rattled off the truths of what was really going on in Israel.

Victor was now getting old and was actually thinking of retiring, perhaps within the next few months. Not once in all the years since they had known him had Harry or Nathan questioned Victor's involvement in government affairs. Now there were questions about Harry's own grandson and Nathan's *only* son. There was a moment when Victor thought about demeaning David's character in order to allow for David to be taken out of the loop and permitted to simply return to Florida. He felt that he owed that to Harry. He thought about not allowing his grandson to get involved in this sticky business of information gathering, but it was too late. David had learned too much, and he knew a great deal about Elanie and her team who were recruiting in Pittsburgh. There was no turning back.

Victor wished he had known all of this in advance, but it had occurred almost overnight when David was seen entering the restaurant and meeting with the group. Before that night, no one in Israel except for Victor knew the name David Blumberg.

Victor got up and walked over to the small gas stove. He picked up the kettle filled with water that had just begun to boil and made himself a cup of tea.

"I want you to listen to me very carefully, my trusted friend." Victor leaned forward in his chair and pushed the teacup aside. "This boy is like family to me. I do not want anything to happen to him. Allow him to provide Uri, Roscoff, Zeitler, Yedidya, and Ross all the information he is able to and then let him go—debrief and release."

The men Victor named were all high-ranking officials that were the nameless men in the embassy briefing room. Admiral Yuri was navy; General Yedidya was second in command in the air force's line of top brass; Zeitler was Military Intelligence; Roscoff was Mossad; and Ross was CIA.

"Will you do this for me?"

"Victor, please. We have known each other a long time, and my loyalty is unquestionable. How can I make you a guarantee when I do not know if I will even be here tomorrow? We are living in very precarious times, my friend."

"Tell me . . . what was David's demeanor during the briefing?"

"He seemed nervous—not that I blame him. Walking into a room with the American ambassador, the prime minister, and all of those faces in front of him was a bit much for even an experienced man."

"How was it that the prime minister was there?" Victor questioned.

"There was a joint operational meeting prior to David arriving. We did not expect him that early. When we learned they were on their way, it was suggested that the prime minister remain for a few minutes for the initial impact. Then he would simply exit through the hidden door behind the drapery when David was engrossed in the briefing. It was purely for show, although the prime minister has a keen interest in this whole matter and wanted to meet David."

"How dangerous do you really believe Elanie and her clan are?"

"I don't know, Victor. There is much we don't know about, and I am not sure."

"What do you mean 'not sure'?" Victor asked.

"There is something beyond this research, something that I can't put my finger on. You see, I have this gut feeling that the research could be a cover for something a lot more important. If you recall, the formula for the new type of gas that our scientists discovered did not go fully airborne like other gasses. The detonation of a small canister of the gas maintained a burst ratio of about three hundred square feet. It spiraled quickly to about ten feet from the ground, but it did not thin out as other gasses did. They were able to release a single burst and the gas would simply form this cloud, dissipating only by the number of inhales per square foot—all of whom would be brain dead within seconds.

When they discovered this, they placed every top-secret security wrap on it. The prototype was almost complete when it was discovered that the research notes had been copied. A special filament woven into the papers disintegrated when exposed to a copy machine, leaving small particles in the paper that one could see when exposed to a special light, similar to ultraviolet. The notes were actually inspected by a security office every morning.

"We know that Elanie has a background in biomedical research and her brother had connections with many laboratories and research facilities. He has deep cover operatives planted at various management and security clearance levels and we must find out who they are.

"Once it was discovered that copies of the research papers were made, the project was halted until we found out how much they really knew. We also wanted to see if there was a lab they started or took over to continue developing this gas or any other biochemical agents. If they had perfected it and were going to use it, we guess that they would release it near the Gaza so that several hundred Palestinians were killed. That would provide just enough bodies for the world to believe that we were the murderers and they were the oppressed. Here is the big problem. About two months after Elanie left and disappeared from sight, a test of the canisters at the lab revealed five empty fakes. To this day, we don't know who has the missing canisters or where they are."

Victor stared at his friend for a moment with a curious expression. He sipped some more tea and then shook his head.

"I don't want this boy placed in any dangerous position. I want him covered at all times, and at the slightest suspicion of anything going wrong, pull him out and send him home."

"I understand," his friend answered.

Victor took another sip of the tea and made a face as if the tea was no longer drinkable. He stood as he took the cup and saucer and placed them in the kitchen sink. He turned and said goodbye to his friend.

Nathan sat at his desk in the synagogue and stared at the picture of David and Rachael. It was an 8 x 10 that was enlarged from a snapshot taken when David was about ten years of age. Nathan loved that particular picture because he could really see the similarities in the eyes and in the smile of his wife and son.

He felt as though his world was falling apart, piece-by-piece, and yet he maintained that it was all in God's hands. He thought about calling David, but he knew that he would surely call home before the weekend— and that was just a day away. Nathan did not want to be a meddling father, but this was his only son. He had a feeling of helplessness lately, and he shared those feelings with Rachael. She felt the same way, as though there were things David wasn't telling them. There had to be more to this than his serving in the Israeli Army after graduation. Nathan had made several inquiries and there was no such program at Tel Aviv University. However, he verified that David was registered as a student. They would not give out any further information over the telephone. He glanced at the small desk calendar from El Al Airlines and briefly entertained making the trip. *Why not,* he thought. *Rachael and I went to Pitt to spend a few days with David, and he welcomed it.* Picking up the phone, he called home. Rachael answered on the third ring.

"Hi, are you coming home early?" she asked.

"Most likely, but that is not why I called you. How would you like to spend a week in Israel?"

There was a moment of silence, and he knew that Rachael was giving the idea serious thought.

"Why do you want to go? The holidays are only a couple of weeks away. Isn't David coming home?"

"Rachael, I talked to David at the same time you did. Did he say anything about coming home?"

"No, he didn't," she replied. She was saddened at the realization that she did not even consider David not coming home.

"I am going to try and call him before I leave."

"That's not fair, Nathan. I won't be able to talk to him."

"I will find out where he will be later, and we'll call him again. Right now I need to know if he is coming home or should we just book a flight. Either way, I have some strange premonition that we need to see him and sort this all out."

Elanie waited by the phone for Yael to call her and give her instructions. There was an urgent alert that came in on the short wave radio from Tel Aviv, and she had relayed the information to Yael earlier. There had been a special meeting at the United States Embassy. The prime minister had attended along with several top army officers, a high-ranking leader in Mossad, IDF brass, and several henchmen that were Israeli Special Ops men.

Something was going on, but their mole had no way of knowing what the meeting was about. It was being kept secret, and no one outside of the people who had attended knew who or what was involved. Yael was very concerned and told Elanie that they might have to leave. The phone rang, and she picked it up hurriedly on the first ring. All she heard were the words, "code one-one," and nothing more. It was Reuben's voice, and now she knew her fears were valid. Elanie put the phone down on the table, purposely leaving it off the receiver. She grabbed her car keys and took her warm jacket from the closet.

Code one-one was a simple way for Reuben or Yael to let her know that their operation had been discovered. They had to leave the United States. All was pre-planned, including their egress from Pittsburgh and passage back to the Middle East. She quickly put on a warm jacket, reached into a special hiding place within the closet and removed a considerable sum of cash. She looked around the apartment one last time, and then left the building. She went out to the parking lot, got into her car and immediately began to shiver. The sun was going down and the temperatures were dropping to below freezing. Then she realized she forgot her gloves and was not about to weather the night without them. She thought that it would also be a good idea to wear a sweater under her jacket. She opened the car door, got out, and headed back for the entrance when she saw the black SUV. The headlights went off the moment she got out of her car. She knew the car had been parked, as it did not pull into that particular space when she first came outside. *Government cars are usually black SUVs*, she thought to herself. She quickened her pace slightly as she walked into the building. She went upstairs and as she turned the hallway, she heard a door slam. She stopped and stood very still, listening for any other sounds.

Just then her cell phone rang, and she felt like her heart would stop. She grabbed the phone from her jacket pocket and pressed the button that stopped incoming calls, diverting them directly to voice mail. She held the button down in the event the caller redialed, and then she just waited. Seconds seemed like minutes. There were no more sounds. She got her key ready and quickly went down the hall and entered the apartment. She shut the door and went to the closet in the alcove and removed a bulky sweater and her gloves. As she closed the door, a gloved hand covered her mouth, just as the cold steel of a gun barrel was pressed against her neck.

~

Reuben entered the restaurant through the back door. He had parked his motorcycle almost two blocks away and was reasonably sure that he was not followed. He did not turn on the lights but rather used a small pocket flashlight. He made sure that the beam of light was pointed down and not toward the windows at the front. He made his way to the restroom and began searching for anything that resembled a bugging device. If they wired the restaurant, they would have planted devices anywhere—and that included the restrooms. It was his first place to search, as it was away from any outside view. He checked under the paper towel dispenser, running his hand underneath and then crouched down to examine the underside of the vanity counter. That's when he saw the tiny device about the size of a dime. He checked the same place in the ladies' restroom and found another. If they had bothered to bug the restrooms, he had no doubt that there were listening and video devices all over the restaurant—including under every table.

How long have they been listening? he thought. Reuben decided not to look any further and take the chance of being spotted. Two listening devices were enough to confirm his suspicions. He crouched down and inched his way toward the counter at the back of the restaurant. If he stayed low enough, he would not be seen. If he were quiet enough, they would likely not pick up his presence with the listening devices. He came to the under-counter dishwasher and very slowly opened the door. He used the screwdriver from his knife to remove the screws from around the panel. Reaching into the exposed inner door, he removed the duct tape from the edges of a plastic bag and removed the bag from the machine. The plastic pouch contained three Israeli passports and three-forged driver's licenses, one for each of them. He placed the package in the upper pocket of his ski jacket and zippered it closed.

Looking at his watch, Reuben realized that Elanie would be arriving at their predetermined meeting place at any minute. He opened a cabinet next to the dishwasher and removed a small package that was wrapped in cleaning rags. Then he carefully removed the inner package that had a single exposed wire sticking out from the side. Pulling one of the wires from the panel of the dishwasher, he twisted the one from the package around it and used duct tape to secure it to the inside of the door. He then closed the door and switched on the locking mechanism while pushing the "dry cycle" button. He stood up and walked to the back door, took a last look around and left the restaurant. Approximately five minutes later, the Pittsburgh fire department responded to the explosion and dispatched two separate stations due to the enormity of the blast.

The arson investigation team would later learn that C-4 explosives with a heat-triggered detonator left nothing of the small restaurant except charred ruins. The FBI and CIA lost three video devices, twenty-three bugging devices, and several high tech transmitters that were on the roof of the building. In both cases, between the fire department and the equipment, it was all taxpayer money. Reuben thought of this fact with pleasure as he sped toward the downtown area and Frick Park.

Reuben had an apartment at the Walnut Towers that was rented and paid for under an American name. There were very little furnishings, no pictures on the wall, and no decorative items. This was their safe house. Reuben alerted Yael within a minute after he called Elanie. Reuben actually stayed at hotels, motels and extended stay properties, alternating his stays and his name in each facility. He never went to the Walnut Towers, assuring that it was indeed a safe place to meet in an emergency.

He was upset that they didn't have more time. They needed one more recruit and were close to getting one when all of this occurred. As his motorcycle turned the corner of the Walnut Towers, he drove a block farther and parked the motorcycle behind another building. They were to meet thirty minutes apart. Yael would be the first, then Reuben and then Elanie. She would be the last to arrive in the event there was trouble.

The building was nestled in a park-like setting and had a courtyard where they were to meet. Reuben looked at his watch as he briskly stepped up his pace, realizing that he was seven minutes late. The wind had picked up, and he felt as though his nose was frostbitten. Upon entering the courtyard area, he saw Yael, who began walking toward him with a look of deep concern on his face.

"Elanie should be here any moment. I am the one who is late. I stopped to get our passports."

"I also called Elanie on her cell phone. The call was cut off and sent to voicemail. Something is wrong."

They knew they had all been discovered. For the very first time in years, they were deeply concerned for Elanie. They would have to proceed and hope that she was okay. They would wait another five minutes and no more. That was the arrangement. She would have to get to the extraction location on her own. They knew she would have no trouble doing so if the FBI had not gotten to her.

~

Elanie had been one of the most promising students during her Krau Maga courses at the university. The I.D.F. taught these classes to security company employees, security operatives in business sectors and certain government employees. It was a method of self-defense that was learned quickly and was very effective in hand-to-hand combat. Elanie had put down men twice her size on the mats during the classes and was uncannily precise for a thin but vital woman.

There was no question that a gun held to one's head is a time for preciseness. She stood perfectly still and was breathing shallow breaths as the man behind her ordered her not to cry out. He said he did not want to use force but would if he had to. He removed his hand and ordered her to go down the steps to the living room. He made one mistake—he lowered his weapon from neck height to waist height and was behind her when they stepped down the first step. Elanie felt the steel of the barrel move from her neck to her waist.

Before he could even react, Elanie twisted her body and fell to the side, grasping the handrail for balance. She kicked out at his shins and his legs buckled. He fell forward and went head first down the stairs. It had happened so fast that he never saw it coming. The gun fell from his hand as his head struck the marble floor. He was stunned but not unconscious. By the time he felt his head to see if he was bleeding, Elanie was at his side with the gun pointed at *his* head. A searing pain shot through his brain as he blinked his eyes and sat up, trying to focus.

"Do not get up," Elanie demanded.

Agent Fowler looked at her. He drew his knees up to him and clasped his hands around his legs so there was no mistake that he was not making any sudden moves.

"That was pretty good. Did you learn that in Israel?"

"Yes," Elanie answered. "What do you want with me?"

"There really is no sense in hiding facts. You and your friends are nailed. We've had that café wired for some time, and as far as I am concerned, you are knee deep in enough federal charges to extradite you to an Israeli prison for a very long time."

Elanie showed no emotional reaction.

"How could you possibly say I have committed federal crimes? If you had the restaurant under surveillance and wired, you heard my conversations. I never once spoke of sedition or treason."

"You're not an Israeli patriot but rather a terrorist sympathizer, Elanie. Who do you think you're fooling? You're recruiting college kids like David to do your dirty work. You lied to that kid. You made him believe he was doing it for Israel. Doing what, planting bombs in Tel Aviv?"

"You have no proof of that, and I have broken no laws in the United States. How is it that the Feds, which I am assuming you are, can come into my apartment and hold a gun to my head?"

"I have a Federal Grand Jury indictment and arrest warrant."

"But you held a gun to my head—without provocation."

"I didn't know if you were armed and for both our sakes, was not about to guess."

"Let me see your identification, and do it slowly, Elanie demanded."

Fowler reached into his jacket and extracted a billfold, holding it out for her to take.

"No," Elanie demanded. "Toss it to me on the floor. Then I want you to push yourself backward about two feet."

Fowler complied, and Elanie picked up the billfold without taking her eyes off of him for a moment. She flipped it open. He was FBI.

"So, Agent Fowler, if I am such an important criminal, then I must shoot you and make my getaway at this time—don't you agree?"

"That's not funny. That would be a murder charge added to the other charges."

"Tell me . . . in all your recordings, did I ever mention even once doing anything that would cause harm to human life or to property?"

"I don't know. I was just sent to pick you up."

"Pick me up? They sent only one of you, without backup? Now I'm really insulted, but very happy you came alone. Are you saying you did not sit in on any of the surveillance?"

"I was listening to some of the conversations but not to all of them. I am also not the agent in charge. They are likely in the process of arresting your brother and boyfriend."

As he made that last statement, Elanie used the handle of the 9MM on the side of his head, and Agent Fowler was knocked unconscious. She was well trained in how to apply just the right amount of force and where to apply it in order not to severely injure a victim. He lay sprawled across the floor with his arms flung out at his sides. She walked into the living room and pulled an electrical cord from the lamp on the end table and bound his hands tightly. She then walked to the draperies covering the living room window, pulled one of the drape sashes, and used it to bind his ankles. She removed his handkerchief that was neatly folded in his breast pocket and gagged him. Just so he wouldn't easily forget her, Elanie went into the bedroom and took one of the pillows off the bed. She returned to the hallway area and placed the pillow under his head.

"You will have quite a headache when you wake up, Agent Fowler, so you will appreciate the pillow until help arrives."

Elanie pushed the release mechanism on the gun and slid the magazine out. One by one, she emptied the bullets from the clip. She put the clip and the bullets in her jacket pocket and then laid the gun down by Fowler's hands. She did not want to get caught with a weapon belonging to a federal officer. She took one last glance around, switched off the lights, and left the apartment. She knew she was very late in meeting Reuben and Yael. She also knew that they would not call her by cell phone, suspecting all their communications were being monitored and GPX could nail their locations.

Yael was right, she thought as she started the car and swerved from the parking lot. She began to skid on some ice and nearly hit another car. *I have to be calm. I must get back to Israel. They will never find me there. I must get to Yael and Reuben.* She also surmised that they had already left and were making their way to New York. She pushed down on the accelerator and when the car nearly skidded out of control on the wet, icy streets, she slowed down and tried to regain her composure. *How far behind her are the police? What do they know? What if they already knew about the safe house?* She could not fathom losing Reuben and Yael. They were her life.

New York was the meeting place if anything went wrong. Each of them knew that they could be separated at any time. If they had to get out of Pittsburgh quickly, Pier #11 at the New York City shipping docks was where they would meet and board their transportation out of the United States. It is where the Lebanese freighters docked, and they could get aboard a ship bound for the Middle East and disappear—if there was a ship sailing that day. If there wasn't a ship sailing, they had the name and address of a fleabag hotel on the lower west side of Manhattan. A Lebanese family owned it, and they would provide shelter and food for them until they were able to obtain safe passage.

~

David hesitated for a moment in his conversation when Nathan asked him about coming to Israel for the holidays.

"There is no one left in our immediate family but you, David. Mom and I really miss you, and we want to see you."

David knew that a visit would lead to questioning about his activities, however David knew he could handle their questions. He loved them and missed them, so perhaps their presence would serve to fortify his courage and spiritual strength. They agreed on tentative plans based on Nathan being able to make reservations and obtaining airline tickets that were reasonably priced. It was the holiday season, and blackout travel usually ruled out any hope of discounts. That's what David was counting on to keep them in Florida and keep them out of harm's way. Nathan said that he would let David know as soon as he was able to make arrangements. He knew that regardless of the price, he and Rachael were going to Israel to see their son. He solved the problem of Rachael not being able to talk to David by making it a three-way call. Rachael spoke with David briefly, and he was grateful for every word she said.

Right after they hung up, the phone rang again. He picked it up, expecting it to be his father calling him back. The voice was stern in demeanor.

"Come downstairs and walk to the road with the line of shade trees." There was a click, and the line went dead.

Now what, he thought. David got up and put on his wool sweater and his winter jacket. He simply reasoned that it was the "van-thing" again. He picked up his gloves from the bed and went down the stairs. He opened the door and saw the security camera above. It was pointed directly down at him. A red light went on the moment he opened the door, and he knew that his picture was just recorded. He would have to remember a reason for leaving his room at that hour in the event he was questioned.

The air was frigid. David tightened the drawstring at the bottom of his ski jacket and pulled the zipper up as far as it would go. As he crossed the road and headed for the trees, he realized that there were no streetlights and it was very dark. What if this was a trap of some kind? Should he be more discerning in accepting these challenges? Then he saw the van. It was parked in the very same spot it had been before, but something was different. The color, the make—he didn't know, but it did not look like the same van. David hesitated for a moment, but not before he sensed someone behind him. He turned to see two men whom he did not know. They were very tall and overly muscular, appearing to be the type that you don't argue with.

"Hi, guys, what's up?" David calmly quipped.

Looking at one another, they motioned for David to turn around. He did, and there was another man facing him that had not been there when he turned around the first time. *This is getting creepy,* he thought.

"David, please come into our van and allow us to speak with you. I assure you that we will be done with our conversation in less than five minutes."

Who are these guys? They have no weapons that he could see and they didn't threaten him. He had better say nothing until they identify themselves.

The man who spoke to him had an accent that was not Israeli. It sounded more Palestinian or Lebanese, but David wasn't sure. He found it difficult to tell the difference between Middle Eastern accents. The man in front of him opened the van door. David saw bench seats inside but no electronic equipment. The man motioned for David to get in, and he did, sliding all the way over in the seat. The man got in and slid beside him. The other two went to the front and got in the passenger and driver's side.

"David, are you at all familiar with this type of meeting?"

David's mind was racing. What should he do now: tell the truth, or try to find out more information as to who these guys were?

"Yes, it's familiar. I was in a van similar to this. I was asked to meet with some guys whom I never saw before. At first I thought Elanie sent them, but then something told me otherwise. I don't even know whom they represented. They did not give me their names, but I thought that they were Israeli. It seemed as though they were fishing around to see if I knew anything." David was beginning to think on his feet, weaving a story that sounded plausible while portraying a facial expression of innocence. The man stared at him for several moments.

"David, we know that you met with these people, and I appreciate your honesty. The Israeli government will often pick up a new operative to see how he reacts under pressure, as we are doing to you right now. We all work together, you know, but we do not reveal that to untrained and unproven operatives. David, *you* are untrained and unproven—but I like your style."

David thanked him and asked why they were testing him. He was not supposed to begin indoctrination until the second semester.

"Let's just call this a friendly surprise visit."

"Sure," David willingly agreed.

"The reason we are here this late is because we just received word that Elanie, Reuben and Yael are en route to the Middle East on a cargo ship. They were able to get passage at the last minute out of New York. Now tell me more about your meeting with the other group."

"They questioned me as to what I was doing in the café in Pittsburgh. I told them I was having dinner! They also wanted to know if I knew Elanie, Yael or Reuben before that night. I told them I met Elanie at the hospital and she agreed to a date. I picked her up and told her that I love Israeli food and could not find an Israeli restaurant. She recommended this café, and we went. I met Reuben and Yael that night while we were there. I went back to her apartment after that, and she invited me to sleep over."

The man who had yet to introduce himself (David was tiring of nameless faces) pondered David's words but could not find fault with his story because it was *almost* accurate.

"Good, then you are in the perfect position to help us even more. Are you saying that the other group did not reveal what branch of the government they were with?"

"No, they did not, and I didn't care. They flashed some identification when they asked me to get into their van, and I thought it looked legitimate. But I can't read Hebrew very well, and I was not about to argue with them. Did I argue with you about getting in *your* van?"

"A good point, and well taken," the man responded. "It's not important to know who I am, David. If you don't know my name, you can't give me up under duress anytime in the future. Elanie and Yael vouched for you. Were they correct in their assumptions of your character, or are you a spy?"

"I am not a spy," David insisted.

"Then we will extend that trust to you—the trust that your story about being innocently contacted by the Israeli authorities; and you were simply being questioned because of your taped conversations with Elanie, Yael and Reuben. Is that a correct assumption, David?"

"Yes, it is a correct assumption, as I told you. However, please correct me if I am mistaken, but are we not all on the same side? I thought we were all working for Mossad? Why does it sound as if Israel is your enemy, instead of us all being on the same team?"

"We *are* on the same side, David, but highly splintered in our divisions and assignments. There is also the possibility that terrorists disguised as Israeli operatives could convince you they were Mossad or some other agency within the Israeli government. If they convinced you of that, you might believe them and be turned against your own people. One must be very careful, but in due time you will gain that knowledge."

"For now, let's discuss the reason of our visit. We've just heard from New York a short time ago. David, I know you haven't been formerly trained and you just arrived here in Israel, but this is an urgent matter. The ship that Elanie, Yael and Reuben are on is carrying a cargo of medicines, clothes, wheat, rice and other products for women and children who lost their husbands in the Lebanon skirmishes and the ongoing Israeli-Palestinian clashes. I know we work for Israel, but even the Mossad has a heart for widows and orphans. They were simply caught up in the crossfire of all this hatred. There are several thousand orphans who are in need of food and medical care, especially at the smaller hospitals. You might call this a humanitarian operation, and it also creates some good will among the civilians. Maybe they will be more reluctant to harbor terrorists if we take care of their needs. There is a small group of us who plays a major role in the distribution of this aide from time to time. We are not sure of the date and time that the ship will dock.

"You see, David, there are terrorists who want these supplies badly, and we must not allow this aide to fall into the wrong hands. It's kind of ironic that we are protecting life-saving aide for innocent Palestinians while trying to protect the cargo being hijacked by radical Palestinians. People would die from starvation and the lack of medical supplies. That is why this freighter must be protected and why we want you to notify the various groups who will be helping us with the distribution. Do you understand this?"

"Yes, of course I do," David answered.

"So, you are saying that you want me to notify leaders of the various distribution organizations of the ships whereabouts at the appropriate time?"

"Yes, that's right. These are brave men who would give up their lives for Israel, but they also cannot stand by and see the suffering of innocents—Palestinian or not. The ship may even attempt to dock here in Tel Aviv unless something goes wrong, or we are alerted that some other outreach organization has already made provisions for these people. Then we'll distribute the supplies where there is additional need."

"I see," David acknowledged. "I would have no problem informing the appropriate people."

David was telling the truth. He had no reservations about a freighter filled with relief aide for victims of terrorism, but why would Elanie and her group do such a thing if they themselves were plotting something against Israel? Who was telling the truth? How can one recognize lies from truth under such complex circumstances? He would have to follow his heart.

David received his instructions and was handed a piece of paper that contained different ports and specific names at each of them. When he received the word from this man, he was to call the appropriate person or persons on the list with the exception of the last name. The name was unfamiliar to David, but he was to drive there and advise this specific authority in person at a designated location in Tel Aviv. David was curious over that last instruction and was told again that the ship's relief cargo could be hijacked to feed and clothe terrorists. If they designated a specific port and there were plans to hijack the cargo, they could not defend themselves with only twelve crewmembers on board. The in-person notification was a safeguard so that the person with the appropriate authority could order the port of entry changed if they suspected any problems. Once David acknowledged his instructions, the door to the van swung open. The two men, without so much as an expression or a word, motioned for him to begin walking back to his quarters. They also thanked him and wished him well.

David shivered as he left the street and pulled his jacket higher around his neck. It was freezing cold. The temperature must have dropped ten degrees from the time he had gotten into the van. He walked to the door of his dorm and punched in the key code on the electronic lock. The door clicked open. As he walked in, the door closed automatically. David looked down this time, as though he was hiding his face from the overhead security camera. He glanced back at the camera to see that the red light clicked off after he passed a certain point—about two feet from the door. He had to figure out another way to go out or bypass the camera.

David pulled the small key chain from his pocket, inserted the key in the lock, and opened the door to his room. He closed the door and leaned against it with his back to make sure it was securely shut. He turned the deadbolt and secured the door chain to the slide. David was in a cautious state of mind, evidenced by his pulling the curtains closed on the single window in his room. He removed his coat and sweater and hung them side-by-side on the coat hooks near the door.

The room was literally one-half the size of his dorm room at Pitt, but he well understood. He was not living in the paying-students dorms, but rather in an employee building that several of the freebies lived in, he being one of them. He smiled in self-embarrassment when he thought about how he used to make fun of those living quarters at Pitt. By comparison, they were luxurious!

He reached into his pocket, took out the paper he was given, and sat down on his bed. He stared at the paper for a few minutes and the names that were written there. Not one of them sounded Israeli, but there were ways to find out. He slipped out of his jeans and into a pair of sweatpants and a hooded sweatshirt that he always slept in since leaving home. He switched on the pole lamp and switched off the overhead fixture. He stretched out on the single bed, held the paper in front of him with both hands, and began to look over the names.

The more he attempted to pronounce the ones he was supposed to call, the more he believed that these were Palestinian names and not Israelis.

Unknown to David, the man whose name was last on the list was a high-ranking PLO official who, if David informed him that the mission was a go, would call the captain of the freighter personally. He would order the ship to put into a designated port. There, Palestinian terrorists under the guise of being regular dockworkers would unload the precious cargo. *This must be Hizbollah,* he reasoned, the organization that purportedly was backed by the Iranians and was responsible for supplying weapons to the Palestinians.

David fell asleep, his mind yet wrestling with the decision to go to the Israeli authorities or let it simply go as an innocent supply of aide.

~

Diane completed her final class for the day at CMU and walked back to her dorm with some friends. Despite the never-ceasing conversations they had as they walked along the campus, her thoughts would often wander off to Israel and David. She prayed for him several times a day and even asked several of her Christian friends to keep the name of "David" in their prayers.

"Pray for his enlightenment and safety," she asked, and her friends acknowledged that they would. She sensed that David was not himself, as the grief of Ruth's death was more than he could handle. His grandparents were a major supportive part of his life.

As the group of four girls approached the dorm, Diane decided to walk over to the library and return several books. Her best friend Susan asked the other girls to take her books upstairs and offered to walk with her. As they headed for the library, they talked about Christmas, seeing their families, and various celebrations. Deep in conversation, they rounded the building and never saw the two men waiting in the shadows of the bushes. They jumped out before the girls knew there was anyone there. Each of the men grabbed one girl and covered her nose and mouth with a rag soaked in chloroform.

Diane struggled for a moment but was quickly overcome.

Susan struggled desperately. Being on the girls' sports teams, she was athletic and would not stop fighting. A few minutes later, she fell limply to the ground. The men's leather gloves held the rags in place until they had dragged the girls behind the building toward the service road where a van was waiting.

Dropping Susan's limp body into the bushes, the taller man helped the other to carry Diane. She was the primary target, and Susan had simply chosen to go with Diane at the wrong time. It was just before dinner, and everyone was showering and changing, preparing for an evening of college social life. No one was around, and no one saw a thing.

The van was parked within fifty feet of the abduction, and as they approached, the door slid open. Two other men were waiting for them. They put Diane inside the van and tied her hands and feet. They gagged her with the same rag but also bound the rag into place with a piece of duct tape. The van was a cargo van with an old mattress on the floor. The two who abducted her stayed in the back while the other two got into the front seats. The driver started the engine, and they sped away.

Even if someone had seen what had happened, the four men wore ski masks, and there was no license plate on the van. They stopped about three miles up the road and replaced the license plate that was removed for the very purpose of not being identified.

The driver was careful to maintain the posted speed limit and drove toward the outskirts of town until he came to a warehouse in the middle of an old, industrial complex that had long been shut down. He pulled into the parking lot and around the back of the building. The other man got out and opened the overhead door. In less than one minute the van disappeared from sight—and so did Diane Kelly.

Chapter Sixteen

Double Jeopardy

Nathan allowed the phone to ring about seven times and then hung up. He had previously told David he would call at this time, and David said he would be at the phone. There were no phones in the individual student rooms, but there was a pay phone in the hallway. When David gave Nathan the phone number, they had pre-arranged a time that David would be there for the call.

This time David did not answer. Rachael waited, and when Nathan hung up, she was visibly upset. It was the third call that Nathan attempted that day. It was about 9:00 p.m. in Tel Aviv, and Nathan assumed that David would be in his room at this hour.

"Where do you suppose he could be this late?" Rachael asked. Nathan shook his head as a father who simply no longer understood the actions of his son.

Nathan instinctively sensed something was wrong. David had not sounded like himself during their last conversation when he suggested their taking a trip to Israel. He was able to buy two tickets at a hefty discount from a last-minute special that British Airways was running just before the holiday blackout went into effect. He sensed that David did not want them there. That could only mean he was in trouble or involved in something he did not want them to know about—such as how he had received a scholarship and how his tuition had been paid in advance for four years. He had not shared these thoughts with Rachael, and it was the first time he ever held something back from her.

Just then, Rachael came out of the kitchen in her bathrobe—the terry robe that Nathan had bought for her birthday last year. It was all white with a white satin sash. She also had on white satin pajamas and looked like an angel. Nathan smiled, walked over to her, and kissed her on the forehead. "You are the most beautiful woman in the world," he whispered as she smiled and kissed him on the lips.

"And you are the most charming man in the world."

Just then the phone rang—it was David. The operator announced the fee, and Nathan heard the dropping of many quarters at David's end.

"David, why did you pay for the call? I was going to call you back in another twenty minutes or so."

"It's okay, Dad. I wanted to speak with you now because I want to go out. I am meeting a friend, and we are going into town for a bite to eat."

"You're going out to eat at this hour?" Nathan questioned.

"Hunger has no time limitations, Dad. I do not have a class in the morning, so I can sleep in if I want to. Besides, in Tel Aviv, life begins after midnight!"

"David, we have tickets, and we leave in the morning. We will be there in two days. I have an overnight in London and then on to Tel Aviv the next morning. Where should I stay, and what is close to you?"

"Tell me your flight number and I'll pick you up. I will rent a car and make arrangements in the morning at a nearby hotel. I need to check on the rates, but I will take care of it for you."

"Great, thank you. And here, your mother wants to hear your voice."

Nathan handed the phone to Rachael, who was standing over the phone like a mother hen stands over her chicks.

"David, are you okay?"

"Yes, hearing your voice makes everything okay."

Rachael could not see the tears beginning to brim in David's eyes. *God, how I miss her,* was all he could think. He took a deep breath so she would not hear his present state of emotions over the phone.

"Mom, I only have three minutes, so they will ask for more money in a few seconds, so know that I love you and Dad very much and no matter what—"

"Please deposit . . ." the operator cut in. David said goodbye and said he would see them at the airport. Rachael hung up the phone and turned to Nathan.

"Something is definitely wrong with our son—I hear it in his voice."

"I know," he admitted, "I heard it, too, when I spoke to him the other day."

~

David walked from his dorm to the main street and continued walking about five blocks northeast of the university to a small neighborhood park. It was very cold, and he would occasionally hear the crunching of ice beneath his feet as he walked. When he came to the path that led into the park, he looked behind him to make sure he wasn't being followed. Those were his instructions when this meeting was arranged. "Make sure that no one is following you."

He entered the park and began to walk along the main path. He walked past a few benches and went to the farthest bench, which was nestled among a group of olive trees. He saw Bill Shanks waiting for him and began to approach him. But he stopped abruptly after seeing another shadow beyond Shanks.

"Is there someone with you?" David questioned with a slight quiver in his voice.

"Yes, David, it's someone that you probably will recognize."

The meeting was prearranged, but Shanks had not said anything about other people being there. David walked slowly, and as he got closer, he saw the man who was present at the briefing. It was dark, but a single pole lamp provided enough light to see his face.

"Hello, David. I think it is time that we formally met. I am General Yedida. I am with a branch of the Israeli military. I am handling this myself because of the secrecy of this operation. I understand that you have some information for us."

Then David heard another sound. "Don't be alarmed, David. You already know Ya'akov. He is covering us while we are here."

David strained his eyes, but he could not see anyone.

"David, you have information for us—please, you do not realize the gravity of this situation," the general stated. "Allow me to fill you in. We are aware that there is a freighter that left New York under Lebanese registration. We suspect that Elanie, Yael and Reuben are aboard that vessel. Is that your information?"

"Yes," David answered.

"David, once they left New York, they were not within the jurisdiction of any law enforcement agencies as they were already within international waters. We are not even concerned with those three. We are concerned with the cargo on that vessel."

"It's aide for widows and orphans—Palestinian families, I suspect," David added.

"That is what the ship's manifest reports and what the inspector in New York Harbor reported during his brief inspection. His workload was already beyond his capabilities when he rushed through that inspection and hardly looked around the ship—so we were told. Clothing, rice, wheat, and the list goes on. Isn't that what they told you?"

"Yes, pretty much, but I didn't think they were telling me the truth. That's why I called the U.S. Embassy and spoke to Mr. Shanks."

"David, call me Bill; no last names, please. And I am CIA, not a diplomat."

"I see," David acknowledged.

"David, the ship we are talking about is a 4,500-ton merchant ship that was purchased by several top ranking officials involved in the PLO procurement department. We suspect that this ship might be carrying arms and munitions designated for Palestinian terrorists. If that is the case, we must make immediate plans to stop that ship from ever reaching us. Once they get here with guns or explosives aboard, it would be a matter of hours to unload the cargo and be on their way. They could even unload outside of the harbor."

"How else could they get the guns ashore?" David asked curiously.

"In small dinghies or fishing boats. That shipment could be on its way to distribution before they ever dock or are boarded by Customs. If there are arms and munitions aboard that ship, we can never allow it to come near Tel Aviv or any other Middle Eastern port."

"If all of this is true, what could I possibly do to help you?" David asked.

"We need to know whom it is you were supposed to notify—their names and especially if there was someone in particular who was the most important person to notify."

"Yes, there is one man who I am supposed to notify in person and not by phone. I was told that I would not receive the information until the ship was definitely scheduled to dock. At that time, I was to call certain people, except for this one man. He is the one who had to be alerted in person."

"What is his name?"

David reached inside his pocket and extracted the piece of paper to the surprise of both men.

"You have a list?"

"Yes, it's all right here."

Before David could unfold the entire paper, Shanks took the paper from his hand, reached into his jacket pocket, and pulled out something that looked like a cigar lighter. He laid the paper on the ground and then took a small, pocketsize flashlight from his other pocket and focused the light on the paper. He held the small object to his eye and depressed a button on the side. A rapid "click, click, click" was heard, and David realized that it was a miniature camera. When Shanks was finished, he picked up the paper and handed it back to David with a sincere, "Thank you."

David refolded the paper and placed it back into the right front pocket of his jeans.

"I know I sound naïve, but I am very new to all of this. Has something like this ever happened before—I mean a ship or boat bringing in guns and explosives? How do they get by the coast guard or the navy? How do you know that this ship has guns on it when it has already been inspected?"

The two men exchanged glances.

"David, the easiest way to catch you up on what's been happening here is to tell you about an actual event that took place. Some time ago, a fishing vessel was seized off the coast of Haifa. It left the port of Lebanon and was headed for Gaza. We had inside information that this vessel was carrying weaponry—although we didn't know exactly what was on board. We decided to capture the vessel rather than sink her. When we did, there were anti-tank missiles, launchers, anti-aircraft missiles, mortar shells, and all of this was going to the Palestinian terrorists. David, even a single bullet that gets into the hands of one terrorist is one Israeli life that will be taken because of that bullet. Think about the devastation that all those munitions could have caused if that vessel had made it to the Gaza."

"I see," David answered.

"So if this huge freighter turns out to have these types of *things* aboard, I will have been part of saving hundreds of lives, correct?"

"More like thousands of lives," the general answered and placed his hand on David's shoulder.

"David, it's not by chance that you have been placed in this position.

Every one of us has the opportunity of doing something for the good of others in his or her lifetime—but not everyone recognizes the opportunity or gets to save thousands of lives. By being part of a team that stops devastating munitions from reaching the hands of those who want us all dead, you get that chance to save lives. "Their hatred of Israelis is a hatred that has been indoctrinated into the minds and hearts of terrorists from the time they were able to understand the word 'Jew.' Allah is their excuse, and mind you, there are hundreds of millions of Muslims who worship Allah and are peace-loving people. The ones we are talking about are all the radicals and extremists. They are the PLO, the Hizbollah, the deranged suicide bombers, and the terrorist cells that exist throughout the world. They call it a blow for freedom. We call it murder."

David's heart was pounding, and he could feel the rush going through him. This was it, the calling from God, the reason he did not attend Yeshiva. This was the mission that would be within his heart for a lifetime. This was the mission he could tell his children about someday. David felt proud, fulfilled, and every fiber of depression was gone, replaced by excitement and feeling good about his life.

"How secretive is this mission, sir?"

"As far as the world is concerned, there is *no* mission and *no* ship. You must not even mention this to your parents if they come to Israel. You would place their very lives in jeopardy."

"I understand," David replied. "I have said nothing to them about any of this."

"Thank you for the list, David. We'll be in touch."

The meeting was ended. David walked back to the campus while the three men went off in another direction.

There was a great deal of conversation going on within the room. There were several guards at the doors to the largest conference room at Kirya. Armed guards with Uzis were positioned in the hallway leading to the room. There were guards on the upper floors above the room, and others who were stationed at all the stairwells. Commandos were stationed in the basement and at every entrance, even within the elevators. No one who did not have a special identity tag with special clearance could even enter this particular part of the building today. The room was filled with every top military officer in the Israeli government. There were officials from Mossad, Military Intelligence, IDF, all the branches of Israeli armed forces, and covert operation specialists from various groups within other agencies. The prime minister sat at the very head of a table that accommodated some forty-two people—twenty on both sides and the two end chairs. The admiral was the first to speak when the meeting was called to order.

"I asked the prime minister to call this meeting because we are faced with another situation on the high seas. The information came to me after our authorities processed it, and I will provide you with the overall Intel we now have. The freighter *Karine Abbalah* left New York with a crew of twelve men. We also know that there are three passengers on board who are civilians and are connected with the PLO and perhaps several other terrorist organizations. We also have information from the United States and Mr. Shanks of the CIA, " the admiral nodded in recognition of Bill Shanks, who was at the table, "that they were fleeing the FBI. The FBI has had their headquarters staked out and wired for the past several months. Their headquarters was a café-type restaurant in Pittsburgh, Pennsylvania. It is where they recruited the American. They were going to be arrested the very night they disappeared."

The admiral picked up a glass of water and took a sip.

"They must have suspected they were being watched or found one of the surveillance items that were planted in the restaurant. They also rigged up what is now believed to be C-4 explosives to a washing machine and blew up the entire restaurant before they left Pittsburgh. For any one of several reasons, they suspected their cover was compromised and had an escape plan in place. They made it from Pittsburgh to New York harbor and boarded this freighter early in the morning the next day. Would you lower the lights, please?"

He nodded at one assistant standing at the lighting controls and another with a laptop computer on a small stand.

The screen was on the far wall and was lowered automatically. The prime minister turned his chair around, as the screen was directly behind him. As the lights dimmed, the first picture flashed on the screen.

"I am mostly concerned with the freighter and her cargo, but let me acquaint you with these three, simply because they are aboard and should be taken into consideration when we decide our ultimate strategy. This first picture is Elanie Feldman, but don't let her last name fool you. She is a graduate of Tel Aviv University and is brilliant in several fields. They include mathematics, chemistry, biology and generally most areas of scientific studies. We know that she was working on a top-level project after graduation. One day, without so much as a word to anyone, she disappeared, and no one knew to where. The first time that we can pinpoint her at any given location was when she applied for the position at a Pittsburgh hospital as an administrative assistant. That's how she met and targeted the American, David Blumberg, as a recruit. He was a patient in the hospital, the result of a mugging while riding his bike one evening. She was able to find out everything about him—his present circumstances and his background. They recruited him under the guise of becoming a member of Mossad and helping the cause of Israel." The admiral took another sip of water.

"The second picture you see is her brother, Reuben Feldman. We know of his adoptive relationship with Elanie. He is extremely dangerous, positively linked to the PLO, and has been in the company of many Palestinian leaders on several occasions."

"The third picture is Yael, who poses as Elanie's brother. We suspect that his name is other than Yael and he has used several aliases in the past. He has known Reuben and Elanie since elementary school days. He is also linked to terrorism through the PLO and has ties to Osama bin Laden. He has been trained in weaponry, explosives, and in almost every field of covert operations. As I mentioned, the three of them practically grew up together.

"That brings you up to date on these three. Here is our biggest concern and objective: We suspect that there are major munitions supplies hidden aboard this ship, possibly covered over with legal goods—likely to be clothing. The U.S. Customs sent a single man aboard to inspect the cargo. He reported nothing that was of a suspicious nature. He was on and off the ship in so short a time that he could not have possibly inspected every cargo hold and storeroom on board. The ports are so busy that they cannot even inspect most of the containers that are coming in and going out. We are here to discuss the possibilities of how to deal with this ship before she reaches our waters or any of the ports in the Middle East.

"The freighter is using international shipping lanes, so the main discussion is whether to take her out or capture her. If we wait until she is in our waters, we have about 161 miles of coastline to protect, for she could lower any one of her life boats, and these three we just discussed would be lost in the darkness of the night. The greater problem that presents itself is the accuracy of the information. Is this ship actually carrying weapons and munitions? That is the one thing we have to be sure of. We believe that Iran and Hizbollah is involved, so we are treading on thin ground if we take her out and she is not carrying arms or munitions. We know this because another freighter, although registered out of Lebanon, is secretly owned by Iranian business sources. That could be the link as to how they were able to get these munitions or weaponry aboard the ship in the first place. We believe that the other freighter might have off-loaded the munitions at sea, and the clothing was dumped on top to cover it up. Again, we have no proof except that one of our reconnaissance planes spotted the two ships tied up to one another at sea. The CIA confirmed this with a satellite picture, as you see here on the screen in the next photo.

"As is obvious from tightening and enlarging this photo, there are cargo transfer lines that can be seen at the aft of the ship. These are where the two main cargo holds are located. This operation will be under air force and naval command during every phase from beginning to completion," the admiral stated.

"Commander Saul Rabene will take command of the operation. The prime minister has asked me to be second in command and head up all air and sea coordination, which will originate from the flagship. The general will be taking his command to the air so he may cover a wide radius between the freighter and the carrier. By circling overhead with sophisticated night vision and hi-tech spy ware, the freighter will be under constant observation prior to her ever getting near Israeli waters."

The prime minister broke in with suggestions that had been made in previous discussions.

"I know we have discussed shooting her out of the water, but that would entail many risks. We would have to insure that there were no other ships or fishing vessels anywhere within miles that could possibly witness us doing so."

"Mr. Prime Minister, our topside guns make a lot of noise when they are fired. If we did this at night, the sound could echo up the coastline. Allow me to offer this alternative. We could use helicopters launched from the carrier to drop several teams of commandos aboard while she is outside of our waters. If we conduct this raid in the middle of the night, they would not expect it. We could scale her in the darkness, and with only twelve crew members and those three terrorists, we could take her before anyone even knew what happened."

"That sounds like a plan worth building some solid strategy around," the prime minister remarked.

"This way, sir, if there was any trouble, we could sink her in deep waters. I would only like to be there to see the Palestinian leader's face in the morning. If I know him as well as I think I do, he is celebrating at this very moment, waiting for the arms to reach his terrorists, and dreaming of our casualties from such a shipment."

"Whatever it takes, whatever resources are needed, I want this ship stopped," was the final statement from the prime minister as he stood. The rest of the attendees stood, as well. Everyone remained standing until he had left the room along with his aides and special guard.

~

Diane sensed the pain from her wrists and ankles before she was coherent enough to realize that she was blindfolded, bound, and lying flat on her back. She could not move, but she thanked God she was alive. Confusion was the first wave of feelings to go through her as soon as her mind was clear enough to try and make any sense of all this. Why did anyone want to kidnap her? She had no money, and her mother was a widow who worked hard and lived modestly. Then it occurred to her that Susan was also with her when this had happened. Was she there with her also?

She heard voices, but faintly, as though they were in another room. It was then that fear began to creep into her reasoning, and tears brimmed under the blindfold. She could smell something strange but could not identify the odor. It wasn't terribly bad, but familiar, like the smell of a garage where cars were being repaired. She did not know how close to being accurate her assumption was. She was lying on the floor of the now closed mechanical repair center for John Deere tractors.

The building had been there for many years, and a newer facility had been built several years ago on the other side of town. This section of the city was run down and had a lot of homeless people who used the abandoned garages and commercial space as shelter from the cold winter. Even the police did not like patrolling the streets of this desolate part of town.

Her back was in pain from lying on a concrete floor. Her earliest memory before this was Susan saying that she would walk with her and then ... nothing. Everything else was a blank. She would soon discover that her life was very much in jeopardy, especially if David did not do what the Palestinians wanted him to do. The motivation for David to cooperate with the PLO was now bound and gagged in a deserted building in Pittsburgh. The terrorists had no problem with the double agent conversations, for it was exactly what they wanted David to do. How did they know about her connection to David? Did they have spies at Pitt or CMU? These were some of the questions going through her mind.

Diane heard voices coming closer, and remained very still, appearing to be asleep. But how long had she *really* been asleep? How long had she been there? The voices became clear as she heard two men exchanging conversation. They were coming closer, but there was an echo to their voices as though they were in a large room or a room without a ceiling or walls—a factory, perhaps, or large garage.

"Did you get the message out to Tel Aviv?"

"Yes, the moment we had the girl."

"Where is the radio?"

"It's in the sales department office on the other side of the building."

"Did you get rid of the van?"

"Yes, I had it disposed of the minute we got here."

"Good, then everything is as we were ordered to do."

~

Captain Omar Akwaite stared at the bow of the ship breaking through the water from the bridge of the freighter. His first mate had just handed him a cup of hot Turkish coffee. Reuben was sitting on the starboard watchchair. He marveled at the blackness of the night at sea.

"If only we could have this kind of darkness when we planned a raid on land," he remarked. Omar laughed and agreed.

Elanie was in her cabin, sleeping, and Yael was with several of the crewmembers playing cards in their quarters. Yael had just pulled a full house and raked in the largest pot of the night.

"Let's play one more round and quit, guys. It's been a long day." The men agreed, just so long as he was not leaving after his winning hand. Reuben was down below, staring at the main cargo hold. He sensed an overwhelming excitement at the thought of so many arms and munitions being below those worthless clothes. It would be the largest shipment brought into Israel in history. He thought about the Pittsburgh operation and the thought of blowing up the café somewhat dampened his spirit. There was a certain enjoyment that he experienced from that small restaurant. It occurred to him that if things had been different, he might have enjoyed becoming a restaurant owner in Israel. Life was what it was, and he was content knowing that in a couple of days, tons of arms and explosives would be in the hands of his fellow PLO members and distributed to the terrorist training camps in various countries.

Diane suddenly felt a hand on her arm. Her reflexes were instantaneous, and she pulled her arm away from whomever it was who touched her. Then the hand caressed her hair, and once again she jerked her body away from the touch. Someone was really toying with her, and she was surely not in the mood.

"Okay, sweet thing," sounded a gruff voice. He was so close that Diane could feel his breath on her face. "I have to leave you alone, but if I had my way . . ." Diane kicked out at him and felt her foot hit something soft but with an underlying hardness. It was the man's cheek, and he reeled and cried out.

Just then a second voice spoke.

"What are you doing, you fool? We have strict orders that she is not to be harmed in the slightest way. Wasn't my warning in the van enough for you?"

"I can not help it. Look at her; she is beautiful," and he reached over and ripped her blouse.

"If you are caught toying with her, you'll have your hands cut off."

She heard the men leave, one telling the other to get some ice for his cheek. She was shaking and began to cry.

She knew that this had to have something to do with or was in some way connected to David. It was the only reasonable and logical conclusion. What else would they want with her if not to use her as a bargaining chip—but for what? What was David involved in that these men would go to such extremes?

~

It was two days before Christmas. The airport was so crowded that Nathan could hardly keep track of Rachael when they weren't holding hands. It took nearly fifteen minutes to get a skycap to check their larger bag because people were pulling up and unloading more and more luggage on the curb. Nathan inched his way forward toward the security tables. Rachael remarked more than once that perhaps this was not such a good idea.

His reply was, "You agreed to the trip, so let's just make the best of it. It won't be so bad once we're in London."

A security officer advised Nathan to please move along and place his carry on bag on the conveyer belt of the x-ray machine, and he complied. Rachael placed her handbag behind it and a box of cookies she had baked for David. Nathan joked with her about the cookies.

"You know, that's an x-ray in there—like a microwave. You should have brought them unbaked and they would have come out the other side all crispy!"

"Very funny," Rachael whispered and poked him in the arm. As he passed through the metal detector, the shrill of an alarm startled him, and he froze.

"Its okay, sir," the guard assured him. "Please step through and wait at that white line." The guard pointed to a place to the left of the security traffic that had a white line on the floor and a glass shield blocking the hallway leading to the gates. He walked to the white line and waited. Rachael came through without incident, and that was when he realized that he had not put his pocket Day Timer in the basket. It had four metal protectors, one on each of the corners of the front and back flaps. A guard approached him, and after Nathan removed it from his jacket pocket, he offered it to the officer.

"That's okay, sir. I am only going to pat you down and run a metal detector over the front and back of your clothes."

"Is all that necessary for one little date book?" Nathan asked respectfully.

"It really is, sir. It's our orders and also a matter of security protocol. Please extend your arms upward and away from you."

Nathan complied and felt like a spectacle as people began to watch to see if perhaps he was a terrorist. It was a good thing that Nathan did not see Rachael standing behind him. She had her hand cupped over her mouth, trying not to laugh aloud at the sight of her rabbi husband being "frisked" by a security guard at the airport! *Of all people,* she thought and continued to giggle into the palm of her hand. After a minute or two, he was convinced that Nathan was not hiding anything and asked that he retrieve his belongings from the plastic bin on the table. Nathan thanked him, walked over to the gray bin, and while picking up his things, gave Rachael a curious glance.

"Were you laughing at me?" he asked with a smile on his face. "I actually did not mind that. It was the most exciting thing to happen to me in a while!"

They walked to their gate. Since they had checked in ahead of time, they already had their boarding passes and seat assignments. It would be a long flight, and Nathan suggested that they just walk up to the next gate and back again to stretch their legs. Rachael began to laugh.

"Did you notice that we just walked from the terminal to gate thirty-seven? And you want to stretch your legs?" Nathan smiled. He placed his arm around her shoulders and drew her near to him.

Nathan remarked that he felt like a robot, following a programmed routine from the time they had arrived at the airport.

Rachael reminded him of something she had read.

"Don't travel to a foreign country with the preconceived notion that you will find everything as comfortable as home. You left home to find things different in the first place."

~

David noticed that he was pacing up and down the hallway, but he didn't really care. There was no one to notice his nervousness. The several students who were boarding in the employee house were gone for the winter break. As far as David knew, there was only one other person on that floor who was not going home. He, too, was a foreign student. All the rest were from Israel and had left the previous day for their homes. He struggled with his role in the ship's cargo matter, which was now becoming a living nightmare and not just a bad dream. He had his instructions and knew that he would do what was right. After returning from the meeting in the park, he knew that he had to inform the Israeli government of when and where the ship was coming in. What if they were wrong? What if there really was relief aide for widows and children of the Palestinians who died? What if this was some sort of plot to simply cut off all food and medical aide to the Palestinians? Fantasy, he told himself. Israel would never do such a thing—but then again, it occurred to him that Mossad might. He had some time to think about it and had to make sure his parents were nowhere near Tel Aviv when it happened. He paced the floor to the end of the hallway, and just as he turned to walk back toward his room, a door opened. David was startled at first and stepped back toward the wall.

"I'm sorry, did I scare you?" the young man asked. David chuckled.

"Just enough for a heart attack."

"Oh, I'm sorry."

"No, it's okay," David insisted. "I heard that there was another student who was staying here for the winter break. My name is David, David Blumberg."

"It's nice to meet you, David. My name is Rajid."

"That sounds more Arabic than Israeli . . . oh, that's right, you are not from Israel. That's why you are staying here."

"Yes, I am from Saudi Arabia, but my family moved to Yemen a few years ago. They are traveling this week, so I decided to just stay here."

"Well, my parents are coming in tomorrow. Perhaps you would like to join us for sightseeing or a meal?"

"Thank you, that's kind of you to offer; however, I have plans for the next several days."

"Are you also going sightseeing?"

"You might say that," he replied. It was a strange reply, but perhaps he was becoming a little paranoid.

"Okay, then, I have to shower and get going. It was nice to meet you, Rajid."

David smiled and extended his hand. They shook, and David promptly walked back to his room and went inside. Then he began thinking about the incident. Rajid? That's Arabic, so how come he's at an Israeli university? How could a "Rajid" be at this school? David knew that he was not going to wait around and find out in some future confrontation. He needed to find out—now.

He quickly changed his clothes to a sweat suit and put on wool socks and sneakers. He waited for a few minutes and placed his hand on the doorknob. He slowly twisted the doorknob, attempting to be as quiet as possible. He swung the door open, walked slowly out of the room, and quietly shut the door. He tiptoed down the flight of stairs, ducked under the security camera, and opened the outside door, quickly exiting the building.

The administration building was across the street. He hesitated before going out into the exposed surroundings and looked around to make sure that no one was there. He ran across the road and up to the building. What was he thinking? No one was here—it was winter break. The building would be locked, and he would have to break into it. If he got caught, he could go to prison. He had to take the chance. David went around toward the back of the building to see if perhaps there was another way in. As he rounded the corner, he saw a stairway going down and a sign overhead that said "Maintenance Department."

David quickly went down the steps to a door with glass panes. Checking to see if there were any magnets or wires to set off a security system, he proceeded to turn the knob. The door was open! He could not believe it and stood still for a moment to make sure that an alarm wasn't going to sound. There was no sound, no guard, and he was inside the building. He slowly closed the door behind him and looked around. The maintenance room was exactly that—a below-level room and obviously sealed off from the inside building. It was strange that they would do that, but for security purposes, perhaps it was a smart move. He had to find out if this boy was genuinely registered at the school. There was something about this that kept nagging at him. He turned and walked back up the stairs to seek another entrance. He had to know if there was a file on . . . *Oh no,* he thought. *He never gave me his last name. The files would obviously be alphabetical. How stupid of me. I could have asked him.* How foolish David felt at that moment, going through all of this and not even knowing his last name. He began walking toward the back entrance area to return to his room. As he turned the corner, two men were waiting for him, and they were both in uniform. They stood in front of a white van with flashing blue lights. The bold blue letters were in Hebrew, but David bet they said "Police" or "Security." One of the men had his hand on his gun, still holstered, and the other was carrying a small machine gun of some kind, which was pointed toward the ground.

"What are you doing here—are you a student?"

"Yes sir, I am. I'm staying here during winter break." The man with the machine gun began walking around David, looking him over.

"May I see your student ID, please?"

Their English was quite good although they both had distinctive Israeli accents.

David reached into his pocket and then realized he had his sweat suit on and not his jeans.

"I was out for a run to get some exercise, and I left my wallet in my room. We can go back there and I can get it for you."

"That won't be necessary. What is your name?"

"David Blumberg."

The man who was questioning him removed a card from his shirt pocket and glanced at it. Then he looked at David and back at the card again.

"Where do you come from, David?"

"The United States, Florida."

"Okay, your name is here. I am sorry to alarm you, but we must be careful—not that there is anything here that a terrorist would want except empty classrooms. By the way, keep your eyes open. You and the other boy are the only one's left on campus."

Another boy! Thank God, there really is a student here, and he must be the one.

"Sir, do you have this boy's name on that card as well?" David asked. The officer reached back into his pocket and read the name.

"He is an exchange student. Why do you ask?"

"Oh, I met him and I forgot his name. I will likely run into him again at the living quarters, and I didn't want to be embarrassed."

"His name is Michael Epstein, and he is from England. However, I don't think you'll run into him, although his room is on your floor. He left yesterday for a trip up the coast with his brother who flew in to be with him for the holidays. I know because I gave him directions to several sites up the coast."

David looked at the officer with a questioning expression.

"Did you say his name is Michael Epstein?"

"Yes, I am sure."

As David went back to the building, he entered the ground floor security point and walked up the flight of stairs but waited. He peered through the glass portal in the steel door and did not see anyone. He opened the door, closing it carefully so that not a sound was made. He walked down the hallway, practically tip-toeing all the way. When he came to his room, he slid the key in the lock and tried to turn it, but it didn't turn. The door was unlocked. David removed his key and turned the knob. He opened the door, and sitting in his chair was Rajid. David attempted to hide the shocked look on his face and simply asked what he was doing in his room.

"I was waiting for you, David. Where have you run to in all this time?"

"I was out exploring the grounds, but what right do you have entering my room?"

"None, I suppose, but then again, I don't usually follow the rules."

He stared at Rajid with a serious look and thought that he was hiding his own fear quite well.

"Do I have any reason to be afraid of you?"

"Yes, David, you do. Perhaps not you personally, but your actions affect others in this world, as you well know. Did you enjoy your conversation with the campus security police?" David was now totally confused. Who was this guy, and what did he want with him? He must have followed him and saw what occurred. He refused to show any fear or comment on Rajid's remarks. Rajid stood up, walked past David, and stopped at the door.

"What do you want, Rajid? State your business and please leave my room."

Rajid laughed as he placed his hand on the doorknob.

We'll talk again, my Jewish friend," he said and left the room.

David stared at the door for about five minutes until he was able to compose himself. This man had to have been with Elanie and her two companions. He had that same demeanor, that fearless look in his eyes that Yael and Reuben had. But what did he mean that his actions affected others? What if Rajid was talking about his parents? They would be in Tel Aviv tomorrow, and what if they were walking into a situation that David created, placing them in harm's way? He had to find out what this was about.

He walked out into the hallway and went to the room where Rajid came out of earlier. He knocked on the door but there was no response. David tried the doorknob, and it was not locked. He opened the door and there was no one in the room. The mattress was rolled up and the linen gone. The closet door was open, and there was nothing on hangers or any sign of personal possessions. David turned and left the room, looking at the wall where he had stood and where he had first encountered Rajid. This was surely the room that Rajid came out of, but it was empty. Perhaps Rajid left, but it was unlikely that he went very far. David reasoned that Rajid had delivered no real message to him but rather made a threatening innuendo. Who was it that Rajid was talking about that would be affected by his actions? If only he could reach his parents. They might be in danger, and if that was what Rajid wanted David to worry about, he accomplished his mission.

~

The airport in London was as busy, as Florida's had been. The noise level in and around the baggage claim area was deafening. People were shouting as they saw one of their bags on the huge carousel, or yelling at someone else who even reached in the direction of their bags. The plane had arrived nearly forty-five minutes ago, and still their bag was not on the luggage carousel. Nathan had watched carefully, visually checking every piece of luggage that came down, but their bag was not one of them. *What a mess,* he thought. *Perhaps I should have come after the holidays, but then David might have been more deeply entrenched in whatever it is he is into.*

No, he had to see his son. He had to get to him, to hopefully reason with him to come home.

Rachael suddenly tugged on his arm.

"You look like you were a million miles away in thought. Any sign of our baggage coming down?"

"No, and it's going on an hour already." They sought out the baggage service center and found that they were number forty-seven in a long line of people who were missing their baggage. A woman with a clipboard and a pleasant smile was going down the line, asking pertinent questions concerning each individual's problem. When she came to Nathan and Rachael, she smiled and asked the reason they were waiting.

"Our baggage has not come down from a flight that landed almost an hour ago."

"I am so sorry, sir," she genuinely stated with a crisp British accent. "What flight were you on, please?"

"The one from Florida," Nathan answered as she flipped through some of the pages on the clipboard she was holding.

"And may I ask your name and see your tickets, please?"

"Yes, of course." Nathan reached inside his jacket pocket and held out their tickets and passports.

"Just the tickets, please, and you hold on to your passport. You'll need it when you go through Customs."

"Our name is Blumberg, Nathan and Rachael."

She ran her finger down a list of names and stopped.

"Yes, there you are, Mr. Blumberg . . . and I see now why your luggage has not come down. Are you not going on to Tel Aviv tomorrow?"

"Yes, we are."

"You checked your luggage *through,* sir. Your bags have not arrived because they were taken to a sealed container at El Al Airlines. It would be a security breech for us to even attempt to acquire that luggage once it is in El Al's space. They are very strict about their security dictates."

Nathan looked at Rachael with a meek expression of apology.

"I didn't know what the baggage handler meant when he asked if I wanted to check my luggage *through.*"

Rachael turned to the woman and thanked her for her help. Fortunately, they were only going to be there one night.

After going through a simple passport check at Customs, they left the terminal and felt the cold December air as the doors opened to the ground transportation area. Rachael slipped on her coat and buttoned it to the top. Nathan had a heavy jacket that he felt was adequate for the forty-five-degree days or thirty-four-degree nights.

Nathan had read that London had over five hundred art galleries and one hundred-fifty museums. He wished they could actually stay a few days and take in the sights. Buckingham Palace, London Bridge, Westminster Abbey, The Tower of London, House of Parliament, Shakespeare's Globe, and so many more that they might not have the opportunity to see again.

They had reserved a room at a hotel near the airport, because their flight left early in the morning. Nathan hailed a taxi and announced their destination. The taxi sped off, and just as his son had noticed when he was in London, Nathan marveled at the fact that the driver was on the wrong side of the car!

Chapter Seventeen

Plans and Complexities

Radio traffic between the navy and the air force was flowing heavily, and every message was encoded for secrecy. There was no doubt in Israel's mind that the freighter had to be stopped. They were convinced she was carrying munitions, weapons, or both, and the source of the information was deemed reliable. They would not allow this shipment to get into the hands of Palestinian terrorists. The possibility of being wrong about the cargo had occurred to everyone involved. If they were wrong, the world would accuse Israel of committing an act of piracy on the high seas. They could live with that, but not the other possibilities if they were right.

At 7:48 p.m. Israeli time, a United States CIA reconnaissance plane flying across the Atlantic, sighted the freighter Karine Abbalah. She was sailing at about 17 knots and keeping within one of the main shipping channels. The captain was obviously experienced, for he was doing everything by the book. It was as though he knew the ship was under surveillance and was not taking any chances. The ship's precise position was relayed to Israeli officials and to the admiral. Below the bridge deck of the command ship, there was a battle readiness and situation room where every sighting was recorded and marked on a huge glass board. The ship's movement by latitude, longitude, and the precise time of every recorded position were carefully charted. Senior operational officers received periodic briefings and every station aboard the ship was patched into the communications board. Combat scenarios were displayed on several mock-up boards, and every conceivable possibility for boarding or attacking the cargo vessel was being explored. Israeli Special Forces teams, (similar to U.S. Navy Seals) were periodically briefed by the executive officer as each new element of information became available.

The briefing board also displayed the complete layout and all spaces aboard the ship. Knowing the various decks and the location of the engine room and crews quarters was critical information. Armed crewmembers could choose any space to hide, once the attack was underway. By projecting her overall course and speed, a specific location was selected just outside Israeli coastal waters. Intelligence predicted she would attempt to either make port along the coastline or drop anchor and off-load her cargo under the cover of night. Distribution of her cargo in either situation could be accomplished quickly, so she would have to be taken before that point.

Precise coordinates were updated continuously and relayed to General Rabene aboard his reconnaissance plane. Three commando teams were being prepared to board Sikorsky CH-53 transports that were standing by and ready to go at a moment's notice. Everything was ready, and all that was needed were the specific orders determining the precise location and time they would strike. Three choppers were assigned, two for the men and one to carry the self-inflating power rafts.

By 9:00 p.m. Israel's time, operation "Take Down" was underway—a little under two hours from the time they received the exact coordinates of the ship's position and her course.

A direct line of communication had been established between the flagship and the prime minister's home. He would be apprised of every critical decision and movement of the operation. There were many political ramifications to this operation, and both he and Israel's military leaders wanted nothing left to chance and no decision left to any one individual. If they were right, they would all celebrate. If they were wrong, there was more strength in numbers. The time for executing the plan was set for approximately 2:00 a.m. or 0200 hours military time.

There were obvious variables and they wanted to leave plenty of room for them. A storm could develop that might force her to change course or any number of other possibilities they had to be prepared for. It was also determined that she needed to be a safe distance from Israel's shores in the event they were forced to sink her. They could board the ship and take possession if she was closer to the coast, but if there was any gunplay or explosions, she had to be clear of any possible sightings from the shoreline. There was also the possibility that the terrorists had rigged the ship with explosives. They had to be prepared for every alternative.

The team to take the crew down would be their most experienced and decorated commando unit, comprised of twenty-one men. There were originally three teams of seven men each and they were merged into one unit whenever a vital and dangerous operation took place. They all wore black seal outfits. They bore no identity, no flags, or any other official insignias to reveal who they were. They were highly trained suppressers of terrorism.

~

It was almost midnight when Rajid answered his cell phone and listened to his coded instructions. The caller was brief but emphatic. Rajid glanced up at the second floor to see if the lights in David's room were still on, and they were. There would be no physical confrontation. It was to be done smoothly and without any harm coming to David. His actions and message would be intimidation rather than force.

At that moment, however, inside room 202, the man whom they counted on to mislead the Israeli's had been praying for divine wisdom. He searched Scriptures for some precedent, something that might give him inspiration, such as what King David did in times of decision-making that could affect people's lives. *After all,* he thought, ***King David came up against his enemies all the time!*** After a while, he felt himself slipping off into a stupor of exhaustion. He desperately needed to get some sleep. He turned off the lights and closed his eyes. Tiny specs of white flashes were appearing, even though his eyes were tightly closed.

Then, there was a sound that startled him, and he instantly sat up and opened his eyes—just as the overhead lights came on. He sat up and thought he saw Rajid. Everything was blurred as he had almost fallen asleep. He strained his eyes to focus, and that's when he saw Rajid, standing at the foot of his bed with a gun pointed at him.

"Rajid!" David cried out. "What are you doing?"

Rajid was expressionless. In fact, David's worst fear began to seer through him. He was eyeball to eyeball with a man who had the eyes of a heartless murderer, a terrorist who would kill for the mere sake of reducing the world's population by one less infidel.

"Listen to me, David, and listen carefully. I am only going to say this once. If you do *not* do exactly what I am about to tell you, someone very close to you will pay the consequence for your lack of obedience. If you do what you are told, she will be set free, unharmed."

"What? What are you talking about? Who will be set free—who is she?" David felt panic in the pit of his stomach. Added to the level of fear he was already experiencing, a wave of nausea began to overcome him. He felt weak and almost at the point of fainting. Rajid also saw this fear and the wave of helplessness in David's eyes, and he reveled in it. He purposely didn't answer him right away, wanting him to wonder who was in danger. Rajid loved the look on the face of his victims—those that knew what was coming. He was morbid and calloused through and through.

"It's your girlfriend, Diane. I am told she is quite beautiful—face and body alike." With that remark, Rajid took on a smirk as though to emphasize the grave danger of being at the mercy of men without conscience. Then a picture fell into place. They had grabbed Diane from her school campus. *Of course,* he quickly concluded, his thought process beginning to work again. *They must have had more of their people in Pittsburgh besides Elanie and her two cohorts.*

David's emotions quickly changed. Anger once again took the place of fear—no, it was more than anger. It was rage. He felt as though his blood was boiling and the anger was seething through his veins. The result was a rush of pure adrenalin, the kind that pumps the muscles and prepares the body for attack. At that very moment, he felt as though he was capable of leaping from the bed and strangling Rajid with his bare hands.

"Does all of this have to do with that ship that Elanie, Yael and Reuben are on? You are ensuring that I make the calls and notify the people on your list, aren't you?" David demanded. Rajid nodded his head.

"You just do what you're supposed to do, and the girl will be set free. If you do not, she will be brutally murdered. It's all that simple."

"Simple!" David cried out in a tone of outrage. His hands were clutching the edges of the mattress, and his knuckles were colorless. His heart was racing, and the muscles in his arms and chest were contracting as he squeezed his fists harder to ward-off the uncontrollable rage. In all of his young life, David never realized that a human being could cross the line of self-control by being literally driven into a state of rage. They were emotions so strong and out of control that they made one human being capable of killing another. Rajid announced he was leaving. He reached for something in his back pocket while holding the .45-caliber gun pointed at David's head. Rajid tossed an envelope onto the bed. He instructed David to open it when he left.

"David, this list is the correct one and not the phony list we gave you at first when we were testing your loyalty. The last man on this list is whom you are to meet precisely where and when the instructions dictate. If you miss one call or fail to appear and provide the information, Diane will be literally dissected—and *your* name will be spoken as they do it." With that said, he immediately retreated from the room.

Of all the contingencies he had thought of when deciding to become a part of this, he never considered Diane becoming a possible victim. Now he knew that every aspect of his world was involved, and he had to figure out what to do. He had the cell phone from which he could call Bill Shanks, but where was Ya'akov? He was supposed to be protecting him.

David got up from the bed and took the water bottle from the dresser. He took a long swig of the cool liquid and began to pace back and forth in the tiny room, allowing his feelings of rage to settle down. Opening the third drawer of the dresser and feeling between some shirts, he retrieved the cell phone and sat back down on the edge of the bed, placing the envelope with the new list of names beside him. He was lost, way out of his league, and too inexperienced in making decisions that effected people's lives. If he called Shanks at the embassy, the Israelis would know every word of their conversation within minutes of his hanging up. He knew that he had to do something, but did not have a clue as to what. He stared at the cell phone for a moment and then placed it beside him. David, of course, had no way of knowing that they already knew every word of their conversation.

Ya'akov had seen Rajid go into the dorm and watched him when he left the building. Surely the Palestinians must know that Israeli officials were on to them. He wondered what back up they had to even think they could pull off smuggling an entire shipload of arms into the Middle East. Ya'akov waited in the freezing December air just long enough for Rajid to disappear from sight. He turned toward the street and walked across to the other side. His car was parked closest to the campus entrance, and his radio equipment was hidden on the back seat. One single word or call by headquarters while Rajid was exiting the building would have blown his hiding place and resulted in an exchange of gunfire. That's why he opted to park far away from the dorm. He reached into the back seat and uncovered his equipment from under a thick, wool blanket. The blanket served to hide the radios when he wasn't in the car and also kept him warm when he was on a stakeout.

David's room was bugged, which Ya'akov had easily accomplished while David was out looking for information on Rajid. It had taken less than five minutes to plant the tiny wireless microphone. Ya'akov recorded every spoken word from the receiver in his car and the information was relayed to military headquarters. There was nothing Ya'akov could do when he saw Rajid enter the building. He knew they needed David to deliver the final message to someone who was high up in the terrorist chain; someone that no Palestinian could approach without exposing this man's collusion in the entire operation. That was the entire purpose of using David. They would simply kill him when it was over, and there was no link to the leaders at the PLO. The military were betting that it was Abdawah, their chief financial man and that the moment David delivered the message to him, he would approve or change the final port of entry.

The plan was in place, but something did not make sense. There was a possibility that out of all the men on the list, only one of them was a real person. Only one man would get the message, and by the time David drove to some destination to purportedly live out the dramatic scene and insure the safety of his loved ones, the message would have already been sent, and the final port of entry for the ship would have been established. David was a decoy, and perhaps so was the last notification on the list. Why did David have to call people who could not possibly have been associated with the higher authority at PLO?

~

These were the scenarios that were being played out in the war room aboard the flagship. The admiral was now in direct contact with General Rabene. In less than forty-eight hours, whatever plans the terrorists made would be played out. They *had* to intercept the ship.

"Admiral, when do you project that the Karine Abbalah will be in open waters where she might not have other shipping vessels near her?" General Rabene asked on the fully secure phone line. The admiral looked up at the ship's course for the past twenty-four hours as it was tracked on the giant glass board. A red luminescent marker was used to track its projected heading. This was based on the ship's recorded positions for the past several days. A blue marker tracked the ships actual course, and a white marker drew lines of comparison between her actual position and her projected position. There were hardly any white lines. The ship had been true to course for several days and continued speeding ahead at seventeen knots.

"General, I believe she will be in that position by 2:00 a.m. tomorrow," and the radio connection was terminated.

"Fast bugger, isn't she, sir?" a radioman remarked.

"Yes, son, she is, but I imagine she is stripped down except for the cargo. They wanted her to maintain enough speed to get here quickly. My guess is she is stocked full of munitions and nothing else." The admiral had no idea how right he was. The ship was totally stripped of all machinery and equipment before sailing to New York. Customs checked her cargo but not the equipment and machinery aboard the ship. All the deck wenches, cargo wenches, everything that could be removed was taken ashore. They wanted her to appear as though she was carrying a normal load of cargo.

General Rabene was in his command jet, circling the ocean area and taking readings from the air in moonlight visibility. He monitored sea swells and other critical criteria that could affect the commandos. There was only a quarter-moon and that was a plus for their nighttime cover.

Nathan handed the boarding passes to the attendant at the gate, and he and Rachael boarded the El Al Flight to Tel Aviv. They never did get to see a London show. Nathan fell asleep on the bed before Rachael could even change her clothes. She smiled and moved his legs to his side of the bed and gently slipped off his scuffed loafers and socks. She covered him, took a shower, and then quietly slipped into bed beside him. She fell asleep within minutes. They were not used to international travel and were quite worn out from all the walking through the terminals, as well as the stress of security checkpoints and the crowds.

Rachael placed a wake up call with the hotel operator that was quite early, although the plane did not depart until the late morning. After breakfast in the café the next morning, they hailed a taxi to take them to the airport. Once aboard the plane, they placed their bag and coats in the overhead compartment and settled into their seats. Nathan expressed his wish that there would not be a third passenger in their row so that they could stretch out. Rachael remarked how excited she was to finally see David, and Nathan agreed that he too was getting somewhat antsy and wished the travel part was over. By takeoff, no one had taken their middle seat.

~

There was no way that Diane could have known the reason for her capture if it were not for her pretending to be asleep and overhearing bits and pieces of her captors' conversations. It was not until she overheard something about an American in Israel that she struggled even harder to hear every whisper. They had moved her into an adjoining room as one of the men apparently spotted a police patrol car that evening. She heard them yelling to turn off the lights and get down out of sight. They obviously did not want any confrontation that could jeopardize their mission. Their orders were to abduct Diane from her college campus, bring her to the abandoned facility, and hold her there. She was not to be harmed in *any* way whatsoever. They would receive a call when the mission was near completion, and they would be given one of two passwords. One was to abandon the site and leave her there tied and blindfolded; an anonymous call would be made to the police with her location. The other password was an order not one of them wanted to carry out. They were political dissenters—not killers.

The four men were Palestinian by nationality and all lived in Pittsburgh. Two of the young men were born in America, and the third, a cousin, was brought to the United States when he was seven years old. He had the most pronounced accent of the three and was the one assigned to tend to Diane. He would see to her needs, including his carrying out the final instructions when the mission was over.

Not one of the four young sympathizers had a clue as to what was really going on. They had met Elanie at a Palestinian celebration at one of the mosques and were recruited specifically for this mission. All they knew was that it was ordained by Allah and would help their people. Meeting other Muslims was not difficult in Pittsburgh. Non-Muslims would not necessarily be aware that there were five Muslim centers (mosques) in Pittsburgh and approximately thirty such places of Muslim worship in the state of Pennsylvania alone.

"We are free, and our brothers in Allah need to be free as well," one of the men commented when Elanie had interviewed him. Elanie indoctrinated them in just a few days, which wasn't difficult to do. They were motivated by the passion of their self-professed plight. Elanie delivered a most convincing sales job that this mission would further their cause more than any previous operation.

"You will be a part of this history," she told them with her glass raised as they drank and ate at the restaurant together with Yael and Reuben.

At this moment in time, however, their only glory was playing cards and sitting outside a room that held a loving Christian girl who did not fully understand why she had been kidnapped.

Diane thought that she had been there for about two days, or perhaps three. Surely her friends would know that she was missing. *Someone at the school would have called the Pittsburgh police by now,* she reasoned. *That police car—it had to have been looking for me.* She continued the scenario in her mind to remain strong and not give in to whatever it was these men wanted. Her faith gave her strength and brought her comfort.

Her back muscles were becoming inflamed from being in the same position for such a long period of time. She was also hungry and thirsty. She began to call out, and within one minute there was someone standing beside her. It was the young man assigned to tend to her needs.

"Stop yelling," he demanded. "If you want something, you need to use the word *please* and I will know. We are right in the next room and can hear everything. Do you understand?"

"Yes," Diane answered in a meek tone.

The man spoke with a foreign accent; however, he sounded as though he had lived in America for a long time. She tried to memorize everything she could of the ordeal in the event the police needed facts to apprehend these men.

"May I *please* go to the bathroom and may I *please* have some food and water?"

"Yes," was his reply, and he untied her wrists and ankles. He then helped her to a sitting position. Her legs and feet were numb due to the long periods in between her allowed movement.

"Please, help me. My legs have no feeling, and I can't stand by myself until I walk a bit to regain circulation." He pulled her up, this time holding onto her perhaps a bit *too* closely.

She could feel his strong arms but was more concerned about the feeling of his nose near the nape of her neck. Diane withheld any comment.

"I may be an American, but that doesn't mean we are different because you came from another country. Why don't you teach me about your beliefs instead of my lying here all day? Perhaps it will help me to understand why you are doing this."

She attempted to open any type of dialogue with him. Perhaps she could possibly find out some more about why she was there. It was an appropriate attempt, but he did not answer her right away. There was a moment of silence as if he were seriously considering her challenge.

"Let's go. I will lead you, but do not take off the blindfold," he demanded.

"I just want to go to the bathroom and have some food and water. I do not want to do anything to upset you, but I am growing very weak and need some nourishment—please."

The man guided her across the room and stopped. He released one of her arms as he reached in front of her and opened the bathroom door. "You can take the blindfold off once I shut the door. Put it back on and make sure it is secure before you come out. Do not open the door—I will do that when you tell me the blindfold is in place. You must understand that if you see one of our faces, we will have to kill you. You are not a threat to us if you do not know who we are." He gently nudged her through the doorway and shut the door behind her. "Five minutes," were his only words. *Kill me? Would they really kill me?* Diane thought.

The incoming telephone call was on his unsecured cell phone. Victor reached into the desk drawer and quickly glanced at the calling number. He could not imagine who had this number anymore, as he only kept the phone around for old friends. None that he knew were in Israel in the middle of winter. He depressed the answer button and put the phone to his ear.

"Shalom," was all he said.

The voice on the other end asked, "Is this Victor?"

He noted that here was a quiver in the voice, the sound of fear and uncertainty. "Who is this?" Victor questioned.

"My name is David Blumberg. Nathan Blumberg is my father. Harry Blumberg was my grandfather."

Victor smiled and felt a fleeting moment of nostalgia, but he also knew this was not a social call. *David must be in trouble,* Victor immediately thought. Victor reacted professionally, as he had done during his entire career.

"Hello, David. I have not seen you since you were thirteen years old."

"Yes, I know," he answered. His voice was beginning to sound calmer as though talking with Victor encouraged him. Nathan had given him the only phone number he had for Victor in the event he needed a friendly face or had any problems while he was in Tel Aviv. Victor had lived in Jerusalem but moved to Tel Aviv after his wife died.

"Where are you now, David?"

"The university campus."

"Listen to me carefully. I don't want you to talk on a public telephone, especially at the dorms. Here is what I want you to do. Go to the street and hail a taxi. Do you have cash with you?"

"Yes," David answered. Victor gave him exacting instructions and hung up.

David was to take a taxi to Yehud, an industrial and manufacturing town that was a short distance outside of Tel Aviv. Victor did not want him anywhere near possible stakeout points that might jeopardize his safety. If anyone were to see him leave and follow him to Yehud, Victor had a plan to insure anonymity. Victor knew that the Palestinian goons were watching David, but not carefully. They had pegged him as a novice who got himself trapped in a situation and regarded him as such when it came to following him everywhere he went. They also knew that he was Jewish and would surely confide in the Israeli authorities. The conclusions the Palestinians had derived about David became his saving grace. When you know everything there is to know about your enemies, you need not worry about them.

David's instructions were to go to the Avia Hotel in Yehud, which was located a few minutes from Ben Gurion Airport. Victor knew other operatives that he could call on if it became necessary. They were all within driving distance of the hotel, in Tel Hashomer, Modiin and Ramia. The hotel was a fairly modern complex with 106 guest rooms and had meeting rooms that accommodated up to 200 people. Victor called the hotel after hanging up on David's first call. He learned there was a Bar Mitzvah scheduled for that day where he and David could simply blend in among the two hundred guests.

Once the arrangements were made and he was certain David understood his directives, Victor called an old friend in Yehud who was a Mossad operative for many years.

"I need help in this one. Can you be available in the event I need you at the hotel?"

His friend was just leaving Ramia and would be nearby at a local restaurant. Victor knew the telephone number.

Victor called the driver who was assigned to him should he ever need to go anywhere beyond reasonable walking distance. Considering Victor's age and his failing eyesight, no one in the organization wanted him to drive on his own. Everyone had expected him to retire by now, but Victor refused to do so until *he* was ready to retire.

Israel's operatives do not have a forced retirement age, nor are they sent off with a turkey banquet and a gold watch. Victor was a brilliant man and could teach every new member a great deal—not forgetting his usefulness in overseeing various aspects of the present operation. He promised himself, however, that that this would be his final mission.

The driver was at his front door in less than fifteen minutes and called him to come down. Victor removed a .38 snub-nose from his closet and tucked it into his jacket pocket. In the old days he would have drawn his .45 or 9mm. Now, he actually considered returning the .38 to the closet before he secured the deadbolt on the front door and went downstairs. The older black Mercedes was parked and waiting.

~

Their plane landed at the airport in Tel Aviv five minutes shy of being on schedule. Rachael collected some of her personal things from the seat pockets in front of her and under her seat. Nathan removed their flight bag and coats from the overhead compartment. Within twenty minutes they were through customs and waiting in the baggage claim area for their two suitcases. He caught a glimpse of a skycap and decided he was not taking any chances of not getting his luggage. He walked up to him, handed him his baggage claim checks, and placed a tip in his hand.

"Our bags are blue, nylon, and both the same size—I think they call it the Pullman size. We'll be waiting for you at that exit door." Nathan pointed to the nearest exit to transportation into Tel Aviv. The skycap palmed the five-dollar bill and thanked him. They put on their coats and walked toward the exit.

"I'm going to check outside for David. You stay here and keep warm," he insisted. He went outside and found that it was no worse than it was in London. Winter was not Nathan's favorite season unless he was in Ft. Lauderdale. Rachael noticed the skycap coming with their two bags on his cart.

"Would you like a taxi or are you taking the bus into town?" the skycap inquired.

"We're being picked up by our son. You can leave the bags right here with me. My husband is just outside."

The skycap set the bags beside Rachael and thanked her as he turned and quickly headed back to the baggage area. Nathan had not yet seen David, his eyes continuously searching the faces of the streams of holiday travelers. He noticed many people bearing the same expression. He called it the "traveled look"—tired, anxious, and thoughts of getting out of the crowded airport with your luggage and wallet intact. After twenty minutes and no David, Nathan went back inside the terminal building. Rachael had to restrain herself from laughing aloud when she saw his face. He looked as though he returned from an expedition to the North Pole. His face was beet red, and he was sniffling profusely.

"It's not that cold out there, but I guess I am just not used to it." He reached into his pocket for a handkerchief. "It appears that David is not going to show up for whatever reason. We should take a taxi and go into town. I'll ask the driver to recommend a hotel near the university, and we'll try to find David after we are settled in. I'm confident that he either forgot the time of the flight or was delayed for some reason."

There were several taxis lined up at the curb. A short, middle-aged man who almost looked American approached them. He was wearing a colorful red beret and a polyester Eisenhower jacket that Nathan had not seen in style since the '70s.

"Shalom—taxi, sir?"

"Yes, thank you," Nathan replied. The man took the bags from Nathan and walked behind his cab to the open trunk. He placed the two bags inside while Nathan and Rachael got into the back seat. The driver closed the trunk with a loud thud.

"Where shall I take you?" the driver asked Nathan as he closed his door.

"I want to stay at a decent hotel that is near Tel Aviv University. Do you know a place that is moderately priced, clean, and within walking distance to the campus?"

"Yes, of course, but there is no school in session now. I should know— my nephew goes there. They are on winter break."

"Yes, I am aware of that," Nathan agreed with a smile. "My son is staying there since we came to see him rather than his coming home to Florida."

"You are from Florida?" the driver asked quite excitedly.

"Yes, why? Have you been there?"

"That's where I am from!"

The man was almost gleeful and turned around as far as he could to introduce himself. "My name is Samuel Horowitz. Please call me Sam. My wife and I and our children moved to Israel almost ten years ago. We live here in Tel Aviv. My brother and his family followed us within a year, and now our entire family lives here.

"That is surely a coincidence," Nathan commented. "My name is Rabbi Nathan Blumberg, and this is my wife, Rachael."

"It is an honor to meet you both," the driver responded. Nathan reached forward and shook hands with Sam Horowitz. He noticed that the man was staring at him with a curious expression on his face.

"You said 'rabbi' when you introduced yourself. Would you be any relation to Rabbi Harry Blumberg from Ft. Lauderdale?"

Tears immediately brimmed in Nathan's eyes, and Rachael looked as though she was in shock. Neither of them could obviously believe what they just heard.

"Yes, he was my father," Nathan replied, holding back a mountain of emotions. Sam was also emotionally overwhelmed. He wiped his eyes with the cuff of his jacket, fighting off his own tears of joyous coincidence.

"How did you know my father?" Nathan finally was able to ask.

"I attended your synagogue in the very early days, about thirty years ago. One day your father stopped me on the way out. He noticed I never hung around afterward and wanted to know more about me, my family, and about our lives. He was a man who really cared about people. We talked for a while, and then we went out to lunch one day. I picked him up in my taxi. I had been a driver in Ft. Lauderdale since I was about nineteen years old. We lived in Delray Beach in the old days when you could still afford a house in Florida."

Nathan was overjoyed and was about to engage in more conversation when a tapping sound came from the driver's window. It was an Israeli soldier tapping and Sam rolled down his window.

"Shalom," was exchanged, and the soldier remarked that the taxi had been parked there for some time and he would have to move.

"I am sorry, but I met a friend from the United States and we got carried away talking."

The soldier took a step over to the rear windows and stooped down to eyeball Nathan and Rachael. He was carrying a very intimidating weapon that was pointed downward. But the way he had his left hand positioned on the gun, he looked ready to engage the trigger in an instant. After looking them over, he gave them a salute and motioned Sam to pull out. He raised his hand to some oncoming cars, and Sam pulled the vehicle from the curb and headed toward the main exit.

~

As the taxi pulled up to the hotel, David asked how he might call the driver if he needed a ride back to Tel Aviv in the event Victor could not take him. The driver gave David his cell phone number. He told him to call thirty-minutes in advance and he would come back and get him if he needed him to.

"Thank you very much," David replied as he paid the driver and got out of the cab. Walking into the hotel, he noticed a great deal of activity in the nicely appointed lobby. Victor had instructed him to be acutely aware of his surroundings, especially of anyone who might be following him. He was to enter the hotel and go directly to the mezzanine floor by using the staircase and not the elevator. The ballroom and meeting rooms were located on that floor, and it would be very busy with guests attending the Bar Mitzvah.

As he walked up the doublewide set of marble stairs to the mezzanine, David looked back and scanned the entranceway. He was relatively certain that no one had followed him. On the ride to the hotel, he was glancing over his shoulder so much that the driver joked, "Is someone following you?"

At the time, David laughed as though it was a humorous remark, but the truth was the driver had no idea how scared he really was.

Entering the foyer area of the mezzanine, he heard the sound of familiar, traditional music. As he rounded the corner, there were people everywhere. Young boys in their adorable suits and ties and precious little girls with pink and white bows in their hair were running all about and playing games with one another. Their parents watched while talking with friends or relatives, sipping a drink and scooping up little pastries from an assortment of trays. There was a very long table decorated in blue and white linen that ran almost the entire length of the mezzanine wall.

David had no idea of what Victor looked like, but he was to go to the main ballroom and proceed to the farthest end of the ballroom on the entrance side. He was to look for table #20, and Victor would be waiting for him there. David walked toward that part of the room. As he came to the table, a man stepped out from an archway located just before the table and placed his hand on his shoulder. Had he not said his name, David would have fainted.

"David, I am Victor. Don't stop and don't greet me. Simply come with me out those doors at the end of the ballroom."

As they approached the exit door, David noticed a sign that read "Emergency Exit" in both English and Hebrew. Victor advised him that the doors led to the hallway adjoining the outer reception area and it was a less conspicuous way of exiting. The problem was in the smaller writing at the bottom of the sign. It warned against using the door except in an emergency—or an alarm would sound. He watched as Victor passed the last table before the exit. With a slight of hand that David could hardly track visually, Victor removed a butter knife from a place setting. The woman was talking and never saw his hand come and go. *Amazing,* he thought.

Victor slid the blade of the knife inside the locking mechanism and held it there firmly, pressing it against the lock so that the latch was depressed. He then pushed on the emergency bar at the center of the door, and they walked through without an alarm sounding. Victor allowed the door to close as he maintained pressure on the blade, but he slid the handle of the knife around in a circular motion so it was outside the door as it shut. Victor retracted the blade of the butter knife from between the doors and discarded it into a wastebasket in the hallway. Victor led him through another door and down a back staircase that led to the basement and boiler room.

When they reached the basement and Victor was certain they were not being followed, he turned to David and placed both his hands on his shoulders. Victor held him back a few inches and gave him the warmest smile David had seen since he was in Israel. At the relief of his pent up emotional anxiety, David wept. Victor put his arms around him and hugged him, reassuring him that this would all work out and he would be okay.

"They have kidnapped Diane," David blurted out.

"Who is Diane?" Victor asked, realizing he did not have all the facts.

"She is a dear friend who I have known since high school in Ft. Lauderdale and was a student at CMU—the university next door to Pitt. I was going to school at Pitt before I became involved in all of this."

"Okay," Victor again calmed him. "Let's take one small step at a time through this. I brought you here so that we could spend private time together. We will go upstairs in a moment to a café off the lobby. I did not, however, want to do this in the middle of the restaurant!" Victor took a small device from his jacket pocket that looked like a cell phone. He switched it on and began to wave it up and down David's body. There were two lights on the front of the instrument. One was covered in an amber plastic sheath, and the other was red. As Victor passed the instrument over David's body, the one light remained amber in color. Victor switched off the device and placed it back in his jacket pocket. "You are *clean*—no bugs—so we can go upstairs to the café where you can tell me about Diane. I promise to help you, but I will need exacting details to every question I ask."

Chapter Eighteen

The Countdown

There were scrambled messages coming in sequentially on the radio aboard the flagship. Each was encoded, and the radioman simply wrote the codes as they were repeated until the last code number was recorded. He picked up the clipboard and literally ran up the stairs to the bridge and saluted the admiral and the captain.

"This just came in, sir." He extended the clipboard to the admiral. The two commanding officers looked over the coded sheet and handed it back to the radioman.

"Very well, go ahead and decode it. Make sure you do so in total secrecy."

"Yes sir," the radioman replied. After saluting, he left the bridge and returned to his radio room. In all, it took about eight minutes to decode the message, which read as follows:

CODE LEVEL TOP SECRET

To: Flagship

Subject: "Operation Take Down."

Coordinates for interception finalized. Receive on Radio TS at 0200 Hours, Channel 3, No naval vessels to come within 1 mile of target. Disburse all teams at said distance. TOTAL BLACKOUT SHALL BE IN EFFECT.

Secure all hands to battle stations at once. Total radio silence.

Condition: "Code Red."

General Rabene, Operations Commander

At 2:00 a.m. or before, on the night in question, the coordinates of the position of the target freighter would be provided to commence Operation Take Down. The captain told the senior officer of the watch to contact the executive officer and ask him to come to the bridge. From this point on, no intercoms or voice communications could be used aboard the ship.

The captain turned to the admiral and whispered, "Would you like to get some rest, sir, before all hell breaks loose?"

"Yes, thank you. Call me at 0145 hours (1:45 a.m.) so I can be on the Bridge when we arrive at the coordinates."

"I will, Admiral."

The admiral left the bridge, and the captain walked down the few steps to the combat room. He went inside, just as the officer of the watch announced, "The admiral has left the bridge."

"Captain on deck!" someone yelled.

"Go about your business, men, thank you."

The captain walked over to the large glass board, picked up a red marker, and wrote the projected coordinates for interception of the freighter. All eyes were glued to every number he wrote. It was an eerie silence that would occur just before something of great relevance to a battle or an operation was being disclosed for the first time. The captain marked a specific point ahead of the ship's position, just where he thought the ship would be on the tracking chart. He then announced that the projections were his own, and the precise coordinates would be radioed to them at 0200 hours the night of the take down.

The captain replaced the cap on the luminescent marker and returned it to the holder on the board. There was a silence among the men and he looked at everyone in the room, meeting their eyes with a steadfast look of assurance before they went to full battle stations. They were previously at battle readiness and had been on duty for the past twenty-four hours. Although they were allowing most to be relieved every four hours for key crewmembers to get some rest, critical staff could not leave their stations. They could rest at the station with a relief but could not go below. "Gentlemen, we go to battle stations at 0200 hours and will remain there until the operation is carried out tomorrow night.

The captain turned and left, and there was silence in the room. Finally, one of the men asked the watch commander if they were sinking her or boarding her. He did not know. In fact, no one knew except the general, who was flying high overhead.

The freighter was still tracking on course but had slowed to twelve knots. The general thought it was somewhat curious but dismissed it to their getting close to the coastline. It was a matter of hours before Operation Take Down, and the general was just itching to get his hands on that cargo. He was one of the officers who had predicted that she was carrying munitions and guns.

~

Victor sipped the glass of iced tea the waiter placed in front of him, and David was nurturing a glass of ice water while attempting to collect both his composure and his thoughts.

"How are your mother and father?" Victor inquired.

Then it hit him. "Oh no!" he exclaimed aloud. "I was supposed to pick them up at the airport in Tel Aviv. They landed late this morning. I was supposed to pick them up with the rental car . . ." his voice trailed off as though he was totally helpless.

Victor appeared to be concerned at their coming to Tel Aviv at such a time.

"David, control yourself. Your father will assume you were delayed or forgot and will take a taxi into Tel Aviv. He will likely get a hotel room near the university and then attempt to find you, or you will find him first. They are adults and can find their way."

David looked at Victor and shrugged his shoulders, commenting, "What other choice do I have?"

Victor took another sip of tea as the waiter approached to take their orders. Victor ordered a salad with smoked salmon, and David simply wanted a cheese sandwich and a cup of espresso—triple if the cup was large enough. The waiter offered to put the espresso in a regular coffee cup. David was growing weary and needed something to jolt him back to an alert state of mind.

"David, tell me about Diane. When did this all occur, and how did you personally find out?" He waited while David collected his thoughts. Victor was listening to David's every word as he explained the entire "Rajid" story. He recounted how he first met him in the hallway and then his coming back at night and what he told him.

"Do you know where they are holding Diane?"

"Not exactly, but it must be somewhere in Pittsburgh."

"Okay, now tell me again about this list that Rajid gave you before he left the room and eventually disappeared."

"It was a second list that he had in an envelope in his back pocket. It had one sheet of paper in it. According to Rajid, the first list was a decoy, and the real list was the one he handed me. The first was supposed to detract anyone from the real people involved. I assume they suspected I might go to the Israeli authorities."

"Do you have the list with you now?"

"Yes, but they said they would kill Diane if I did not cooperate and do as they said."

"And that was to call all the people on this list after you were notified and reiterate what you were told—except for the last name on the list?"

"That's correct."

"I see," Victor said as though he were deep in thought. He removed a cell phone from one of his jacket pockets and dialed a number.

"Hello, this is Victor. I need you to go through regular channels and find out if a missing persons report was filed on a Diane . . . what's her last name?"

"Kelly," David replied.

"Diane Kelly," Victor continued. "It would have been filed with the Pittsburgh Police Department in Pittsburgh, Pennsylvania, in the States. If there was a report filed I need to know the name of the police officer who is heading up the investigation and what progress they've made in their search for her."

Victor cleared the call and proceeded to make a second one.

"Hello, this is Victor. I need you to inquire at the hotels near the university, probably near Lebanon and Einstein Streets where the student dormitories are situated. I need to know if a Nathan and Rachael Blumberg have checked into one of the hotels. If you locate them, call me back and let me know."

Victor closed the phone and put it back in his pocket. "David, may I please see the list that Rajid gave you?"

"If I give you this list and there is one screw up by *anyone,* I will have sent Diane to her death. I am not about to live with that for the rest of my life. And what about my parents? Rajid mentioned them, and he *knew* they were on their way here. What if he tracks them down and uses them as a back-up bargaining chip?"

"David, you will have to trust me. I was a close friend of your grandfather for many years. I attended his funeral in Florida when he died. Your dad stayed with me when he graduated Yeshiva and came to Israel. When I was at Harry's funeral, I saw you as a mature young man with a promising future—with your whole life ahead of you. I am saddened that you have chosen a different course, but perhaps it is what God has planned for you, and you may even wind up saving thousands of Israeli lives—who knows?"

David thought of the words and remembered that they were almost identical to the speech Elanie had given him back in Pittsburgh. Even Bill Shanks told him the same thing a few nights ago. It was the "saving lives" speech that had gotten him into all of this in the first place. He realized now that he must have been an easy mark. He was a disgruntled Jewish kid whose only burden in life was his wanting to make a difference in the world and not just preach from a synagogue pulpit. He also realized that Victor was quite different than Elanie. He was a Jew and knew his immediate family. Elanie was a lying terrorist who didn't care if he and his family lived or died. Victor interrupted his thoughts at that moment, and David snapped back into reality.

"David, let me tell you a story about the people with whom we are dealing. You have no concept of what really goes on here in the Middle East—the truth, I mean. Your news stations and their journalists, in fact most of the world does not have a clue what the truths are behind the terrorist events that shake the very fiber of our society. David, the radical terrorist organizations involved in getting this ship into safe waters for Palestinian distribution are connected with the same terrorists who were responsible for the Lebanon marine barracks bombing back in 1983. You were just a twinkle in your mother's eye back then, but it was a terrible event. About two hundred Americans were killed—blown up by these radicals, these religious fanatics who believe Allah will reward them with virgins and a place in paradise forever. Their families get money, and they are deemed heroes and martyrs for Islam. In 1992, they attacked our embassy in Argentina, and twenty-nine of our people lost their lives.

We have inside information that this ship is carrying enough munitions to wipe out half of Jerusalem. We also believe that the Iranians are in collusion with this operation. On the Palestinian side, it goes all the way to the PLO top leadership. Hizbollah has been linked to the launching of this ship and co-conspired with the PLO in creating its cover until they picked up the cargo. Some of their most notorious operatives are directly linked to this operation. Like it or not, David, you walked into this—nobody dragged you. Now you have information that could help us not only capture the freighter and its cargo, but some of the terrorists involved in this operation. If we get the ship, we get the cargo. If we do not get the cargo from this ship, and we are right about its content, thousands upon thousands will die as a result. That shipment is headed right for the Gaza and the Palestinian radicals."

David sighed and finally handed the paper with the list of names, to Victor. As Victor took it, he instinctively looked around the café to make sure that they were not being watched. He looked at the list and became very serious.

"David, are you absolutely positive that this man calling himself 'Rajid' told you that the *first* list was the decoy and this was the right list?"

"Yes, that is exactly what he said."

Victor studied the names again for a few more minutes. He took out a pen from his pocket and a small notebook and began copying the names and telephone numbers. He also wrote down the last name on the list, the one with whom David was directed to meet. He double checked the list against his writing, folded the sheet of paper, and handed it back to David. Within the next half hour, they were on their way back to Tel Aviv in Victor's car. His parents had checked into a hotel near the university. Victor noticed that David had finally calmed himself and was chatting away during the entire ride.

Nathan walked around the lobby of the City Hotel while Rachael was using the public rest room. Their luggage sat beside the bellman at the front desk area. Nathan looked into the restaurant and checked the menu that was posted on the wall. It was nearly 2:45 p.m. and they had not had any lunch. He noticed that there was also a coffee shop and decided they would have a sandwich and some coffee before they went upstairs. He thought to himself, *a long hot bath, a nap with Rachael in my arms, and dinner in the dining room when we wake up*. The thought was to calm Rachael from worrying about David. Nathan had a plan and walked back to the front desk and registered, opting for the "deluxe" accommodations with a larger bed than the lower priced rooms. He saw no way that they could get a decent night's sleep in a double bed when they were used to their king-size bed at home. Nathan presented a credit card and signed the registration form.

"Are there many attractions or historic sites that we can visit within walking distance or that are a minimal cab ride away?" Nathan asked.

"Oh, yes, Rabbi Blumberg," the clerk replied. "There are many places for you to visit. There is the Dispora Museum, also known as the Beit Hatefutsot. It chronicles over 2,500 years of exile and Jewish life in different parts of the world. It is something you do not want to miss while you are in Tel Aviv. There is also the Tel Aviv Museum of Art and many other historical sites. You should make ample time to appreciate each one. How long will you be staying with us?"

"About five days, I think, but I am not sure. I want to go to Jerusalem and spend several days there, as well. Do you need to know right now?"

"No, not at all, but as soon as you know it would be appreciated if you advised us."

"I will, of course, and thank you for everything."

Nathan turned to the bellhop and asked that he watch their bags for a little while. As he was speaking to him, Rachael returned and gave him a playful hug. He explained to the bellhop that they had not eaten and were going to the coffee shop. Then he realized that the bellhop could simply take the bags up to the room. *What was I thinking?* Nathan laughed and told the bellhop to take the bags upstairs, handing him a tip.

"We can eat in the café and then go to our room, take a bath or a shower, and get some rest before we go out to find David. That is, if he does not find us in the meantime," Nathan whispered to Rachael. He slid his arm around her waist and guided her toward the coffee shop.

"Good idea. I'm famished."

~

"I asked that you meet me here because it is private and the crew can not hear any of our conversation. What orders do you have from the authority regarding our destination?"

Omar looked at Reuben with inquisitive eyes and asked why he wanted to know.

"Because your orders are about to change, that's why. I do not know how much you were told."

"What are you talking about?" Omar challenged with a tone of total resentment to what he just heard.

"I am the captain of this vessel, and no one gives me orders except..."

Reuben placed a hand over his mouth and demanded that he lower his voice. "You are in a cargo hold, you fool. Your voice is echoing off the steel bulkheads."

Reuben had asked Omar to secretly meet him in the #1 cargo bay at a preset time so that he could speak to him secretly.

Omar reached up and literally pulled Reuben's hand down and forcibly pushed him away.

"When did you receive new orders or any information about our destination?" he challenged.

"Just before I got on the ship in New York. Yael and Elanie know nothing about it. They believe it was a mere twist of fate by Allah that this ship just *happened* to be leaving for the Middle East at the very time we needed to be miles away from the United States."

"Who gave these new directives to you?"

"It was handed to me by our operative in New York who received it directly from a senior PLO authority. It was given to him just before he flew back to New York, less than a day before we left. I had a cell phone number for him that I received from our headquarters. That is how I knew it was authentic. I called him before I signaled a code for all of us to get out of Pittsburgh. I also spoke with him personally just before we boarded the ship. He was waiting for us on the docks and stayed out of sight in the event we were followed. Your ship is "hot," and everyone wants to know why. Whom did you talk to about this cargo?"

"No one, absolutely no one," Omar insisted.

"They know about us, and it could have only been leaked by one person—you."

Omar looked surprised, but he admitted he suspected that one of the crewmembers could be dirty.

"What makes you so sure the Israeli's know about the cargo?" Omar asked.

"Because we have our own Intel and know that there is an alert at sea." The fact is, they know, and no one besides you had the knowledge of this cargo."

"How do you know it was *me?* Are you insane?" Omar cried out.

Reuben turned around and walked a few paces as though he were totally exasperated. He turned again and walked back toward Omar. He was holding a gun with a silencer attached, and it was pointed at Omar's stomach.

"What are you doing—are you crazy? Put that thing away."

Not a sound was heard as Reuben pulled the trigger. The bullet shattered his pelvic bone and splinters from the bone fragments tore through him. The second shot was directly through the heart, killing him instantly.

Reuben looked closely at his face after he drew his last breath.

"I know because *you* told them, traitor. You sold us out like a capitalist American pig."

No one was listening, and Omar was dead. Reuben unscrewed the silencer with a handkerchief. It was still hot as he wrapped it and placed it in his outer jacket pocket. He tucked the gun into his back pants pocket. He walked over to the piles of clothes, grabbed a handful, and threw them on top of Omar's body. He repeated the process until Omar was completely covered beneath old shirts and pants. He knew the smell would attract curiosity in a few days, but in less than twenty-four hours they would be at their destination. Reuben knew that his people would take care of getting rid of the body.

Their own intelligence had warned them that there was activity at sea and that scrambled communications were intercepted between a plane overhead and an aircraft carrier. *It has to be a trap,* Reuben sensed. *I know exactly what we must do,* he thought as he climbed up the ladder from the cargo hold. When he was on deck, he closed the hatch, raised the bolt to slide under the u-shaped clamp, and tightened it down so that the hatch was secure.

When Reuben returned to the bridge, the second mate knew exactly what was happening and when it would occur. He was already on the bridge, waiting for Reuben, and advised the watch that he was now in command of the ship. No one questioned him—not one of the sailors would dare inquire, for they knew that the ship was directly under the control of the Palestinian authorities. To do anything about the present situation would mean a bullet in the head at sea or when they returned to port.

"Send a message to the frequency I gave you that 'Mother is ready to come home,' were Reuben's instructions.

Shariff instructed the man on watch to go to the radio room and give those instructions to the radioman. He then handed him a piece of paper with the radio frequency on it.

How did a man like Omar, who had served so many years, turn against his people? That was the question on the mind of Shariff as he took command of the vessel. No one knew the plan or what was really going on except Reuben. He had heard every detail from the Palestinian Authority's contact in New York just before they sailed.

The details relayed by Reuben were received directly from their operative in New York before Reuben, Elanie, and Yael boarded the ship. He told Reuben that several months ago, while the ship was on a trial voyage and docked for a maintenance check in Yemen, a top-ranking official in Israeli Intelligence had approached Omar. He was cornered and he knew it. They had known about the ship and had a pretty good idea about their plans, although they did not know when or the extent of the cargo. They offered Omar fifty thousand dollars in cash, and a pardon from the entire mess when it was over. All he had to do was inform them of the port from which the final drops were going to be made and the extent of the cargo.

Omar agreed to the deal. He had turned, and gave up his ship, his people, and their cause. For that he had to die, and Reuben was the one assigned to do it. Reuben had a direct line to the top. He was an insider, and Shariff knew it. Reuben was feared, and his word was final. Omar had betrayed them, but he also never knew that the intelligence agent in New York was a double agent. He had received a great deal of cash from both sides every month in exchange for revealing certain details of who was in on this operation on the Israeli side, and who it was that was calling the shots for the final drop on the PLO side. The only problem was that Reuben never knew this.

Reuben glanced at his watch and saw that the sun was going down. He knew he had to advise Elanie and Yael of the plans for that night.

"I am going below now, Captain," Reuben told Shariff and the personnel on the bridge. The former second mate liked his new title of captain and nodded to Reuben as he descended the ladder from the bridge to the upper deck of the ship. The air was chilly, and with sunset on the horizon, he zippered his jacket to the top and pulled it up around his neck. He entered a bulkhead door opening just aft of the rear of the bridge deck. As he did, he turned to close the door and laughed. *I forgot, they took off the steel doors from the passageways.*

There were four cabins on this deck—one vacant and one for each of them. He slowly opened the door to Elanie's cabin and saw that she was sound asleep. Her long tan legs hung over the skimpy bed that looked more like a cradle and mattress. She was covered with a down blanket, and her hair was strewn across the pillow. She was beautiful, he admitted. He had just bent down to kiss her when a gun was in his face, and he jerked backward in shock.

"Oh, I'm so sorry, Reuben . . . forgive me. I heard the door open and I panicked."

Reuben began to laugh and so did she.

"That will teach you to stay in your own cabin," Elanie mused.

"I have something to tell you," he practically whispered and lay down beside her. He leaned on one elbow, facing her, and placed the other hand in front of him, holding one finger over his lips. Elanie drew closer, and he leaned toward her ear.

"Omar is dead. He was a traitor and had made a deal with an Israeli agent. The trouble was he never knew the agent was dirty and fell into a trap. I was ordered to take him out of the picture. I was told that it was possible he had made a deal to tip off the Israelis as to what port we were entering."

"Where is the body?" Elanie whispered.

Her facial expression showed no regret for Omar's death. She had become hardened and very matter of fact about life and death, and Reuben knew she was ready for anything that would be thrown at her. She was a survivor and loyal to the Palestinian cause and honoring the memory of her parents.

It was difficult for Reuben to deal with the reality of his romantic feelings for Elanie. However, he justified these feelings by considering her not to be a blood relative since she was an *adopted* sister. They were told that if they remained pure, there was no reason they couldn't marry. They both agreed to abide by that premise and planned to marry when the shipment was safe in Israel and they could get away together to Europe.

"What are the plans?" she whispered to him as he removed his arm and was about to turn over.

"I will tell you as we go. This way you can't be blamed for anything that goes wrong." Reuben closed his eyes. He had just taken a human life, but he had no trouble falling asleep. Perhaps Elanie was no different than he was or any other terrorist. Human life was cheap—it was all for the *cause*.

~

David watched as Victor removed the kettle of water from the old fashioned, black and white porcelain stove. There were so many chips running along the edges that David wondered if they might be notches for every terrorist Victor had taken out during his career. The kettle appeared to be very old and was singed with black starburst patterns running all around the bottom and up the sides. He poured the boiling water over a teabag in a china teacup on the sink counter. Then he replaced the kettle on the burner and turned off the gas.

"Do you drink tea, David?" Victor asked as he continued to stir the tea bag in the water.

"No, thank you. I've never developed a taste for tea."

They talked for a time, mostly David giving Victor a capsulated version of his young life. Victor apprised him of his feelings regarding the situation, as well as some minute details about his involvement with Mossad and military intelligence. David was captivated by the intrigue of it all and hung on every word of the conversation. Victor also explained to him that he (David) was being set up as a pawn in a very large chess game.

"David, every move is calculated and recalculated. These are not suicide bombers, but highly trained warriors who know all the tricks and schemes of obtaining their objectives. They will stop at nothing to carry out whatever it is that they are planning, and their plan is to dock that ship with its massive amounts of munitions and guns. Believe me, David, this shipment is larger than any arms smuggling operation the PLO has ever attempted.

This is not a ship filled with relief supplies for the Palestinian widows and orphans. A cheap trick, but you bought it just as they knew you would. You are totally inexperienced in this area of deception, and you are filled with values and ideals. They knew this, and that's why they recruited you."

David listened attentively and knew that every word out of Victor's mouth was true.

"Our ideals have been replaced by a life of violence, espionage, secrecy, and counter-terrorism. It is a daily struggle in the simple art of survival. We *are* survivors, David, and we will never lay down for terrorism, or anyone attempting to cut off our entitled presence in a land that was given to us and occupied by us long before the Arabs did."

David nodded in acknowledgement. He was in total awe over the type of life that thousands of Victors have led in the fight to remain free and protect their homeland at any cost. When it came right down to it, Israelis were willing to sacrifice their own lives for the cause of human dignity and religious freedom. Without those enjoyments, there was no life.

"The fact is, David, Jewish roots to this land preceded the Arabs by at least a few thousand years. Did you know that it was Jews who actually settled the city of Medina?"

"No," David replied, being more attentive as he pulled his chair closer to the table. He did not want to miss a single word that Victor had to say: his knowledge of Israel, its history, the Scriptures, and just about any other subject that Victor talked about.

"Before Islam, the city was originally known as Yathrib. When Moham-mad invaded Medina, it began what is known as the seventh century Arab conquest of Arabia. It was during this time in history that our people were nearly eliminated. David, have you ever heard of the Cave of Machpelah?"

David thought for a moment, and his eyes widened. "Yes, isn't that the cave that Abraham purchased?"

"That's correct. It is that cave in which Abraham buried his wife, Sari, when she died. Later, Abraham was also laid to rest there, as well as Isaac, Jacob, and Leah. These were our patriarchs and matriarchs. My point is that we are the people who walked this land long before it was taken from us. What has been regained is actually quite small compared to how things were nearly 4,000 years ago. Your namesake, King David, was the conquer-ing hero of Jerusalem, then known as "The City of David," after the capture of Zion. The entire world is led to believe that we are the invaders and the

Palestinians are the downtrodden. This is our land, David, and we are up against the entire Middle East. Yet we prevail—every single time they try to take away what is ours."

"I know that, Victor, biblically and spiritually. That is one of the reasons I went along with Elanie, Reuben and Yael. I *wanted* to believe I could make a difference."

"Noble, but unrealistic in terms of what you have gotten yourself involved in. You have had no formal training and possess very little knowledge and understanding of what is really going on here. However, should this all work out in our favor, *you* would become the modern-day David who will help put a stop to the Goliaths of terror."

David looked at Victor and for the first time, there was actually a look of humility about him.

"David, I need to make a private phone call, and I will go into the bedroom to do so. When I complete the call, I will have some more definitive information about your role in all of this. I need to find out more about these two lists."

~

Captain Lutz was just finishing dinner as the phone rang, and his wife answered it. Her reaction to whoever the caller was told him that it was official. Hyman Lutz was the section chief for the Tel Aviv police patrol units. It was his job to insure civilian safety by efficiently disbursing his troops when they were needed. The troops served to cordon off or conduct evacuation of any areas within the city where violence was expected. Intelligence would receive bomb threats or have informers or double agents who tipped them off on an intended terrorist attack. They gathered all the information they could, and then it was Captain Lutz who was called to get troops to the area and take action according to the directives given. He had met and served alongside most of the top military officers, but a call from the general drew immediate concern—especially to Mira, his wife.

"Yes, sir. Good evening, General. I am honored, sir."

The general was talking to him from his plane, high above the waters of the sea. He listened as the general told him he must be ready to deploy troops at a moment's notice and cordon off the piers at the waterfront. "Which ones, sir?" was his question.

"All of them," General Rabene stated. "No one goes in, and certainly no one comes out. Deploy all the men necessary to accomplish that once the order is given. This is a high priority as well as a top secret operation, and no one is to talk to anyone outside of the usual chain of command."

"I understand, sir. It will be carried out as you ordered."

"Very well, thank you. Keep in mind, however, that you will only have minimal notification to deploy your men."

"I understand, sir," Hyman replied.

The general said goodbye, and the call ended. Hyman looked at his wife and shrugged his shoulders.

"Why would General Rabene call you himself and not have a junior officer make that call?" his wife questioned. Hyman thought about it for a moment, knowing that a top-secret project meant absolutely no information was to be given to spouses.

"Who knows?" He shrugged his shoulders again, dropping the matter entirely. Mira knew exactly what that meant—don't ask.

The red phone on the night table beside his bed was a direct line used to forward calls from military intelligence to the prime minister's home. Any calls to this phone were also scrambled in the event of satellite eavesdropping. There were only three callers who could be patched through to this line at any time, day or night, without question. One was General Saul Rabene; second was the admiral; and the third belonged to General Sam Zeitler of Aman, Office of Military Intelligence. The phone rang, and the prime minister answered it before the second ring. It was a conference call including all three men. General Rabene began speaking first.

"Mr. Prime Minister, from new intel in the past hour, we believe that the ship will be in range of optimal striking conditions near 2:00 a.m. The young man who was recruited in the States, David Blumberg, has a list of contacts that Ross got to us through the embassy. David was instructed to call the list of names first, but then go in person to advise the last person, who is none other than Abdul Abdawah. He will be waiting to give the signal to eleven fishing boats that he has paid to disburse the cargo into several areas. We don't yet know which areas, though we suspect most will end up on the West Bank. We also believe that a portion of the arms and ammunition for those arms are slated for several terrorist training camps."

"It appears that you have this under control?" the prime minister questioned.

"Not exactly, Mr. Prime Minister. Ross called me less than an hour ago after he received a call from Victor. It seems that there is a second list with different names and telephone numbers, and Abdawah is *not* the final person on that new list."

"Who is?" the prime minister asked.

"Sir, it is Jamas, the Palestinian naval commander."

"That's what they would like us to think, since it's an at-sea operation. However, the second list could be a ploy to distract us from the primary list. Palestinian procurement would usually have no actual part in a high-seas mission. It's a clever ploy, but not overly brilliant. PLO procurement purchased the ship and ultimately its cargo. In the past, the PLO used procurement to seed purchasing funds to Hizbollah. Iranian factions would be paid cash for guns and ammunition. No legitimate trace on the weapons could be made, and the Hizbollah agents would smuggle those guns into Palestinian territories. Perhaps we have a simple repeat of their past tactics and we are looking too hard for what is obvious. The second list is likely to have an assassin assigned to kill the boy. Do we know for sure, beyond any doubt, that the cargo is what we suspect it is?" the prime minister questioned.

"No sir, not absolutely. However, the probability is very high that it's weapons."

"Very well. Keep me informed, regardless of the hour. My guess is that the first list is the true list." The prime minister hung up his phone.

~

Victor left out the part about Diane being held hostage by Palestinian extremists. He did not want anyone to know until he heard back from several contacts in Pittsburgh. If he could locate Diane's whereabouts through his CIA contacts in Philadelphia, he vowed to get David and his family out of Israel. He was retiring in a month and did not need the death of a friend's grandson on his conscience. He was even beginning to grow fond of David, something he never allowed himself to do about *anyone,* in all the years he served the government. He had lost far too many friends and relatives in the battle for Israel's total freedom. There were enough ghosts floating around from his past, but this one would not become one of them.

~

Diane had no sense of time. Night was day, and day was night.

There were no windows in the room she was in. She was not permitted to remove her blindfold except for the times that she was allowed to use the bathroom, and it had to be replaced before she opened the door. They untied her hands from behind her back and took off the ropes that were on her ankles. They had become sophisticated in the past twenty-four hours, although Diane was sure they were first-timers at kidnapping. A single video monitor had been set up in the room, and they no longer had to bind her or check on her every half hour. She was being monitored on a fifteen-inch portable television screen that sat on the hastily made wooden table that her captors sat around each day. The men talked, continuously went out for pizza, drank large bottles of soda and basically attempted to keep themselves amused as best they could. Diane knew this from both their conversations and the fact that she was getting the same food to eat—but surely less of a portion than they were eating. There was one catch to their act of kindness, however. If she removed the blindfold or attempted to escape, she would be shot. They were most convincing, and Diane had no intention of finding out if they really meant it. She felt that they were not out to really harm her.

Lying there on the floor, hour after hour, straining to listen to voices in the next room was wearing thin on her tolerance, and usually there wasn't much she couldn't deal with. She had no idea how much longer it would be and could not understand why the police were not searching abandoned warehouses. She must have been reported as missing by now. CMU would have called her mother in Florida to ascertain if she possibly had gone home. Her mother would be devastated and would likely take the next plane to Pittsburgh right away. If only she knew where she was and who these men actually were. She also thought that surely Susan, once revived, would have reported the incident if she was not being held hostage as well.

~

It took about two hours of explanations and answering questions before Nathan and Rachael were not even remotely up to date with the complexities of their son's life. David had decided to tell them everything. He met them at the hotel, and after heartwarming hugs and a joyful reunion, he asked them to accompany him to the café so he could explain everything and get something to eat. Victor advised him that at any time until this was over, something could occur that might place his parents in harm's way. How would they know what to watch out for, what to be cautious about, or how to protect themselves if the terrorists came after them?

Rachael was in total denial that this was what their son had gotten himself into. David felt no sense of remorse or shame. He insisted that he did not knowingly come to Israel to become a flunky in some terrorist's plan.

"I had to find my own destiny, a purpose for my life. This is only a single journey towards finding that purpose. I promise you'll soon understand."

David became silent and gave his parents a chance to ask a question or make some kind of remark. They both sat there, eyes fixed on David, and their expressions were of utter disbelief. During their conversation in which David did almost all of the talking, Nathan sat with his arms folded and never moved from that position. He stared intently at his son and did not even raise an eyebrow or crease his brow in a frown or look of curiosity.

Now that David had paused for a moment, Nathan stopped staring at him and reached for a glass of water. As his hands clasped the moist cold glass, his hand began to shake ever so slightly, indicating the nervousness he was experiencing. His calmness had now ceased, and the fear of what might happen to David began to clutch his heart. There was also no question that Nathan had just heard the details of a situation that he would never have believed possible. This was not hearsay or someone spinning a tale for a novel. This was coming from their son's own lips. Nathan took another sip of water and cleared his throat.

"David, I understand your zeal in wanting to do something heroic and useful with your life, but I believe you have no idea of what you're actually dealing with here."

Rachael looked into his eyes and drew her chair closer to her son.

"David, the struggle between Palestinian or Arab and Jew has been going on for thousands of years. In all the plans, the talks, the truces and cease-fires, the results have always been the same. A lot of people die and many of them innocent bystanders—just like you. They are blown apart or shot to death. Those who thought peace was in the making drop their guard and make foolish mistakes. They are the casualties of the peace talks. They also bear the heartbreak when fighting or terrorist bombings resume all over again—when the peace talks break down. Do you think your father and I do not know anything about the Middle East?"

David was seriously considering his mother's words, and Rachael knew that she was getting through to him. Nathan did not know what to say, a perfect indication that he was totally overwhelmed by all of this. *How could my son get himself involved with seasoned assassins and terrorists?* Nathan thought. None of this made any sense, and he was already tuning out the conversation and looking off into the streets of Tel Aviv outside the café window. It was at that moment that a car pulled up to the curb practically right in front of the window where they were seated. A man emerged from the back seat and peered into the restaurant. Nathan was seated at one end of the table, Rachael at the other end, and David at the facing seat in the middle. The man stared straight into the café. Nathan watched him curiously and thought that he looked familiar.

It's Victor, Nathan realized. He turned to David.

"Didn't you say that Victor's driver dropped you off at the hotel?"

"Yes, I see Victor here now. He must have come to see you and Mom." David waved, but through the glare, Victor could not see him. He walked into the hotel entrance and came directly into the café, standing next to David with a big, warm smile.

"Hello, Nathan. You've gotten a little older since Yeshiva." Nathan stood and smiled at Victor, and the two men embraced.

"Please, sit with us Victor, have a coffee. . . . no, a tea!"

"You remembered after all these years?"

"Of course, how could I forget? You served it with every meal. I couldn't even find one single scoop of coffee in the whole apartment!" They all laughed.

Victor turned toward Rachael.

"Here we are, talking about us while your beautiful bride is sitting here. I have not seen Rachael but twice—the photograph you wore out when you came to Israel almost twenty years ago and, of course, at Harry's funeral. Hello, Rachael." Victor extended his hand, took Rachael's, and held it while he smiled a knowing smile that Nathan had made the right choice.

"Hello, Victor. I am so glad to see you again. The last time I saw you I was not very conversational. David told us about your meeting with him, but he refused to tell us any of the details. Victor, what could possibly be happening that should involve our son?"

Victor glanced over at David and released Rachael's hand. He pulled the empty chair out and sat down. Nathan leaned forward and had his elbows practically in the middle of the small café table, as though Victor was about to reveal some incredible spy plot. Victor signaled the waiter and when he approached, asked for a cup of tea and a glass of water. The waiter acknowledged and returned shortly with his tea.

"I can't think without my cup of tea," Victor stated, and David smiled a knowing smile. After the tea and water were set down in front of Victor and he had sufficiently pressed every last ounce of tea from the bag, he took a sip and looked up into Nathan's eyes. The explanation took nearly an hour. When Victor had finished, his parents didn't know if they should rejoice or cry for their son's seemingly heroic act. However, it did not alleviate their fear for his life.

~

There were voices shouting orders and the sound of gunshots that echoed through the walls. Diane's body jerked in spasms as the sounds woke her from a deep sleep. She jumped to her feet and instinctively ran to the far corner of the room. She knew where it was because she walked the perimeter of the tiny room practically all night long so that she would sleep during the day. She wanted to sleep while they were awake and then stayed awake while her captors were sleeping. This way, she would not have to overhear the vulgarities and blasphemous humor coming from the other room. Previously she had strained to hear every word. Now she could care less. She wanted out of this. The shouting continued, but they were American voices.

"Keep your arms in front of you and face toward the floor. Don't even think about flinching even once or we'll kill you."

My God, Diane thought, *is it the police? It has to be the police!*" That was her last thought before the door burst open and a man declared,

"FBI, miss. You're safe."

Her hands were outwardly poised in front of her as if to ward off any bullets. Now she instantly moved her hands to her face as she began to sob uncontrollably.

They were sobs of relief, thankfulness, and the reality that it was over. The man who burst into the room was holding a gun with his right hand, and he slowly removed Diane's blindfold with his left, dropping his gun hand to his side. The light from the clear bulb in the ceiling socket was extremely bright, but her eyes quickly adjusted.

"Thank you, thank you, God bless you," she sobbed. She almost threw her arms around the man in the suit before her. He was FBI Agent Steve Sims of the Langley, Virginia Office. He had been in Philadelphia on another assignment. He and six other agents had overwhelmed her four captors before they could even draw their weapons. The shots she had heard were fired into the air to immediately convince her captors that they meant business. Simms shifted her to his right arm after he holstered his weapon, and slowly walked with her toward the outside warehouse. As she walked into the light of the warehouse, Diane saw her captors being handcuffed and their faces in the dirt. They appeared so very helpless, four young men who had threatened to kill her just a short time ago.

"They are cowards, ma'am," one of the men called to her as he clicked the handcuffs tighter. The man beneath him omitted a squeal of pain.

"Miss, why don't you come over here and tell these cowardly excuses for men what you really think of them," the husky agent encouraged. Simms looked at Diane and dropped his arm. He noticed that beneath all that dirt and the dirty streaks from her tears she was a very attractive young woman, and he smiled at her warmly. He also saw that her blouse was badly torn, and he removed his jacket and draped it around her shoulders. Diane thanked him with a soft smile of gratitude.

She walked forward and stood near the four men, who now looked rather pathetic.

"Turn your faces toward that girl, you cowards. She has something to tell you," Simms commanded.

Burns, another agent, was standing guard over them with an automatic weapon. He turned to the other two beside him and asked if they wanted odds on her *not* getting physical against any of them.

"How do you know?" one of the two asked as another agent drew closer to the men on the ground.

"I know because she has a presence about her of non-aggression and a look of pity more than hate. She's got to be a believer."

"Oh, I forgot, you're a Christian—and you know this from just looking at her? I'll go ten to five against that poetic, spiritual conclusion." The other men stated they were in on the bet. They did it in whispers, and Diane never heard them.

The four men on the ground turned toward her and she looked each one of them as she circled around them.

"'I pity all of you, not just your ignorance, but the ignorance of your parents and the parents who teach their children hate instead of love. I pity you because you will close your eyes one day after taking your last breath and realize that you have been lied to. There are no virgins waiting for you, no mansions or eternal rewards—just the flames of hell, eternal punishment for taking lives and hating without any real justification except for hate itself."

Tears streaming down her face formed more white lines over the smears of dirt already staining her cheeks.

"You don't deserve to be American citizens and should be stripped of every right and deported back to the Middle East. I pity you, and I'm sure you'll have ample time to think about your lives that you've just locked up behind bars so you won't do this to anyone else."

She turned away from them and walked toward the open door. As she did, she felt the winter air, cold and damp. But it changed the stale, ware-house smell in her nostrils to the fresh breath of freedom.

The agent by the door stepped aside and looked up at Simms. He shook his head and he took another few steps to the right so that the door was open to her as she slowly walked through and into the night air of Pittsburgh. It was cold, and she only had Simms's jacket around her shoulders, but she did not shiver. The Lord had carried her through this, and she was grateful. Her eyes closed, her head tilted heavenward, and her lips began to move ever so slightly in prayer. When Simms came outside, he watched as her arms began lifting upward. In the reflection of the single light overhead, he imagined he saw an angel. He nodded his head as his tough heart was softened by joy for the first time in a long while. This was one of the more pleasant endings he had experienced in his young career.

The other agents were coming out now, leading the men in handcuffs to the awaiting black SUV trucks parked on the other side of the building. They all looked at Diane praying in the winter cold, her hands still uplifted. Every one of them nodded to each other as if to say, "This is one I will always remember."

Burns reminded them of their bet! Simms finally walked over to her as she opened her eyes and looked at his face.

"You saved my life, and I don't even know your name."

"Oh, I'm sorry, Diane—I know yours. I thought I told you. My name is Agent Steve Simms."

"It is wonderful to meet you, Agent Simms."

Diane threw her arms around him and kissed him on the cheek. She looked right into his eyes and whispered,

"May God bless you and keep you."

Steve smiled. When she dropped her hands, he placed his arm around her shoulders and escorted her toward one of the waiting cars.

"We'll need you to come with us to Langley, Virginia. We have already flown your mother there, and she is waiting for you. You're a lucky girl. We weren't sure if they would have allowed you to leave there alive."

"I know, I thought of that, but I am also a blessed girl. I had company and strength all the time I was there."

She smiled a knowing smile as Simms opened the car door for her, and she slid into the front passenger seat of the black SUV.

~

The embassy radio had been silent most of the night while its operator, Bill Simmits, sat in his chair with his feet up on the desk. His ear was tuned to the radio, listening for any semblance of a single crackle of the broadcast he was waiting for. He was a bodyguard and the head of security at the embassy. He had served twelve years as a marine M.P. and was shot in the line of duty in Lebanon on a policing operation. Lebanese thieves had been pilfering the supply depots so they could sell American goods on the black market. Government-issued goods were a very real commodity in any war zone area where there was nothing left of value. The supplies brought in by the army and marines (usually boots, blankets, helmets, socks, and anything in the way of rations or candy) brought a high dollar on the black market.

Any one of the locals were willing to risk their life to get into one of the supply houses and get out with an armload of stolen goods. The trick was not winding up with a bullet for the effort. Military police were ordered to treat *any* non-military personnel found on the base as suspected terrorists. After the Beirut attack, kindness was a forgotten virtue.

Simmits had been on security patrol the night two men decided they were going to try their hand at robbing one of the supply depots. The major difference this time was that they were armed. For the most part, it was common knowledge that they were just smalltime thieves who were trying to get a day's pay out of a wool army blanket or pair of army green socks.

Maybe that's why Simmits never even drew his weapon when he cornered one of these men in the base storeroom. There was only one, and he ordered the intruder to put down the stolen goods and place his hands in the air. He never saw it coming but the man had a small caliber weapon in his belt. From where he was standing behind a pile of boxes, he never saw the gun.

After a small steel plate was surgically placed in his skull, a Bronze Star and a Purple Heart, Simmits received a one-way ticket to Washington. Once there, he received a security assignment to be at the side of the ambassador to Israel while he was visiting the president. There was a top-level meeting in the Oval Office concerning the Israeli-Palestinian crisis, and Simmits was at the ambassador's side at all times. When the ambassador met with the president, it was Simmits standing side-by-side with the marine guards on the other side of the closed doors. The ambassador grew fond of him, but mostly felt safe with Simmits and made the offer for the security job in Israel.

Simmits suddenly heard a break in the radio silence as a coded message was repeated twice. He looked at his watch and began to line up the encrypted letters and numbers of the transmission. Beneath his desk was a single button that had a wire running through the wall. He pressed the button on the buzzer three times in short succession. Several minutes later, the ambassador and Bill Shanks came through the door. Simmits stood out of respect, although the ambassador always motioned for him to sit down.

"Sir, I've received this coded message from General Rabene."

Astor nodded at Shanks as both he and Simmits walked over to a wall and removed the picture of the president to reveal a small wall safe. Shanks turned around as Simmits turned the combination two times. Then Simmits turned away, and Shanks dialed in the final numbers, opening the safe. A single plastic envelope containing a sheet of paper was removed and handed to Simmits. The message was decoded within five minutes and handed to Ambassador Astor.

"They did it, they got the girl—she's safe. They escorted her back to CMU, allowed her to shower and change, and took her to an all-night diner. After they all ate, they flew her to Langley for debriefing. She was tired and dirty but unharmed."

"Good news, Mr. Ambassador," Simmits beamed, and Astor asked him to call him Joel when no one was around.

"I am sure that Victor will be pleased, as well as the young Jewish lad who can now go home. However, the intelligence boys want to debrief him for a day or so before he leaves the country. I understand his parents came to Tel Aviv?"

"Yes sir, they did, and Victor met with them."

"Let's get this good news to them and get some rest."

"Sir, in all due respect, may I suggest waiting until later—just to be sure he is not actually needed in some way to contact anyone on that list they gave him? It could hurt the entire operation if he walks away too early in the final hours. It's only another day."

"I agree," was the response from the ambassador.

With that said, the ambassador turned around and walked out of the room, bidding them a job well done as he closed the door behind him.

~

Reuben held on to Elanie as they both clung to the side of the berth bed. The ship was bow-first into gale-force winds that had come out of nowhere. The captain was at the helm and steered the bow *into* the storm to avoid being hit broadside by twenty-foot swells. A giant swell coming over the decks could carry away the ship's stacks, flooding the engine room and boilers, and she would go down quickly. The new captain however, had steered many ships through wicked storms as a first mate.

The bow rose with the swells and slammed down with a huge thud that echoed through the hull. The vibration was so powerful that it felt as though the hull would split wide open from bow to stern with each new pounding. Elanie became violently ill, as it was her first time at sea in a major storm. Reuben had been at sea several times. He had his sea legs well planted on the deck of the cabin floor as he filled a glass of water for her.

Yael was on the bridge, keeping an eye on the new captain. He had made some excuse that he could not sleep and asked if he could ride out the storm on the bridge. The view was really great from the watch stations, and he assured the captain that he would not bother anyone. He was only there because Reuben told him to be there. They could not trust a man who would help them execute Omar. Reuben finally told Yael what had happened.

No honor among thieves, Yael thought as he strapped himself in an observation chair. He actually thought that the huge swells crashing over the deck were beautiful in a powerful way. Living in the desert for so long allows one to appreciate the sea, even in its fury.

The admiral studied the course markers on the board and saw that there was a slight irregularity in the tracking of the freighter. He went to the radiomen's desk and took the clipboard with the weather reports at sea by longitude and latitude, searching for their approximate position. He immediately saw that there was a major storm in the area of the ship. *Perhaps she will sink in the storm and save us a lot of trouble,* he thought to himself as he walked out.

The officer of the watch announced, "The admiral has left the deck."

This relaxed all hands on duty, and they simply went about their work. Some of them even cracked a joke, and a faint chuckle replaced the barking of details, locations, and the seriousness of the watch. The admiral went to the mess deck and entered the officer's mess hall.

The captain entered right after the admiral, and the two men began planning the coming night's operation. The admiral had brought a chart of the area where they planned to engage the freighter.

"I make it to be between 12:20 and 1:00 a.m. when we will be in the exact position to carry out our mission. I'll update the previous message that called for a 2:00 a.m. broadcast of coordinates. Weather reports show calming seas and a quarter moon, so there won't be very much light. Since we are already at full-dress battle stations, we'll relax the men for a few hours until we get to right about here . . ." and the admiral pointed to a specific location on the chart.

"I would like the men to be reminded that any sound, anyone dropping a tool, or any metal object could send a sonar-detectable sound to the freighter. Our guns will be within range at that time, and we'll be prepared to sink her if the signal is given by the general."

"I understand, Admiral. I fully agree, but as of yet, I do not know the whole plan."

"Don't feel left out, my friend. Neither do I, since Rabene is calling the shots on this one. He will also be the one to implement the raid by the commando units from the helicopters if that's what he decides to do. It will likely be a last-minute call. They want to insure that there are no crew-members on deck who might warn the others or set-off any explosives if the ship is rigged and ready to incinerate the cargo, crew, and our men who board her. We are not taking any chances with this one. It will be done by the book, but not by all the rules."

Chapter Nineteen

Operational Events

The conversations had all been positive, and David was grateful for Victor esteeming him to his parents the way he did. His father seemed resolved not to meddle in David's plans or attempt to sway him from his convictions. His mother, however, was upset, as David expected she would be. She feared the possible loss of her only son. Victor drove David back to the campus and waited until he was safely in his room. His father said he would pick him up in the morning and they would all go sightseeing together. Sleep came quickly, and the night passed like a momentary blur as the morning sun shone brightly upon the winter-chilled land of the Chosen People.

~

Several key leaders of the Palestine Authority sipped their strongly brewed coffee in small cups and talked quietly among themselves. It was early morning when Abdul Abdawah walked into the conference room at PLO headquarters. The others became silent as he greeted them and sat down at the head of the conference table.

"We have a situation that has just been made known to me," Abdawah began. "We must decide how to handle this before I apprise our leader. We should also render a suggested solution. Apparently, one of our own agents approached Reuben before he boarded the ship and declared that Omar was a traitor. He cited our office's authority to assassinate Omar once they were at sea."

The four men in the room immediately expressed shock and dismay over this news. Omar was a loyal and trusted officer of the Palestinian Authority, having served for over twenty-five years in their leaders own Fattah group. It was not Omar who was the traitor but rather the agent. Abdawah went on with the briefing.

"It seems that less than eight hours before Reuben arrived in New York, our man was cornered by federal agents and arrested for espionage. He was threatened with spending the rest of his life in prison. They never actually took him to jail or to a place of interrogation. They had him in the back seat of a car and made a deal with him. He could become a double agent and work with them, or he would take him directly to a prison facility where he would never see the light of day again. They also told him that he could even be executed. Espionage carries the death penalty, and they had more than enough proof to convict him. His life, freedom, and money were the lures that he could not refuse. After all, he was on American soil.

He was then turned over to a CIA operative who took him handcuffed into a warehouse on the dock and further threatened him by showing him pictures of his wife and children in Gaza. They would be dead before he could escape back to the Middle East if he did not do exactly as he was told.

Our agent, who after accepting the deal from the Americans along with an undisclosed sum of money, became a double agent. He was to bribe the second mate and turn him as well—also for an undisclosed sum of cash. We do not know for sure that the second mate believed the double agent, or went along with all of this to gain his captain's bars.

It is thought that a faction of the CIA set up the entire plan. They were working with the Israeli authorities, and one of their own men, a Mr. Ross, is headquartered at the United States Embassy in Tel Aviv. As of now, we have no reliable information as to what the intentions of this second mate are in conjunction with this operation. He is now the captain of the ship and can do whatever he pleases, including putting into a port that has been pre-arranged by the CIA and Israeli Intelligence. Reuben was told that not only was Omar a traitor, but that the second mate was planted there by our office to take over the ship after Reuben carried out his orders of killing Omar."

Abdul went deeper into the facts by presenting the entire plan to the group, beginning with the purchase of the ship. They were not previously told so that if this plot were to be discovered, not one of these known leaders would be linked to the operation.

"Our plan was to sail this freighter around the Middle East from port to port, picking up various cargos of food, clothing, grains, and appearing totally legitimate. Eventually the ship would make its way to the United States where we would load a large cargo of surplus clothing. We would sail the ship to Yemen and unload the cargo, establishing the ship's international legitimacy. We registered the ship as a Lebanese freighter carrying and distributing humanitarian aide throughout the Middle East. I personally arranged the purchase of the freighter. She is now returning from her second voyage to the United States. The ship was to take on two cargo loads. The second cargo that was loaded on top would hide the first cargo. There would be thousands of pieces of clothing for widows and children in war-torn areas.

Both these cargos were to be supplied by another freighter that would rendezvous with our ship about ten miles off the coast. Since we would be in international waters, no one could interfere with the transfer. They would unload the main cargo ship to ship and then the clothes to cover that cargo." He stopped and sipped a glass of water.

"When they arrived in the United States, customs would find nothing but clothing, accounted for on forged papers and contributed at another port. The ship's itinerary would state that they were in New York to pick up even more clothing that was being contributed by two legitimate, Lebanese-owned clothing manufacturers.

United States Customs would not sift through thousands of pounds of bundled clothing. They might prod, but our main cargo would be buried at least ten to fifteen feet deep."

He paused once again, as though concentrating on the precise facts.

"The plan was almost infallible, but none of us foresaw anyone turning. Reuben was not supposed to be aboard, but it seems that the timing of being discovered in Pittsburgh and this incident could be interpreted as no more than coincidental. We believe that it was a set-up by the CIA. It had to be, but we are not absolutely sure. That is where we stand at the moment."

The leaders began to ask questions and appeared annoyed that they had not been apprised of these events before now. The ship was due to dock the next day. Now, if the second mate was turned and was running the ship, how could they be sure that he was not going to order his crew to overpower Reuben? He could simply denounce him as the one who killed Omar and a traitor. He could have Reuben locked-up in a stateroom along with Yael and Elanie, and possibly even kill them as traitors and toss their bodies over the side.

He could then dock the ship at a port prearranged by Israeli intelligence. The discussions, proposals and counter-proposals went on for most of the morning. The chairman was attending an international peace conference with various leaders from the United States and Israel. He could not leave the meeting or even appear to be involved in any way with this operation. They would have to come up with a plan and make sure it was one that would insure the success of this mission. The second mate of course, fully intended to keep his deal secretive and simply spend the CIA's money and enjoy his freedom. He knew he could never step foot on American soil again and would have to watch his back, but he was still loyal to the PLO. If he brought the ship in safely, he would be the new captain.

~

Inside the main offices of the Sayeret Matkal, Arri Ben Joseph was reading a coded message from General Rabene. This was the most elite of the special operations forces. For many years they handled operations that were deemed almost impossible. Their main function was counter-terrorism, and they were the best of the best. Each man was highly trained in the most up-to-date aspects of warfare and tactical operations. This was the group that turned out nearly every Israeli leader. General Rabene was also a part of this group many years before, as well as the former and present prime ministers of Israel. They were now being briefed on the operation in the event the freighter somehow slipped past the intended trap and made it to a sympathetic port. The Israelis vowed that this ship would never off-load her cargo. Everyone, every team member on and off duty was available and ready to go if called upon.

~

The day at hand left David somewhat apprehensive. No one had contacted him, and as far as he could figure, the ship must surely be close to Israeli waters. They had breakfast at the crack of dawn, and then Nathan wanted to drive to Jerusalem, though David wasn't sure that he would be able to enjoy the trip.

It had been nearly nineteen years since Nathan had stood before the temple wall and prayed. He joked about the rapid passing of time and toyed with Rachael and David over finding the piece of paper he stuffed into the wall when he was there. Rachael returned his humor by telling him that if he wanted to find the paper, he would have to dig through nearly nineteen years of other papers stuffed in on top of it, and she was not ready for an archeological dig! They all laughed and were in a far better mood than when they were filled with apprehension and fear over David's well being.

They approached the border and slowed as they saw an Israeli barricade and soldiers searching the cars. Nathan remarked that he thought there were a lot of soldiers on the road for a chilly winter's morning. Nathan was worried about the time, as he thought they might have to have David back in Tel Aviv by that evening. They handed over their passports for inspection to an officer who came out from the small border patrol building. Looking at David and his passport picture several times, he then asked Nathan to pull the car over to the side. All of them were to accompany the officer inside the building.

"Is there anything wrong?" Nathan questioned with a tone of slight anxiety.

"No sir, not at all. If you are the Blumberg family, I have been asked to escort you to our senior officer. It appears that there is an urgent message for your son and for you, as well."

Nathan complied with the officer's request and pulled the car off to the side of the road near the entrance to the small building. They exited the car and followed the officer inside the building and down a small hallway to an office at the end of the corridor. He knocked and opened the door, motioning for them to go inside. A tall man in green fatigues was standing behind his desk, waiting for all three of them to enter.

Nathan saw a beret tucked neatly into his left shoulder strap. Both shoulder straps displayed a gold star. *A general?* Nathan thought. Nathan moved closer to the desk to allow David to enter behind Rachael.

"Shalom, Rabbi Blumberg, Mrs. Blumberg, and our young American hero, David. I am General Arri Ben Joseph. I came to this station to intercept you before you continue on into Jerusalem."

Nathan introduced Rachael and then asked the general why he called his son an "American hero."

"Please, be seated. Would you like some coffee or tea, or perhaps a cold drink?"

"Yes," Rachael spoke up, "I would love a hot chocolate.

"Of course, I will be happy to accommodate you. And what may I get for you, Rabbi? Perhaps something for yourself or for you, David?"

"No, thank you," they both answered.

The general picked up the phone and ordered a hot cocoa to be brought in.

"Rabbi, as you well know by now, your son is involved in this major cargo operation, which, I must inform you, is labeled top secret. This means that you are not privileged to ever discuss or divulge a single word of anything you have learned about this operation, now or within the next day or so. We must have your assurance that you will comply with these instructions."

Nathan looked at Rachael and then to David, and they all nodded affirmatively.

"You have my word and the word of my family."

The general smiled and thanked them.

"David, have you informed your parents about your friend from school,

Diane Kelly at CMU in Pittsburgh?"

"No, I did not."

With that said, Rachael turned to David with a shocked expression.

"What about Diane—what happened, David, and why didn't you tell us?"

"I could not tell you because I was not sure myself until I saw you and Dad. I only knew that it was someone close to me and it was a woman. I was threatened that if I did not want to see any harm come to her, I had better do as I was told."

The general interrupted any reply by Rachael.

"Excuse me, Mrs. Blumberg. David was following orders of silence and secrecy—from both sides. David, Diane is safe. She was rescued last night by an American FBI team from an abandoned warehouse. She is presently in debriefing at Langley. She is unharmed. She needed only a long, hot shower, a decent meal, and some sleep."

David's tears of relief turned into convulsive sobs, and his shoulders began to tremble. Rachael got up and put her arms around her son to comfort him. Nathan simply shook his head in disbelief at any of this being a reality. He thought that he might just wake up and realize it was all a bad dream.

"How was she involved in all of this?" Nathan asked.

"She was used as a back-up—a guarantee, if you will—that David would do what he was told to do. If he didn't, they threatened to kill her."

"My God!" Rachael cried out and held David even tighter.

After David had sufficiently drained several days of explosive emotions, the general provided them with details about the rescue operation. There was, however, a caveat to all of the good news. They still wanted David to make the calls on the first list.

"Absolutely not," Rachael ordered and looked to Nathan for support.

"Mrs. Blumberg," General Arri broke in. "Please, sit down, drink your cocoa, and allow me just a few minutes to explain some things to you."

Nathan nodded to Rachael and they both waited until they heard what the Israeli General had to say, before drawing any conclusions.

Reuben waited for the radioman to conclude the encoded message sent to the freighter. It was for his eyes only. The first message demanded that he be called to the radio room when the formal message was sent. Reuben was trained for decoding messages from the Palestinian Authority, and he was to instruct the radioman to leave the room while he did. He waited until the man left and settled into a chair behind the radio. He took a pencil and a piece of paper and waited. It was but moments later that the message was transmitted. Sounding more like a weather report than a message, he recorded every word, striking lines through letters as he counted from the first letter through each consecutive letter of all the words. The string of words was simply run-on letters and numbers that after decoding represented new orders and a latitude and longitude location.

Reuben was also told that he was in danger and that his new captain was a traitor. Reuben had been set up, and his leaders knew it. He must eliminate the second mate *only* after he has brought the ship to a destination provided for in the message. Once they reached the specified destination, Reuben was to assassinate him. Then a new captain would be brought aboard to guide the ship to a location where the cargo could be safely off-loaded.

Reuben looked at the word "some" for several moments and decoded it again to make sure he was reading it correctly. Some? What about the rest of the cargo? Reuben followed orders. He realized now that it was a set up by the CIA. They weren't going to arrest them—they had needed him to kill Omar so that the turncoat, the second mate, could steer the ship to a port where the entire Israeli Army would likely be waiting for them. He felt sick for a moment that he had killed Omar, knowing his background and years of service to their people. *I should have known,* he told himself. But he realized all he could do now was obey his orders. It wasn't his fault and Elanie and Yael would agree . . . but should he tell them?

Reuben located a book of matches in the desk drawer. There was a metal ashtray that was bolted to the steel desk. That way, in rough seas, no one had to worry about the ashtray falling into the papers all over the floor and setting the radio room on fire. Reuben tore the message into pieces and then lit the small pile until it was burning in the center of the ashtray.

Taking a clean sheet of paper, he wrote a new code that was decoded as, "New Orders, Palestinian Authority," with the new coordinates written out. Reuben made sure that the previous papers were burnt ashes with no traces of writing. He took the second sheet of paper with the coordinates and tucked it in his pocket and left the radio room. He climbed the ladder to the bridge and explained the new orders. The captain ordered the change of course and full speed ahead on the new heading.

~

"She is changing course, sir," the second lieutenant announced.

"Someone get the admiral right away," the commander of the watch ordered.

A seaman bolted for the door and headed up to the bridge. The admiral was in the control room within minutes.

"What's going on?" he asked. He was shown the change in course of the freighter, now tracking on a new heading that would take the ship over ten miles from their originally projected interception point.

"What are they doing?" he wondered aloud and began to examine the charts for the area she appeared to be headed towards.

"If she steams at seventeen knots, she will be in this area," pointing to the chart as the captain looked on. He had arrived within a few moments of the admiral.

"It completely changes our plans, as she will be within sight of the coastal cities. We could never fire upon her that close to the shoreline."

"That's a hell of a distance from the usual shipping lanes or any other commercially traveled route that I know of," the admiral commented.

"Do you think she might be attempting to off-load at sea, admiral?"

"It's entirely possible," he replied without looking up from the charts.

The admiral turned to the first officer standing to the right of the captain.

"Notify Rabene aboard his command jet. Perhaps they can track the ship for us. We need to know if she slows or another ship approaches her."

"Very well, sir." The first officer took leave to carry out the admiral's order.

The admiral continued to examine the charts, questioning in his mind, *what are you up to, heading for waters so far out of the plotted path? Are you up to something shrewd, or are you just running because you found out we are watching your every move?* It was going to be a very long night.

David, Nathan and Rachael arrived at Intelligence Headquarters, having agreed to participate—providing that David would not be in danger at any time. They sent a military escort to pick up Victor and once they were all together, the plan was discussed until every aspect of the operation was decided. Nothing was left to chance when it came to David's safety. Victor insisted on being the point person and overseeing whatever David was involved in.

It was far too risky to allow David to make the required telephone calls from his dorm. There were several entrances to his living quarters and the campus was relatively deserted. Providing enough manpower to maintain an acceptable safety level would put him more at risk rather than protect him. Too many people would alert any terrorists watching David's room.

Victor made a suggestion, and their communications specialist was called in to affirm the viability of Victor's plan. They would rig a telephone in the office where David, Nathan and Rachael were. This telephone would have the same telephone number as the payphone in the hallway of the dorm. David would receive his instructions and make the calls on the list from right there. He would never be at risk.

"What if someone checks on the dorm to see if he is there, looking for a light or even movement within his room? There is a window and someone could be watching for activity," one of the strategists on the team remarked to Victor.

"Place a decoy there," Victor answered. "Find one of our own men, a young recruit who resembles David, and place him there beginning this afternoon. It shouldn't be too hard to find a tall young man with a lot of hair!"

After some further discussion, it was deemed an acceptable plan. David was asked what he usually wore when he was hanging around his dorm room.

"My sweat suit—I usually wear it around the dorm and even sleep in it."

"Excellent," Victor commented.

"Send this look-a-like to the dorm and have him change into David's sweat suit and hang around. When it gets dark, we'll have him switch on a small light in the room and pass by the window a few times with his back to it. Does the sweat suit have a hooded top?" Victor asked David.

"Yes, it does."

"Excellent. We'll have him wear the hood all the time so there's less chance of being recognized as someone *other* than David."

The plan was put into motion. Victor left to make some calls and find a young trainee or recent graduate of their intelligence school who might bear some resemblance to David. It took less than an hour to find Michael

Lipkin, a twenty-one year-old graduate who was without assignment and eager to get a taste of doing something more than studying field manuals. Victor had him brought to the office, where he briefed him and introduced him to David.

"We *do* look alike," David commented as the two young men shook hands. Victor briefed him on the operation, gave him David's keys, and instructed him to change into the sweat suit he would find in David's room. He was to simply hang around the dorm room.

"They will likely be watching from afar to avoid campus security people, so you may never see anyone, but proceed as though you were being constantly watched. Make sure that the hood of the sweatshirt is covering most of your face at all times," Victor added. "Do you have your weapon?"

"Yes sir, I do."

"Good," Victor added. Let's hope you don't have to use it. That would mean your cover would be blown."

After receiving all his instructions, Michael left. David would remain there with his parents, who were fully briefed on the plan. They expressed a great deal of gratitude for Victor protecting David. It was all arranged, as was the telephone number.

The telephone company was called, and a phone was installed in the office within the hour. At Telephone Central, it was arranged that if the phone in the hallway at the dorm rang, the phone in the office would ring as well. If the number were being traced, the same telephone number as the public telephone would come up on the trace. The arrangements were completed, and David was safe within the walls of Headquarters. Intelligence was betting on their conclusion that the in-person notification on paper was legitimate as far as the person and title were concerned, but the PLO official named would never be there.

Instead, it was assumed that David would be left as a murdered example of anyone attempting to meddle in PLO affairs—especially a young Jew from America. This would not be the case. The location for the in-person meeting was screened, and traps were set as of late afternoon. A sniper or anyone attempting to hide in the cover of the two buildings on the property would not be able to get in or out without being detected.

Victor sat down with David and began to coax him on how he would be making the calls. They practiced many times so that David would have a feel for it when the hour came. There was a small round table with four chairs in the middle of the room. Nathan, Rachael and Victor sat there together. Victor explained to them that all of this was part of the Intelligence group taking every precaution in the event the ship got through. Nothing could be left to chance.

"David may never even make these calls if we are successful in taking the ship before she reaches her destination." They were all relieved, and the conversation turned from operations to family. They talked about Florida, the synagogue, the old days, Harry, and the recent ordeal with Ruth. Victor was anxious to hear everything. Despite the distance between them, Victor felt connected to the Blumberg household. Nathan filled him in on the last six years since he had been in Florida. The officer in charge of the watch sent in sandwiches, pastries, a pitcher of ice water, and two thermos bottles—one with hot cocoa and the other with hot tea. Someone remembered.

At the opposite end of this rectangular room was another desk. A young man sat there in front of a radio and wore a headset so that no sound would be heard if the phone call came in earlier or later than expected. After investigating the numbers that were on David's list, it was learned that they were various parties who were involved with the off-loading, the transport, and the distribution of the cargo. The first list was actually found to be correct, and the second list the cover up. Had David pulled out or refused to do his part in the operation, the second list would have never surfaced. They would have also called-off the men on the first list. Because of David's agreement to make the calls, the real distribution network was now made known to the Israelis. They were the men who would have received the goods, set up the appropriated counts for each part of the shipment, arrange the specific transportation and deliver each shipment to its destination.

As Nathan and Rachael were informed of these developments, they never dreamed they would be sitting in an office in Israel and watching their son play a major role in a counter-intelligence plan for the Israeli government.

~

The Journey Begins...

General Rabene and the admiral were in constant communication, and they agreed that their biggest problem was the 164 mile-long coastline of Israel. Every naval patrol boat was called out that night, and the inland water traffic was heavy. They were fortunate that it was Christmas and there were not hoards of fishing boats scattered about. The freighter was rapidly approaching the coastal waters, steaming on the same heading at about seventeen knots. She showed no further sign of slowing or changing course, and the final call had to be made. It appeared as though she was going to try to get as close to the coastline as she possibly could.

After David made the first call, fishing boats would be disbursed. The ships crew would dump the cargo overboard, wrapped in waterproof plastic, and the boats would pick them up. The fishing boats would then bring the cargo to a designated shore location. These were the conclusions that Intelligence and the commanders agreed upon. Night vision scopes were being used, and as many docking possibilities as humanly possible were being watched as darkness enveloped the entire coastline. The general's primary concern was that not a single bundle get off that ship and get picked up by a fishing boat.

If the freighter dumped even a portion of her cargo before they got to her, many of the bundles could literally float into coastal areas and be picked up by Palestinian civilians. The PLO would spread the word quickly, and there would be cash rewards offered that would send out hundreds of poor Palestinians scouring the shorelines for waterproofed packages. That could only result in a military blockade of the entire coastline, and on Christmas it would be a tactical nightmare.

Secondly, should the freighter dump her entire cargo, hundreds of the packages would wind up afloat and would likely be picked up by fishing boats. It would be impossible to stop and search every fishing boat off the coastline at one time. The odds were that several would get through with their cargo of arms. It would be far more expedient if they could get to the ship *before* the calls were to be made by David.

~

Reuben and Yael were on the Bridge of the freighter, monitoring the sophisticated radar and sonar equipment that was aboard for this operation. It was the type of equipment that the general would not have guessed would be aboard a freighter—but it was. Just before the midnight hour, the general's jet was detected flying in a circle high above the sea. Yael adjusted the scope and read the range and size of the plane.

"It's an Israeli recon jet and they are circling us, Reuben. They know we're here, but do they know what's aboard?"

"I don't know," Reuben replied. "We have radar, not a crystal ball. We will have to make a call on this and radio in for Authority approval. We are not to act unless we are in immediate danger of being sunk or boarded."

The radar and sonar equipment was brought aboard in New York, installed by their New York operative's technician before sailing.

"What is our estimated time to be close to the first fishing village?" Reuben asked.

"We are approximately an hour or so from that point."

Reuben was betting that the Israelis would never suspect an operation that far from the coast. He turned to Yael and placed his right hand on his shoulder.

"It's time, my brother. Get Elanie and change into your wet suits. They are especially made for below zero temperatures. The seals on the cuffs and the ankles were made to allow water to become trapped in the suit at a very slow rate of intake. This way, the body temperature rapidly adjusts. The seals will not allow any additional water into the suit once the optimum amount has been attained. The one-man subs were anchored a short distance from here as a contingency, in the event they discovered our ship or our plans."

Reuben opened a chart and pointed to a circled designation.

"Take the designated bundles, and you know what you have to do. Let Elanie handle the bag with the toxic label on it; you take the other bag, and may Allah be with you."

The two men embraced, and Yael left the bridge to suit up with Elanie. Their drop off point was getting nearer by the minute, and there was no time to waste. Reuben turned his attention to the captain and began giving him instructions while also maintaining an occasional feel for the gun under his jacket. This traitor would never make it off the ship, but for now he had to maintain an air of trust.

"I don't want you to slow the engines until you are within one thousand yards of the drop-off point," Reuben instructed, and the captain acknowledged.

"If we begin to slow, they will be able to track our slowest point and figure out that we must have made a drop of some kind."

Reuben walked over to the chart table and motioned for the captain to join him there. He examined the top chart and pointed to a specific red circle.

"When the ship arrives at this point, (pointing to a designated coordinate) I want you to be prepared to immediately cut the engines. That will slow the ship enough for Yael and Elanie to go over the side safely. As soon as you cut the engines, have the engine room bring the engines back on line for just two seconds and then cut them again. Repeat this several times and then bring the engines to twenty-five percent. Increase them slowly until you are at full speed. They will think that we had some temporary engine problems. All I want to do is confuse them long enough so they don't think that anyone or anything went overboard. That will also shut down the screws long enough so that Elanie and Yael will not be caught in the undertow of the ship. If you bring the engine back up slowly, they will have enough time to swim clear of the full wake before the engines reach the first twenty-five percent thrust."

The captain acknowledged Rueben's directives and returned to the bridge window to carefully watch the ever-increasing sight of the coastline of Israel. Reuben made this decision and felt that it was the right move under the circumstances. In the event he felt the mission was threatened in any way, this was the contingency plan that would bring the most important bundles of the cargo into Israel.

~

The call came in for Hyman Lutz at 7:42 p.m. He was ordered to disburse his units to cover specifically designated routes along the coastline in Tel Aviv and along the major roadways and intersections leading from the coastline. In the event the cargo was brought ashore for transport, roadblocks must be set up at every major crossroad into and out of Tel Aviv.

It was Christmas Day, and the roads were already busy as people were coming and going to Bethlehem and various landmarks along the way. There were not many Israeli soldiers who were *not* on duty. Of all the days of the year to be involved in a covert operation, Christmas was not the best time for security assurances to civilians. There were too many of them around. General Rabene sensed that their timing was purposeful and in some way had to hand it to them for working it out that way. Radio communications to Army Intelligence accounted for more than 75% of the air traffic during this hour, as additional patrols were being sent out to guard the roads into Bethlehem and into Jerusalem. Rabene believed that he had every angle covered. For the first time in a very long struggle with terrorism, he sensed they were truly on top of this situation and Israel would prevail. Then the call came in from the admiral.

"We have received a new directive from the prime minister. There has been a change in plans, and the new orders are to be executed immediately. We will intercept the freighter when she is approximately one hour off the coastline with our Special Ops teams aboard the choppers. The new coordinates are being radioed as we speak. The choppers will fly within several miles of her so they are not spotted.

They are carrying three high-speed inflatable power rafts that will carry seven men in each raft. The teams will be heavily armed, and their rafts will be equipped with scaling devices. We are going to intercept her, hook onto her, and scale her in the darkness. They will never know what hit them, and there are only fourteen men and a woman aboard the ship—the twelve crewmembers and the three PLO terrorists. I need cover from your recon patrols in the event they have any other ships or smaller vessels meeting them. If one of the vessels or the freighter itself fires upon us before we scale her, our men have orders to drop back, and within the next mile she will be sunk to the ocean floor. We have several gunboats on their way, but we are hoping there is no major engagement."

"Daring," Rabene commented, "but a good plan. I assume your teams will sneak aboard and round up the crew as combatant terrorists?"

"Yes, we will attempt capturing them and taking them as prisoners with charges of attempted smuggling, covert operations against Israel, and a long list that is being drafted by the Cabinet members as we speak. No one is getting very much sleep tonight."

"I understand, Admiral, and we'll provide the cover you need."

~

The clock on the wall read 22:40 in military time, or 10:40 p.m. Rachael had drifted off to sleep, her head resting on her arm on the small round table. The two cups of cocoa had managed to make her sleepy, as it had been a very long, emotionally draining day. Nathan was talking non-stop with Victor, who noticed the man at the radio writing feverishly on a pad, and he appeared to be excited. As he put down his pencil, he held the pad in front of him, re-reading what he wrote, evidently making certain he was correct. He removed his headphones just as Victor nudged Nathan to draw his attention to the radioman. Victor instinctively knew that something had come over the radio that was pertinent news about the operation. The radioman practically ran to the door and left the room, slamming the door behind him. Nathan and Victor looked at each other, exchanging "who knows?" glances. Nathan saw that David had also noticed and asked him if he was okay.

"I'm fine, Dad, it's just all this waiting. This chair is not that comfortable, and I haven't had much sleep in the past several days."

"I can appreciate why," Nathan replied with an understanding look.

Just then the door opened, and the general entered with the radioman.

"I have some news for you. There has been a new plan ordered, and we do not think the calls will become necessary—but don't celebrate yet. The entire matter of making these calls depends on whether the Special Ops teams reaches their objective before the call comes in for David. The timing will be critical since the ship will be taken within minutes before or after the calls—whichever turns out to be the first line of action."

"When do you think this will occur?" Victor asked the general.

"Very soon now, but it all depends on the weather. There's a small storm brewing, but it's not enough to stop our people or present any danger to the mission. We have to wait and see, but I believe it will all happen right around midnight or shortly thereafter."

Nathan glanced at the clock and saw that it was just over an hour from now, and then noticed that Rachael was still soundly sleeping. He appeared puzzled and asked the general why the calls were so important in the first place.

"It was a matter of linking the PLO to the ship's cargo of arms. There was discussion all along of allowing the ship to begin off-loading as well as seeing if the Palestinian Authority could be implicated at the highest levels. Several men on that list are linked to terrorist activities. If they were called and actually answered their phones, it would implicate them in this operation and we could arrest them. Right now, they are a name on a list and that is not enough proof to convict them. The decision to not allow the ship near our shores was made in the interest of safety for the thousands of civilians that are on the streets tonight. We cannot afford a single shipment being smuggled ashore and a chase or battle to ensue. It was too risky, so the objectives were changed to the priority of preventing the cargo from reaching us. We were also concerned that she could begin dumping her cargo for fishing boat pick-up, but we believe she is far enough out that she won't try that. If she does, we will be there. We also have heavy patrols that were dispatched to cover the shoreline from that point on and road patrols for major roadways. We have already set up roadblocks at strategic intersections. We will all remain here until we have the word that the mission has been completed. Until then, I am sending out for some more food, and, of course, a fresh pot of tea."

Victor smiled and thanked his commander.

"Can we go home now?" Rachael jokingly asked. They all laughed; however, Rachael had woken up several minutes ago, heard all that was said, and was very serious. David told her that it was a matter of less than a couple of hours, and they would all have accomplished the reason they were there in the first place.

"It's almost done, Mom, and I have not yet been exposed to any danger."

"By the way, Victor, I meant to ask you before. Did you have anything to do with Diane's rescue?" David questioned.

Victor shrugged his shoulders as though he had no idea what David was talking about. The general shot a "well-done" glance to Victor.

No details of the operation would be prematurely leaked to the media. Not a word would go out about the operation until the Prime Minister was thoroughly briefed. They also wanted to insure that the cargo was completely inspected and the fifteen men who were on board were identified as Palestinians. Many pictures would be taken of that cargo. It would all be used to demonstrate to the world what the PLO was up to while their leader was participating in peace negotiations with both the president of the United States and Israeli officials. This was to be an example of their ongoing deceit and manipulation of the world news media. The next day, the prime minister would expose to the world the truth behind the Palestinians claim.

All along they had orchestrated that their goals were twofold. First and foremost, they claimed they wanted peace. Then they wanted to live on their own land, free from Israeli occupied rule. Smuggling tons of munitions into Gaza to kill Israelis simply didn't fit with those expressed goals of peace.

The Journey Begins...

Chapter Twenty

Operation Takedown

The coordinates that Reuben had given the captain were within a few thousand yards. Reuben was on the bridge and notified Elanie and Yael below. He watched intently as the distance closed and waited for the precise moment to order the engines stopped. There was very little moonlight due to winter cloud cover and only a quarter-moon. Reuben waited for the word from below that they were ready, and within a few minutes the whirring sound of the ship's telephone informed him they were equipped and ready to go. This had been a long, painful and emotional ordeal for Elanie, and she did not want him to remain aboard.

"Why can't you go with me instead of Yael?" she demanded, her anger emanating from a gut feeling that she would never see Reuben again. "There is something you're not telling me," she insisted.

Reuben assured her that he had to stay with the freighter until it either docked or the cargo was off-loaded. He took her into a compartment where they could not be heard, and he whispered the entire situation with Omar and the new captain and what he had to do. She understood but was still upset and hugged him tightly. Then she abruptly left him to finish suiting up. The ship came to the precise point where Reuben intended for them to jump and he ordered,

"Engines all stop."

The captain repeated the order to the ship's engine room below, and the engineer pushed the engine levers fully downward, indicating a cut in all engine power. The ship slowed as the captain maneuvered the bow into the wind to cut the speed more quickly. At an exact moment determined by their position, Yael and Elanie went over the side and into the water. Two large waterproof bags were dropped to them. They had but seconds to attach the nylon towline from the steel cable that secured the bundles to their waists.

They had to swim away as quickly as possible, pushing heavily on the rubber diving fins to propel them out of danger from the ship's screws. The ship's engines revved up again and then stopped for a few seconds as they cleared the ship's wake. The process was repeated several times. Finally, the engines came up to full power, and the ship pulled away. Elanie checked her compass and the two swam about a thousand yards to the anchored, one-man power subs waiting for them.

They resembled torpedoes, had a steering mechanism and throttle and were battery operated so they could run silently. They had been brought by a fishing vessel and anchored at the precise coordinates just after sundown. Elanie and Yael headed for those coordinates and the one-man subs that would bring them to the shoreline just off the Israeli coast.

They would go ashore at the tip of Haifa, just on the Mediterranean side of Galilee, and be virtually unseen in the darkness of the winter night. Then they would go inland by car, in an older model Mercedes that was waiting for them in a clearing off the main road. Inside the trunk were a change of clothes, passports, two, micro Uzi's with extra clips, and false driver's licenses. Although Reuben had identical documents for the three of them in Pittsburgh, new ones with new identities were necessary. They could not take a chance that the FBI hadn't provided their old, forged identities to the Israelis by now. They did not want to be stopped and identified by some army road patrol.

Yael took the towline that had been secured to the two large water-proofed bundles bobbing in the water next to them and snapped the eye-hooks onto the towing line of their one-man subs. He tested both lines, raised his right hand, and began a circular motion to signal Elanie to start the engine on her machine. When both of their engines successfully turned over, Yael motioned to her to follow close behind him, and he turned the throttle to full. They sped away in the night, their bundles secured to the machines and towed behind them. Within the cover of darkness, their black rubber suits and black torpedo-like subs, gave them autonomy on the surface of a huge dark and cold ocean.

Behind them, the ship grew farther and farther away and finally disappeared from sight. Elanie glanced back and Yael could not see her tears in the water—tears of knowing that Reuben would never come home to her.

She knew that's why he sent the younger Yael who had loved her since they were in elementary school. Out of his friendship and respect for Reuben, he managed to keep his feelings silent all these years. If anyone survived this mission, Reuben wanted it to be Yael and Elanie. He had to stay with the ship.

It had been less than twenty minutes since Elanie and Yael had slipped into the icy waters when two F-15A fighter jets passed overhead. The fighters were providing protective cover for the helicopters that were now coming up behind the freighter. It had also been less than ten minutes since the new captain had gone below to get some sleep. He had manned the bridge for nearly twenty-four hours, taking the ship through a violent storm and then remaining to insure all went smoothly in the ploy to stop and start the ship's engines. The new second mate was at the helm of the ship, and watchman stood at the port and starboard stations. Both men had also been on duty for too many hours and were half asleep. All the other crewmembers except for the engine room watch were sound asleep.

As the Israeli helicopters closed in from behind, the teams aboard could begin to see the wake of the freighter below them. It was just before 1:00 a.m. The two choppers closed in and were just about at the point of jump-off when the pilot switched the engines to whisper mode and only a slight swishing sound could be heard. Aboard each helicopter, last minute checks of gear and wet suits were almost completed as the men readied themselves to disembark. They were lined up in a tight row and held on to a cable that ran the length of the overhead. Over the helicopter's door, a yellow caution light began to blink, signaling they were within one minute of their jump location.

The helicopters descended until the green jump light appeared. Without a word, the men jumped into the sea in rapid succession of each other from each of two helicopters. Twenty-one men were now operating as one powerful and deadly unit. Their orders were to get aboard the freighter, overpower the crew, and take possession of the ship without jeopardizing a single life.

Just ahead of them, the third helicopter dropped three powered inflatable boats. The moment they hit the water, each automatically opened from the air-powered pumps aboard them.

As each man broke the surface of the water, they swam for the rubber boats and climbed into them by teams. The engines on the heavy rubber rafts were space-age technology and were actually manufactured in Israel. One switch of a waterproof knob, and the plastic-enclosed control panel started a rear propeller that could be maneuvered with a single small lever, similar to those on an electric car's control device. The propeller was housed in a casing that could be controlled to turn the propulsion system an immediate 45 degrees in any direction. The moment all the men were aboard their crafts, the helicopters rose and disappeared out of sight, and the three rafts raced rapidly toward the freighter. Within minutes their rafts came alongside the ship, now traveling at an estimated twelve knots. The ship was now in the channel and legally within Israeli sovereignty. One of the rafts went port side, and the other two went starboard side. An air-charged line gun fired a nylon lead line up the side of the ship and over the railing onto the cargo deck. The top piece was similar to a large steel fishhook and had four claw hooks to grab onto the cable of the safety railing on deck.

The men in the raft noticed that the ship was riding somewhat low in the water, the black painted hull line just under the surface. This indicated that the ship was carrying a heavy cargo. This was a slight contradiction of previous intelligence, which had suggested she was light and running fast. It was evident that her engines were larger and more powerful than they had thought. There must have been extensive modification since her launching and filing of the original specification documents.

The hooks of the lead lines caught the railings as each team shot its line guns. The threaded lines pulled the heavy nylon lines taught within seconds, and the rafts nearly jerked out of the water from the sudden thrust of being pulled by the freighter.

The first three men that climbed up the lines were the team captains. They used the large knots that were tied every twelve inches to climb quickly and were on deck within moments. Checking that they had not been seen and that no crewmembers were on deck, the signal was given, and the rest of the men proceeded to climb aboard, silently and swiftly. Each of the men was equipped with night vision glasses that were strapped over their wetsuit hoods. Besides giving them sight in the dark, they served to hide their faces. The element of surprise and the darkness of the interior of the ship were their advantages, and the men knew precisely how to use them.

Once all the team members were aboard and had checked their gear, the commander of the joint teams would signal for them to disburse. Each man knew precisely where to go and what to do. They were well drilled and had the means, along with the combat abilities, to prevail.

The first team drew its weapons from their waterproof carry sacks and headed for the Bridge. The second team sent three men to the engine room and four men to the cargo hold. The third team made its way below. They single-filed down a ladder to the inside deck and down a corridor toward the crew's quarters, where they were somewhat surprised as there was no watertight door! They noticed that *all* the doors were missing. Now they did not have to turn a handle or open a door that might wake up the sleeping crew. The team members silently entered the quarters and positioned themselves at equal distances between the two rows of bunk beds. When they were all in position and had checked their watches to insure enough time for the other team members to reach their objectives, one man turned on all the lights and they began to yell. The sleeping crewmembers were startled and jumped up, some hitting their heads on the bunk above them. The moment their eyes focused and they were able to see the menacing sight of black wet suits, night-vision goggles and assault rifles pointed at them, every one of them raised their hands in immediate surrender. After all, how could sleepy sailors in boxer shorts possibly resist?

Elsewhere aboard the ship, like shiny slivers of black rubber in the dim, winter moonlight, the other men silently slipped up and down ladders and passageways until they had secured the bridge and the engine room. Still in their underwear and their hands behind their heads with their fingers clenched, the crew was brought to the mess deck where they were blindfolded and plastic wrist binders were used to detain them. They were seated on the deck, facing the bulkheads, and were ordered to be silent and not to move or they would be shot.

Not a word was exchanged among the teams of the Special Ops forces before this warning to the crew. Hand signals were used for every command. Not a shot was fired, and not a hint of resistance was offered. The entire operation from helicopter drop to full control of the freighter was accomplished in under fourteen minutes. The senior officer began counting personnel. When he had completed the count, he motioned for two of his men to follow him outside to the upper deck where they could talk and not be heard.

"There were supposed to be twelve crew members and three terrorists aboard the ship. That's fifteen all together—fourteen men and one woman.

There are only eleven male crewmembers accounted for so far. That leaves one crewmember and the other three still missing. Take a team and search the ship from bow to stern."

~

The radio had been silent for the last hour. Rachael was now awake and talking to Victor about Harry. David sat by the radioman and was looking through a day-old newspaper. A slight crackling sound came from the radio and the radioman secured his headset. He picked up a sharpened pencil and the code pad and began writing in Hebrew code. Everyone was watching the expressions on his face, as he seemed tense at first. He then broke into a big smile of relief, and they knew it was good news. He pulled off his headset, tore the single page of writing from the pad and headed for the door, but not before he looked at Victor and with a smile and gave him an affirmative nod. Victor held up his hand for everyone to wait and be silent. He wanted to give the radioman time to notify the general. Then they would hear the news from him. It was a matter of respect and protocol.

As anticipated, the general came into the room within minutes, followed by his aide and the radioman.

"We have some news. It appears to be good news, but we are not completely sure. It seems we have the freighter under our command, but the captain is missing and so are the three terrorists. They are conducting a complete search of the ship as we speak."

Victor appeared concerned.

"Have our men searched the cargo hold to ascertain the nature of the cargo?"

"I believe they are searching *every* area of the ship, *especially* the cargo hold."

"Well, David, it appears you are not going to have to make those calls after all," Victor stated with a tone of thankfulness in his voice.

Victor then asked the radioman if he would please call David's dorm and tell the young operative who was posing as David, the good news. Rachael went over to David and embraced him. The general smiled and nodded to Victor that he may as well see them all back to their hotel. Anything that occurred beyond this point would be privileged information, and there was really no sense in keeping them there. The general said he would notify the operatives at the site where David was supposed to meet the Palestinian official and have them stand down. No one would be meeting anyone that night except for the commandos who took possession of the ship in the name of Israel. Although it appeared that the situation was well under control, David was eager to learn if the cargo was indeed what they had suspected.

"I can't discuss that with you, David. As I said, I do not know all the details at this moment. The ship is being searched, and I suspect we will find exactly what our intelligence has informed us of. It is a blessing that we were able to stop this delivery, and you have been highly instrumental in the success of this mission—more than you will ever realize. I expect that the prime minister will want to be in contact with you and your family within the next day or so. Will you all be staying at the same hotel?"

Nathan looked over at Rachael and informed the general that they would likely be going to Jerusalem and might change hotels—but he would let Victor know where they were. Handshakes and congratulations were exchanged as Victor ushered them out of the room and into a waiting car. Victor knew that the night was far from over and that something was not right. He felt it, but it was more important to get the three of them out of the middle of this operation and safely tucked away in their hotel beds. Nathan insisted that David stay at the hotel and asked Victor to call ahead and book David a room adjoining or on the same floor. Victor suggested that they not use David's real name, and register him under a different name for security purposes. Nathan agreed, thanking Victor for thinking of that detail. Unbeknownst to Nathan, Victor also arranged for a security detail to watch over them around the clock until this operation was over and the three terrorists were located. Something wasn't right and Victor knew it. He had been around these situations far too long.

~

Elanie and Yael changed their clothes inside the car, shivering and exhausted from the ordeal. Even with battery-powered propulsion, it had taken them well over two hours to reach land. Once out of the water, they had to work their way inland to the waiting car and supplies, carrying the two bundles from the ship. The packages were extremely heavy and they had to stop every few minutes, as Elanie was not used to carrying such weight over any distance. The four canisters were light but the explosives were weighing-in at more than she was used to carrying. The wet suits had done their jobs, but getting out of them and drying off subjected their bodies to a drastic temperature change, and Elanie could not stop shivering. Yael grabbed several blankets from the trunk and wrapped her tightly, rubbing her skin and massaging her hands and her feet. Once they were changed, she began to feel better; however, she was obviously at a point of physical collapse.

"We will rest for a while before we start out," Yael suggested, but Elanie shook her head negatively.

"We can't. It will be daylight soon, and we must make it to the first checkpoint before sunrise. There will also be a lot of traffic this morning, and we don't need to be caught up in a huge line of cars at some Israeli roadblock. Can you drive?"

"Yes," Yael assured her.

"Good, then I can just crawl into the back seat and rest for a short while and then I'll drive while you get some rest."

"No, its okay, I can take us in. I want you to rest," Yael insisted.

"I will rest when I know that Reuben has made it into port and the ship's cargo has been off-loaded and distributed."

"I don't like that business about the agent in New York and all of the allegations about traitors. It doesn't add up, and I have been uneasy since Reuben told me about it."

"I know," replied Elanie. "I feel the same way. I asked him how he could be so sure that Omar could have possibly been turned after all his loyal years. It was then that I saw the look of doubt in his eyes. He himself was unsure."

"Let's not dwell on it. These packages must get to Jerusalem."

Elanie crawled over the front seat and into the back of the aged Mercedes. She took the two damp blankets and covered her legs. She then curled up and fell asleep within seconds. Yael began to load the two bundles into the trunk of the Mercedes, but the second one would not fit and was preventing the trunk from closing. He took his knife and began to cut away some of the waterproofing and foam around the outer package. When he had managed to reduce the outside dimensions by several inches, he wedged the bundles into the trunk and closed it.

He was now shivering out of control from having stood in the cold for the past ten minutes. He got into the car and turned the ignition key, his foot firmly on the clutch. The diesel engine sputtered for a moment and then turned over, releasing a cloud of black smoke from the exhaust pipe. He released the handbrake and did not turn on the lights. He waited for a few moments; his window slightly open as he listened for any sounds to insure there was no one watching them. He shifted the car into reverse, inching his way slowly along in the dark until he had backed out of the tiny clearing and onto the road. He shifted into neutral and waited, once again looking in all directions. There was no sign of movement, so he shifted the car into gear and drove off into the night, switching on his lights only after he was sure no one was behind them.

Reuben could hardly breathe. He was wedged into the tight space that housed the wench-lift motor and pulley system for the cargo hold. It was a matter of split- second timing, that moment when you catch a glimpse of something out of the corner or your eye and you instinctively react. As he descended the ladder from the bridge, he saw the line of men boarding the ship. He froze, hardly even breathing as he watched them make their way down the deck. They had split up between both sides of the ship and silently scurried off—obviously to capture the crew and the ship.

It was then that Reuben realized he had come down to the main deck by the narrow engine room ladder. It was used for the maintenance crew. There was no particular reason for his selecting that way down—he just did. He realized that the teams would have layouts of the main decks and ladders between them, but might not have considered the ladders used for emergencies. He had to think quickly, realizing that he only had a minute or two before they would overrun the ship. He had to make it to the cargo deck and get into the #1 cargo hold. Within an instant, he knew what he had to do, but he also knew that it was over for him. Perhaps Allah would be merciful and he would die a martyr's death.

All Reuben's beliefs and convictions were at conflict within himself as he inched his way along an emergency crawlspace between the engine room and the lower cargo area. Inch by inch he crawled, his knees hurting from the bolts in the steel deck and an occasional loose bolt sticking into his back as he squeezed through the narrow passage. All he could think about was Elanie as she hugged him and looked at him as though she would never see him again. *She knew . . . she just knew,* he thought, and she was right. *Yael has always loved her and he's young and vital. I will simply cherish the years we have had and we will meet again when Allah brings us to paradise.*

He slid from the tiny passageway onto the deck of the cargo area and waited, hesitating . . . listening for the slightest sound . . . there was movement. . . . they were in the cargo hold. He knew the invaders were sure to make their way there. It was what they were after, what they came for, and he was not about to let them walk away with it. Reuben knew they were Israeli commandos, and with only a pistol, he did not stand a chance of fighting them off. They were walking around the cargo deck, inspecting the outer perimeters of the hold for any type of wiring or rigged charges. All that was visible were piles of bundled clothes. Reuben slowly slipped behind a large gearbox and pulled his knees to his chest and his head between his knees, attempting to not even breathe too deeply . . . and waited. Then he saw the winch and the small crawlspace that housed the motor. Slowly, he inched his way along the short distance from the winch gearbox until he was able to wedge his body between the motor and the space beyond it. Reuben was now one with the darkness, hidden from the eyes of the Israelis.

Perhaps they would abandon the mission as useless if they didn't dig deep enough into the thousands of pieces of clothing to find the munitions. Anything was possible, but there were limited options open to him.

~

General Rabene was now on the ground and back at his field office. He immediately called the admiral and discussed the progress of finding the munitions. The admiral provided an update and informed him that Apache helicopters had been sent to recon the mission. They were to circle the freighter and search for any signs of unfriendly fishing boats that might have been sent to off-load the cargo at sea. The word came back that the sea was clear: no shipping traffic, no fishing boats and no activity. It was the day after Christmas in the Holy Land, and all was quiet.

Admiral Yuri asked the general to please stand by. He was receiving an urgent message from the major who was in command of the Special Ops group.

"Sir, it appears that we might have been wrong. My men are now at about six feet into what appears to be thousands of pounds of old clothing."

"How deep did you say you were down into the cargo hold?" the admiral asked.

"About six feet or so, and we are continuing. The only way we could do this was to form a line of men and begin removing the clothes to the upper deck. A great deal of this cargo seems to be loose and there is no way of separating it. Perhaps hoisting a pallet up might be the best way, because it looks like it was literally dumped into the cargo hold from above."

"That makes me even more suspicious, so keep digging," the admiral ordered. There was another point of information that the admiral did not disclose. He had reliable Intel that the ship had a false water line and there was another ten feet of depth that wasn't disclosed in the ship's blueprints when they were officially filed upon registration.

Yael strained at keeping his eyes from closing. His instructions were to stay close to the coastal roadways, traveling from Haifa to Hadera, Netanya, Herzilyya and on into Tel Aviv. He was to cross over into Jericho and on into Jerusalem. With the bundles from the ship now safely in the trunk, he was to drive cautiously and under no circumstances do anything to draw attention to the car or to them. As he continued on the coastal road, Elanie awoke and saw that Yael was falling asleep.

"I'm up and I feel rested. Thank you for letting me sleep, but I would not suggest you continue driving at the risk of killing us both after all we've been through."

Yael slowed the car and pulled over, now spotting the headlights of a car that was coming up quickly. Elanie waited until the car had passed before she got out and exchanged places with Yael. It took less than a minute for him to crawl into the back seat and pull the two wool blankets over himself. He was sound asleep and snoring before Elanie even started the car again. She checked her map that Yael left unfolded on the front seat. Checking the time and fastening her safety belt, she looked behind her before pulling out. It was still early and the traffic was light.

~

Nathan peered out of the window in their room as the morning sun began to cast a wall of light on the hotel building. Rachael began to stir and stretched, omitting an almost moaning sound after very little sleep.

"We haven't even slept a couple of hours and you are up already?"

"Yes, I am still excited over the events of this entire matter—a rabbi from a small synagogue in Ft. Lauderdale, Florida, in the midst of international intrigue, terrorists, and contraband cargo!"

"You are definitely in a melodramatic mood—but why did you open the curtains? We could have slept a little longer."

"I would actually like to check out of this hotel, leave Tel Aviv behind us, and drive to Jerusalem. We'll check into a hotel there if I can find a vacancy, stay a few days, and go home. Perhaps we can talk David into coming with us."

"I believe that if he were approached in the right way, Nathan, he just might come back with us."

"Do you really think so?"

Nathan was unsure of David's state of mind at this juncture.

"Yes. I think he has had enough of seeking his destiny. This experience has fulfilled his inner desire to do something worthwhile. Perhaps this is all he really needed. After all, Nathan, he did have a major role in a rather big and important operation. Victor told us how important this operation was and how instrumental David was to its success. I believe that some loving support right now might just bring him home."

"Okay then. Why don't you get dressed and let's call David's room when we are ready to leave? He can join us for breakfast and we can discuss it all then. He *is* going to accompany us to Jerusalem, so we will have a few days to sort this all out."

"I agree," Rachael replied, "but for right now, at this moment in time in the great nation of Israel, I'm taking a shower! Why don't you call the concierge and see if he can get us a nice hotel room in Jerusalem."

The concierge was not on duty as of yet, but the front desk clerk answered the phone, and Nathan explained what he wanted to do. The clerk stated that he would make some calls on his behalf and ring him back in a few minutes. As Nathan finished dressing, he heard the shower being turned on in the bathroom.

Playfully he knocked on the door and complained,

"There is only one shower and two people—not enough time for individual showers!" he chided.

Rachael laughed and told him he was "one lathering too late." She would be out as soon as she rinsed off.

Just then the phone rang, and it was the clerk.

"Rabbi Blumberg, I will shortly deliver a printout from the internet on the hotels in Jerusalem. I attached information about a hotel I thought you might enjoy, as it is located within walking distance to both sides of the city, old and new. After you have decided, call me and I will make reservations for you. Will you be checking out then?"

"Yes, I will, after breakfast."

"I will prepare your bill, sir."

Nathan thanked him, and less than five minutes later he heard a knock at the door. The bellman handed him a printout on the King David Hotel in Jerusalem. It appeared to be a famous landmark and was in walking distance to the Old City.

Rachael came out of the bathroom at that moment and was towel-drying her hair.

"The clerk sent up this information on a hotel in Jerusalem. It's in the Old City and appears to be very nice," he said, handing the sheet of paper to Rachael.

She sat down on the edge of the bed and began to read it when the phone rang. Nathan picked it up, and it was David.

"Good morning, son. Did you get a few hours sleep?"

"Yes, and I am feeling much better. Are we all going to Jerusalem today?"

"How about after breakfast? It appears that there is a room available at the King David Hotel, and we may as well stay there for a couple of days."

"Can I stay there with you and Mom and not come back tonight?" was the request from their son, and Nathan's eyes brimmed with tears. Rachael saw him become emotional and knew they were tears of joy.

"Of course you may. Why don't you pack your clothes that are back at the university and we'll see where God leads us over the next few days? We'll drive you back after breakfast and then leave for Jerusalem after you pack. You can always come back if you decide to, but at least you will have your belongings with you in the event we all want to fly home from another destination. Mom and I will wait for you in our room, so knock on the door when you are ready to go down for breakfast." Nathan slowly cradled the phone.

"He's coming with us, isn't he, Nathan?"

"Yes, and he consented to our driving him back to school and pack all his clothes so he can take them to Jerusalem."

Rachael smiled and jumped up from the bed. She smothered him with hugs, and then playfully sat on his lap in the overstuffed easy chair. She began kissing him with love and a spirit of rejoicing. In her heart, she felt that in David could possibly be coming home!

"God is so good," she exclaimed. They simply held each other, sensing the blessings of finally feeling whole again.

The message came in from the captain of the Special Ops group aboard the freighter. They had continued removing clothes and were another foot or so down without finding anything. It had been a very long night. The ship was anchored, and there were two Israeli gunboats alongside. The ship's crew was undergoing intense interrogation by Army Intelligence personnel who were brought aboard on the gunboats. Just then, one of the team members called out to their team leader.

"Sir, there is another compartment that is adjacent to this one that our men reported an unusual smell coming from it. It almost smells like a decaying body."

The team captain got on his radio and reported the incident to the captain aboard the flagship. The information was immediately conveyed to the admiral. "Investigate it and report back to me" was the admiral's response.

The team captain followed his team member toward a hatch at the end of the cargo area about eight feet in length. He had to bend over and almost crawl the eight feet. His man led him through another hatch about half the size of a normal hatch and into a cargo hold stacked with clothing—mostly jackets and old coats. Again, they noticed that the hatches and openings were without doors or hatch covers. They finally understood how the ship was able to shed so much weight. The smell was unmistakable. It was the smell of a dead human being, but it was not bad enough to indicate he had been dead very long—perhaps several days. With the lack of airflow in that area, the odor was more pronounced. They followed the smell to a far corner and then began to remove the pile of clothing that covered the body. He had captain's bars on his epilates. His wallet told the rest of the story.

"It's Omar, the former captain of this vessel. That explains why he was not among the men we captured. He was shot in the abdomen at point blank range and also through the heart. But who would kill him? He was a Palestinian! I need to report this to Admiral Yuri right away. Something is not right in all of this, and the three terrorists are still missing. Get another man and some plastic sheeting, and get the body topside into a cool area. Wrap him carefully to preserve any evidence."

The captain made his way back to the passageway and to the main cargo hold. Moments later the admiral and the general both had a new situation to ponder.

"I want the cargo searched to the bottom of the cargo hold. According to our engineering charts of this ship, there should be another fourteen or so feet to the bottom. We must be sure, and we will not be sure until we have scraped the bilges of that ship."

Unbeknownst to them, there was another set of ears hearing the very same orders. Reuben, who by now could not move his legs from the cramping of having not been able to move for the past several hours. He had heard every word. When he realized that the teams searching the cargo hold was going to get more men and strip it bare, he knew what he had to do. In just a few more feet they would come to the plastic sheeting that covered the munitions. Slowly he began to massage his left leg and then his right leg, attempting to get the circulation going so that he would be able to slide out of the space and onto the deck. He glanced at his watch and realized that he must have fallen asleep for a short time. He could feel the pins and needles in his thighs and calves as he began to move his legs, leaning backward onto his elbows. He rotated his body so that his legs were slowly being lowered from the space and outward toward the short drop to the deck. It was painful and arduous, as he was wedged in a jackknife position facing the other wall of the tiny space.

He knew that sooner or later they would use the hoist to bring some of the bundles up to the deck. Then they would have more room for digging. The main bundles had been brought up, and all that was left now were piles of loose clothing. The arms and munitions had been carefully wrapped in small bundles and then covered and taped in waterproof sheeting. In this way, any of the bundles could have been tossed overboard and would have floated until picked up by their fishing boats. In all, there were over twenty tons of weapons and munitions.

It would not be long before they hit the first layer. Reuben suppressed crying out from the pain in his legs as he inched his way onto the deck and waited, lying on the deck, stretching his legs, moving his ankles and regaining movement. There were but two men left. They were walking around the cargo hold, assessing the possible amounts of clothing that needed to be removed. In his right pocket, Reuben carried a grenade. One was enough if he could slip into the hold and dig his way down far enough to reach some of the rockets. If he could cut through the plastic sheeting and get the grenade within the center of a bag, then paradise would be his next destination in his long career of fighting the Zionists. The entire ship and all aboard would be blown to bits, but only the crew would be with him and their virgins for eternity.

Chapter Twenty-One

A Twist of Fate

Mrs. Kelly was asleep when the knock came at her door. She sat up in bed and rubbed her eyes. The second knock told her she wasn't dreaming. Putting on a bathrobe, she walked to the front door and looked out the side window. There was a man and a woman wearing blue jackets with FBI printed on them in large white letters. She opened the door a few inches but did not remove the chain lock.

"May I please see some identification before I open the door?"

The agents both held out their identification. Mrs. Kelly sensed a rush of immediate apprehension as the door swung open and the female agent asked if they might come in.

Mrs. Kelly opened the door all the way, and they removed their caps, also imprinted with "FBI." Brittany Stein introduced her partner and herself and assured her that Diane was all right. There had been an incident in Pittsburgh that Diane was involved in. After topically explaining some of the details, she asked her to quickly pack an overnight bag as there was a jet waiting for them at Ft. Lauderdale Airport. Her partner would drive them, but Brittany was personally escorting Mrs. Kelly on the flight. She was assured that on the way to Virginia, Brittany would fill her in on all the information she had. Within fifteen minutes, a bag had been hastily packed and they were on their way to the airport.

~

Reuben listened intently to the voice of the Israeli commando as he called to his teammate on the upper deck to hoist some of the bails of clothing out of the cargo hold. They did not have an inch of space left to place any additional clothing they extracted. The rest of the teams were interrogating the crew in an attempt to learn what happened to Omar and who killed him. There were questions upon questions, with several Israeli Intelligence officers interrogating individual crewmembers in different compartments of the ship.

Below, Reuben had slipped into the hold, which was now near a ten-foot drop. Landing on clothing did not produce the slightest sound, and the commando at the other end of the cargo area continued to eat his sandwich and sip his coffee. They had all taken a lunch break. Reuben inched his way over to a corner of the hold and slowly began to lift pieces of clothing as he slid beneath them. He proceeded doing this one single layer at a time, quietly and methodically, until his hand touched plastic. He felt around blindly, as he was now under several feet of clothing. He was having difficulty breathing, much less viewing what was beneath him. His hand touched something hard and realized that he was above a package of automatic weapons and not the munitions he was seeking. He would have to continue searching, and time was not on his side. Once the teams had eaten and rested, they would all be back down to continue searching. He had to find something with an explosive content such as gunpowder or plastic explosives. Then he realized that perhaps his hand was not touching a gun barrel at all, but rather the shaft of a rocket—a long-range rocket! There would be but one in a package and altogether, one dozen in each case. His heartbeat increased, and Reuben knew that it was fate and his own destiny.

He painfully managed to get his right hand into his pants pocket and extract a small knife, struggling to open the larger blade with his fingers. He poised the knife between his fingers and began slowly cutting away at the plastic. If he could just cut an opening the size of an apple, he could get his hand down far enough to explode the grenade at the rocket side of the bundle. The C-4 plastic explosives that were with the shipment would have been perfect to blow the entire ship to pieces—but they were not there. Elanie and Yael had taken them along with the four canisters.

~

Hyman Lutz had been patrolling since the pre-dawn hours along a designated stretch of highway. He and his driver were securing the checkpoints in and out of Tel Aviv. Except for some holiday traffic after minight, the roads were basically deserted.

At the very moment he was about to call in his hourly report, one of his men spotted a car coming on fast, well above the speed limit. Hyman told his driver to position their jeep facing the other jeep and create a narrow but passable opening in the event the car did not stop. He was not about to get anyone killed on *his* watch. The driver maneuvered the jeep, and all four men got out of their vehicles. The driver of the second jeep took a rolled up red flag and stood a few feet back from the vehicles. He began waving it at the oncoming car as a signal to stop. The approaching car was a sedan, an older Mercedes. As it approached the jeeps, it slowed and came to a stop. Hyman exhaled a quiet breath of relief and then approached the driver's side of the vehicle. The driver rolled down the window about one-quarter of the way.

"Good morning, Officer. Is there anything wrong?"

"No, miss," he answered. He paused for a second as he was somewhat taken back with the beauty of the woman driving. Her smile was instantly compelling.

"We are looking for someone. May I please see your driver's license?"

"Of course you may," she answered in the sweetest tone of voice. Elanie removed the forged license from her wallet and handed it to him.

Hyman studied the license and handed it back to her. Then he noticed a man in the back seat, sound asleep. It was perfectly normal; however, he was covered in wool blankets in such a way that Hyman could not see his face.

"Is that your husband in the back sleeping?"

"Yes, it is, officer. He was *very* tired from the medication he had to take for his asthma and could not stay awake, so I offered to drive."

"Very well, thank you. I will need to just take a peek in your trunk if you don't mind. It will only be a minute."

Elanie glanced into the rearview mirror and saw that Yael was listening to the entire conversation. Under the blanket, his hands were wrapped around the Uzi. Elanie had to think of something or there would be a blood bath that could possibly hinder their prime objective.

"Actually, Officer, I have a problem. The trunk is on a separate key, and I left it at the house. We didn't need any luggage, so we didn't even think about it."

"I see," Hyman replied.

"Don't you have a trunk release within the car?"

"No, this is an older model as you can see, and if there *is* one, I surely have not found it!" Elanie began to laugh. Would you like to look for it under the dashboard?"

Hyman would never know this, but his next decision saved his life. Yael was prepared to open fire on him and the other three soldiers and would have killed them all if necessary. He would have sprung from the back seat on the side of the others, and before they could even draw their weapons, they would have all been dead. Elanie would have taken out Hyman without hesitation. A 9MM automatic rested between her legs and had a round in the chamber, ready to fire.

"Its okay, go ahead and drive safely."

"Thank you so much, Officer, and have a pleasant day."

Hyman waved them through the checkpoint. Elanie pulled out slowly and then accelerated to a normal speed. She didn't see Officer Lutz standing in the wake of her diesel exhaust, staring after the car. He instinctively knew it was them, however he had no way of knowing what weapon the man in the back seat had hidden under the blanket. He also saw the driver's hand resting between her legs and thought she was also hiding a weapon. He didn't want to die tonight, and all his men had families. He turned when she was out of sight and headed for a phone.

~

Reuben was perspiring so profusely that he was beginning to feel dehydrated. His breathing was becoming labored and he knew that he could not remain buried beneath the clothes much longer. Taking into consideration the height, width and depth of the cargo, the weight factor of even the lightest materials were weighing heavily against his back. It made breathing even more difficult than just the lack of circulated air around his face and body. He would either have to set-off the grenade or get out and try again later. However, he knew that wouldn't likely happen once they removed another layer of clothes and began to see the plastic wrappings. He could not hear any sounds from above as he tried to shift his position to create a small air pocket around himself. It was a grave miscalculation.

High above, one of the Ops team members saw the slight movement below. In a whisper, he touched the tiny microphone button that was on a wire under his chin and alerted the squad captain. Quietly and within a few seconds, the captain stepped in from the outer deck and signaled him to draw a bead on the movement. The signal was given to load an armor piercing round. If someone were hiding in the clothes below, a bullet would have to penetrate many feet of clothing. The marksman inserted a single, armor-piercing cartridge in his sniper rifle, quietly drew the bolt back, and chambered the round.

Then the captain realized that there were supposed to be munitions below those clothes and he waved the sniper off. He held up a hand signal for him to wait.

The man nodded and watched closely, pointing again to where he had seen the movement. By this time, three other men were surrounding the hold and had guns drawn on the fixed location. Suddenly, there was a muffled explosion. It sent a sound shockwave through the bulkheads of steel with such an echo that the men thought their eardrums would burst. They saw clothing flying everywhere below and became fearful. If there were indeed munitions in that cargo hold, the entire ship could be torn apart.

The reverberation of the single shockwave ceased, and there was quiet. Reuben had been dead wrong. It was a case of AK-47 rifles, equipped with huge silencers. To a blind touch, the top of those silencers could feel like the shaft of a rocket. The grenade that was pushed beneath the six inches of plastic sheeting that he cut through, uncovered nothing more than the barrels of the rifles. There was not even a single round in their chambers to explode when the grenade went off. There was a large amount of fragmentation that resulted from the explosion, contained only by Rueben's body as the shrapnel tore through him like hundreds of tiny scalpels. He never knew what hit him.

"If this was supposed to be martyrdom, something is drastically wrong with the terrorist philosophy," remarked the squad captain.

~

Admiral Yuri and General Rabene had been discussing the latest developments in Operation Takedown.

"I believe that we should confirm this information with the prime minister," the admiral said to General Rabene.

"Yes, he will want to shove this in the face of the Palestinian Authority. There is supposed to be peace talks tomorrow. It's the day after Christmas, and I believe the Palestinian Authority thinks this shipment is safe and being off-loaded in some port."

"Does it really mater?" the admiral asked with the certainty of his years of experience.

"Don't you agree that except for the very fact that we eliminated enough munitions and arms to save thousands of Israeli lives, world opinion doesn't really matter because the majority of the world doesn't truly give these things a second glance—after the emotions of the initial story. Everyone is caught up in his or her own form of terrorism. If it's not a terrorist, it's a serial killer. If it's not a killer, it's a flood or an earthquake. We all have our trials to deal with."

"With a shipment of arms and munitions this large, the prime minister wants to make sure that the news coverage is extensive. He wishes he could be at the Palestinian Authority Headquarters when they see their ship on the news and the cargo spread out all over Israeli docks for the world to see. They are expecting that cargo to surface at any time now," the general commented.

"Where are you having the ship towed?" the admiral asked.

"Into Tel Aviv, since the television crews from the United States and Europe are all there. Before they leave from covering the holiday in Bethlehem, we want to give them something spectacular to report to the world."

"Who was the poor guy who got himself blown up under the clothes?"

"We don't know for sure," general Rabene answered. "Immediate identification is virtually impossible. It will take Forensics and DNA to know for sure. We *do* know that it is either Reuben or Yael. The crew is all accounted for with the discovery of Omar's body, so it must be one of the terrorists."

"Where do you think the other two are?" the admiral asked.

" I believe they are headed for Tel Aviv. When the radio report went out to all police and military stations, one of the sector chiefs reported that he stopped a Mercedes with a man and a woman inside. The description of the woman matches that of Elanie. From the officer's account of the incident, the man was in the back seat and he could not see his face. He was purportedly sleeping, and his face was covered by the edge of a blanket. However, he did say that the man had black hair. Reuben's picture shows a reddish brown. I believe that was Yael in the back seat of that car, and it is Reuben's body in the cargo hold of the ship. Elanie and Yael obviously made it over the side of the freighter, prior to boarding her with our teams."

"Couldn't we have sent out their descriptions on the wire sooner than we did?" the admiral asked.

"It wouldn't have mattered. Ordinary police patrols couldn't stop those two. We would have had four casualties on our hands. The officer made the right decision, in my opinion. The problem is that nobody has seen either of them recently, and the girl could have dyed her hair or disguised herself."

"She and her boyfriend or her brother are on the loose, and she is going to be a very angry terrorist shortly."

"Why is that?" the admiral asked.

"She will know about the ship and also about the body under the clothes within the next twenty minutes—when it hits the airwaves. We are also claiming the ship as salvage since it was party to a plot of espionage against Israel and its people. The Palestinians are going to be madder than hell."

~

Nathan was singing, David was singing, and Rachael could not stop laughing. It was like old times when David was much younger and they took weekend trips together. No matter where they went, they sang and they laughed. They were the "Three Musketeers of Ft. Lauderdale" and would chuckle at the very mention of that title. However, with all of her natural beauty and attributes, Rachael could not carry a tune. Nathan would always chide her about her "tin ear" being very cute and just the right size for nibbling instead of music. She would call him a chauvinist, and they would all laugh as she strained her voice to sing a specific tune. There were times that David laughed so hard that he begged them to stop because his sides hurt.

The drive to Jerusalem was a reminder of the wonderful times they used to have, and David realized that he still wanted more of those times in his life.

"David, how about you and I playing a quick game of Israeli trivia?"

"Okay, you start—want in on this, Mom?" he asked.

"No, thank you, I'll let you two brainy guys compete with each other."

"Okay, David. Let's see . . . how many names are in the Scriptures for Jerusalem and in what chapter and verse can they be found?"

"That's not fair. You know Scriptures a lot better than I do!"

"No excuses, you went to Hebrew School. Here is the first, *Salem*, and it is in Genesis, chapter fourteen, and it means City of Peace.

David thought for a moment and excitedly recalled one name specifically—"Holy City, and it's in Isaiah, chapter fifty-two."

"Good one, but easy," his father teased. "Okay, as long as you went to Isaiah, I've got a long one for you—Zion of the Holy One of Israel, Isaiah, chapter sixty."

"Okay, Dad, I have one more left in my memory banks. Jerusalem, and it means Foundation of Peace. It's in Joshua, but I can't recall the chapter off hand."

Nathan changed topics, and they went on for some time. It was not competitive, but rather in fun and keeping sharp on their knowledge.

They decided to see some sights before checking into the King David Hotel and drove toward the Wailing Wall. Nathan was still betting Rachael that after all these years he could still find the paper he stuffed into the wall. It was becoming the family joke, and every time he insisted, David and Rachael raised the stakes. They were now up to betting the synagogue, the house, all worldly possessions, and a week's vacation at the Sonesta Beach Hotel to relive their honeymoon. Rachael stopped laughing long enough to wipe the tears from her eyes and calm her breathing.

"Where do you want to visit first, Nathan?"

David called out, "The Wailing Wall—I want my inheritance when he can't find his piece of paper." They all began laughing again.

"Okay, you two," Nathan retorted, "that's enough. You win and you can have all I have—but I still want to go to the wall. I can't for some reason get that view out of my head when we came toward the area."

"What do you mean, Dad?" David questioned.

"The Dome of the Rock, the Muslim Mosque that stands out so dominantly where the Temple of our God once stood before the Romans leveled it. One wall—that's all that is left standing. At just about all the temple gates, you have every representation of religion and we only have a wall!"

"I don't think I understand," David stated with some confusion.

"The Old City, David, where we enter, there are gates. You have the Zion Gate and directly beyond it is the American Quarter. Then you have the Dung Gate and *then* the Wailing Wall! Then you have a Muslim Mosque, the Al-Aqsa Mosque, and as you look to the right, there is the Jewish Quarter. It has all never really made sense to me in terms of the entire layout of the Old City and how much of our heritage we have given up."

"Perhaps that is what the battle is all about," Rachael suggested.

"No, it's not about the land—not the land itself. It's more about thousands of years of hatred, instilled one generation at a time."

"Dad, go on about the layout. I want to visualize it so when we get there I will recognize it all."

Nathan thought for a moment. "Let's see, I was talking about the Dung Gate and the Jewish Quarter. Yes, then there is the Temple Mount, as it's called, and dead center upon it is the Dome of The Rock. Below that area is what they now call the St. Stephens Gate, which was the Lions Gate of old, but was renamed to commemorate Stephen, the first Jewish-Christian martyr who was stoned for his profession of Christian faith. The famed Saul, who later became the Apostle Paul of the Christian religion, looked on and said nothing. Then there is Herod's Gate and the Muslim Quarter. I am not sure what is on the far side. I believe it might be The Christian Quarter, and there is a church there as well. It is all our Israel, and yet our Israel belongs to the world and not to us—not in a sense of exclusivity."

As Nathan went on about the Old City, the shops and the vendors, it all began to become a living reality in David's mind. When they arrived,

David could see first-hand what his father was describing. The streets were a combination of wide and drivable, as well as walking-only streets that were narrow and winding. There were all types of shops and vendors along the way. As Nathan maneuvered the car around several trucks, a car pulled out from the side street, nearly hitting them, and Nathan declared it a blessing.

"A blessing? The man neatly hit us and you call it a blessing?" David questioned.

"Yes, my son. We now have a parking space."

Rachael laughed aloud, and Nathan maneuvered the car into the side street. Sure enough, it was the only parking space available.

"Come, let's walk from here."

Making certain that they placed anything that appeared to have value in the trunk, Nathan walked around the car and checked all the doors to make sure they were locked. The air was a bit chilly, but the temperature was up to the 40s, the usual January temperature in Israel. They began to walk, and Rachael took Nathan's arm on the left as David took his mother's other arm. Rachael turned and smiled at her son, and as she did so, he remarked, "We *are* the Three Musketeers, you know!" Rachael was beaming with the delight of having David at her side again.

"When we get to the gate of the Wailing Wall, Mom will have to remain among the women on the screened side, and David, you will need a head covering."

"I want to pray with you at the wall, Dad," David insisted, and Nathan's smile could not have been any brighter. His son was asking to pray with him, side by side at the wall of the Temple of old; the wall where he had prayed some nineteen years ago for Rachael to be his wife and for God to bless them with a son; the same wall that he had pressed that tiny piece of paper into, so long ago. He knew in his heart he could never find it, but he had a sense that it was still there. Something had drawn him back to the wall. Something had brought the very people that comprised his life—his wife and his son—to a wall where he once prayed that they would indeed be the main parts of his life—after God, of course.

This was almost surreal to Nathan, as he began sensing an uneasiness that was mounting within him. It was a queasy feeling that he suddenly remembered having at one time before, but he dismissed it as tiredness.

As they approached the wall area, David could not help but notice all the soldiers with their machine guns slung on their shoulders and ready for any situation. *A holy place of prayer and men with killing weapons are all over the streets, watching and checking out every person and staring suspiciously at every package that appeared too large or was held too tightly.*

Rachael found a spot among the women and said she would wait there for them. Women were permitted to pray at the Wailing Wall, but there was a special area separated from the men. It was a screened area just to the right of where the men prayed. Nathan hesitated, as he did not want to leave his precious half of his life alone. They walked around the women's area and over to where hundreds of men stood before the wall, praying, crying, pleading, or simply giving thanks to God. As they came to stand at the perimeter of the large open courtyard surrounding the wall, Nathan stopped for a moment and lifted his eyes toward the heavens and prayed aloud.

"I lift up my eyes toward the hills, where does my strength come from. My strength comes from the Lord, the Creator of heaven and earth."

This Psalm was one of Nathan's favorites, and he murmured it to worship God before he went before the wall of his ancestors to pray for peace. David watched his father and smiled as he covered his head. The two men walked toward the wall, father and son; one a rabbi, and one whom Nathan wished with all his heart would become one. For the moment, however, he was content to simply be standing side by side with his son.

"Dad, wait up a minute. I can't believe the sight of this."

Nathan looked at the expression on his son's face and smiled. It was the same look of awe that he must have had when he stood before the wall for the first time. David was visually scanning it from one end to the other. There were fern-like plants that were growing out from crevices at varied places and heights. David could not help but notice the variation in the stones: some narrow, and some vertical with huge horizontal blocks just above them, as though they were nested and resting upon one another.

At that moment, Nathan sensed that same nervous feeling again. David noticed his change of expression.

"Is something wrong, Dad?"

"No, it's just this feeling of queasiness in my stomach. I must be hungry," Nathan quipped.

"Dad, I never thought I would stand before a wall of stones with some bushes growing out of the cracks and think it was so incredible."

"I know exactly how you feel, David," Nathan answered.

Nathan remained quiet. He stood at his son's side and sensed that he was deep in thought, allowing him these moments of personal thinking. They were likely the very same thoughts that he and most Jews have when they stand before this huge reminder of history, for the very first time.

~

The prime minister paced the floor and kept looking at his watch. Several of his staff stood nearby, watching him, well understanding his apprehension. They had uncovered all of the clothes and found what they had suspected they would find. It was all over the news. The cameras of the world were carrying the live coverage of the largest capture of arms and munitions in the history of the Israeli and Palestinian conflict. The Karine Abbalah was towed into port and was declared a captured vessel under the Arms and Munitions War Act that forbid commercial vessels from carrying or concealing any weapons within the coastal waters and ports of Israel.

That was not the worst of the news for the PLO. Under heavy military guard with troops lining either side of the dock at the Port of Tel Aviv, navy personnel formed a human conveyer belt from the freighter's deck to the piers. Cameramen, news people, commentators, reporters, and media representatives from around the world were at the entrance to the pier, crowding one another with television cameras banging into each other as they waited for the military guard to open the roped off barricades that blocked the pier.

The prime minister's orders were explicit. He wanted every last box and bullet to be off-loaded from the ship.

"I want those guns to be uncrated and laid out one by one beside each other, even if they stretch all the way to downtown Tel Aviv. I want every rocket launcher side by side, and every long and short-range rocket for those launchers to be placed in front of them. Whatever is there, I want the world to see. I want the shipment to go on the cameras of the world, having the most devastating appearance and shown as the largest shipment of arms and munitions in history. I want this to take place while the

PLO leader is talking about peace with the United States and members of our own cabinet. I want the world to see their hypocrisy, their deceit, and understand that dealing with the PLO is simply courting death with diplomacy."

The general and the admiral well understood, and his orders were being carried out to the letter. As the men brought more and more munitions to the docks, General Rabene ordered several battalions to assist the naval personnel. Before long, the media people began to realize that this was one of the biggest seizures of illegal arms ever captured anywhere in the world. It was war history in the making, and the word spread worldwide. In the United States, every newsperson on Fox News, CNN, and all the networks carried the live coverage.

Pictures of the off-loading were being beamed to every affiliate and every news station around the world. All major newspaper chains were holding their headlines and front pages, awaiting the electronic sending of photographs of the ship, the crew, and the seemingly endless lines of guns, rockets, mortars, machine guns, hand grenades and so much more. All the crates from which all the weapons were unpacked were brought ashore. Although they were empty when they reached the dock, the prime minister ordered that they be brought to the docks. He wanted them stacked two or three high in a long line with their stenciled identity turned outwards. Then the cameras could get a perfect view of their dangerous titles: DANGER—EXPLOSIVES—ROCKETS, and they stretched all the way down the pier. It was a news media field day. Within a few hours, the lines were opened up, and the camera crews rushed in for position.

Commentators stood before a section of the contraband and told the world what they had pieced together of the mission: the capture of the vessel, the killing of the ship's captain by one of their own, and weaving the story as they went. It would seem that all the Israeli officials could now rest easy. It was over, and it was successful. Not a single life was taken during the capture. The only death was by the hand of a terrorist, and the other death occurred while that same terrorist blew himself up while attempting to blow up the cargo. In Palestine, the PLO was declaring Omar and Reuben "martyrs," and demonstrations began to block all the streets on the West Bank. Earlier, the streets were already flowing with dissidents and militant Palestinians holding up hastily made signs accusing Israel of taking their property (the ship) and planting the munitions. They claimed it was nothing more than Israeli propaganda to thwart the peace talks going on in the United States at that very moment.

The prime minister called an emergency meeting and asked several members of the cabinet to join him. It was done hastily, and several of the prime minister's assistants were on the phones and sending cars for the members he trusted—those who he knew were supportive of his efforts to bring resolve to the PLO problem. It took about an hour for the six men to arrive, and when they were all seated in the emergency meeting area, an aide poured coffee and ice water while they waited for the prime minister to join them.

A dangerous situation presented itself less than ten minutes before the prime minister called for this meeting. The call came from a major, who was assisting the naval personnel in searching every inch of the freighter. He was going through the captain's quarters when he discovered a hidden plastic envelope, taped to the bottom of the captain's desk. When he opened the envelope and saw the word "Manifest," he immediately called the prime minister. It seemed that this was the legitimate cargo manifest and contained a list of individual items and the quantity of those items that were aboard the ship. The prime minister ordered that he tell no one about this discovery, place the list back inside the original envelope, and try not to handle the envelope or the list without gloves.

"It's winter," the prime minister jested. "It should not be too difficult to find a pair of gloves. Tell me, was the envelope open, or was it sealed when you discovered it?"

"It was sealed."

"Good, put it in your pocket and come directly to my office. No one is to know that you found it, have it, or that you're bringing it here."

It was twenty minutes later when the prime minister read the list and understood why the army major was so concerned. The manifest of the cargo was discovered after General Rabene and a team of army personnel took an inventory of the cargo that was off-loaded. Two bundles were unaccounted for. They were C-4 explosives and five biological canisters. There was no description of these canisters or any indication of what they contained. The canisters could contain gas or biological weaponry. How much of it, they didn't know.

The prime minister drew a deep breath and thought, *Elanie, her research years ago. My God, could she have stored or maintained possession of the biological gas they were working on?*

The prime minister's thoughts poured through his mind. Finally he left his office, entered the meeting room, and began addressing the members of his cabinet.

"I have in my possession the manifest from the freighter. We have accounted for just about all of the cargo, right down to the ammunition for the AK-47s."

"Almost everything?" his most trusted friend repeated.

"Yes, almost everything, and that is the reason for this meeting. The general was called into the cargo hold when one of his men found two empty crates that someone apparently tried to hide in another compartment. They were not labeled, but one of them had a number '4' stenciled about six inches high on each side of the box. The question at first was did the '4' mean that whatever was inside the two crates were four in number or four parts of something that had to be put together? We simply didn't know. The general called me and apprised me of his findings. Then we found the manifest. The '4' on that crate represented 'C-4,' and we estimate by the size of the crate and the discarded packaging and safety material that there was approximately one hundred pounds or more of C-4 explosives in that crate that are now missing. The other crate was labeled 'Toxic Canisters,' and we have no idea what might have been in those canisters. We have some suspicion that is based on what Elanie was professionally involved in at one time, but we would rather not even *think* it was true. I have spoken with both General Mofazz and Admiral Yuri, and they reminded me that Elanie and Yael were both still missing and last seen heading for Tel Aviv in an older model Mercedes. As you may recall, the older model had the larger, box-type trunk in which they could have easily placed those bundles."

The cabinet members began talking among themselves and just at that moment, General Rabene entered the room.

"Ah, you are here," the prime minister said, and he hugged his old friend. "Gentleman, I have asked General Rabene to join us so that we may immediately expedite some appropriate counter-measures. If these two fanatics are driving around with over a hundred pounds of C-4 explosives and possibly some type of toxic material, I do not want to even speculate what they could do if they are not apprehended right away. General, what do you think?"

"I have been in contact with intelligence, and we have been running several model theories as to where these two might be headed and for what reason. I also contacted all of our top men in every department of both defense and intelligence and asked that every piece of information or news about their whereabouts be sent directly to my cell phone. What I am most concerned about is that they may be attempting to smuggle the C-4 out of Israel and into Lebanon or Syria. If these explosives were to find their way into a terrorist training camp, the consequences could be devastating. At first I thought they might try the old underground route between Egypt and the Gaza that we discovered they were using in the past. I immediately ordered a guard unit to Rafah.

"I am convinced, however, that they had a definitive backup plan in the event the freighter was sunk or captured. If they could not dock and off-load the cargo or even dump the weapons so fishing boats could retrieve them, they would certainly have their day in the limelight with some horrific explosion. The question, of course, is where. If it were twenty-four hours ago, I would have bet on Bethlehem, but now, I don't know."

The prime minister did expound on the toxic canisters. This situation was more than disturbing. It could become catastrophic, and they all agreed they must avail themselves of every possible means of stopping these two.

"Let us not forget that Elanie and Yael are shrewd. They have been well trained, and Elanie possesses many talents. She is a terrorist of the most dangerous kind—a brilliant one, who is quite familiar with this spectrum of destruction. We must act at once, and I am not recommending we keep this as a low-profile event. We need to expedite every measure of search and seizure available to us while somehow warning the public. We don't need to begin an all-out panic, but we do need to tell them we have received information that has led us to believe a terrorist attack is imminent. Let's get this message on the wire to Tel Aviv, and I would also recommend alerting the border patrols. We may even want to include Jerusalem in the alert. There is nothing so far to make me believe Jerusalem could be a target, but I also do not think we should take that chance."

"I agree," the prime minister somberly stated, and the cabinet members agreed as well. They had to be stopped at any cost. The prime minister dismissed the meeting but whispered to Rabene to join him in the office next door. Once inside, the door was closed, and the information concerning the canisters was related to the general. His reaction was one of horror.

"What if it's actually that air-born gas? Where would they attempt to release it?"

The prime minister simply shook his head and commented,

"We can pray and we can search for them. We can't do any more. We can sound alerts and deploy troops, and we will do so, because we will tell the media we are not taking any chances. Make a personal statement. Go down to the pier and allow them to corner you. Let the world media know that if the Palestinians can stoop to smuggling arms and munitions while peace talks were underway, they could be up to even more despicable terrorism. Expose Elanie and Yael so that we have civilians watching for them, as well. Get their pictures on the news wire. We will simply tell everyone that we are not taking any chances.

"That's exactly what I'll say, Mr. Prime Minister."

Helicopters soared over the city. They searched the miles of roadways leading in and out of Tel Aviv. Sirens were sounding at military installations and facilities, and a state of alert was declared to all military personnel. The government offices were under evacuation, and all major military sites were brought to full alert with increased guard units.

General Rabene left the meeting and went directly to his headquarters to deploy the necessary personnel. He would personally command this operation, and asked Admiral Yuri to assist by having patrol boats secure the port at Tel Aviv. He also wanted gunboats to patrol the shorelines of the coastal waters. They were thankful that it was winter, or they would also be forced to close the beaches in the resort areas. They were out there, and they had to be stopped. It was a double-sided coin, so to speak. On one hand, the Israeli government was sporting their captured arms and munitions along the docks of Tel Aviv. They were declaring how many lives were saved because they intercepted this shipment. Camera crews were making this into one of the biggest stories of the war on terrorism while the whole world looked on. Everywhere people resided, sirens were being sounded to alert the public to the dangers of a possible terrorist attack. It was attributed to the missing explosives that were on the very same ship.

As the general's jeep pulled up to the piers and the guards at the entrance snapped to attention, all cameras were turned and trained on the general. He stepped out of the jeep just a few feet from the Fox News cameras and reporters. As he pretended to avoid them, one newswoman ran up to him with her microphone.

"General Rabene, please, why are there sirens and alerts being initiated all over Tel Aviv? You captured the arms and the terrorists, so what is going on that we are not being told about?"

Ah, a direct challenge ... smart girl, Rabene thought. He turned around as though he were somewhat annoyed and approached her as the cameras from all the networks turned and were trained on the general.

"I will make a statement, although brief, as we have much to do. The terrorists plotted to bring these munitions and arms into Israel for distribution to their various terrorist groups. If they could sink to such lowliness as to bring weapons of human destruction into Israel on the day their own leader is talking about peace with the president of the United States and our own representatives, we cannot trust their intentions. We are not taking any chances that there was more to this plot—especially with all of you here, the eyes of the world. We want to insure your safety and the safety of our people. Hence, we have initiated full alerts and full-scale preventative operations. Thank you."

The general turned and walked away with a dozen or more reporters screaming questions after him, but he did not turn around. He got back into his jeep and told the driver to take him to his headquarters. The prime minister watched on the television in his office, smiling contently over Rabene's mannerism and answers. *Rabene is not only a good general but a showman as well,* he mused to himself.

General Rabene arrived at his office from the piers and was sitting at his desk when the phone rang. It was one of the unit commanders from Jerusalem.

"Yes, Ari, what do you have?"

"General, I know that there is a top-priority alert in Tel Aviv; however, we have been told that there is a possibility these terrorists might come into Jerusalem. If that's a possibility, I am considering going to full alert. Less than an hour ago, an abandoned Mercedes Benz with the trunk wide open was found in the Old City." The general jumped up from his desk, and his face turned ashen.

"Oh, my God," were the first words that General Rabene could say. He immediately began dictating orders. He called the prime minister and informed him of their conversation. He then called other military leaders in an attempt to head off the terrorists. He now had a hunch as to where they were going.

~

Nathan and David approached the Wailing Wall and walked toward the furthest part so that Nathan could be closer to and possibly speak with the Orthodox rabbis who sat at their tables. Several were gathered around the entrance to the underground caves that were beneath the city. There was also a sheltered office for them within a few feet of the entranceway. David had heard of this entrance to the underground at the far end of the wall. He knew that it led to a series of tunnels that spread out in all directions beneath the entire city. It was said that no man could find his way through all of them, and that there were passageways and tunnels that even the most experienced and knowledgeable explorers of the caves have yet to find.

Some time ago when David was involved in an intense study concerning the Ark of the Covenant, he read about these incredible stories. Rumor had it that the Ark, the Tablets of Moses, and Aaron's staff, were hidden underground in a secret tunnel beneath Jerusalem. It was further rumored that only several of the highest ranking Orthodox rabbis of Israel and the prevailing prime ministers through the ages knew the location of the Ark and were allowed one visit to the hidden tunnel in their lifetime.

As Nathan and David walked toward the end of the wall, they could not help but see the incredible reverence that emanated from just about every man who was praying. David caught sight of an older man who appeared to be an American. He leaned against the wall with his arms stretched above him and his palms against the wall. He was weeping bitterly, but his prayers were aloud, rejoicing that he had seen the Wall of the Temple of his people before he went to be with the Lord. They stopped, father and son, marveling and being touched by the same moment of reverence. ***Perhaps we are really not that far apart in our love for the Lord and our*** *people,* Nathan thought as he glanced at the glistening in his son's eyes over the sight of the weeping, elderly man.

They continued walking, and when they came just about to the end of the wall and the area where the rabbis were located, David could not help but notice that military personnel were heavily guarding the entrance to the tunnel at the end of the wall. Soldiers were standing on either side of the opening with automatic weapons, and they were not pointed down. They were actually aimed straight ahead toward the courtyard area. David also noticed that they were both giving him and his father the once-over and kept their eyes on them as they approached the rabbis. David sensed their level of awareness as they both spontaneously placed their left hands on the top portion of their weapons; as though to ready themselves to aim and support the recoil should they have to fire. An unsettling observation, to say the least, and David called out to his father.

"Yes, David?" Nathan responded as he slowed his approach to the rabbi's table.

"Dad, I think we might slow our pace a bit, and you really should greet the rabbis in Hebrew with an immediate introduction. Those soldiers are not looking happy about our approaching them."

Nathan glanced over at the soldiers, who were less than twenty feet from them. "I agree, and thank you." Nathan slowed his pace and about ten feet away called out, "Shalom." In Hebrew, he introduced himself as Rabbi Nathan Blumberg of Ft. Lauderdale, Florida and his son, David.

One of the rabbis who was standing near the table walked toward Nathan and extended his right hand, palm-up in front of him, as though to say, "Wait until I come to you." Nathan stopped immediately. David also noticed that the soldiers were actually in a firing stance with both hands on their weapons. They did not relax that stance until the rabbi approached them.

Nathan began to talk to the rabbi in Hebrew, and David waited, as he also observed six armed soldiers above them. He marveled at the security, but at the same time he was saddened at the need for such stringent measures and such a showing of military presence at this holy place. Each of the soldiers above were carrying the same automatic weapons, facing straight down at the area where the rabbis were gathered.

Just then he saw the rabbi who was speaking with his father embrace him, and as he did, David watched the guards relax their demeanor and take their left hands off the weapons. *The hug must have done it,* David mused to himself. The soldiers above, however, did not relax their stance. Nathan motioned to David to keep behind him as he followed the rabbi toward the table where apparently the head rabbi sat. The rabbi who was talking to Nathan leaned over and said something to the older head rabbi at the table, positioning himself between the rabbi and Nathan. David was still behind his father and decided not to move until he was instructed to do so.

The older man stood and extended his arms toward his father, who walked up to him and embraced him in respect. They exchanged several words in Hebrew, and the older rabbi sat down again. But this time, a chair was brought from the side of the area for Nathan. Nathan said something in Hebrew to the older rabbi, and he motioned for David to come to the table.

"Shalom," the rabbi greeted David, and David greeted him and shook his hand. Speaking only in Hebrew, Nathan was explaining that this was his only son, just as he was an only son. He went on to explain how his father, Rabbi Harry Blumberg, came to Israel often and would come to the wall to pray with his friend Victor.

Before Nathan could get the next word from his mouth, the older rabbi repeated Victor's name and asked Nathan, in Hebrew, if he was related to Victor. Nathan explained the relationship, and it seemed to please the older rabbi greatly—that Nathan was indeed like family to Victor, as they all knew him very well. The older rabbi appeared saddened as he explained that he knew Rabbi Harry Blumberg and had prayed with him when he came to Israel. Victor would always be with Harry, and they would all pray together. He also explained that at one time, years ago, Victor was in charge of the security at the gates and at the wall.

Just then, several rabbis came out from the tunnel entrance at the wall and walked over to the table as the head rabbi introduced them to Nathan and David. Nathan stood and greeted each of them and shook hands with them. Several chairs were brought out, and they all began speaking in Hebrew; about what, David had no idea.

Just at that moment, and for what reason he didn't know, something caused David to look back toward the wall and the people behind him. It was a strange feeling, almost likened to having a sudden sense of danger or apprehension—you suddenly feel a gnawing pang in the pit of your stomach.

Of the many people who were milling about, David happened to notice two rabbis walking toward the area where they were seated. There was something odd about them, especially one of them that caused him to originally take notice. They were still about fifty feet away, and David didn't have a clue why he was drawn to stare at them. He began to turn around again but stopped and looked back at them a second time. Goosebumps instantly formed all over his body, and his heartbeat increased.

What is going on here? he thought. He glanced over at the two guards who were standing on either side of the entranceway and noticed that neither of them responded to the two coming toward them as they did to him and his father. They seemed preoccupied with what was going on around the table and the rabbis all laughing and exchanging conversation.

He looked back at the two rabbis who were nearing him, and there was definitely something very strange about the one walking on the side closest to the wall. He appeared to be purposely remaining just a step behind the other, attempting to be hidden by the other as they walked. His head was lowered and his jacket collar pulled high around his neck and past his chin. *What was it, God? Is there something you are trying to tell me, Lord? Something about them I don't understand? They are Rabbis, they are . . .*

And then David saw what his eyes had seen but what his brain had not yet registered. They were wearing a rabbis long black coat, black pants and black, large-brimmed hats, but were also lugging huge knapsacks on their backs. This was very peculiar for rabbis to be carrying knapsacks at the Wailing Wall. They were also quickening their pace as they came closer. There was another noticeable difference, something that was missing. Neither of them had any facial hair. The one on the outside appeared to have *some* facial hair, but the rabbi on the inside had no beard or any curls coming down from his head. The inside one had his hat pulled down so far over his brow that. . . . wait . . . it's the skin—too smooth for a man, too perfect of a nose, the eyebrows, the face, the face of . . . a girl?

David jumped to his feet as the two rabbis were almost at the table, less than twenty feet away. The one on the inside saw him suddenly get up. David saw his hand slowly reach into his jacket. He quickly looked at the face and realized that he was looking into the eyes of Elanie! His eyes darted to the other one, and it was Yael. *My God, she's reaching for a weapon!* David ran toward the side of the wall and screamed at the top of his lungs. . . .

"TERRORISTS—STOP THEM—THEY HAVE GUNS!"

Elanie and Yael both drew micro Uzi's from under their coats, and machine gun fire erupted on both sides of the rabbi's table. David threw himself on the ground a few feet away from where he was standing. He cut his head as he slammed against the concrete, but instinctively covered his face with his arms. Screams came from overhead, from the spectators, and from the women's corner.

It was bedlam; people running in every direction and screaming, as continuous machine gun bursts were exchanged. The air was filled with the pungent smell of gunpowder. Between the screams of spectators, one could hear the clanging of hundreds of shell casings echoing off the pavement as they bounced. The shiny brass casings began reflecting slivers of light, as they finally settled on the ground. When the gunfire stopped, all that could be heard were the sounds of screaming women and children, crying out in shock as they called the names of their husbands or relatives who were at the wall when it all began.

David removed his arms from around his head and slowly lifted his body so he could turn toward the table and entrance where the gunfire began. It was apparently over. It looked like there were a thousand brass shell casings scattered all over the ground as his hand came down on several of them. They were still warm. He was attempting to lift himself to his feet, but he remained in a semi-sitting position, steadying himself with his hands stretched before him. He then realized there was blood dripping down his face and into his eyes. He wiped the blood away to clear his vision with his sleeve and then fully sat up. His vision was blurred and his thoughts hazy, but he realized the blood was from the cut he sustained when he dove for the pavement.

Besides the blood from his head, there was blood everywhere and several bodies lying across other bodies. It seemed that most of the gunfire came from overhead, from the soldiers on the railing who were above the rabbis. There was a sound of one of the rabbis asking for God to have mercy on Israel and his family as he gasped his last breath. He closed his eyes as his right arm dropped to the ground. He had been sitting on one of the folding chairs that were at the rabbi's table. Now he was slumped over with blood dripping down his arm and his hand from the bullet holes in his body.

A siren sounded, and many soldiers and officials were clearing the Wailing Wall as dozens of uniformed soldiers came running toward them from every direction. David was dazed, stunned by feeling the presence of danger that caused him to turn around in the first place. He was in shock over seeing Elanie and Yael, and finally, he had never heard nor had he ever been near gunfire. They were awful sounds that shut down his senses after the first reaction to dive for cover. He sat where he was, trying to focus his eyes. He was facing the outer area and saw soldiers putting up wooden barricades while a line of soldiers guarded the scene. They were not allowing anyone to cross the barricade that stretched almost toward the very end of the wall where the women's side was located. The sounds of sirens from ambulances could be heard, and several men in civilian clothes with Red Cross armbands came rushing past the barricades. They each carried medical kits and began kneeling among the bullet-torn bodies in a desperate attempt to find a pulse, a heartbeat—one rabbi that might still be alive. None were. Not one survived the exchange of gunfire from below and above. David turned toward the end of the wall and realized, *my father . . . the rabbis,* when he saw the two men.

It was his father, lying across the body of the head rabbi with his arms spread-eagle across him as though he were trying to shield the old man from the bullets that were fired. David screamed a gurgling sound he didn't even realize had erupted from his throat. Panic and fear swept over him as he watched the life blood of his father seep onto the concrete and a large crimson puddle form that was growing larger by the moment from the holes that were in his father's back. Many soldiers were now on the scene, and two of them grabbed David's arms and slowly lifted him from the ground as he screamed and cried, struggling to break free.

"You have a head wound, let me bandage you," one of the men with a medical armband pleaded.

"I want to hold my father, let me go!" he screamed.

Just then a man with stars on his epilates walked over and signaled the two soldiers to release him. David lunged toward the grotesque dead bodies of his father and the head rabbi and knelt beside them. He could not see his father's face as it was turned toward the wall. As the man with the stars on his epilates knelt beside David, placing his hand on David's shoulder, he attempted to comfort him—as though that would have been enough to control his sobs of agony over the sight of his dead father. It was then that he heard the scream from his mother as she was escorted by two female officers after having told the officers behind the barricades that her husband and son were down there. They knew right away who she was because they were looking for the Blumberg family in Jerusalem.

Victor had learned that the clerk had made reservations for them at the King David Hotel and they had checked out early that morning. He was confident that the Wailing Wall would likely be their first stop for Nathan since his son was with him. Victor and two other operatives rushed to Jerusalem by helicopter, but they were apparently too late.

Rachael ran to David, still kneeling at the body of his father. He had stopped choking on his sobs and was simply staring at his father with tears streaming continuously down his face. His tears began to fall on the cement like tiny droplets that quickly evaporated from the heat of the cement. His hands were upon Nathan's back as though he were trying to cover the bullet holes and stop the bleeding. Rachael knelt beside him. She held her hands over her mouth to muffle the sobs from the agony of seeing her husband, bleeding and lifeless before her.

She tried to stop herself from shaking and reached for David. Mother and son embraced, crying with one another, trying to silently comfort one another but not able to deal with the reality of what was beside them. By that time, General Rabene and Admiral Yuri were also at their side and had ordered a guard detail to surround them. They did not want the cameramen above to take any pictures of their moments of grief.

~

The prime minister nodded his head over and over again in silent affirmation as the details were relayed to him on a secure cell phone. Admiral Yuri and General Rabene were to meet him. He was en route by car from a helicopter that landed in a safe area away from the site. General Rabene was explaining the situation and the fact that they had found the C-4 explosives.

"The entire 120 pounds was strapped to Yael. That was not the worst of it. Elanie had four canisters of the gas she was working on when she was with Biotechnology, a gas that instantly destroys the brain. It is obvious to us what they were trying to do. The explosives would have been detonated under the city in the tunnels. They wanted the C-4 to disburse the gas all through the tunnels so that it would seep into the streets across the city. The gas would have killed thousands. Once dissipated, the Palestinians would have taken the weapons from the ship and would likely have attempted to invade every military installation while the leadership and our military intelligence would either be reduced in numbers or attempting to help those affected.

"Had it not been for David being there at the precise moment they attempted to enter the tunnel, they would have gotten through because the element of surprise was on their side. The soldiers just glanced at them but were pre-occupied with what was going on at the table. Additionally, the explosives themselves would have caused entire streets to cave in, taking down buildings and thousands of people with it. David crying out instantly when he saw Elanie and Yael disguised as rabbis, drew gunfire from the soldiers positioned overhead. The two guards on the ground by the tunnel entrance didn't have a chance. By the time David yelled out the alert, Elanie and Yael had opened fire on the guards at the tunnel and killed them instantly.

"The problem was, Mr. Prime Minister, both Yael and Elanie kept firing into the rabbis as they attempted to back into the tunnel entrance. They were being fired upon from above, and they continued to fire in front of them as though they were going to take them all with them—and they did. The amazing thing was that they were both killed just inches from the tunnel entrance. Another step and they could have run inside and set off the explosives. The men above would have never reached them in time. There were detonators in both packs, with wireless triggers in their pockets. I can only guess that they did not detonate the C-4 and the canisters because they had both hands on their automatic weapons and were under fire. They were actually killed before they could even get one of their hands into their pockets. They could have, before the gunfire brought them down, but their own evil desire to take everyone with them was their downfall.

There are seven rabbis and Nathan Blumberg, David's father, all dead. What is most compelling is the fact that apparently Rabbi Blumberg threw himself across Rabbi Grossman. He was covering him with his body and spreading his arms as though he were attempting to protect him from the bullets!"

"I see," the prime minister responded in obvious grief and sadness. Rabbi Grossman, the head rabbi, was a long-time friend of the prime minister, and so were several of the other rabbis. The prime minister sat back in his seat as several tears dropped to his cheeks. He had seen his share of grief and had lost many a friend in the on-going war of religious hatred, but this was a sadness he could not hide. He had lost an old friend. Additionally, Rabbi Blumberg being killed at the Wailing Wall of Jerusalem was not a pleasant national news event for the coming evening news. The terrorists had managed to thwart the story of the munitions and the ship with an event that would be more widely and exclusively covered by the media. Bloodshed and an American being gunned down at the Wailing Wall would surely get prime time over any other news.

"Did they recover the four canisters of gas?" the prime minister asked.

"Yes, sir, they are safely on their way to a facility."

"Debrief David and ensure that he knows nothing about this gas being part of their plot. It would produce international sanctions and cause a great deal of trouble and panic."

"I understand, Mr. Prime Minister."

The flags at every military installation were flown at half-mast the next morning. At Kirya, an honor guard was at the main gate of the Israeli defense complex in honor of the fallen rabbis, the two soldiers at the tunnel, and the one American rabbi at the wall. Rabbi Grossman was a former member of the Sayeret Matkal and had served with the prime minister during his own tour of duty in their most elite Special Operations group. Although he chose the rabbinical life and dropped out of the military prior to what might have been a handsome retirement, he would receive the highest military honors.

It was later detailed that Rabbi Nathan Blumberg had literally thrown himself in front of the prime minister's friend. Nathan had tried to shield the elder Rabbi from the bullets of the terrorists, but they had passed through both of them. David was described on the international news that night as a "true son of Israel," a hero, who, had he not been there at the very moment that God's providence placed him there, one if not both of the terrorists would have set off explosives in the tunnels under the city. In the right location, it would have resulted in the deaths of thousands of people. They were calling it "David's Destiny" because of the incredible timing of him being there and recognizing the terrorists.

The news media continued emphasizing the sorrow of the prime minister and all of Israel at the loss of David's father, Rabbi Nathan Blumberg. David and Rachael were asked to remain in Israel for a few days by the prime minister and all the top Israeli officials. They accepted their offer, partly because they were far too grief-stricken to travel back to Florida. They suggested allowing them to bury Nathan among the heroes of Israel.

"It is what Nathan would have wanted," Rachael stated in an interview by Fox News at the American Embassy.

Joel Astor, the ambassador to Israel, conveyed the condolences of the President of the United States, who also issued a statement regarding the heroism of both David and his father. It seemed that politically, the heroism of an American was quite timely, as there were several issues over the Palestinian problem between Israel and the United States. So timely was this needed, positive heroic act of an American, that the president personally called Rachael and David in Israel to express his condolences. That too, was a top story on the evening news. Politics was flowing as usual.

The funeral was conducted with full military honors. Victor, Admiral Yuri, and General Rabene flanked David and Rachael, and the prime minister remained with them throughout the ceremony.

Several days later, before they were due to fly home, Victor called Rachael at the hotel and told her that he would appreciate it if he could pick them up and escort them to a location outside JDL Headquarters. Because there was a military guard assigned to David and Rachael at all times, Victor called the commanding officer of the guard detail and cleared the short ride with him. They would accompany them with a patrol unit, forward of Victor's car, and remain behind them at all times. When the commander learned of their destination and why Victor was taking them there, he assigned a guard detail to surround the area where they would be, even before they arrived.

The prime minister told General Rabene that they were to be guarded until they were safely on a plane back to the United States. In less than thirty minutes, a soldier knocked at Rachael's door and then at David's door in the adjoining room. Rachael and David came out, and the guard escorted them to the elevator where two other guards were waiting for them.

They all took the elevator to the lobby, and David could not believe that there were three more guards waiting for them outside the elevator doors. After opening the doors for Rachael and David to Victor's armor-plated Mercedes, the guards who had accompanied them out of the hotel got into jeeps in front and in back of their car. The jeep in front had a blue light on the crash bar, and it began to revolve as they pulled out and headed for the JDL property. There was also a huge machine gun on the crash bar, and David wished he would never see another weapon for the rest of his life.

When they reached their destination, there was an area they walked to that had white cement benches and sprawling flower gardens. It was a place that very few people knew about and very few people came to—except the families of the people who were engraved on the plaques affixed to a huge marble tablet. The people who came here were the relatives of the fallen heroes of Israel. This tribute would insure that they were never forgotten. In addition to the names already inscribed from every branch of government service, Rachael and David read:

In Tribute and In Loving Memory
Rabbi Nathan Blumberg
He died protecting our country and its people. His memory shall be honored among all Israelis who served God's given land. He shall be a true son of Israel for all time."

~

Upon their return to American soil, David and Rachael were flown to Washington and were invited to meet with the president at the Oval Office of the White House. The Secretary of State and the Ambassador to Israel accompanied Rachael and David. Also present at the ceremonies were several congressmen and senators who had supported various financial aid bills to Israel in the past. It was a political extravaganza.

Later that afternoon in the Rose Garden, the television cameras of the world were rolling as the president bestowed the Presidential Medal of Freedom in memory of Rabbi Nathan Blumberg. It was placed around Rachael's neck on behalf of her deceased husband while David stood at her side, holding her hand. The medal is one of the two highest civilian awards in the United States and is considered the equivalent of the Congressional Gold Medal of Honor.

She wore a black dress and hat and looked so beautiful that women everywhere admired her poise and dignity. She stood before America as the widow of a man who, in the words of the president, "Gave his life out of love. If the people of the world would learn a lesson from this rabbi's heroic and unselfish act, peace would reign instead of wars. I pray that perhaps both the Israelis and the Palestinians will look upon this act of unselfishness, and consider taking the first step toward peace with one another."

David managed to hold back his tears as the president presented him with the same medal for his heroic actions. Rachael held his hand tightly and looked at him adoringly as the president shook his hand. It was on all the Florida news channels and needless to say, once they returned to Ft. Lauderdale, everyone came to sit a delayed *Shiva* (A mourning period where the family is supported by visiting friends and neighbors) out of respect for their beloved fallen rabbi. There were lines out the door and around the block. It was an outpouring of love for a man who had left his mark on the world and on the Ft. Lauderdale community.

~

Four years had passed since that terrible but heroic day in Israel. Four long years, during which nothing could fill the emptiness that was felt in the Blumberg household. Nathan's study was never touched, although David would pray there every day. Ruth's room remained as it had been, although David's clothes had hung in the closet for nearly three of the four years.

It was a typical Saturday morning in South Florida. It was summer and quite humid. The air-conditioning in the synagogue founded by Rabbi Harry Blumberg some thirty-five years ago was sufficient, but no one was wearing a jacket or dressed as they used to. It was actually a very comfortable setting for the one-and-a-half-hour service. The Ark was opened, and the Torah was laid out on the reading table.

In the rabbi's words, "The Torah is before you as a symbol of our inheritance from God—His guidelines for living a just and worthy life. The Torah can be observed by *all* of mankind, for its message is about creation, sin, deliverance, and God's word. The Old Testament provides the words of all the prophets and their prophecies that man should look upon as living truth."

The rabbi delivers not a timely sermon, but rather a message of what life in the reality of these times was all about.

"It is about patience and understanding—tolerance of differences and the ability to make the right choices. It is about caring and fostering good will rather than arrogant superiority. It's about looking at one another as all of God's children. It is about giving out all the love you are able to in a non-personal and uncaring world of hatred and bitterness. It is about loving your neighbor regardless of their loving you. It's about respecting and honoring God's unconditional love."

The rabbi continues speaking, and every set of eyes and ears in the nine hundred plus seats are tuned in, watching and listening to every word. Rachael is sitting in the same front row seat she has always sat in; the same front row seat she sat in the day her husband was ordained as the synagogue's rabbi; the same row and seat she sat in when Harry died during her son's Bar Mitzvah; the same front row seat of what is now the largest Reformed synagogue in Ft. Lauderdale.

In the past four years, the building has almost tripled in size. The houses on both sides and the back parking lot were willingly donated to accommodate the expansion. Although many who came were not Jewish, they enjoyed attending the new services because of the teaching of the Word of God and a message of salvation for the world. It was about mankind and God's love for His creation that Rabbi David Blumberg preached. It was no longer "our people" or "their people" but rather *all* people, and they came to listen to him from every walk of life and different beliefs. It was amazing what could be accomplished among all people when you love on *all* people and not just your own people.

Those who were heeding his words were from Ft. Lauderdale as well as other cities and states. They came to hear this young rabbi who preached that love was an attribute of God. He stated that love was soulfully instilled in every human being as they drew their first breath of life. The emphasis was on *every* human being.

David was invited to speak at other synagogues and even the two Messianic synagogues, one in Boca Raton and the other in North Fort Lauderdale. Some of the largest churches throughout South Florida also invited him as a guest speaker. His message of love was like a sweet sounding trumpet in the midst of a world overcome with oppression and blood-spilling terrorism. Some looked at David with awe. So much tragedy, and yet he vowed to bring everlasting meaning to the lives of his grandfather and his father. He told Rachael one evening that he wanted to insure that his own son would one day find his individual destiny, that predestined path that God picked for him alone.

Rachael's thoughts turned to Nathan and how he would have been so proud of his son and his grandson. She gazed down with enough love for both of them, hers and all that was within her heart of Nathan's cherished memory. She was holding her grandson in her lap that morning, and she saw the distinct resemblance to Nathan in the baby's eyes. She was sitting with her daughter-in-law Diane at her side. Both women looked up to the bright light that shone out of the darkness and bitterness of the past. Rabbi David Blumberg was standing behind the pulpit that he had so long rejected.

Apparently, it was his destiny—or was it? Quite often, destiny can have a very long path that either lures us or compels us to continue following. Was this the end of David's path or had he just begun?

Epilogue

It took several years for the grief of Nathan's death to be reconciled within the hearts of David and Rachael. It was a long and painful process for both of them. Many barriers had to be overcome in their lives, and many concessions were made toward old ways of thinking.

David became a Reformed Jew and slowly moved the synagogue in that direction from its conservative past. It was not a decision based upon a lack of respect for his conservative upbringing, but rather his desire to encourage Jewish and non-Jewish people alike to come and share in the Word of God. David began teaching the Bible in an expository method, (chapter by chapter and verse by verse) and people listened and learned. This opened the doors to countless seekers who had never attended services in the past—any kind of services. Before long, the synagogue was overflowing with people who wanted to learn the Scriptures. They wanted to know more of Gods Word. The teaching went beyond Torah to include the Prophets, the Psalms and Proverbs, Esther, Ruth and Job. Hearing God's Word produced a growing hunger in every heart for further Biblical knowledge.

Rachael and Diane gradually grew closer, and as they did, Diane and David began to give more consideration to their relationship. It wasn't long before their deeply rooted love of the past brought them together forever in a beautiful marriage ceremony that took place in their home. Only a few close friends and Diane's mother attended—who became Rachael's best friend. Rachael adored Diane, and within a few months, her first grandchild was on the way. They agreed on the name Joshua, and for the first time in many years, with the exception of the absence of Nathan, the Blumberg family appeared to be at peace with their lives. Rachael succumbed to absolute tears of joy, the first Friday night that Diane lit the candles that ushered in the Sabbath. David also opened up his heart to learn from Diane and they both shared a love for God, together, one day at a time.

It is said however, that one never knows about tomorrow or when the past will one day intertwine with the future.

Some in the Middle East have said that terrorists never forget. The Bible teaches us, "Vengeance is mine, saieth the Lord." In the fallen world of these times, it is also said that the enormity of the loss to the terrorists would *never* be forgotten.

There was a single point of information that no one thought of, although it was something that David wanted to forget: the night his racing bike was stolen by four thugs during a snowstorm. Not only did they steal his bike, but they also stole his wallet. The items in that wallet were later sold to an underground document forger who sold passports, licenses and credit cards to people who needed false identities. Terrorists were certainly among his most valuable customers, and as a result, the name David Blumberg was now widely recognized throughout the world's most dangerous terrorist circles.

$$\sim$$

In the second book of the trilogy, the terrorist's actions begin with unthinkable retaliation from the very first page of the book, and then it's non-stop, pulsepounding action until the very last page. Be sure you watch for the release of

Days of Destiny
The Journey Continues . . . Book Two